WARWYCK'S CHOICE

BY ROSALIND LAKER

The Smuggler's Bride
Ride the Blue Riband
Warwyck's Woman
Claudine's Daughter
Warwyck's Choice

Warwyck's Choice

ROSALIND LAKER

Doubleday & Company, Inc., Garden City, New York
1980

ISBN: 0-385-15649-9
Library of Congress Catalog Card Number 79-7803

Laker

WARWYCK'S CHOICE

Chapter 1

He had forgotten there would be a full moon. At any other time Tom Warwyck would have welcomed its glow, particularly since he was about to keep a highly promising assignation that could only benefit from the romanticism of its silvery aura. But as it happened, he was not able to enter the grounds of Radcliffe Hall by the gates, but must secure his entrance by stealth. It made the moonlight a distinct disadvantage as he made his way, hand over hand, along a branch that was conveniently dipping his weight down on the inner side of the ancient wall of Sussex flints that encompassed the estate.

Abruptly there came a splintering sound and the sharp crack of snapping wood to disturb the balmy night air. The branch lurched downward and he grabbed in vain for another, missing it by an inch. Losing his grip completely, he plummeted down amid a shower of leafy twigs to land with a breathtaking thud on soggy moss and tussocky grass, his long limbs sprawling. He sat up, swearing softly the rich cuss words of the old prize ring learned in early youth from his grandfather, which were more than adequate for any occasion. He was far more concerned for his new suit, a natty gray check, than for his person, which somehow always managed to escape unscathed from falls and tumbles.

All seemed to be well, nothing torn or snagged. He stood up, tall and lean and firmly muscled, to comb back with his fingers his thick, brown hair. His features were well formed in the Warwyck mold of broad brow, large, straight nose, and strong chin, which characterized the males of the family. A final straightening of his cravat, a flick of cuffs into place, followed by an inspection to see that no pieces of grass or damp leaves still clung to his clothes, and then he was off through the trees, making for the landmark of the Radcliffe folly, which was a specially constructed classical ruin that had been built as a fashionable whim at the turn of the century. It was the arranged trysting place with the girl named Laura Bannerman.

The wood was full of night sounds. An owl hooted somewhere near at hand, and there were scrabblings on all sides as small, wild creatures darted away at his approach. Although he kept up a good pace he was alert and watchful at every step, well aware of the danger of his mission, his pulse racing. Not that he was a stranger to perilous circumstances, having been caught up in trouble and involved in escapades throughout the nineteen years of his life, and recently getting sent down from university in the process. But he was always exasperated by any delay in getting what he wanted, and in fancying a girl allied to the Radcliffe household he was having to overcome a deal of otherwise unnecessary risks, for the feud between his family and the Radcliffes had reached the third generation with unremitting bitterness. His own grandfather, Sir Daniel Warwyck, would most surely have exploded with wrath to see his youngest grandson stalking his way across territory that had been forbidden to him since he had first learned that anyone bearing that hated surname of Radcliffe was never to be trusted.

Emerging from the woods, he could see the Hall in the distance, looming in silhouette against the starry sky, some windows lighted and showing gold as if a lamp had been placed behind a cardboard cutout of the many-chimneyed mansion. He was faced with a choice of paths to follow between high box hedges, but he knew which one to take, having explored the grounds many times in his earlier days out of bravado or in response to a dare from

schoolfellows who, like everyone else in the neighborhood, knew of the feud between the two families. In any case he had always believed that rules were made to be broken, and had cheerfully done his best to keep up that tradition at every available opportunity.

Gravel scrunched underfoot, as swiftly and quietly he took a path at his right hand, the box hedges casting deep moon shadows. He came out by the wide lake where water lilies, showing colorless and waxen, had left space enough for an inverted reflection of the ruins to lie shimmering in the dark depths. Another few yards were soon covered, and he reached the marble steps of the folly.

"Laura," he called softly as he entered, his voice echoing uncannily. There came no answering whisper, but he was not surprised. It was not quite midnight and in any case she would not arrive before time. Yet—? He glanced about with a new alertness, not entirely sure that he was alone there and straining his ears for the slightest indication of any hostile presence. Nothing. He should have felt at ease, but he continued to listen warily for a few minutes longer before persuading himself that his heightened senses were playing tricks on him. Thrusting his hands into his pockets, he sauntered deeper into the ruins. With the single exception of the chamber that he was making for, all the rest were roofless and open to the stars, so that dried leaves from the previous autumn whispered about his feet as he passed through the archways from one into another. The only furnishings were scroll-ended stone benches and statues set on plinths, some staring with their blank eyes out of the strangling clutch of ivy which had broken through to take possession of the walls. One inner chamber of considerable size flaunted a curving marble staircase, without balusters or rails, that went up to a narrow balcony backed by the uncompleted wall, and it seemed to him to be a folly within a folly, so purposeless was it. He went underneath the overhang of the balcony into the innermost chamber of all, where he sat down on a bench to wait. Overhead the moonlight, coming in through high apertures, picked out the faded paintings of cavorting Roman gods that decorated the only ceiling in the ruins. It could have been specially fashioned as a lovers' retreat. Perhaps it was. Laura would know it was the spot where she would find him.

He let his mind dwell on her in sensual anticipation. Full young breasts threatening to burst forth from a high-necked bodice, a handspan waist, and a pretty wantonness about her that promised laughter and soft fumblings and ultimate surrender. She was the type of girl, for all her good breeding and high social status, who was destined to be labeled a minx throughout her life by jealous females who lacked her charms. He wondered if she smoked. He'd wager she did. She looked game for anything. Absolutely anything.

He had first seen her on the promenade of Easthampton, which lay no more than two miles away, the sea-bathing resort that his grandfather had founded in 1827 out of a humble fishing hamlet. Many changes had taken place since those days, the resort having grown and expanded almost beyond recognition over past decades, but the promenade still followed its original course above the shingle and the golden sands of the bay, and it was there Laura Bannerman had twirled her scarlet parasol, the fringe dancing like beckoning fingers.

He had been engaged in talk about the boat he was planning to build with one of the fishermen, a burly, good-natured fellow who knew all there was to know of the tides and winds that buffeted the Channel coast, when he had caught sight of her. She was more than eye-catching with the bustled drapery of a cobalt-blue dress accentuating curved hips, and wearing a wide-brimmed hat ornamented by a brilliantly plumaged bird of uncertain origins splaying its wings as though held in its death throes by the very pin that skewered the *chapeau* to the owner's golden head. His gaze had become glued on her. She strolled with an air of boredom, keeping pace alongside a wicker bath chair in which an elderly lady in black was being pushed by a chamois-gloved manservant neat in dark gray with a high-crowned hat. Tom guessed from the girl's impatient, often neck-craning glances over her shoulder at the traffic approaching along the road which ran parallel to the promenade that she was anticipating the arrival of an equipage to put an end to what appeared to be a dreary expedi-

tion for her. He decided to enliven it, and at the same time see if
he could not strike up an acquaintanceship. The occupant of the
bath chair, who sat stolidly, holding a black-and-white-striped parasol between herself and the sun, was probably stone-deaf and
shortsighted, and he foresaw no problems there. Leaving the
fisherman, he began to saunter after the trio.

She made no secret to him that she knew he was there. He
guessed that the slight pause she had made in his vicinity to study
the passing flow of vehicles before catching the bath chair up
again had been to encourage the very diversion he was offering.
There began between them the age-old and pleasurable pastime of
letting eyes meet as if by chance, her head turning as if for the
continued sole purpose of assessing the traffic, and the exchanged
looks became a little longer each time; his bold and compli-
mentary, hers affecting a mischievous disdain until, with perfect
timing, his wide, handsome grin won an upcurling of the lips
from her. He knew she wanted their acquaintanceship to develop
as much as he did. In fact, she wanted what he did, however
much on later, closer terms she would pretend otherwise and need
to be coaxed and wooed and persuaded exactly as he knew how.

His chance to speak came when the three ahead of him reached
the end of the promenade where it gave way to a rough path rising to meet the cliffs that formed the westward curve of the bay
that made Easthampton such a sheltered resort. The manservant,
turning the heavy bath chair to retrace the ground they had covered, was unfortunate enough to lodge one of the large wheels in
a rut caused by recent rains. The bath chair dipped to one side,
bringing a cry of alarm from the old lady and expressed consternation from the girl.

Tom rushed forward. "Pray allow me to help, ladies," he offered
gallantly, but hardly had he put a steadying hand on the wicker
arm when the old lady gave a hiss of outrage, snapping shut her
parasol and whamming it down on his fingers.

"Get away from my chair, you Warwyck!" she thundered aw-
fully. "Get away, I say!"

He stepped back in dismay, recognizing the wizened face of
Mrs. Olivia Radcliffe beneath the veil that trimmed her out-

moded bonnet, the pigmentation of age dark about eyes that glit-
tered venomously at him, almost with a touch of madness. The
girl intervened hastily, uncomfortably aware of turning heads and
curious stares at the astonishing little scene.

"The gentleman only wished to help, Mrs. Radcliffe."

"Bah!" The old widow shook her parasol threateningly as if she
would have struck out at him again if he had not moved out of
range. "No Radcliffe associates in any way with a Warwyck, Miss
Bannerman. Surely you've learned that much during your friendship with my granddaughter? The Warwycks contaminate the
very air that a Radcliffe breathes." She turned her fury upon the
manservant, who had righted the bath chair. "Idiot! Simpleton!
Take me to my carriage immediately! Where is it?" She thumped
her parasol on the arm again with as much force as if a Warwyck's fingers still rested upon it. "Where *is* the brougham?"

"It's coming, madam," the manservant answered on a note of
relief, having sighted its approach. As it drew up with a clop of
hooves he assisted Mrs. Radcliffe out of the bath chair and into
the brougham. Miss Bannerman followed quickly in a rustle of
petticoats, seemingly not daring to give Tom a final glance in
deference to the old lady's outrage, and possibly in fear of an ex-
tension of what he could see had been to her a highly embarrass-
ing incident. He was not surprised. To come at close quarters to
such an expression of the feud must have been decidedly nerve-
racking for a stranger. But his interest in her had not waned. He
intended to find out all he could about her.

It did not prove difficult. Gossip about local families abounded,
and later during a croquet game he learned that Laura Bannerman had attended the same school as the widow's granddaughter,
and both girls were staying at the Hall, Laura until she sailed to
rejoin her parents in India, the other girl for an indefinite period.
With them were four of the Radcliffe-Stuart brothers: Hugh, Bertie, and the inseparable twins, Roger and Oscar, grown sons of
Olivia's only child, Sophie, now deceased, the ages of whom
ranged from twenty-three to Tom's own age. They, in turn, had
brought a number of friends to join them in their customary
early-summer sojourn at their grandmother's residence. Of the five

older brothers in the family, all were married and lived the lives of Scottish gentlemen in the Highlands, no longer descending upon the Hall in droves. It was always said that old Mrs. Radcliffe had brought pressure to bear on her son-in-law, James Stuart, insisting that the family surname be tacked onto that of Stuart if he wanted his children to inherit from her, but whatever the reason, he had acquiesced, and it had had the effect of firing every one of his offspring into carrying on the feud against the Warwycks as fiercely as on the day when it had first come into being. Perhaps that was precisely what Olivia Radcliffe had hoped for, but who could say?

He saw Laura the next day and the day after with the same tantalizing exchange of looks and smiles and glances before he was able to make contact with her, for each time she was with Hugh and Bertie, who failed to notice him leaning nonchalantly against the promenade rails, his eyes absorbing her wickedly under the brim of his straw boater. Everything turned completely in his favor when the following warm and sunny afternoon he sighted her on the beach in a far from amiable mood, her color high, her splendid curves heaving, and with a mulish set to her mouth as she upbraided Hugh Radcliffe-Stuart for failing to be in time to obtain seats in a pleasure steamer, which had left the pier and was already some distance out to sea, flags fluttering overall. From where Tom was leaning his arms on the railings of the promenade he was able to watch the exchange of sharp words between the two of them, and was amused by the discomfiture of one of his old enemies, a black-haired, aggressively good-looking fellow who usually cut a dash with the girls.

"All right! All right!" Hugh's voice suddenly boomed on a louder note, reaching Tom's ears above the splash of waves and the sea gulls' crying. "I'll go and get tickets for tomorrow instead." Abruptly he turned from her and stamped back to a striped tent ticket office that had been set up to deal with bookings, ignoring her taunt thrown after him if it rained she would not go. And it was then that she saw Tom at the railings. Immediately she bit into her lower lip provocatively, looking up at him through her lashes, and the smiles they exchanged spoke volumes each to the other. Deliberately she took the handle of her parasol in both hands and guided the ferrule to write large in the sand: *Radcliffe folly. Midnight.* With a twinkling look over her shoulder at him she hurried off to take a flight of wooden steps away from the beach. Hugh, seeing her go, ran after her, waving two tickets.

In the folly Tom took his gold watch out of his waistcoat pocket and peered at it in the moonlight. Two minutes past midnight. She would be here at any second. A rustle of leaves in one of the outer chambers brought him to his feet from the bench. She had come! Desire was high in him. Throbbing with anticipation, he moved to the archway to greet her, but what he saw banished all else from his head beyond an instinct for self-preservation. Facing him, still two chambers distant, but advancing steadily, was a phalanx of Radcliffe-Stuarts, backed by some other youths whom he did not recognize, showing that whoever else was staying at the Hall had been drawn in to deal with the Warwyck who had dared to trespass. To the forefront was Hugh, such a temper upon him that Tom was left in no doubt that the purpose of his being there was not unknown. Bertie looked no less furious, and the twins' expression was one of rancor and menace, making them appear mirrors of each other.

"There he is!" Several voices raised the shout spontaneously, but following some previous instruction they did not make a rush at him, simply continuing their inexorable approach, knowing he was trapped with the closed chamber behind him and no means of escape. Hugh, who was in his waistcoat ready for battle, smacked one fist into the palm of his other hand and ground it as if preparing his knuckles for the blow he intended to smash home at the offending Warwyck standing in the archway ahead of him.

Tom's face tightened. There were more than a dozen of them altogether. Slowly and deliberately he took off his jacket and waistcoat and commenced to roll up his sleeves. "Which of you am I taking on first?" he challenged with high arrogance, ignoring Hugh's priority. No one answered him, and with an uncomfortable knotting of his stomach muscles he saw by their malevolent expressions that there was to be no individual combat, mass punishment having been lined up for a Warwyck's temerity in aiming for a girl whom a Radcliffe-Stuart had earmarked for himself. That, far more than the trespassing, was the certain cause of their pent-up aggression. Moreover, it was easy to see they had been drinking, probably not with the intention of getting drunk, but sitting on at the dinner table with port and brandy after the cloth was drawn until the time had come for them to snare their quarry in the folly. The mob harm they could inflict upon him under the sway of alcohol, with all reason fled, would be severe in the extreme. He must secure a position where he could not be attacked from all sides and could meet oncomers squarely.

Without seeming to, he took stock quickly of his position. The apertures in the walls around him were out of reach, and there were no footholds in the smooth walls of the enclosed room in which he had been trapped. He must make a dash for the marble staircase leading up to the balcony in the intervening chamber, through which his adversaries were already advancing. He took a few leisurely paces forward as if preparing himself without haste to meet the first onslaught, and without warning sprinted for the stairs.

"Get him!" Hugh roared, leading the rush forward, all breaking into yells, some tallyhoing as if in the hunting field.

Tom was already on the plinth and with his foot in the crook of the statue's arm was high enough to throw himself forward onto the curve of the flight. He would have succeeded in getting there if the statue had not begun to tilt, causing him to lose his balance. He made a grab for the edge of a stair and hung suspended while behind him the statue and the plinth crashed to the ground with an impact that made the whole folly shake.

They were on him at once. He kicked out desperately, but his legs and ankles were seized and down he went, his fall broken by those who were floored with him, brought level by his weight. Not being unprepared, he brought up both fists to crack one against Hugh's chin and catch somebody else a blow in the middle of the forehead that made the fellow collapse back again. The resulting confusion gave Tom a much-needed chance to scramble to his feet. He had been taught the science of self-defense in boxing gloves as his opponents had in their public schools, but oddly, almost as if it were inherent in him, all that his grandfather had taught him of the old bare-knuckle tactics came to the aid of his clenched fists. With lips tightly closed to protect his teeth, of which he was justly proud, he fought as if he had been born to the prize ring that Daniel Warwyck had known, raining chopping blows of exceptional ferocity that had never been experienced before by those seeking to overpower him. His scything punches and kill-bull right-handers met undefended ribs and throats and jaws, and he rendered three of his attackers senseless and put another two out of the fight before the rest overpowered him through sheer weight of numbers while he struggled violently and in vain to free himself. There was blood in his mouth and nose and more gushing from a cut across his brow that he did not remember receiving. Hugh, his own nose streaming blood and one eye blackened and closed, grabbed Tom by the hair and jerked his head back.

"Damn you, Warwyck! You need a dousing to cool you off for more reasons than one!" He released his hold with a wrenching forward and a throwing back that made Tom's neck crack and the muscles sear with pain. "Into the lake with you!"

Uttering triumphant whoops and yells, the gang of them bore him forward at a run through the echoing chambers and out into the night air, thumping and punching and kicking him as they went, he without chance to defend himself, both arms held wide and pinioned. He lost his footing on the steps, sagging in the grip of those holding him, but the haste with which he was being borne along did not slacken. Almost at a run they continued on along the bank of the lake until they reached the ornamental bridge that spanned it. Although he renewed his efforts to free himself, doing some damage in the process, he was overpowered again, going down under pummeling blows. His shoes were wrenched off as he was lifted bodily, still struggling, up onto the parapet of the bridge. Oscar, who had lost a front tooth in the fray, was wild with rage, half suffocating Tom with an arm while his twin was among those with Bertie shoving and pulling with brutal force in readiness to send their victim down into the water.

"Now!" Hugh shouted.

A great thrust sent Tom over it and downward, unable to save himself. He saw his own reflection hurtling to meet him before he hit the water with a tremendous splash and went plummeting down into its chilly depths. Instantly he recovered himself and began to kick out to surface again, not much hampered by what remained of his clothing, for he was a strong swimmer, but there was danger in the weeds that flicked against him, and in the tangled undergrowth of the lilies.

He took a great gulp of air as he surfaced, treading water as he looked to see in which direction he should swim. With angry dismay he saw that Hugh and some others were putting out in the two rowboats kept by the bridge, intent on continued punishment. Immediately he struck out for the opposite bank, not realizing that the lilies would bar his landing until he began to flounder among the stalks like a fish in a net. Turning, he saw his foes were gaining on him, and he dived down under the surface, where he swam through waving weeds, making for the far end of the lake, where the lilies thinned out to leave the water clear.

Amid the dark ripples under the bridge he bobbed up for air and was unnoticed by those jeering and shouting in the boats, who were plunging their oars in among the lily pads, thinking he was sheltering somewhere amid the foliage. Without a splash he sought the depths again, and when next he came up for air the bridge was some distance behind him and the bank he had been aiming for was within easy reach. A few more strokes, and then his bare feet were touching sticky mud. With water pouring from him he waded out of the lake and climbed laboriously on hands and knees up the bank to collapse face downward on the grass, shivering violently with cold and exertion, his teeth chattering. But he was to be allowed no respite. A shout came from amid the trees near at hand where he had least expected to be observed.

" 'Ere! What's going on? 'Oo the 'ell are you?"

It was a gamekeeper on the night watch for poachers. His stern challenge had resounded far in the still air, alerting those still searching among the lilies for their vanished quarry, and their voices took on a fierce, deeply ominous rumble at the trick that had been played upon them. Tom lifted his head almost imperceptibly, watching through the dripping fronds of his hair as a pair of gaitered legs and booted feet stumped toward him, the barrels of a shotgun gleaming. Both rowboats had changed course, oars once more in impatient hands, and as the first of them came plowing its way out of the lilies to shoot under the bridge, Hugh, seated in the bow, cupped his hands about his mouth and bawled out an order.

"Don't let him get away!"

The gamekeeper had no intention of letting that happen. "On your feet, boy!" he ordered Tom grimly.

Tom made an attempt, reeled, and fell to his knees, bowed over. The man, seeing that he appeared half drowned and in no state to abscond, came closer to investigate, giving him a dig in the ribs with the toe of his boot that was far from gentle.

"'Ere, you! Get up, I tell you."

Tom obeyed, but not in the manner that had been expected, moving with a speed and strength that was born totally of desperation. A chopping blow against the man's wrist sent the gun flying, and it was followed with a left-hander to the belly that doubled him up to meet a crack on the chin, which in turn sent him flat on his back as though poleaxed. But Tom did not wait to see where the man landed on the grass. The boats had put in to the bank and his pursuers were spilling out of them, shouting to each other to spread out and cut him off. He had no choice but to run in the direction in which he was being hounded, which was away from the distant gates or any other escape route he might have taken, and he crashed through shrubberies, dodged trees, leaped steps down into sunken gardens to race past playing fountains, and up again. All the time the moonlight pursued him as relentlessly, seizing upon him whenever he emerged from cover. Somewhere behind him the shotgun was fired twice, a signal to other gamekeepers that there was an intruder in the grounds, and he faced a new danger of a potshot being taken at him from any who might come from the direction in which he was running. Twice he fell as he pounded along, doing himself no harm the first time, but afterward he tripped and went hurtling down on a flagged path, hitting his knee, and when he ran on again there was a limping gait to his pace, slowing him down.

He was almost level with the Hall. His mind raced. None of his pursuers would expect him to be crazy enough to seek any kind of refuge there and were thinking that they could run him like a hare until he dropped. He was not far from that state of exhaustion, his lungs sore with breath gasping, his legs heavy, and his knee making him stagger; at least he was no longer chilled, but pouring sweat from every pore. Dodging low, he switched direction toward the house.

Radcliffe Hall soared hugely above him when he reached the rose garden that flanked the east wing. He had never been so near it before, but he knew there was a large conservatory attached to the house not far from the arbor, and he made for it cautiously, his pace slackening as he stooped down to skim past the windows on that side, some lighted, but most in darkness. He reached the glass door of the conservatory and turned the handle. It gave! Still crouched down to avoid detection, he almost fell through the door, and once on his knees made no fruitless effort to rise again, but shut the door after him and crawled past flowering pot plants and groups of ferns setting off the seclusion of wrought-iron tables and cushioned basket chairs where doubtless the widow Radcliffe sat with her family for tea on coolish days. He reached a far corner and lay there on the russet tiles amid the greenery, his heart still hammering against his ribs as if it would never accustom itself to a slower beat again, his throat working convulsively on every rasping intake of air. For the first time since he had been alerted to danger in the folly he turned his thoughts to Laura Bannerman and her betrayal.

What a fool he had been! He had seen she was a born flirt, flippant and perverse, who out of pique and temper made that assignation with him with the coquettish spite in her common to such girls who liked to play one man off against another. She had let it be known that a Warwyck would be waiting for her at the folly at midnight. The duplicity of women was beyond belief. He had learned a bitter lesson, and he would never be caught again.

The door from the house into the conservatory opened, a lamp spilling arrows of light across the floor between the plants. He held his breath, not daring to move, and heard slippered footsteps crossing the tiled floor. They came to a halt. Whoever it was must have come to peer through the glass in the hope of catching some glimpse of the chase outside.

To his dismay the footsteps had paused only briefly, and were coming toward the place where he was lying. Still he hoped to escape detection, hidden as he was in a corner, but as the lamp drew nearer, sending the shadows of exotically shaped leaves and blossoms leaping up on all sides, he glimpsed the tiles along which he had crawled and saw that he had left a telltale trail of blood drops. Well, a Warwyck should not be caught skulking in the darkness. He would get to his feet and defend himself again somehow. Pushing aside the plants that were shielding him, he made no attempt at silence and was rising when some drooping palm leaves were held back by the bearer of the opaque-globed lamp and its light fell full upon him. It was a girl who stood there. Not Laura, but one whom to his knowledge he had never seen before, in a throat-to-toe robe cascading lace over a nightgown, her dark red hair flowing down her back, her oval face taut and angry and hostile. At the battered, gory sight of him she drew back a pace, her eyes widening incredulously, and she looked aghast, her gaze taking in every detail of his appearance from the wet and matted state of his hair to the shirt hanging in tatters from his bruised body and the torn trousers caked in mud, but in no way did her bristling animosity abate.

"How dare you set foot in my grandmother's house!" Nicolette Radcliffe-Stuart's voice shook with anger. She had seen his stealthy approach from her bedroom window and had rushed down to order him out herself, thinking that he was persisting in a meeting with Laura, who had provoked Hugh unmercifully with the disclosure of the arranged tête-à-tête, which anybody else but a besotted swain could see she had no intention of keeping. Nicolette had felt exasperated with the two of them, but had held her tongue. Now the unpleasant task of banishing the intruder had fallen to her, and in spite of all he appeared to have suffered at her brothers' hands he looked as if he would not go willingly.

"Leave at once!" she ordered again and more fiercely than before, since he had made no move. "No Warwyck is welcome in these grounds!"

Tom, from where he leaned against a wall for support, glared at her wrathfully. So this was the youngest child of the Radcliffe-Stuarts. He knew about her. There was little that the two families did not know about each other. Nicolette was the spoiled brat of the brood; only daughter after nine sons to be born to a doting mother who had never allowed her precious darling to visit the Sussex coast with the boys. Old Mrs. Radcliffe had had to bestir her creaking bones up to Edinburgh every time she had wanted to see her favorite grandchild.

"I'll come again if it suits me!" he retorted in the same fierce tone. "And I'll still come alone. But I'll make sure of a vantage point next time and not allow myself to be caught in a trap. In the meantime I'll not let you light the way for my would-be captors." His arm swung out and she saw the state of his raw, split knuckles in the instant before he knocked the lamp from her hand. It crashed to the floor, the light going out, and the conservatory was plunged once more into its patterns of black and silver. He made to reel past her, but staggered and would have fallen if she had not reached out instinctively to grab his arm and steady him.

"That was most courteous of you," he jeered angrily, pulling himself free, "but I can manage."

He took two steps away from her and fell flat on his face. She eyed him with delicate scorn, smoothing the palms of her hands down the sides of her robe as if to remove the feel of him. All she had heard of the stiff-necked arrogance of the Warwycks was more than true. As he struggled to rise to his knees she jerked her head up sharply, her attention caught by sounds of the search moving into the vicinity of the Hall. Quickly she went to the glass and looked out, able to see figures running past in the moonlight, one breaking away to take the path branching toward the conservatory. Her mouth parted softly. It was Lawrence Payne, one of Hugh's friends, who had taken a fancy to her and, if she cared to admit it, she a tender liking for him. She glanced down again with a wrinkling of her brow at Tom, who had collapsed once more, his forehead resting against the cool tiles while he strove to summon up whatever energy he had left, for he had heard the approach of the others as clearly as she had. Skirting him where he lay, she brushed her way through the plants and hastened to open the door that led out into the garden.

Lawrence sighted her, slowing his pace over the last couple of yards. "What are you doing downstairs, Nicolette? You said good night a couple of hours ago." He sounded worried that she should be witness to any part of what was taking place, and she guessed that he wanted to spare her any fright or glimpse of violence.

"Who could go to sleep without finding out what happened?" she replied, pleased with his concern for her.

He reached the door, panting heavily from all the running he had done, and clapped a hand against the jamb, glad of a rest. A punch he had received in the ribs was causing him a deal of pain. "Tom Warwyck got away from us, but he's still somewhere in the grounds, and we intend to finish off the lesson he deserves before chucking him out through the gates. Where's Laura? Awaiting his head on a platter?"

"She's shut herself in her room, but her light is still on."

"Hmm. Is it? She'll get a shock when she sees Hugh and so will you, but he's not the only one who's suffered a black eye. We're searching the stables and outhouses now for the enemy, and if you'll just step aside I'll take a quick look around the conservatory."

In the shadows of the palms Tom groaned inwardly. Now she would give him away. He had managed to get to his knees and intended to use the same tactics as he had on the gamekeeper, although his arms were drained of the power that had been there before, every muscle plagued with tiredness, but he would do what he could in the circumstances. Then her next words made him catch his breath incredulously and with relief.

"There's no need. I've been keeping a lookout all the time. You had better catch up with the others and I'll lock the door to make sure there's no chance of his getting in here."

Lawrence was reluctant to be dismissed. Coming across Nicolette on her own in garments that should never have been seen beyond the bedroom door had put enticing thoughts of another kind of chase into his head. He thrust himself forward and held the door even as she would have closed it.

"I'd better check anyway." For a moment it seemed to him that she would have struggled with the door if she thought her strength could have matched his, but as it was she let it go and stepped back gracefully in a drifting of lace.

"Whatever you say, Lawrence. We'll share the chore. You search the east end of the conservatory and I'll take the other."

Because he did not believe Tom Warwyck would have ventured anywhere near the house, let alone enter into any section of it, he indulged her whim, and after making a perfunctory search among a few plants he went back to meet her as she diligently combed her way through the foliage. He took both her hands into his.

"There's nobody here," he said in a low voice. "Nobody except us." He stepped forward to draw her to him and a piece of glass crunched under the sole of his shoe.

Tom, who was lying flat on his stomach again, Nicolette having pressed his shoulder down warningly when she had passed him by, saw that shards from the smashed lamp lay scattered all around. But the fellow she had addressed as Lawrence had more on his mind than glass underfoot. Between the plant pots Tom observed her small, slippered feet draw nearer the man who was taking her into his arms, and her heels left the ground as the embrace tightened. He shook his aching head wearily and let it sink once again onto the tiles. There was nothing he wanted less than to be within earshot of a loving exchange, but both speech and movement were magnified by the odd acoustics of the conservatory, and there was no escaping it. He could almost hear the intensity of the kiss that was taking place, the passion of one mouth bearing down upon another that was softer, gentler, but no less willing. Uncomfortably he found himself physically stirred by the image conjured up of her responsive lips, his own seeming to know the contours and moistness of them, his tongue the honey taste of her.

The kiss that she might otherwise have enjoyed was ruined for Nicolette by the intrusive presence of a stranger, even though he was out of sight and could not possibly see them through the thick greenery. But he was there. Animosity and resentment emanated from him with such force that she was acutely affected by it, disappointment soaring in her that Lawrence should have proved so insensitive as to choose such a time and place to enfold her to him in a first kiss. She knew the labeling of blame to be irrational since he in no way suspected that Tom was there, but inevitably it made her less disposed toward him. Abruptly she broke away from his arms.

"You must go, Lawrence," she said hastily. "The others will miss you and I should not be down here anyway."

He knew she was right. At any moment somebody might come resummoning his help in the chase, and he had no wish to compromise her; moreover, if that old dragon of a grandmother should get wind of them being alone together, he would be told to leave the Hall without further ado. But it was hard to do what was wise. Resignedly he made to follow her toward the garden door, where she stood waiting to bolt it behind him, and again he stepped on glass. He looked down. There was glass everywhere. He frowned, suddenly suspicious. Did it come from a broken pane?

Through a gap between the plant pots Tom saw Lawrence's hand descend to pick up a piece of the glass, and the sweat stood out on his brow. He should never have resorted to refuge, but kept on his feet somehow, for by giving in to the exhaustion of his lungs and limbs he had gained nothing, every nerve and sinew in protest against the further combat that must come. Lawrence's voice spoke on a new note, wary and on guard.

"Close and lock that door, Nicolette, and then go into the house out of possible harm's way. There's a lot of glass around, and I'm going to find out where it has come from. We may not be alone after all."

Tom heard her give a tinkling little laugh and the lace hem of her robe swirled forward. "It came from the lamp I dropped." Her fingers snatched up a curved fragment. "See! It is opaque. Look closer at the pattern in the moonlight."

"A lamp? What happened?" He sounded surprised and dubious, but his fingertip slid on the fragment as he examined it.

A whisper of lace as she shrugged. "In the excitement of the moment it somehow flew out of my hands. Fortunately the moonlight showed me all I wanted to see without bothering to fetch another."

"Where is it? If it's leaked all its oil it could be dangerous." He was persistent. "We had better find it."

Tom knew where it was. Lying on its side, it was no more than a foot away from him. Already Lawrence was hunting about, dangerously near. If he could just get it to roll against her slippered toe! Carefully he reached out and prodded the lamp, and in the same instant she moved out of range. He cursed his luck. The lamp clanked horribly as it rolled, but she must have been expecting him to aid her, and she snatched it up.

"I've found it," she announced triumphantly, "and it hasn't spilled a drop of oil. Now you really must go."

Outside the door Lawrence waited until she had turned the key, her moon-bathed movements held in the glass panels as if in a frame. When the lock clicked reassuringly he gave her a wave and departed, making for the stables at a jogging run, his hand pressed to his painful ribs. She leaned back against the door and expelled a long breath. An appeal to Lawrence on Tom's behalf would have been in vain, for he was Hugh's lifelong friend and their loyalties were shared. To approach any of her brothers with the same request would be equally fruitless, because she knew the Radcliffes' stubbornness, having a fair share of it herself, and they hung on like bulldogs when their minds were made up on a matter. She did not dare to contemplate their fury if ever they should learn that she had sheltered Tom Warwyck, but since she would have given succor to any ill-used animal or harmed bird she could not in all conscience turn a human being loose to suffer more punishment at their hands. Never had she felt more shocked than when she had clapped eyes on Tom's pitiable, blood-soaked state through which his fierceness had shone undefeated. He was an antagonistic, disagreeable young man, a Warwyck in every sense of the word, but she was compelled to shelter him a while longer.

As she moved from the door she glanced down at the floor. The blood he had left did not show in the shadows, and she had been on tenterhooks all the time in case Lawrence should strike a match. At the first chance she must wash it away. There were pools of it where he was lying. The fronded palm leaves danced behind her as she stood looking down at him.

"You can't stay here," she said coolly. "It isn't safe."

He looked up over his shoulder at her, postponing the moment when he must exert himself and struggle to his feet. "I know, and I appreciate what you did for me. I'll get away as soon as the hue and cry has died down. I can't believe they'll look for me all night."

"They will if they think you're still in the grounds. You wouldn't stand a chance. There'll be a watch on the walls and at the gates. If you take off the remnants of that sodden shirt and hold it against your face to stop blood dripping everywhere I can get you up to my room without anybody knowing. Nobody would think of looking for you there, and you can stay until I find out when it's safe to leave."

He regarded her steadily, his brown eyes very bright under his deep frown. Her face was as composed and hostile as it had been from the start. Her dislike of him was transparent. "Why?" he asked bluntly. "Why should a Radcliffe help a Warwyck?"

"I'd not turn my worst enemy out to suffer what would still be in store for you," she answered crisply, "and after all, you are my worst enemy, I suppose."

He croaked a laugh, but she saw nothing amusing in what she had said and raised her eyebrows disdainfully. Thrusting himself up by the flat of his hands he kneeled and then reeled to his feet. Curiously, one button was still fastened on his shirt, and as he fumbled with it, barely able to see, she brushed his fingers aside impatiently and undid it herself. But she was gentle in helping him remove his rags, showing that she understood the agony his pummeled muscles were giving him, and it was she who folded the shirt into a neat pad to press against his face. Then she put her arm about his waist, told him to put his around her shoulders, and together at a stumbling pace they went into the house.

She took him up a servants' rear staircase to the second floor, where they crossed a landing to reach her bedroom. She had left a light burning, and he had a quick impression of pastel-hued walls and dark furniture. She let go of him to pull a chair forward.

"Sit down," she said authoritatively, completely in charge, and went to pour from a ewer into a basin on the washstand.

He obeyed her reluctantly, thinking she had the kind of imperious manner that he disliked in a woman, and he resented being ordered about. However, he tilted his head obediently this way and that at her instructions, although with some slowness to assert his own masculine superiority, while she bathed his cuts and his swollen eye, the water she had poured into the basin turning red. He observed her with his good eye as she carried out her self-imposed duties, the gas lamp suspended from the ceiling showing him details of her features and her figure that he had barely grasped through rage, pain, and blood before dashing the lamp she had carried from her hand. She was slender and stalk-like, her small breasts barely making any protrusion under her robe, the lace of which had lost its pristine whiteness through contact with him, and her neck was longer than was normal, giving a proud look to the way she held her head.

As she leaned close to him her breath was warm and fragrant in his face, making him aware that he smelled strongly and pungently of sweat and grass and lake mud, and her nostrils were curved in an almond line in a nose that was well shaped and a trifle pert. Her eyes, intent upon her task, were hazel, a definite blend of green and gold and brown. For himself, he preferred a girl to have blue eyes even as he liked hair to be fair with curls to ring about his finger, although after Laura's treachery he doubted if he would ever trust those colors again.

She finished fastening a clean linen bandage about his head and stood back to study it critically. "There. That should stay in place. Now you had better get some sleep. I'll wake you when it's morning."

He closed his eyes, thankful to surrender to sanctuary and the bliss of sleep, which overtook him even as she set a cushion behind his head. He did not feel her lift his legs by the ankles onto a stool, or know that she covered him with a blanket taken from her own bed.

Once more she left her room. This time she took with her a petticoat from her chest of drawers to use as a washcloth, and in the conservatory she wiped away all bloody evidence from the

tiles that an injured man had been there. Outside everything was
quiet. Her brothers and the rest must have concentrated the hunt
through some of the woodland, a natural choice for a fugitive
seeking cover. How odd it was that she, who had always scoffed at
the name of Warwyck with everybody else in the family, even
though she had never seen one of them until this night, should
have gone against kin and tradition and the whole conditioning of
her outlook toward the feud. And within the first ten days of her
coming to the seat of her forebears, which was to be her home
from now on.

As she took the stairs again she mused over the events of the
night, hoping that her involvement was not an omen of as much
trouble awaiting her in this seaside district of Easthampton as she
had left behind in Edinburgh. Living with her father's second
wife for almost six months had not been easy, for Felicity Stuart
was only a few years older than herself, and had set about, upon
her return from the honeymoon trip, to eclipse all memory of the
woman whose place she had filled, wanting to be called
"Mamma" even by Hugh and those of his brothers still attached
to schools or universities. Nicolette had led the rebellion and
knew Felicity was never to forgive her for it, dooming any chance
of an amiable relationship developing between them. Nicolette
was sickened as much by the sight of her mother's rings being
flaunted on another woman's fingers as by her father's infatuated
attendance upon his new wife, his behavior more suited to a boy
in love for the first time than to a gray-haired, middle-aged man
with a portly figure. He had been no more than a day out of the
year's mourning when the marriage had taken place. In the
church Nicolette, resentful and bewildered, had stood with her
five elder brothers and their wives, the younger boys in the pew
behind, and listened to the service, unable to comprehend why
her father should have chosen such a very young woman. Felicity
was well-bred, poised, and pretty enough, but quite apart from the
difference in their ages, he had nothing in common with her either intellectually or aesthetically, for unlike Nicolette's mother
she never opened a book, and liked no music unless it had a jingly
tune to set her frivolous toe tapping.

It took Laura, who had had older men hotfoot after her, to explain a few facts to Nicolette and widen her basically innocent knowledge of the marital realm and all appertaining to it. Nicolette did not doubt the truth of it, and by the time every one of her mother's treasured possessions and favorite pieces of furniture had been removed to the attic, Felicity was *enceinte,* a perfectly healthy state that she used as an excuse for tearful hysterics and tempestuous scenes whenever Nicolette came near her. The battle was soon won and Felicity the undoubted victor. Nicolette well remembered her father's stern announcement to her in the privacy of his study that for the sake of his wife's peace of mind and the well-being of the unborn child, he was sending her to live with her grandmother. He was overly stern to hide his distress at sending her away, but Nicolette welcomed the deliverance. The Edinburgh house was not home any more. She had noticed before, among the residences of her friends, that when a beloved wife and mother died the very spirit of the home died with her. Some houses never recovered.

She opened the door and went into the bedroom where Tom sat slumped in the chair in deepest sleep. Some part of the blanket had slipped off him, and she pulled it up again, tucking it more securely about his neck. His poor face was a sorry sight. Compassion moved her strongly. For a moment, not quite knowing why, she wished his name was anything but Warwyck.

Chapter 2

Tom awoke to a shaking of his shoulder and he sat forward sharply, alert to danger, but it was only Nicolette who stood by him in the dawn's light that came through the windows. She was fully dressed, a bonnet tied with ribbons in a bow at the side of her face. There was a freshness of morning air about her, revealing that she had already been outside.

"Come on," she urged in a whisper. "It's time for you to leave now. The hunt was given up an hour ago, but to be on the safe side I'm going to drive you out of the grounds myself. The sooner all this business is over and forgotten, the better it will be."

He moved stiffly out of the chair, twinges of pain stabbing all over him, which came as much from sleeping awkwardly as from the ordeal he had been through the night before, and he gave an involuntary grunt, which sounded loud in the stillness of the room. She was pulling on gloves and spun about toward him, knowing from a family of father and brothers how men could never bear small inconveniences stoically. She put a finger to her lips with some impatience. "Shh! Don't make a fuss."

He glowered at her. A *fuss!* What was he doing anyway, sheltering behind her skirts for protection? He would walk out of this damn house with his Warwyck head held high and take on all comers if they liked to set on him again. His strength had returned, the rawness had gone from his lungs, and altogether the three or four hours' sleep had done him a power of good. He began to flex his arms and shoulders where he sat, intent on getting his muscles back into shape with banishment of the pain.

"There's no need for you to drive me anywhere," he said, not ungraciously, but wanting her to know that he would take no more orders. "I'll leave by the way I came in, but at my own pace this time and in full view for all to see." He broke off. She had gone quite fiery with anger, clenching her small fists and bringing them shoulder-high on bent elbows before thumping them down again in exasperation against the brown silk of her skirt.

"You really are the most inconsiderate and hotheaded fellow it's ever been my misfortune to meet! It's certainly true that you Warwycks think only of yourselves and ride roughshod over everyone. *You'll* strut off in full view of the house? Marvelous! Wonderful!" She chucked her chin about on the vehemence of her words. "And who will be left to answer questions as to where you could possibly have spent those hours of hiding? Who will be the one to explain away again a dropped lamp? Suppose some telltale smears of your gore have been left on the conservatory tiles, because after all I had only the moonlight to aid me in the mopping up? If nobody is suspicious then nobody will look, but your fine departure like a knight going home after a battle could be enough for my grandmother to decide against giving me a permanent home and send me back to Scotland in disgrace!"

He got up out of the chair and limped toward her, his knee less rested than he had expected, but he ignored it, concentrating on her. There was the glint of despairing tears in her eyes as well as a very real dread of being sent away. "I didn't think," he explained apologetically. "Of course I won't do anything to bring trouble down on your head. Look what you did for me. I'll do anything you say."

She gulped and nodded, mollified. "That's more obliging of you. I realize we're bound to fight like cats and dogs all the time we're together. It's inevitable. Let us go without further delay."

She took him by a different route out of the Hall, avoiding the servants' stairway, for in the kitchens life was already astir. They went silently down the main flight and out through a gardening room where flowers were arranged for the house. A horse and dog-cart, which she had had brought from the stables, awaited them under a covered way, no one in charge.

"Get in," she urged, "and lie down quickly. We can't be seen from the house here, but there's always the risk of someone coming along."

He did as she told him, and when she took the driver's seat she unfolded a plaid traveling rug over her lap, spreading it wide so that it completely covered him. He was left in its red, woolly glow, curled around her feet, jogged by the rhythm of the wheels as they left the house behind them.

"How will you explain this expedition?" he asked her.

Her voice came back to him. "I've been twice for a ride along the Easthampton sands in the early morning, and this time I'll take a drive around the countryside instead, after leaving you at the Grange."

He felt his face gingerly with his fingertips. It needed expert treatment if his bruises were to heal quickly. "Would you take me to Easthampton House instead of my home?" he requested. "As you must surely know, my grandfather was a bare-knuckle pugilist in his younger days, and he'll know exactly what to do for me."

"Very well. You're fortunate to have the healing ministrations of a onetime Champion of England at your disposal," she remarked dryly. "My brothers and their friends are less lucky. Those who bore the worst brunt of your fists at the folly hobbled in like wounded men, and as far as I could see when I went to the head of the stairs upon their return, there was not one who escaped some unsightly damage to his features."

"I'm glad to hear it," he commented with ruthless satisfaction.

She said nothing. Her silence was icy. She loved her brothers and would countenance nothing against them. At the gates he heard her exchange good-morning greetings with the gatekeeper, who came hurrying from the lodge to open them up for her. He waited until they had passed through and were out of earshot before he spoke again, not wanting their association to end in a complete breakdown of communication.

"What has made you decide to make your home at Radcliffe Hall? I noticed you revealed a distinct aversion to Scotland. Didn't you like living in the north?"

She was compelled to defend her birthplace. "I loved it. I'll always love Scotland. But my father married again. I don't want to go back there."

"Why did you never come to stay at the Hall as your brothers did?"

"There was a time when I was not considered robust enough to take the long traveling, and when I was older my mother's health was in a decline and she could scarcely bear me to be away from her side for any length of time."

As she followed the country lane, making for the sea, she recalled her early years when she had been dosed and purged and confined to bed at the slightest sniffle. For herself, she believed that more fresh air and less cosseting would have given her the color in her cheeks that was always missing in those days. As she approached young womanhood and began to break the shackles and assert her spirited independence, she took to riding and tennis and walking and swimming with enthusiasm, feeling she could never get enough of the open air of which her lungs had been long deprived. To go to the local day school for the daughters of gentlefolk had been another breakthrough after a succession of governesses, none of whom had met her mother's exacting standards, and her friendship with Laura had developed from the first day. They had been in a number of scrapes together, all harmless and quite hilarious at times, but these small escapades had paled into insignificance beside the glorious tales always told by her brothers upon their return from visits to Radcliffe Hall of clashes with the detested Warwycks on pier, beach, and neutral lawns. Well, now she had been part of one of those clashes, and it had been a deal less glorious than those legends of the past, which most probably had been embroidered and exaggerated to impress a young sister and—later—her extremely attractive friend.

Easthampton was coming into sight, veiled here and there by the lightest of sea mists. Within minutes she would be in the outskirts of the town that was the root and cause of the whole feud, for her grandfather, Alexander Radcliffe, had totally opposed Daniel Warwyck's development of it as a sea-bathing resort out of a peaceful fishing hamlet in the early part of the century. She knew that her grandfather had had the highest motives for his objections, his concern being for the humble inhabitants as well as for himself and his well-to-do neighbors, none of them wishing to see the growth of a fairground sprawl of tawdry buildings and tasteless attractions that could ruin both the area and the very countryside that surrounded it. Yet many of those fears proved to be unfounded, only the best of architecture gracing the resort from the colonnaded Assembly Rooms to the home of the founder himself, and for a long time it remained a tranquil and genteel place patronized only by persons of quality, including a number of royal visitors, but the savagery of the feud did not abate. Alexander was dead when the first railway branch reached Easthampton, and he never saw the first signs of the changes he had always dreaded, when cheap fares and excursions opened floodgates to mobs of folk who had never been able to afford trips to the seaside before. Inevitably, the resort began to cater for their less sophisticated tastes, driving the elite away to foreign spas and more exclusive abodes. Coinciding with the arrival of the railway's link with Easthampton, the Warwyck grip on the place slipped beyond recall, much of the property and land being sold into more mercenary hands where it was exploited shamelessly, but Daniel Warwyck could do nothing to prevent it, having suffered severe financial losses in other directions. Over the past decade the resort's decline had culminated in a veritable explosion of vulgarity, restraint thrown to the winds, nothing too gaudy or too bawdy to keep the seaside holiday makers happy and the money flowing from their pocketbooks and purses. Nicolette had heard her grandmother say many times that her dear Alexander must be turning in his grave.

But, oddly, there was never any softening of tone when he was mentioned. Indeed, there were times when Nicolette, observing the bitter lines etched in her grandmother's face, the hardness of eyes and mouth, wondered if there was more behind the feud that had never been revealed. Admittedly, no hint of a dark secret had ever been given, either on her grandmother's many visits to Scotland or since her own arrival at the Hall, but the impression remained, something that could not be dismissed although doubtless, if there was any foundation to it, the truth would die with Olivia Radcliffe and perhaps with Daniel Warwyck too.

The plaid rug slipped from her lap as Tom flung it back, having had enough of the stifling atmosphere, and half raised his head inquiringly. "Where are we?"

"In Victoria Avenue," she answered. Passing by on either side of the dogcart were some of the later houses of Easthampton, built in the past thirty years since the coming of the railway, their solid red brick, Gothic ornamentation and large gardens spreading the boundaries of the resort far beyond its original confines.

"Not far now," he remarked, resting an arm under his head as he looked up at her, her profile under the high-perched bonnet neat against the sky and the trees that were following one another in orderly succession. "I had better keep low until we reach Easthampton House. It wouldn't do for anybody around here to see us together either. Word could get back to your grandmother."

"I had thought of that."

He chuckled where he lay, his sense of humor suddenly getting the better of him. "This is a fine kettle of fish, is it not? A Radcliffe and a Warwyck conspiring together."

She glanced down at him. His grin was impudent, but without malevolence or design. Against her will the notorious Warwyck charm almost melted her frosty attitude, but she forced herself to remember the damage inflicted on her brothers, which had appeared to be every bit as severe as that which he had received. She kept before her the image of Oscar, always her favorite, with the ugly gap in teeth that had been faultless and even. Yet as she turned her long-lashed, stony gaze once more on the road ahead she knew that in spite of herself Tom's grin had held them momentarily in limbo as if the feud were no responsibility of theirs and could not mold their lives.

As the dogcart progressed, there came squares flanked by the elegant terraces of the resort's earlier days, with fanlighted doorways, delicately canopied balconies, and pastel stucco. As one commercial street met another the windows of the emporia and stores of every kind reflected Nicolette and the equipage as she drove past, red wheels spinning, the horse stepping high. Everywhere the bakeries, already open for business, wafted out the appetizing aromas of new-baked bread and currant buns, causing Tom's belly to rumble with hunger.

Reaching the seafront, they continued on past the many hotels and the stretch of gaudy souvenir shops that stood side by side with the waxworks museum and other sideshows that catered for the tripper trade. Beyond the promenade the waves of the wide bay were rolling in like liquid silver over the white sands, the last traces of the mist dissolved into sparkling atoms irradiating the sun's rising brilliance. Along the chain pier the flags made confetti spots of color, not yet alive in the unnatural stillness of the early morning.

She did not have to ask where Easthampton House was to be found, for not only had she recognized it from its description on her first ride through the town to take a canter on the beach, but none could escape seeing it from almost any part of the resort. It had been built on a green hillock overlooking the stretch of Ring Park down to the sea itself, and as she turned the horse toward it she thought again that it was a remarkably beautiful mansion with its pure lines, tall windows, and graceful frontage, some trick of light and position giving it an iridescent quality as if it were fashioned out of a giant seashell.

She reached the horseshoe curve of the road at the north end of Ring Park, so named for the old prize ring, and drew up at the gates of Easthampton House. "We've arrived," she said.

"Good," Tom acknowledged, but did not rise from where he lay. The gates screeched slightly as a gardener's boy opened them.

"You had better get out quickly," she advised, glancing about her. Admittedly only a milkman with his handcart was to be seen, but she felt remarkably conspicuous sitting there in a Radcliffe dogcart outside the Warwyck gates.

He stared up at her incredulously. "Aren't you going to drive me to the entrance?"

It was no frivolous request, for the drive up to the house was long and took several turns as it wound like a ribbon to follow the slope of the hillock. It would be no easy walk for him with his painful knee. The rosy softness of her lips set stubbornly.

"I'm not crossing onto Warwyck land."

For a moment he seemed scarcely able to believe what he had heard, and then his temper flared. "Well, I must say!" he exclaimed inadequately, sitting up and clapping his hands down on his outstretched knees. "If that isn't the limit! Fair's fair! Remember I happen to have spent half the night on Radcliffe territory."

"That was your choice," she retorted. "You came to see Laura. There's no one I want to spoon with at Easthampton House."

He gasped, outraged. She could not have used a taunt to needle him more, and he tore at the plaid rug still entangled about an ankle to free himself and get out of the dogcart. Quite apart from anything else her statement had been like a personal rejection, and inexplicably his pride was hurt.

"That's it, then. Goodbye." The inflection in his voice gave emphasis to the parting. He got out of the dogcart and would have limped through the gates without a backward glance if she had whipped up the horse immediately, but when she did not, he turned on one heel to stay between the dolphin-headed gateposts, seeking the cause of her delay. She looked nonplused by his turnabout.

"I just wanted to make sure you could get up the drive on foot," she said confusedly.

He set his hands on his hips. "I'll manage," he said without rancor, in a wry reminder of his use of those same words in the conservatory, his eyes narrowed as he watched her. It came, the smile he had hoped for, illuminating her face as though from a candle within, and the raw disgruntlement that had descended upon him

at their parting lifted and dispersed. She cracked the whip and departed smartly. He began to limp up the drive and took shortcuts
across the lawns, avoiding the turns, absorbed in his thoughts. His
grandfather's booming voice from an open window startled him
out of his reverie as he drew near the steps of Easthampton
House.

"What in the devil's name have you been up to?"

Tom stopped and looked up, remembering what a sight he
must present in nothing but a pair of torn, mud-stained trousers,
his torso covered with bruises, his face a rare combination of reds
and purples, with a bandage about his forehead. "I've been in a
fight, sir. I hoped you'd patch me up before I go home."

The stern visage of Daniel Warwyck did not change expression,
but he nodded and indicated with a silken gleam of dressing-robe
sleeve that Tom should enter the house without further delay.
Drawing away from the window, Daniel resumed the grooming of
his thick, gray hair with the silver-backed brushes that his late
wife had given him on one of his natal days. Beneath the mask of
age in the looking glass there was an undoubted likeness to the
young scallywag who was the dearest of all his grandsons, and the
thought pleased him. Whether he had ever been as wild and trou-
blesome as Tom was difficult to say, but he had certainly never
been as undisciplined, having been trained from an early age for
the prize ring, and it was the very habit of that training that sat
upon him still, making him rise at an early hour when other men
of his advanced age would have snoozed on under the coverlets.
He was troubled by rheumatism in his right shoulder and a
stiffness in one leg due to injuries sustained during his last fight,
which had made him Champion of England and brought about
his retirement in glory from the prize ring. Otherwise, apart from
stone-deafness in one ear caused by a much earlier bout, he had
little to complain about and much to be thankful for. He put
down the brushes and turned when a knock came on his door.

"Come in, Tom."

The lad entered, not subdued by a battered appearance, but
cockily as if he had won a bout without a scratch. "You should
have seen the others, Grandfather," he joked incautiously.

Daniel was unsmiling. "Indeed? And who is caring for them?"

"They'll not lack for attendance."

"I'm glad to hear it. After a mill, no matter how grueling the combat had been or how many injuries sustained, one always inquired solicitously after one's opponent and made sure he lacked for nothing. That was sportsmanship of the best, a long tradition of this country of ours."

Tom wondered why old people always forgot they had made the same statements countless times before, and brought them out as if fresh come into their heads. "But this wasn't exactly a mill. More of an ambush."

"Oh? By whom?"

"Do I have to say?"

"Not unless the law was broken in any way."

"I hadn't thought of that. I was trespassing, and I did floor a gamekeeper."

Daniel passed his tongue over the inside of his cheek, but refrained from smiling. The boy's honesty was like a draught from a crystal-clear stream. Tom was never afraid to own up to what he had done, never made excuses, and it had been the same throughout his boyhood. "I think you had better take a bath before we discuss the legal aspects of the matter, and while we are sorting things out I'll see what I can do for those cuts and bruises of yours. You've left them a bit late. How long? Four hours? Five?"

"Six, I suppose. I couldn't get away before, but don't ask me about that."

"Very well." Daniel let the matter pass. "You carry on with your bath, and I'll get the oils and unguents that I need from my dressing-room cupboard."

Tom found the adjoining bathroom still faintly steamy from the bath his grandfather took at five o'clock each morning, although it had been dried out by a servant and fresh towels of snowy softness put on the mahogany towel horse. The hot water gushed from the taps and did wonders for his tired limbs. He pulled off the bandage around his head, yelped when it stuck and reopened the wound, but nevertheless soaped the lake mud away from his tangled hair as well as his body. When he returned to the bedroom, wearing a towel about his hips and holding another to his forehead, stemming the renewed trickle of blood, he found his grandfather fully dressed except for his coat, with an array of bottles and jars laid out neatly on a white cloth spread on a side table under the window, a kitchen stool sent for and placed ready by it.

"Sit here in the light where I can see better," Daniel said, putting on silver-rimmed spectacles. "My eyes are not what they were."

With skill and care he dealt with his grandson's injuries, the blended aromas of the balms he was using subconsciously arousing nostalgia for the days when his old trainer, Jem, dead for more than forty years, had ministered to him after a bout. Yet he kept his mind from the past and concentrated carefully on the present, tilting his good ear forward as he bandaged up the stitch he had put in Tom's forehead, not wanting his deafness to hinder his listening to a selected explanation of what had occurred: a place of venue had been arranged with an unnamed young lady on an unnamed estate where the sons of the household and their friends had taken umbrage at the intrusion and set upon the lad. Suspicion stirred dangerously. He'd wager a sovereign he knew where the fight had taken place.

Tom, hoping not to have to reveal names or places, adopted a man-to-man attitude that seemed appropriate to the moment. "I can't think why I fancied that filly anyway. Wenches like her are ten a penny. She manipulated me to revenge herself upon—well, upon somebody else."

Daniel was not interested in the blowing hot and cold of his grandson's amours. "How many did you level in the fight apart from your knocking out of the gamekeeper?"

"Five at least. I think I used every prize-ring punch and thrust you ever taught me."

"Tell me about it."

Tom obliged, well pleased with how he had acquitted himself now that he had time to look back over the affray, and feeling increasingly relaxed and at ease. The unguent smeared on his lower lip had reduced the swelling already, his blackened eye no longer throbbed under a soaked pad, and his hands were dabbling lux-uriously in a bowl of aromatic oil balanced on his knees that was taking the stiffness from his knuckles. He thought as he recounted the details that he was surely feeling a little as his grandfather must have felt long ago when giving a blow-by-blow account of the championship fight to George IV, a great patron of the ring, at Buckingham Palace itself. The illusion was soon shattered.

"You should never have made for the stairs." The still-powerful hands massaged liniment into the muscles in Tom's back and shoulders. "Had you remained where you were you would have stood a better chance of dealing with your antagonists face to face. Not that you should have been on Radcliffe property in the first place, by God!"

Tom almost shot off the stool under the sudden abruptness with which the treatment of his torso was completed, barely sav-ing the bowl of oil from tipping down onto the carpet. Daniel, his face wrathful, snatched it from him and proceeded to pad his knuckles and bandage them. Neither spoke, Tom practically hold-ing his breath as to what was to be said next, but not until the condition of his knee was pronounced a slight strain and duly dealt with did the subject of the Radcliffes come up again.

"Nobody has any legal right to beat up a trespasser," Daniel pronounced, his back turned as he stood at the side table recork-ing bottles and screwing tops back onto ointment jars. "Not even if he's caught red-handed with poached game in his pockets, so there is no excuse for the Radcliffes' unprovoked attack upon you. You'll hear nothing more of the matter, you can be sure of that, because Mrs. Radcliffe knows that I would immediately sue for as-sault on your behalf since you were invited onto the premises in the first place."

Tom released a grateful sigh. "That's good news. Thank you, Grandfather."

Daniel spun about and pointed a terrible finger at him, breath-ing heavily. "Don't dare to thank me for anything to do with this scrape of yours! Of all the young women to be had in this town you were addle-headed enough to pick on one with Radcliffe con-nections and shame the very name of Warwyck by blundering into a trap that made you look both ridiculous and inadequate! A laughingstock! A clown who returns home in nothing but his breeches! Had you leveled the whole lot of your attackers you might just—and only just!—have come out of the whole business with some scraping of dignity to save your face!"

Tom went white. Never before had his grandfather shown such displeasure toward him. He was used to his father's irascible impatience, his mother's alcoholic indifference and even thinly veiled dislike, but he had never had anything but support and tolerance from Daniel. "Nobody had laughter in them when I landed my right- and left-handers," he declared hoarsely. "Neither is the feud anything that they or I will ever forget for one instant. Maybe the score has been left in some part unsettled, but never fear that I'll waver in extracting full payment sooner or later for all that occurred."

Daniel breathed deeply, nostrils flaring, and lowered his arm. He took a few steps across to the window and stood looking out. "Go along to your father's old room now," he advised gruffly. "I'll have breakfast sent on a tray. Try to sleep afterward. There'll be no anxiety about you at the Grange since you stay overnight at Easthampton House often enough and keep a supply of clothes here, but I'll let your mother know you'll be remaining with me for a few days. No need while your father is in London to give her a fright with your present appearance. Don't you agree?"

"Yes, sir." Tom made for the door, still pale and taut, his spine a ramrod. He was halfway out of the room when Daniel halted him.

"Tom."

"Grandfather?" In a tone impatient to be gone for the time being.

Daniel's gaze remained fixed on some point beyond the window. "I was outnumbered in a fight on the beach once where my attackers used rocks and stones and iron bars and bludgeons with nails. Those were rough, bad times. The ambush was instigated by a rogue named Brown, allied to Alexander Radcliffe and his cronies, whose sole aim was to kick me out of Easthampton. There were no by-laws concerning the shore then, and Brown thought to bar my full rights to remove shingle in my wagons from his bathing-machine site for my building projects—as if there were not enough for all. What did I do? Set up bathing-machines in opposition and drove the fellow out of business." He looked around at his grandson. "A Warwyck always makes his enemies settle their accounts. I see you know that. And five is no mean number of opponents to have leveled out of a round dozen. Just make sure you do better another time in meting out justice."

Tom's eyes held his in perfect understanding. "I will, Grandfather."

In the room that had been Richard Warwyck's boyhood room Tom slid between the sheets of the bed and let his head sink back into the soft pillows, his bandaged hands resting on the brocade coverlet. Hugh was his main adversary as Alexander had been Daniel's. And what of Nicolette? She was his enemy as much as the rest of them with her inherent hostility, her fierce pride, and her spurning of Warwyck territory and all appertaining to it. But it was hard to think of her in any other way than as someone who had taken a great personal risk to shelter and help him, and he could not dismiss that lightly. In fact, he did not see how he could dismiss Nicolette at all. He had never met anyone quite like her before.

He closed his eyes and saw her smile again: wistful, enchanting, and suddenly and immeasurably shy. The image held with a treasure house of secrets behind it. To gain the key to it would be to unravel sweet mysteries of Nicolette that would be barred to all others. And barred most of all to a Warwyck.

Chapter 3

In the first-class railway carriage Richard Warwyck folded his copy of *The Times*, put it to one side, and looked idly out of the window at the passing spread of the Sussex countryside. The glass reflected the well-molded, intelligent face of a man in his early fifties, whose glossy hair had darkened from its original fairness over the years to a dark wheat color, speared attractively by wings of gray spreading back from the temples, and upon whose broad shoulders was set a coat of immaculate cut, his cravat pin a rare, greenish pearl.

He had left Victoria Station and the traffic jams of London less than two hours ago, and with the junction of Merrelton slipping away behind the train he would be in Easthampton on the dot of noon. It was an excellent train service, kept good time, and enabled him to travel between his office and the Grange without harassment or delay. Now that he was able to relegate complete responsibility for most of his affairs to his eldest son, Lennox, who had the sharpest of business brains, far more leisure time was opening up at his disposal, and he was able to remain at Easthampton for longer periods than ever before. Once he had hoped to have four sons in the business with him, but his second son, Cedric, had been set on going to sea, and after enlisting as a midshipman had died less than six months later of a fever off the Windward Islands. At the thought of his third son, Richard frowned deeply, the firm mouth tightening. Jeremy was a thorn in his side; weak, spoiled, and a wastrel, who had been forced through laziness and financial incompetence to return ignominiously to live at home, completely penniless except for a moderate allowance settled through necessity upon him out of Richard's own pocket.

And there was Tom. Richard sighed, shifting in his seat. The lad had intelligence, wit, and ability, but the same cursed love of the sea that had afflicted Cedric ran through Tom's veins. Both had inherited it from their mother, but whereas Cedric had wanted only to go into the Navy, Tom's sole ambition appeared to be to build and sail his own craft, with nothing planned beyond it. The lad was not indolent or shiftless and could work as though possessed when his interest was captured, and it was Richard's resolved intention to divert that disciplined power into one of the many enterprises that he had under way. It was not as though there was not a wide field for his son to choose from. One of his factories was turning out every kind of bicycle from ordinaries or penny-farthings, as they were more popularly called, capable of a speed of twenty miles an hour, to dual-seated models on which cyclists could pedal side by side between high wheels, all finding an ever-eager market in the current bicycling boom. On a secret list in another factory he had engineers working ceaselessly on designs for a horseless carriage in a bid to forestall competitors engaged in the same race to be first in the field. *That* was where the future lay! In horseless carriages! That was where Tom would have a wealth of opportunities to engage him. But had he been able to convince his son of that? No, he had not, and it was a bone of contention between them.

As for himself, Richard knew he had always had the knack of being able to look ahead with foresight in all realms of business, and as a result success had crowned him many times over. Unfortunately he had been less clearheaded in personal affairs. Had he not made a disastrous marriage when he was twenty-one a deal of his initiative would never have been lost to Easthampton, and

there would have been on the Channel coast a watering place of
splendor with every amenity to rival any resort on the French
Riviera or in any other part of the world for that matter. Instead,
on the rebound of losing the love of his life, he had gone away
with Meg, a fisher-girl from the beach of Easthampton, and married her. Afterward he had returned briefly now and again for a
day and sometimes for a weekend, but only ever to see his mother,
who was dying, and for her sake he had made peace with his father; otherwise Easthampton had seen no more of him after his
mother's death until he purchased the Grange some years later
and—by sheer chance—in time for Tom to be born there. His
reasons for buying the house were his own, reasons he had not
disclosed to anyone, but Meg in her possessiveness and jealousy
had made a guess at them and deliberately destroyed the peace of
mind and heart he had hoped to find there.

The train was slowing down. Residential areas of the resort
were beginning to close in on either side. Looking at the density
of the buildings and the gardens, Richard thought that few would
ever suspect that once there had been nothing but brickfields
there, but the seam had run out long since, adding to his father's
financial losses that had cruelly coincided with his own departure
with Meg. As the platform appeared he stood up, took his silk top
hat from the rack and put it on, buttoned his gloves, picked up
his cane, and as the train came to a halt, stepped out as a porter
opened the door. He decided that he would stop at Easthampton
House on the way home and see his father. He liked to keep an
eye on him, although fortunately the old man was still strong and
active, with all his senses about him in spite of his advanced years.

"Richard!"

He turned his head sharply, recognizing his sister's voice, and
saw her hastening amid a flow of raiment and feathers toward
him from a compartment to the rear of the train. "Good day to
you, Donna," he greeted her, retracking a few paces along the
stretch of platform to meet her. "I had no idea you were on the
train."

"I caught it at Victoria by the skin of my teeth," she confessed,
laughing as she slipped her hand companionably into the crook of

his arm. They had always got on well together, always been good friends, the only son and daughter of Daniel and the late Kate Warwyck to survive childhood. "Have you a carriage meeting you? . . . Good. You may give me a lift home to Easthampton House and stay for luncheon."

"I had already planned to do that," he admitted good-humoredly. "I've been away a month this time, but now I've left Lennox in charge at the head office in London, and hope to spend most of the summer at Easthampton. It will give me a chance to see Father quite often."

"That will please him." She stepped ahead of her brother into the waiting carriage.

"You're looking very grand," he complimented her when they were both seated and being drawn out of the station yard.

She preened a little, tilting her head in acknowledgment of his praise, the feathers of her hat wafting against her hair, which was brightened artificially to a reddish brown. At the age of fifty-one she still had a remarkably young complexion and a slim figure, enabling her to hide the true passing of years by at least a decade to those who did not know the truth, and she always dressed well, if somewhat eccentrically in the aesthetic style favored by those allied to the arts. Years ago she had inherited handsomely from their Uncle Harry, their father's only brother, although Richard had been his heir and received the bulk of his fortune, and she gave her patronage generously to struggling artists, which was the reason why she sometimes went to London. She had never married, but Richard had not been surprised by that, for her fiancé had been drowned in tragic circumstances, and from that time forward she had channeled her frustrated energies, first of all in support of Daniel's political career, and then into various good works until her patronage was sought for a penniless young artist of promise. She had continued to indulge the arts ever since.

"I'm pleased we met today," she said, the sunlight passing over her face as they bowled along. "It will save me making a special trip out to the Grange to see you about a matter in hand. I have at last found a woman who would make an ideal companion for Meg."

"Have you?" He was both relieved and wary. Admittedly he trusted her judgment implicitly, but he wondered whether she comprehended fully the recent deterioration in his wife's condition. It would take a companion of stamina to deal with Meg.

Donna seemed to know what he was thinking, and she put her gloved hand lightly on his arm in reassurance. "This woman, Mrs. Constance Meredith, understands exactly what is expected of her. Her husband was one of my artists a few years ago until he drank himself into an early grave. Recently I met Mrs. Meredith again. She is desperately in need of employment. Life has been hard on her."

Richard looked faintly unconvinced. "After close contact with one drunkard, how can she contemplate looking after another? I can think of nothing worse."

"You're wrong there. It's much, much worse to be poverty-stricken and homeless in London, with only one terrible way for a woman to earn a crust of bread. My meeting with her was providential. I saved her in the nick of time. She will rejoice in a roof over her head and security. All her tasks will be light to her."

It sounded promising. Whether Donna had been the salvationist she imagined herself to be was immaterial if the woman proved honest and capable and was able to deal kindly and firmly with Meg. "Have you arranged everything?" he inquired.

"Everything, subject to your final approval. I'll bring her to the Grange at the end of next week. I imagine you would like me to be there to present her to Meg."

"Yes, of course. Where is Mrs. Meredith now?"

"At a modest hotel in London."

"For which you are paying?"

Donna flicked a hand nonchalantly to ward off any suggestion of munificence on her part. "I couldn't let her sleep any longer under a borrowed blanket in a corner of someone's studio. She will be well clothed and well fed when she presents herself at the Grange. I could do no less."

They arrived at Easthampton House. Donna sailed up the steps and was the first to discover Daniel, who was reading in the library, a spaniel at his feet.

"Papa!" She kissed him on the cheek before he could rise. "See whom I've brought home with me! Richard and I met at the railway station."

Daniel was on his feet to shake his son by the hand, and Donna dipped to embrace the spaniel, who was named Barley after a pugilist her father had once met in the ring, but his reception of her was no more than a few thumps of a tail. He made no secret of preferring his master's company to anybody else's, which piqued Donna, who was fond of all animals and had an exceptional liking for dogs. But she had not kept one herself since her beloved Toby had died many years ago, leaving her determined never to shed such tears or experience such a sense of loss over a pet again. Even as she straightened up he padded across to flop down again on her father's foot. It was useless to coax him into following her, and she went alone upstairs to change out of her traveling clothes.

Daniel and his son conversed comfortably until it was disclosed that Tom had gone home only that morning after spending a week there. Richard was far from pleased to hear it. Meg always complained that their son cared more for his grandfather than he did for anyone else, and there would be more than the usual tirade to listen to after such a length of time spent by the boy at Easthampton House, particularly since it had coincided with his own absence.

"I hope that at least you talked some sense into him while he was here, Father," he said grimly. "It's high time he buckled down to earning a living. Why, when I was his age I had been working with you for two years, and before that there wasn't a workshop or a site where I hadn't spent some time during my school vacations to gain a wide knowledge of the building industry."

Daniel had reseated himself in his crimson leather wing chair, and he looked across at his son, who had taken up a stance with his back to the marble fireplace that was kept filled with garden flowers behind the fan-shaped brass screen in summertime.

"I would say that Tom has followed your example there," he remarked mildly, leaning forward as he fondled the head of the spaniel that was leaning against his knee. "That boy hasn't missed a chance to learn all he could about boatbuilding ever since he was old enough to go out alone."

Richard snorted. "Helping the fishermen build their boats is a pastime for any number of boys, but knowing how to hammer deck planks and wield a tarbrush is of no use to him."

"I disagree. He gained a sound practical knowledge there and from other sources, which is revealed nowadays in the models of his own designs that he makes. He was working on the latest while he was here. I happen to remember that when he was expelled from school it was for playing truant in a boatyard instead of attending chapel and his lessons."

Richard shrugged irritably, clapping one hand into the other behind his back. "The less said about that, the better. Three times he was warned—three times out of special consideration for his academic ability!—and then he played truant again, the young fool, and I was asked to remove him without delay."

"You should have put him to an apprenticeship with a boat-builder then."

Richard raised a cynical eyebrow. "I'll remind you that just a month ago he was booted out of university for having a young woman in his room. What sort of apprenticeship should follow that?"

"Now, now." Daniel shook his head benignly, tolerant toward his grandson as he had never been with the son who was displaying such an impatient mood. "He was neither the first nor the last to be sent down for being involved in capers of that kind, and in any case that particular misdemeanor is not under discussion. He has his mind made up as to what he wants to do with his life, and it does not include following your footsteps into the financial empire you have built up for yourself with factories and mills working around the clock. He is content to leave the lion's share to Lennox."

"I'll see about that." Inexorably.

Daniel regarded him penetratingly. "You'll not grind the sea out of Tom no matter how hard you try. He is Meg's son as much as he is yours."

Richard's retort was bitterly derisive. "I thought you as a champion prizefighter never resorted to blows below the belt."

Daniel's attitude toughened. "None of us can pretend that Meg does not exist, however much you would wish it. She comes from fisherfolk who have cast their nets in the waters off Easthampton for generations, probably even before the Romans came. You cannot wonder that the strain should come out in at least two of your children. You let Cedric go to sea. Why are you so against Tom following it in his own way?"

"Cedric had no business acumen. He was a fine boy, bright and amiable and a son to be proud of, but you know as well as I do that he would have run away to sea if I had not let him go. But Tom is different. Tom could outshine Lennox if guided along the right lines. I have any number of exciting projects under way, and Tom could have his choice, but I'll not throw money away letting him turn into little more than a beachcomber for months on end while building a boat to no purpose."

"Has he asked you to finance him?"

"No, but how else can he do it?"

"I think you should wait to hear what he has to say about it before you make up your mind. I'll add no more other than I approved all he confided to me, and I hope you'll do the same."

"Oh, I'll hear what he has to say," Richard conceded uncompromisingly, "but you must remember that I also listened to Jeremy when he presented a plan to purchase stables and breed racehorses. Against my better judgment I let him have his way for his mother's sake, but the whole enterprise failed, and at the age of twenty-six he is an aimless bankrupt and I had thousands to settle for his gambling debts alone. That's what listening to my third son cost me. I'll not countenance any nonsense from Tom."

Donna overheard his last words as she re-entered the library. She had changed into a floating shift of multicolored silk. "Who's talking about my dear nephew? Luncheon is served. Let us go into the dining room."

It was late afternoon when Richard drove along the avenue of oaks that led to his fine home. The Grange was set in acres of gardens and woods, the former owner having planted an additional stretch of woodland to keep away the sound of the trains that chuffed past across a strip of land which had once been part of the estate. Only the occasional drifting of smoke over the treetops showed when another locomotive had gone by. When his father had owned the Grange years ago it had been a hotel, which had enjoyed a short spell of success, but it had been designed for the extremely well-to-do, who withdrew their favors with the closing of its gaming rooms and the cessation of the prizefights that had been held there for private entertainment, new laws of the land having been passed to deal harshly with such gentlemanly pastimes. It went up for sale and became a family home once more as it had been in the past. It was upon the death of the owner that it had come onto the market again and Richard had purchased it.

He had never regretted his purchase. It had been good to come back to Easthampton after so many years away from it. Always he glanced up and around at the house before entering, taking pleasure in its mellow gray stone, splendid parapets, and the mullioned lights that gave such grandeur to the high-ceilinged rooms within. He saw that as usual every window in his wife's apartments stood open. Sometimes it took much persuasion to get them closed in bad weather, it being her main complaint that she would most surely die in the house she hated if she could not feel the clean sea air upon her.

In the entrance hall he met Tom coming down the great Tudor staircase and they exchanged greetings. Richard noticed that there was a newly healed scar on his son's forehead. "What happened to you?"

Tom's eyes glinted wryly. "I walked into something."

"Oh?" Richard's thoughts were already elsewhere. "I want to talk to you later, but now I must go and see your mother. How is she?"

"Not very pleased with me at the moment."

Richard's brows descended in a sharp frown that creased the bridge of his handsome nose. "I know why. It was deucedly inconsiderate of you to absent yourself for a full week at Easthampton House."

"Really, sir? Jeremy was here." Tom's tone was not insolent, merely matter-of-fact. When Jeremy was at home with his mother no one else existed for her. While she was fond of Lennox and grieved for Cedric she adored Jeremy beyond all reason, but her last and youngest son she had never cared for, using him as a butt for her ill temper whenever it suited her. Perhaps that was why she missed him in his absence. She had certainly made up for it upon his return.

Richard opened his mouth to reply that Jeremy was never to be relied upon, but he thought better of it, clamped his lips together, and went upstairs to go to his wife's room. Sometimes he almost wished he had been born without a sense of duty. It would have made life much easier. He could have put Meg in a residence of her own and never set eyes on her again; instead, pity overcame revulsion, compassion conquered dislike, and he, who was notoriously ruthless and hardheaded in business, could never have found it in his heart to abandon her to loneliness and despair. When he reached her door he experienced the usual sense of depression when going into her presence.

Downstairs Tom thrust his hands into his pockets and sauntered out through some open casement doors onto the terrace. The grounds of the Grange stretched out before him in patterns of lush green and blossoming flower beds. A couple of miles beyond the forest where the trains went by lay Radcliffe Hall. Where was Nicolette at this hour when the sun's rays were beginning to lengthen? Strolling across a lawn with Laura? Playing tennis with her objectionable brothers? Or sitting in a shady bower with Lawrence and repeating the kissing episode he had been compelled to be a witness to in the conservatory?

His face tightened. It was useless to deny the fact that instead of forgetting her and the whole unfortunate incident, he could not put her from his mind. One of the reasons he had stayed on at Easthampton House beyond the first couple of days had been the growing knowledge that he was beginning to be haunted by her. It had compelled him to go down on the beach at early morning in the hope of seeing her out riding as she had mentioned, but she was never there. Each time he told himself that he was glad he had not seen her, it being for the best, but by breakfast time he was overcome by disappointment that she had not appeared. Had she not given him that wisp of a smile at the moment of parting he would never have given her another thought except in association with an unpleasant experience. Or was that true? Hadn't the spell already been cast? Yet, going over all that he could remember of their time together, not a second of it had been devoid of hostility. What made it impossible to forget the piquant, wide-eyed face of Nicolette Radcliffe-Stuart?

A step on the terrace made him turn. Jeremy had come out through the casement doors. Tall, black-haired and black-eyed, he had the sort of dangerous looks that appealed to women, and few saw weakness in the sensual, worldly mouth or suspected until it was too late the callousness behind the charm. He was holding a gilt-edged invitation card between finger and thumb, which he waggled at Tom.

"Would you like this ticket for a charity ball at the Assembly Rooms this evening?"

"Why?" Tom was suspicious. Jeremy never gave anything away.

"I'm not able to use it after all. Something more intriguing has come my way."

Tom hesitated. He did not much care for dancing on warm summer evenings in white gloves and stiff shirtfront unless escorting a girl of his choice, but his father had mentioned a talk with him later, and he was in no mood for a dressing down, the turmoil of his thoughts about Nicolette having set him unusually on edge and uncharacteristically at a loss. Better to use the ticket and be absent until tomorrow when he could prepare himself for logical explanation and argument as to why he did not want to spend the rest of his life putting machines onto the roads of England and the rest of the world.

"All right," he said. "I'll take the ticket."

Jeremy handed it to him. "That's two guineas you owe me. I'd be glad of the money now."

Tom told himself he should have known. He took his last two sovereigns from the gold fob case on his watch chain and raked about in his pockets for change. Jeremy's waiting palm did not close upon the money until a halfpenny and two farthings had made up the amount.

"Thanks, old chap. Have a good time." He went back indoors.

Tom studied the invitation. It was in aid of a local orphanage patronized by the ladies of the district, commencing at seven-thirty and including supper. He hoped the supper would be good. He didn't expect to enjoy the rest of it very much.

It was half past eight before he arrived at the colonnaded front-age of the Assembly Rooms, which faced Ring Park and lay within sight and sound of the sea. The ball was in full swing, lights and music and a buzz of chatter greeting him as he handed over his ticket and stood looking about him to see whom he recog-nized. He acknowledged several nods, waves, and smiles from friends and acquaintances, seeing that he would not be short of company, but was not ready yet to commit himself to one group or another, and let his gaze take in the dancing couples on the floor. It was a polka, being fun to dance with the right partner, for it was necessary to hold a girl's waist tightly as the pace grew more frenzied, but to dance with those who soaked half-moons of per-spiration under their arms and ended with tumbled hair or some other disarray could be decidedly unpleasant. Round and round went the dancing couples, coattails flying, bustled skirts swirling out like liquid scimitars from tiny loops caught on little fingers. Silk and satin and velvet and gossamer lace. Bows and frills and flashing heels. Surely every color of the rainbow caught up in a variegated and riotous whirl. And there was Nicolette! His heart gave such a thud that he swallowed convulsively.

She had not seen him, but that was not surprising, there being at least a hundred couples circumferencing the polished floor, and as it was she was lost from his sight almost immediately. He craned his neck, but she was somewhere in the thick of the whirl-pool. Quickly he glanced along at those standing around or occu-pying the sofas and chairs arranged amid potted palms set back from the floor, and tried to see whom she might be with. When he noticed Bertie Radcliffe-Stuart talking to someone on the stairs he guessed that a family party would be gathered at one of the

tables on the gilded balcony which extended horseshoe-shaped
above the dance floor. He was right. When the dance came to an
end he caught a glimpse of her going up the staircase with her
partner. Without a second's hesitation he darted up an alternative
flight and came to the balcony some little distance from her.

There were at least twenty people in the Radcliffe-Stuarts'
party. Lawrence was there, Hugh and the twins, as well as Laura,
and also an older matron acting as chaperone with her husband,
who looked a military man. The rest he did not bother to observe,
concentrating the full force of his gaze upon Nicolette, who had
an aura about her where she had seated herself at the table from
the brilliance of the crystal gasoliers that illuminated the ballroom
below. Gas brackets on the crimson walls gave additional light to
the gallery, but deliberately the whole area was bathed in a more
intimate glow, and he was in shadow as he leaned a shoulder
against a pillar, watching her.

She was in white tulle as befitted a young girl, much trimmed
with pink satin ribbons and bustled drapery, her shoulders bare
and creamy-smooth, her hair elaborately dressed, and her arms
covered to above the elbows with white gloves. It ran through his
thoughts that he alone out of all men everywhere had been alone
with that beautiful girl in her room, had felt the softness of her
night garments brush against him, and inhaled the fragrant bouquet of her in the dark hours. Were it known, innocent though
their encounter had been, the scandal would have wagged every
tongue in these Assembly Rooms. She was sipping a glass of
champagne sparingly, displaying no need of anything to revive her
after the violent exertion of the polka, nothing in her pristine appearance and the neatness of her coiled tresses to show that she
had been danced almost off her feet by her exuberant partner.

He willed her to turn her head and look at him. The force of
his desire that she should see him there was so strong that it was a
physical ache. But not once did she glance in his direction. Instead, her neck and shoulders took on a kind of rigidity as if under
stern control as to which way she should look and at whom it
should be. Suddenly he understood why. She *knew* he was only a

few yards from her, knew it and would not acknowledge it either to herself or to him. If she ignored the sensation afflicting her it would go away. He would go away. A surge of exhilaration went through him. *Look at me, Nicolette. Look just once. That's all I ask. That's all I'll need to be able to discover whether I have been in your thoughts as you have been in mine.*

She fought him. Her smiles, her laughter, her glances, and her attention were all for those around her. Once Lawrence leaned toward her, their heads coming together as he related a confidence that caused her some superficial amusement, but Tom ignored the play. His stare on her was unwavering, almost unblinking. *Nicolette, Nicolette, Nicolette.*

She was going to dance again. With the military gentleman this time, who moved to take her down the far stairs to the floor. Tom bolted back the way he had come, and keeping under the balcony to avoid being spotted by the Radcliffe-Stuarts, he dodged between bystanders and chattering clusters of people to reach the foot of the staircase that she was descending, one hand gliding down the baluster rail, the other holding up her skirt by its silken loop. Her lashes were down as she manipulated the treads amid the flow of frills about the toes of her satin shoes. *Nicolette!*

Her cheeks hollowed, but her will was as strong as his. He saw how delicately her nostrils flared as she breathed deeply, and still she did not raise her eyes to his. She was so near when she passed by him that he had only to lift his arms to enfold her gently within them, but with her fan swinging on a cord from her wrist she let her partner lead her to join others into the steps of a quadrille.

Tom left. Hurt, offended, and deeply angry he flung himself out of the building and charged down the street until he reached the promenade. There he thumped his arms down on the railings and glared out to sea. She could have *looked* at him, couldn't she? But no. She was a Radcliffe through and through, despising all Warwycks on principle, and she had made it savagely clear that what she had done for him was over and forgotten, totally without importance, and never to be acknowledged in any way again. Perhaps hatred for him because of his name had surged back to destroy the flicker of gentler feeling that he had glimpsed in her face at the gates of Easthampton House.

The clock on the Assembly Rooms struck ten. It was too early to go home, and he did not want to return to the charity ball. With a suppressed groan of frustration he looked over his shoulder in the direction of the house on the hill. Windows were still alight. He would go up there and spend a couple of hours with Daniel, who was always willing to set aside a normally early bedtime for a game of chess with his grandson.

But when Tom arrived at Easthampton House he discovered his grandfather had already retired, and it was his Aunt Donna who was writing a letter at the bureau on her own in the Green Drawing Room. She was delighted to see him and put down her pen.

"This is an unexpected pleasure." She moved across to the sofa, her strange garments wafting about in points of chiffon that appeared to have a life of their own, and she patted the seat beside her. "Come and tell me all your news. I haven't seen you since—" She broke off, looking distressed.

Tom cocked his head at her. "Since I was sent down, you mean?" He had ignored her suggestion that he sit by her and was prowling restlessly about the room. "Ah, well. I'm not grieving over that. I didn't want to go to university in the first place."

"You didn't get sent down on purpose, did you?" she questioned, aghast.

"Good Lord, no. But it taught me a lesson in the pointlessness of letting other people mold my life for me. In future I'll go my own way."

"Your father only has your own good at heart."

"He has what he sincerely believes to be my own good at heart, and that's not the same thing."

"Nobody should go against parental wishes," she reproved primly. "Not a well-brought-up son or daughter anyway. Everybody knows that."

"Come, come, Aunt Donna," he chided laconically. "Don't tell me that you always did exactly as you were told."

Her expression grew ruminative and troubled. She looked down at her hands in her lap, playing with a ring. "I did once lock myself in my bedroom when I was a little older than you are now, and I refused to come out. I nearly starved to death then and afterward." It was a nightmare time for her. Her face and figure had become skeletal, and the monthly function normal to a woman ceased and never recurred, leaving her with the knowledge that she was as barren as it befitted a spinster to be.

"Why did you lock yourself away?" It was a tale Tom had never heard before and he was intrigued by it. "Don't tell me that my grandparents were trying to force you into marriage with someone you didn't love?"

"Quite the reverse. They had approved the man of my choice, but he was drowned tragically, and I was left unable to face up to life any more, loathing myself for my own weakness."

"Oh, yes." He knew about the drowning, but it was curious to think of Aunt Donna of the bright front and bizarre garments acting the recluse. "How did you overcome your troubles?"

A wry, sadly triumphant look that he had never seen before passed over her face, hardening her mouth. "Your grandfather had need of my help. *My* help." Her twisted smile was mirthless, born out of some long-ago personal anguish. "He had never had any patience with me, and I was a constant disappointment to him, but suddenly his whole future was dependent upon my actions, and I cannot tell you what that did for me. It proved that in my own way I was as strong as he, as able as he, and in that moment of victory I knew that I would never despise myself again, never feel inadequate again."

"What did you do to help him?"

Her mouth fell open slightly at the directness of the question, almost in dismay as if in the companionable quietness of the house she had said more than she had intended to her attentive listener, but with that aplomb that made her such a resourceful person she recovered herself, lifting her head proudly. "I took no small part in getting your grandfather into the House of Commons."

Tom's interest waned. The oft-told tales of the zest with which

Aunt Donna had thrown herself into Daniel's political campaign were legion. She, who had always been quiet and retiring, although capable, had worked with a tireless, almost frenetic fervor that was said to have amazed everybody at the time, and Daniel had spoken of it with unstinted praise. But Tom had thought that she was about to disclose something she had kept to herself over the years and never spoken of before, so faraway and pensive was her expression, but he had been mistaken. No wonder she placed such importance upon what she had done during the political campaign if it had given her the fresh interest she had needed so much at the time. He changed the subject to a more mundane level.

"I haven't had any supper. I left the charity ball before it was served. Do you think there's anyone still about in the kitchen who'll produce some food for me?"

"You poor boy." She was all concern, fussing maternally. "How dreadful that you should be hungry. Ring the bell. Something shall be brought at once."

He tucked into cold chicken sandwiches and half a bottle of wine while she finished writing the letter at the bureau that his arrival had interrupted. Afterward they played a game of backgammon, which he won, and upon seeing that she was tired by the lateness of the hour, he got up to leave.

"I left Jones with the carriage in the forecourt at the Assembly Rooms," he said, "so I'll walk back there now and be driven home. Good night, Aunt Donna."

"Good night, Tom."

She saw him to the door herself, closing it quietly after him in order not to disturb her father's sleep. It had been a most pleasant evening, for Tom was especially dear to her. She liked to think that if ever she had had a son he would have been like her youngest nephew. Stroking her tired eyelids with the fingertips of one hand, she reached out almost blindly for the baluster rail at the foot of the staircase, and her palm encountered the newel-post. Instantly her eyes stretched wide and she clenched her hand in revulsion as she jerked it back hard against her chest. Flashing images came in upon her memory of a man's head smashed in against the newel-post, a mess of blood and brains and spattered gore. She had not touched that gilded globe since the night when that terrible, secret murder was committed, and although she had had no part in the slaughter that had taken place, she had been instrumental afterward in concealing the crime. It had plagued her conscience ever since, and yet, if she had her time all over again, she would do exactly what she had done then.

She gulped, hurrying up the stairs. She had tried to atone. God alone knew how she had tried to settle her account with society, the political campaign a way of getting a good man into Parliament, and then working ceaselessly to help the poor and the needy and the unfortunate, as well as to bring some beauty into the world through those artists and sculptors who would not survive without her patronage. One of the reasons she had taken to the aesthetic style of clothing not usually worn by someone adhering to the morals and standards of a conventional way of life was that they made her feel detached from the past and totally different from the gaunt-faced, self-starved girl who had worked under the cover of night to conceal a man's body with a face so battered that his own mother would not have known him.

At the head of the flight she stopped and leaned against the wall, her heart hammering against her ribs. Talking to Tom about her youth had made her doubly receptive to the horror of touching the newel-post. Normally she passed it day in and day out without a glance, going across the hall and through the doors without the slightest recollection of what had once occurred there, for other, happier days made the house dear to her and there were the echoes of love and laughter in every corner of it. But tonight she had smelled the sweaty, bloody smell of the body again, heard the strain of the rope that dragged it slithering and bumping behind her horse through the damp night grass to the railway line where the speeding wheels of the late train out of Easthampton station had removed forever any suspicion of murder from her own father.

Turning her head, she looked down into the hall. She had come to this very spot when the noise and the cries of her mother and half sister had brought her from her bedroom to see what was amiss. There was her father, hammering his pugilistic fists into the face of a man named Ben Thompson, who had been drummed back against the newel-post and was pinned against it helplessly, suffering punishment worse than anything that any of the retired champion's opponents in the prize ring had ever known, for her father, who had never lost his temper during a bout, had been dealing out his blows in a blind, white-hot rage, and had it been a fair fight he would have let his man slide unconscious at his feet. But it had been no contest. And Ben Thompson had been a blackmailer who had offended against her mother. There could have been no greater crime in Daniel's eyes. He had gone on punishing the man long after he was dead, not knowing the skull had been smashed in against the newel-post, and there was no telling how long the madness would have possessed him if his by-blow, Lucy, the cause of all the trouble in the first place, had not knocked him out in desperation with the base of a heavy vase. He never knew he killed the man. When he recovered consciousness her mother and Lucy told him Ben Thompson had left, never to return. It was true. She, Donna Warwyck, the daughter for whom he had never had any time, always critical of her shortcomings and lack of courage in the saddle, was secretly disposing of the body and saving his neck from the hangman's noose.

A sigh shuddered through her. Her darling Mamma was dead these many years, but it was doubtful whether Kate Warwyck, kind, compassionate, gentle creature though she had been, had ever suffered a twinge of conscience over the rights and wrongs of the awful incident, for although she would have grieved that even an unscrupulous blackmailer should lose his life, she would have gone to the gallows herself if she could have saved her husband in that way. As for Lucy, her part in the concealment of the crime had been small but necessary, a cleaning up of all evidence before the servants' return from an evening off duty. But, living a distance away in the county of Kent and happily married as she was, with a prosperous husband and three pretty daughters who had recently wed well, it was unlikely that she ever gave a thought to that night when she had been desperate to do what she could to protect her father—the father by whom she had been conceived during an adulterous relationship with a married woman named Claudine Attwood. It was to silence Ben Thompson, who was threatening to expose the truth, that Kate had invited him to the house, intending to give him the sum of money he had demanded. Instead, Daniel, returning unexpectedly with Lucy from the Grange, had inadvertently and terribly silenced him forever.

Donna started, as a door from the kitchen opened in the hall beyond her line of vision, the butler being on his rounds to make sure all bolts were fastened for the night. She hastened away in the direction of her own bedroom. Was she never to have peace of mind over what she had done? Would the awful face of Ben Thompson never be erased from her memory? She could feel one of her depressive headaches coming on as they always did when her conscience was stirred.

Reaching the Assembly Rooms, Tom met departing carriages, the ball being at an end. He dodged the horses and went into the forecourt, seeking out his father's carriage, in which he had ridden in style earlier that evening. The steps of the building were aflow with people moving into their equipages, which were drawing up in turn, one behind the other, and he spotted the coachman, gray-coated and top-hatted, looking in that direction for him while waiting in line.

"Jones!" he called firmly, thinking to attract the coachman's attention and draw him out of the queue of vehicles, but in the general crush and confusion he went unheard. Quickly he mounted the steps and threaded his way through those thronging there, to approach the Warwyck carriage from the colonnaded side, and suddenly and unexpectedly he was face to face with Nicolette, a light, silken wrap about her shoulders. They were each taken completely by surprise, she knowing he had gone from the ball long since, he intent only upon getting home, and their eyes met fully and deeply with no chance of avoiding the encounter. The effect was unlike anything that either had ever experienced before. Not a drowning, because it was akin to rebirth. Not a losing of identity, although it was a fusing of two hearts. Not happiness or joy, because each knew of the terrible consequences portended by that holding of each other's gaze, but neither could look away. He saw her shiver involuntarily as if on the premonition of doom, clutching her wrap a little closer about her, and something of the chill that had touched her communicated itself to him. He would have spoken had she not turned away in the same instant, hastening after those she was with, and he realized the whole encounter had lasted no more than a few seconds. Nothing could be the same for either of them ever again.

Chapter 4

Richard, wearing a velvet smoking jacket, came to the open doorway of his study, a glass of brandy in one hand, a cigar in the other. "Is that you, Tom?"

"Yes, sir." Tom turned from going in the direction of his own room and came into the stronger rays of light from the study. He was not altogether surprised to see his father still about, for he always kept late hours.

"Come and have a drink with me," Richard invited benevolently. "I've been waiting to see you. Did you enjoy yourself at the Assembly Rooms? A charity ball, wasn't it?"

"That's right." Tom followed his father into the study, neither giving the other anything in their splendid height. "I'd like a brandy, sir."

"Help yourself." Richard sat down comfortably in a large leather chair and stretched his long legs out on the footstool in front of him. He liked his study with its paneled walls and framed Gillray cartoons that he had collected over the years. It was a retreat. A place that was truly his own. Meg never came into it. He watched as his son settled himself with a glass, swilling the golden liquid gently, his youthful face not tired, but curiously self-absorbed, his gaze distant and abstracted. Richard prompted his attention. "You don't look too exhausted by your gallivanting for us to have that talk I mentioned to you, but say so if you are."

Tom collected himself with a start. He would have preferred to wait until morning, but from the beginning his father had wanted the discussion to be that evening, so he might as well get it over and done with. After all, nothing was going to turn him from the path he had chosen. "Er—no, sir," he answered. "Not at all."

"Good." Richard regarded his son benignly, feeling mellow from wining and dining extremely well on his first evening home after an absence of several weeks. "The question of your future career must be settled, and with everything quiet and the house more or less to ourselves I think this is a splendid chance for both of us to air our opinions on the matter."

Tom spread a hand. "Whatever you say."

To his father he appeared almost detached, prepared to listen with one ear while his thoughts dwelt elsewhere. Not for the first time Richard crushed down a feeling of irritability at the unapproachable attitude of his youngest son. Had it always been the same between middle age and youth? He could remember how he and his father had always exploded into wrathful quarrels, but Tom was different, set on getting his own way quietly and without fuss. "I think we must both be in agreement that you've frittered away enough of your time to date, but I'm prepared to be lenient and draw a veil over the past, which need never be mentioned again." Richard was determined to be fair as well as firm. "I was young myself once, and I understand you a great deal better than you think I do, so I see no reason why we should not settle everything amicably and to our mutual satisfaction."

Tom's eyes narrowed slightly. He was alert now, emerging from amorous clouds to settle what must be settled before all else. "Nothing could please me more, sir. I hope this means you will allow me to show you the final line drawings of the yacht I have designed, as well as the molded half-section model of the hull, which gives a true indication of its shape and proportions." It was a challenge that he voiced. Always his father had dismissed out of hand any reference to a future linked with boats, and never had he been given the chance to express his most cherished ambition as he had with his grandfather in confidence many times over. Almost holding his breath, he waited for his father's reaction.

Richard had not been unprepared for the challenge and knew what Tom was about; moreover, after Daniel's words of caution he had given much thought as to how he should bring his son to heel, and had decided that tolerance and leniency would bind the young rebel tighter than the parental domination that was generally accepted as every father's right. "I will look at them, of course. As I understand it, you would like the summer in which to complete this project of yours. Well, I daresay I can stretch a point there and grant you a few more weeks of freedom."

"No."

Richard raised his eyebrows. "What do you mean—no?"

"I mean the summer will only be a time of preparation, ordering timber and other materials, getting the place ready in which to build the craft, and so on. I plan to make a start in the autumn, which means the vessel will be ready to compete with any other new designs early next year."

"A hobby for winter weekends. Most commendable." Richard had no objection to that and felt some relief over it as he continued speaking without pause, thinking that such an arrangement would fit in with his own plans quite admirably. "I hope to spend most of the summer at home myself, but when I do have to go to Town or visit any of the factories you will be free to come with me and take your time over deciding in which branch of the business you would like to set your future career and whether it should be in an administrative capacity or the engineering field, the choice being wide and the best of men available to train you to the top of the ladder."

Tom shook his head. "No, sir. Thank you, but my mind is unchanged. I thought you realized that. I want to make my own way in the world and let my achievements come on my own merits."

"But you would have ample scope to make your own mark in my concerns. Good Lord, Tom! You have only to prove yourself and you will have every encouragement. Young men of initiative and foresight are always in demand."

Tom frowned as he appeared to study the brandy in his glass. "That's just it. Everything would be made easy for me. I don't want that, and in any case my interests do not lie with the Warwyck Company."

Richard's tone hardened angrily. "You'd not have it easy, I can promise you that. The very opposite, in fact. No concession would be made because you and I bear the same name."

"Had I felt able to consider your proposition that assurance would have weighed with me, but I can't."

"Can't, damn it! Won't, you mean!" Richard was shaken by a tempest of exasperation. "I've a good mind to kick you out of this house until you come to your senses!"

Tom's jaw tightened, but he eyed his father steadily. "Naturally I should regret being barred from home, but it would change nothing. I'm linked to the sea, the seaside, and to boats. Not to wheels and looms and horseless carriages."

Richard thumped a fist on the arm of the chair. "Confound it, boy! Have you no ambition in you? Does it mean nothing that a Warwyck machine could be the first marketable one on the road, outstripping all competitors?"

"That is your ambition, sir. I respect it. Mine is to build the fastest sailing yacht in the world one day. Toward that aim I'm making a start with my first boat, and later will come my own boatyard." Tom's long-held enthusiasm was taking over and shining through his face as he spoke, leaning forward. "Sailing is growing as a sport. There is keen research going on this side of the Atlantic and the other to get yachts faster and more maneuverable. The boat I have designed is no more than forty feet in length, but I believe I'm heading in the right direction."

In searing disappointment, Richard could not hold back a vengeful taunt. "Well, it will not be the first floating craft you've ever made. I remember the coracle you built and paddled on the lake when you were seven years old. Had a gardener not hauled you out when it sank you would have drowned. Or perhaps you are basing your ambition on the two rowing dinghies that came next? I seem to remember that neither was particularly successful

—one capsized and the other bore you out to sea on the tide, twisting like a cork."

The dark color flooded into Tom's face and he drew back in his chair. "You're making sport of me, Father. I was no more than ten or eleven at the time, and in truth I bless the day that Wally Burns, the fisherman, picked me up in his boat after I lost the rudder from mine. He taught me the rudiments of boatbuilding, and from that point onward I have continued to gain experience and make progress." Some of that experience was to his credit during his university days when he had designed and had some part in making a rowing scully with which races had been won, but as far as he knew his father was not aware of it, the subject of boats being one that had usually been avoided between them over recent years. Often the clashes between them had been caused by his mother's displeasure that he should hobnob with fisher-folk and the trouble she stirred up over it, Richard being bound to support her while being no snob himself, never dreaming in the earliest days that by occasionally turning a blind eye to his youngest son's gratis trips out to sea with the fishing nets, Tom's path was being set on a course far different from anything he planned.

"How are you going to finance this expensive venture?" Richard had already regretted the taunt, but his anger would not abate, giving a rasping edge to all his words. "You'll not get a penny-piece out of me toward it, I can tell you."

"I have it all worked out."

"Indeed? Even counting in the fact that your allowance has stopped from this very hour of going against my wishes?"

A faint shrug of broad, young shoulders. "It stopped when I decided to secure employment for the months ahead. I could not in all conscience use any money but my own toward a project of which you so heartily disapprove."

Richard was taken aback. "What employment have you secured?"

"I was going to join the fishing fleet for the summer—"

"What?" Richard slammed down his glass, his face corded with outrage. "I forbid it! No son of mine is going to be a fisher-boy!"

It was as if Meg had wreaked some special vengeance on him, no matter that she would have cared for the prospect of their son taking to the nets as little as he.

Tom was shaking his head. "It's all right, Father," he said placatingly. "I'm not going to do that now. Something else came up quite unexpectedly. I'm going to work on the Pier. An assistant manager was suddenly needed to run the roller-skating rink in the Pier Pavilion, and I got the job."

"Indeed! You are full of surprises," Richard ground out savagely. He was severely shaken and his hands clenched involuntarily upon the chair arms. "Your grandfather put you up to that, no doubt."

"I admit Grandfather told me there was a vacancy. The fellow who held the post ran off with somebody's wife, taking the cashbox with him. Naturally it couldn't have happened at a worse time, with the season already under way, and the pier manager needed a replacement urgently. The decision as to whether I should be appointed was left to him, in spite of Grandfather owning the Pier, and he was glad to take me on, because I do know the ropes, having helped out at various times during previous summers when I've been home on school holidays. The manager approved a few suggestions I made about holding a roller-skating carnival as well as other attractions, and I'll practically have free rein."

"When do you start?"

"Right away. It should have been tomorrow morning, but I said I must have another day to make all my arrangements. What I earn there, plus a bonus on any of my schemes that meet with success, will tide me over until I receive my share of Great-Aunt Jassy's legacy, which is to be shared equally between Lennox and Jeremy and me. I have approached the bank manager for a loan against the legacy, and it will be forthcoming."

"You were not idle during your sojourn with your grandfather." A bitter retort. "Where do you imagine you will build your yacht? I need hardly say that you'll have no building or land of mine."

"I have secured a site."

"Oh?"

"It's the Tudor barn that was once used for storage by the Warwyck brickworks in the old days when Grandfather was building Easthampton. It has plenty of headroom and huge doors. He has agreed to let me use it."

"The devil he has!" Richard's mood was not improved by the revelation of his own father's complicity in aiding the lad's waywardness. The barn and the land on which it stood were Daniel's property, and Richard himself had no jurisdiction over it.

Tom continued evenly. "Wally Burns's brother is going to work with me there. He's a boatbuilder of long experience, but he's had no work in that line since he lost his leg at the knee in an accident at a Southampton boatyard a few years ago, when he had to return to fishing off Easthampton for a livelihood."

"Hab Burns is a scallywag of the first order."

"I like him. Everybody does. And he's keen to get started. Already he has made a start in clearing the barn as if it were tomorrow instead of summer's close when work will commence."

Richard passed fingertips over his forehead and brought them to the bridge of his nose, forcing himself to some degree of calmness with the reminder that orders, threats, and raging tempers had never won his father a point from him when he had determined upon a course to be taken. Tom was a true Warwyck with his independent spirit and unswerving resolve to go after his own goal, a trait Richard recognized only too well from his own character, and it was that same determination never to be beaten that had made Daniel a master of the prize ring in his day. With a suppressed sigh Richard realized that however much it galled him, he must let Tom try out his scheme. He must give his son the time needed and wait to see what happened. He raised his head as Tom spoke again.

"Later on, when I'm able to expand and take on more men, Grandfather has promised me the land that runs through from the meadow where the barn stands to the sea. It crosses Hoe Lane, but that's no problem since it's a private road and he owns that as well."

Richard stared as if he could not believe he had heard aright. "That is Honeybridge House land. Part of it is the old orchard, and it runs to the west of the house's garden wall that shuts off the old stables and the yard to the rear." For many years a sign threatening that trespassers would be prosecuted had protected the land, keeping it inviolate simply because it was adjacent to the environs of Honeybridge House, which had been kept locked and bolted ever since the death of Richard's mother over twenty-five years ago, and Daniel never went near the place or allowed anyone else to go into it. It had been his wife's haven, the house she had loved as their first home together, and even after they had moved into the far grander Easthampton House she had kept it as her own sanctuary. Now it had become an unvisited shrine. After Kate Warwyck died, all that she had possessed had been taken from Easthampton House and stored there, and Daniel's own portrait of her, which had been covered over on the day of her death, had been removed from its place of honor in the Green Drawing Room at the house on the hill to Honeybridge with everything else, he unable in his terrible grief to set eyes again on the face of the woman he had loved more than life itself.

Tom had followed his line of thought. "The gates into Honeybridge are padlocked, and not I or anybody else from the barn will go near them. We'll be too busy anyway."

Richard gave a nod. "Your grandfather has granted a concession indeed, both with the loan of the barn with its proximity to Honeybridge and with the promise he has made you. I hope you take it as a measure of his deep affection for you." He was controlling his own chagrin.

"I am sensible of the honor, sir." Tom leaned forward, resting his arms on his knees. "What was my grandmother like? I've never seen a likeness of her and rarely heard her name spoken by anyone in the family. I suppose when I was younger I never thought much about it, but over recent years I've often wondered about her. Now and again local people have mentioned her, always telling me that the like of Kate Warwyck is never seen these days, and that she helped this one or that when there was sickness or ill fortune of some kind. Was she very pious?"

"No, she wasn't. She had a strong faith, but there was nothing in the least sanctimonious about her. Far from it. The charitable work that she did was a matter entirely between her and those she was helping, and there was no parading about with baskets of largesse in the manner adopted by so many ladies when visiting the poor and performing other outwardly good deeds. Nobody knows just how many people Kate Warwyck helped in her time, and peer or prostitute, it was all the same to her. She suffered an injury to her side, which was the indirect cause of her death years later, through going to the aid of a villainous rogue who fell under a wagon wheel. It was during the great fight on the beach, which you have heard about, and she was attending the injured."

"Grandfather mentioned that incident to me only the other day." Tom chuckled. "I'd have liked to take part in that affray. Grandfather's pugilistic fists must have knocked the majority of those ruffians into kingdom come."

"Not far from it, I would say. I cannot give you an eyewitness account of his victory, because it happened a few months before I was born, but from the way it has passed into local legend I daresay you're right."

Father and son each became aware that the tension had gone between them. Richard felt no different over Tom's defiance, but at least they were still on speaking terms; no unbridgeable gap had widened between them, and it left the door open for further negotiations in the future, should Tom's plans come to naught. It crossed Richard's mind that the mention of his mother's name had somehow set them on a better track. As he remembered from his childhood and later in young manhood, being no more than twenty-three when she died, Kate Warwyck had always had the power to calm and comfort, a deep warmth in her personality that touched all who knew her. He did not agree with his father's rejection of memories, it being the only way Daniel had been able to find to go on living without her, but he could understand it. Easthampton House had become a hollow shell at her death for her husband, family, and her many friends. Whether something of her personality still lingered at Honeybridge House he had never discovered. On the one occasion, several years ago now, when he had asked for the key in order to inspect the condition of the house, Daniel had struck him. Struck him with all the force that still lingered in the master fist. He had not taken offense, see-ing such a wild despair in his father's eyes that anything belong-ing to Kate should be disturbed; he had nursed a sore jaw for weeks and never mentioned Honeybridge to Daniel again.

"How did my grandmother feel about Aunt Lucy?" Tom ques-tioned. "It's never been any secret in my lifetime that Lucy Bar-ton is Grandfather's daughter by an adulterous affair with another woman."

Richard, caught off guard, felt old wounds again. After all these years the pain of loving Lucy in his youth could still come back to him. He had fallen in love with her before the truth had come out for either of them that they had both been fathered by Daniel. It had been on the rebound of that terrible discovery that he had become inextricably involved with Meg and married her. He did occasionally see Lucy when his homecomings to the Grange coincided with her visits to see their father, but he was no longer the young man he had been, and she of the red-gold hair had become a matron with a life entirely of her own in which he had never had any part. They could talk, exchange news, even laugh together, but it was the ghost of the girl she had been that had prevented him ever loving another woman as he had loved her. He had never been faithful to Meg, not after the first year or two anyway, but love had not come his way again; affection some-times, infatuation once or twice, but never love. He brought his thoughts back to the present, answering his son's question.

"Kate Warwyck knew how to forgive and forget, a rare enough quality in human nature. Realizing that she was dying, she did ev-erything in her power to bring her husband and his daughter to-gether. She was thinking only of him, not wanting him to be lonely when she was gone, because your mother and I were al-ready married and living away from Easthampton, and he and Donna had only recently become on better terms with each other, partly through a change in her that I never really understood. Donna had always been a rather timid person, much browbeaten by him into believing herself to be less of a person than she was, but practically overnight she seemed to cast aside her shell and emerge in her true character." He shook his head ruminatively. "I never understood how it happened, but happen it did, and all for the better." He rose from the chair, putting an end to any more questions, the purpose of the original discussion having come to naught. "It's late. You need your sleep, and it's many hours since I left London. Promise me one thing, Tom."

His son faced him. "If I can, sir."

"Should you change your mind about your boatyard at any time, I ask only that you reconsider what I have put to you."

"I have to say that I can't foresee those circumstances arising."

"But if they should?"

"Then you have my word on it."

"Well spoken." Richard shook Tom's hand seriously. As they made to go from the room together Tom paused, intent on one further piece of information.

"Aunt Lucy's mother once lived here at the Grange, didn't she?"

Richard suppressed a sigh. He had wanted no more questions about Lucy that night, but he answered evenly. "That is correct. It was over fifty years ago. Her name was Claudine and she was married to Lionel Attwood, whose family had owned this estate for many generations. She was said to be a radiant beauty, and tragically she died quite young. Why do you ask? What's troubling you? Your grandfather's indiscretion? He wasn't always old, you know. At the height of his fame as the prize ring's Champion of England he was said to be one of the finest-looking men in the land."

"No, it isn't that." Tom's brow was furrowed. "I've just remembered hearing once that Claudine Attwood was Mrs. Olivia Radcliffe's sister."

"So she was."

"Well, it couldn't have helped the Warwyck-Radcliffe feud if Grandfather was having an illicit affair with a Radcliffe sister-in-law, and she another man's wife."

"I'm sure it added to the bitterness, but needless to say, for Lucy's sake it's a skeleton to be kept in the cupboard."

"Yes, of course," Tom agreed. It was none of his concern, and he would not want through idle talk to cause his Aunt Lucy any distress over the old scandal. Not that he saw her often, but he had always liked her, and as a boy he had appreciated her generosity toward him at Christmas and on natal days. It was simply that his interest in all things connected with the Radcliffe household, present and past, now held a new fascination for him. "One thing more, sir. Grandfather has offered me the hospitality of his home again while I'm working at the Pier. It does mean that I'll be much nearer than at the Grange, and since you'll be home most of the summer I would like to take advantage of his offer."

"I trust you'll not be too busy to visit your mother or me."

"No, of course not. I'll be coming and going here all the time."

"Then I've no objection. Good night, my boy."

"Good night, Father."

Tom went to his own quarters, his thoughts returning fully and cherishingly to Nicolette. Quite apart from his own plans for his future, if his father had offered him the chairmanship of the whole Warwyck empire that night he would have refused it, for it would have taken him away from Easthampton and all chance of seeing her again soon.

At Radcliffe Hall, Nicolette, unable to sleep, sat by her window, looking out into the night-clad grounds. She was afraid, afraid as she had never been before in all her life, and her fear was for Tom, for herself, and for that tender, vulnerable emotion that had ensnared the two of them in that unguarded moment of meeting on the steps. If she had not lingered for a few extra minutes to bid good night to others in the vestibule, she would have been safely in the landau with Laura and the colonel and his wife. But would it have made any difference? Sooner or later she and Tom would have met again, and the inevitable would only have been postponed for a short time.

Not that she had expected him to look at her in the way that he did. It had been her own feelings she had been seeking to hide, to crush down, and to put away from herself in a struggle that had lasted since her parting from him. Her whole being had become tinglingly aware of his arrival at the Assembly Rooms. She had *heard* his silent appeal for a glance from her in her head, and had blamed her own heightened nerves for the intensity of the message received, not dreaming that his feelings were on a par with her own. Then his eyes had captured hers, and such sweet passion had consumed her in its flame that she had trembled with it, aware that the whole map of her life was changing.

Restlessly she sprang to her feet and paced the room, the candle glow from the bedside throwing light and shade into the billowing ripples of her nightgown. Should she go away? Should she make an escape while there was still time? But where? Not back to Scotland! Never there! To India with Laura in a few weeks' time? Her father would never allow it; the old myth of her delicate health that had been perpetuated by her mother would be against her going to such a hot climate, and in any case she had had more than enough of Laura's company, aware that she had outgrown the schoolgirl silliness that Laura still retained. Where else was there? Or, more to the point, was there anywhere that she would be allowed to go?

She came to a standstill by her reflection in the cheval glass. How desperate she looked. How darkly her eyes glistened as if tears were not far away. And yet there was something else as well in her face, a secret terror and jubilation as if she found herself truly on the brink of fulfilled womanhood, her inner self possessing an inherent wisdom of deep, sweet longings of which she had no true knowledge. She shivered. All she did know was that it was impossible to flee from love. To think how deliberately she had given up riding on the sands to take no risk of seeing him on her own, only to come face to face with him in a crowd and exchange looks in which more had been said by the eyes than any words could have covered on a deserted shore.

She caught her breath on the realization that she had acknowledged the existence of love. *Love.* She had said that magical, beautiful word, not only in an awareness of its first ever awakening in her heart, but in connection with Tom. She must accept that the die had been cast and her fate set. There was nothing that she could do to stop the run of it. To try to escape from love was as foolish as trying to evade death when the time came. A soft moan escaped her. She had been stricken again by the sense of doom that she had experienced earlier.

She clasped her hands and stood with them pressed against her chest, her head bowed, her dark red hair a-tumble about her shoulders. "Tom," she whispered. "Forget me while there is still time, because I am lost. I can't forget you. My heart defies me and bars all escape."

She stood there, still and unmoving, while the candle drowned in its own wax and the dawn began to lift the sky over the sea.

Chapter 5

"So you're going to build a sailing boat, are you?" Meg commented dubiously after listening to her youngest son. It was morning, and they were in her boudoir, which was furnished to her taste, every inch of it cluttered with knickknacks and heavy draperies. The Gothic bed was vulgarly ornate, an exact copy of one displayed at the Great Exhibition, which she had spotted afterward in a shop window and known no peace until it was hers, for she had considered it to be the handsomest bed she had seen. And she had been hungry for rich clothes and pretty things during those first months of marriage, thinking she had only to deck herself out finely enough and lavish love and passion on her new husband to win him away forever from the memories that haunted him and kept the look of dark despair in his eyes.

"I'll be ready to start on it at the end of the summer, and I'll have the skill and experience of Hab Burns to back me at every turn," Tom explained to her. She had taken the news better than he had expected of his taking charge of the skating rink, but no doubt she imagined him swanning about under his surname of Warwyck with everybody bowing left, right, and center, which was far from what he had in mind. In any case, quite by chance he had caught her in a fairly amiable mood, which was enabling him to talk more easily with her than was usual. She had been drinking, for it was impossible for her to start the day without some alcoholic beverage, but as yet she was free from the ill humor and maudlin self-pity that overcame her all too frequently.

She was somewhat appeased. "Oh, I see. You'll give the orders and he'll do the work."

"Not at all. Every inch of that boat's timber will pass through my hands at one stage or another. There'll be many a time when I'll be taking instruction from Hab on what to do."

She shook her head firmly, making some straggling tendrils bounce. "It don't sound like no gentleman's occupation to me."

She was obsessed with gentility, loathing her own rough origins which had been instrumental in making her less than the wife she had wanted to be for Richard's sake. After Richard had given her his name she had scorned all whom she had known in her humbler days, thinking that by cutting herself adrift from the past there would be nothing to hamper her being accepted into the London circles in which he moved, but that had not happened. With the Sussex dialect thick upon her tongue, and with her rosy, sea-weathered complexion and square, workaday hands, she had been ignored and looked down upon at social gatherings while Richard with his fine bearing and handsome looks had been made much of, particularly by the ladies, who had been the cause of many a stormy quarrel between them. One of the worst quarrels in all their married life together had been through his love for another woman long gone from his life, for without consulting Meg he had purchased the Grange, and she had known as if it had been shouted at her that its links with his half sister, Lucy, who had once lived happily under its roof, were the reasons why he had bought it. He never admitted the truth of it to her, even though she nagged and shrieked and goaded him almost beyond endurance, but went stubbornly ahead in removing her, almost at her time in a fourth pregnancy, and their three boys to the Grange. She had frightened them and alarmed the servants already installed there by screaming when she had stepped from the carriage and stood facing the house. She had screamed and beaten her breast and torn her hair, not so much for returning to

Easthampton, which she had thought never to see again, but because the Grange represented the woman who had robbed Richard of his love, leaving none for her, and she was going to have to live within the confines of those hateful walls until the end of her days. When Richard had tried to calm her she had clawed his face to blood, ignoring the terror of young Lennox and Cedric as well as the sobbing of little Jeremy, clinging to her skirts. "You'll not find her in this house!" she had screamed at Richard. "I'll see that you don't! I'll make every day in it a hell for you!"

He had overpowered her in his arms and dragged her kicking and yelling into the house, where she was seized with such birth pangs that she had collapsed against him, slipping to her knees. He had lifted her up and carried her to the bedroom, where Tom had been born two hours later. She had refused to look upon the infant, wanting to hurt Richard by her rejection of his child, wanting to show him that she had meant every word that she had said, so that when finally the pain of her milk-swollen breasts compelled her to take the infant into her arms, she knew only dislike of her burden and distaste for her task, the maternal love she had felt for her other children completely lacking. She had never changed her attitude toward her youngest son, and yet perversely she was jealous of his affection for others, unable to stop herself finding fault with Daniel or anyone else whom her son held in high regard.

"I'm not concerned with the social status of my venture," Tom answered her patiently. He was the only one of her surviving children to show continued tolerance and understanding toward her, Lennox and Jeremy always thankful to escape her presence, although that did nothing to soften her toward Tom since she attributed her eldest son's coolness to his reserved nature and Jeremy was without fault in her eyes. "All that matters to me," he continued, "is getting this yacht of my own design into full sail on the waves. I'm certain I'll find a waiting market for her, and then I'll be launched quite literally into what I've wanted to do all my life."

Meg looked faintly contemptuous, diving her plump fingers into a box of colored cachous on the table at her side. In her youth she had been a pert, quick-moving girl with a liveliness about her that had attracted many an admirer, but all that had gone long since, crushed from her by a marriage that had been calamitous to both partners, and over the years she had put on weight, lost pride in her appearance, and never looked or smelled particularly clean. Lady's maids of any pride never stayed long, and other maidservants who attended her were easily bribed to smuggle in extra bottles to supplement the amount of alcohol that Richard allowed her, which she considered meager, forever accusing him unjustly of meanness, refusing to acknowledge that it was his concern for her that made him place a limit on her daily intake. Although it was almost noon she was still in a peignoir, its frills and flounces bunched about her ample figure as she lay back against the satin cushions, and her brownish hair, which had retained its natural curl, had yet to be brushed and dressed, one side flattened from where she had slept on it during the night. No morning visitors ever called on her at the Grange, and since the housekeeper managed adequately there was nothing to spur her into making the most of any day. Tom's high-flying ambition offered no interest. The time when she had known how to sail a fishing boat better than any man belonged to happier days long past.

"That's as may be," she commented, using the ball of her thumb to push some powdery sugar from the cachou into her mouth, "but we're not put into this world to do what we want. If I've said it once I've said it a thousand times, you're willful and headstrong and don't never do what's fitting for the son of a gentleman and the grandson of a baronet."

She had said it as many times. The phrase was as repetitious as if played on one of the new talking machines known as a phonograph, which he had first heard at an exhibition of its wonders at the very Assembly Rooms where only a few hours before he had looked again upon Nicolette. He stifled a sigh at the monotony of the reproof and thought to give his mother something to look forward to later on.

"I'll take you for a sail when the yacht is finished, Mother.

You'll enjoy that. It will be like old times for you to be on the sea again."

She shot forward from the waist and struck him a ringing blow across his ear, her mouth pursed up with temper, her eyes blazing. "None of your lip! I'll have none of it, I say! I won't have no mention of the days before I married your pa. I'm a lady now and as good as the best of 'em, however toffee-nosed they act toward me. Nothing can change the fact that I'm Mrs. Richard Warwyck, and every one of those damn women what gives me those icy smiles and talks in la-di-dah tones would give ten years of her life to be in my shoes." She flung her feet to the floor and sprang up from the chaise longue in a flurry of lace and a pervading odor of unbathed flesh. "God Almighty! I need a drink." She stamped across to the cabinet, swung open the doors, and took from it a decanter of gin and a glass, which she half filled and drank down as though she had developed an unquenchable thirst. She poured the same measure again, left the decanter conveniently within reach on top of the cabinet, which she rested against when she turned to face her son, the glass to her lips for a more leisurely gulp, and she let the liquid run about in her mouth before swallowing it. He had risen from the chair where he had been sitting, and she found it amusing that he showed his indignation at the blow she had dealt him. She liked to see him displeased. It gave her satisfaction to inflict some of her own misery upon him. "You get more like that damn grandfather of yours every day," she taunted, making an insult of what he would have considered a compliment from anyone else. "Same scowl when your brows meet. Same mulish set to your mouth. Same aggressive jut of the chin. You've spent too much time in his company instead of being at home, which is your rightful place." Her tone became heavily sarcastic. "I don't know why you bother to show your face here at all, I really don't." She swung her glass about, careless that the contents swilled over. "Why don't you stay at Easthampton House all the time? Or you could live in the barn with the bloody boat while you're building it for all I care. You've never donated nothing but shame to me, being chucked out of those posh schools where education was being handed to you on a plate—the sort of learning that was denied the likes of me, what would have jumped at the chance." She advanced a pace toward him, her expression becoming a grimace in her animosity to him. "And what happened when you went to university? You couldn't behave like a well-brought-up son of a gentleman should do, but had to bring down more disgrace upon yourself by—"

He interrupted her tirade, pale but controlled, ignoring her taunts through long experience, and was rigorously courteous as always toward her. "As it happens, I shall be living more at Easthampton House and eventually with my boat than here during the months to come. Father is in agreement, and I'll be coming home and calling in often enough."

His quiet statement, disregarding her display of ill temper, somehow served to antagonize her still further. "You get out then!" she shrieked. "Go your own way! See if I care! Why should I? You've never cared tuppence for me, your own mother. You and your father would like to see me dead and gone. Dead and gone, I say!"

Wearily Tom turned for the door. "I'm leaving for Easthampton House after luncheon."

"Leave whenever you damn well like and don't come back!"

He closed the door after him and had no idea that she had hurled her glass at him until he heard it smash against the panel. Left alone, she darted back to the cabinet, took another glass, her hands shaking with temper, and poured gin into it up to the rim. When Richard returned that evening from Merrelton, where he had had business and social engagements, he found her lying in a drunken stupor on her rumpled bed, still in her peignoir and nightgown from the morning. A couple of bottles that he did not recognize lay on the floor. He sighed, pulling the covers over her, and hoped that when Mrs. Constance Meredith came she would seek out the hiding places where his wife kept reserve supplies of spirits and put an end to such pathetic degradation.

*　　*　　*

In the orange-red glow of the sunset through open doors the Tudor barn presented a vast area of clean-swept flagstones under the soaring hammer-beam roof, which in itself was the shape of an inverted boat. Tom, who had walked to the barn from Easthampton House, where he had comfortably installed himself that same afternoon, stood with feet apart and hands in his pockets as he surveyed the interior with satisfaction. Now that so much of the accumulated rubbish of years had been turned out, the interior looked even larger than before, and he felt quite dwarfed by its size. It had not been used for farm purposes since Daniel had bought the land on which it stood years and years ago in the days of building Easthampton, but had become a warehouse for bricks and tiles until the local clay seam had run out and the Warwyck brick-building industry had ground to a halt. Some stacks of that old produce still remained, thick with dust and bits of straw, waiting to be carted off by Hab when next he came to finish his chores there.

Tom took a few steps forward, his feet clacking on the flagstones, and he wished that Nicolette were with him that they might talk of other things than the fraught topics that had engaged them previously, because most of all he would have liked to tell her of the enterprise he planned, and to enable her to see with his vision the way it would be. Here beneath the huge crossbeams his yacht would take form, a sloop of new design and yet rising traditionally from its building board, not to be built upside down as many smaller boats were, but taking shape from its wedged keel, sharp and purposeful as a shark's fin, until all the work was finished inside and out, and then in the open air the tall mast would rise up on her as if to touch the skies. For as long as he could remember he had thought, read, used, and researched boats and methods of sailing to this end. Nothing written by the famous yacht designers of the past thirty years had escaped him, and among his most treasured possessions was an original lines drawing of the famous yacht *Jullanar* with her revolutionary underwater profile, the cutaway forefoot the inspiration for his own design with the drawn-out forebody, which he was convinced would enable her to sail closer to the wind than *Jullanar* herself when at last she was released upon the water, the product of his keen mathematical mind and extensive sea knowledge.

He continued to look about him with satisfaction. In one

corner was an old boiler he had managed to get for a few shillings, which would be more than adequate for the steaming box needed for making the timber pliable, and he had no other tools to buy, Daniel having allowed him a choice from the stacks of stored planes, chisels, screwdrivers, drills, saws, and innumerable other items kept from the Warwyck building days. On an ancient side bench, much scarred over the centuries, he would be able to spread out his lines drawing, the tables of offsets giving measurements to plot the lines to full size, and all the specification drawings over which he had spent such time and care. In addition there would be the mounted model of the hull carved out of a single piece of wood to give scale to dimensions for Hab's benefit, more to set him at ease than anything else, for he was used to a visual guide in the old traditions of boatbuilding. As for himself, he knew every nut and bolt that would go into his yacht's making, and he could picture her when finished with the spray rising from the slender bow and the sails billowed full. She would be a beautiful boat, created solely for speed, a very star of the seas.

He grinned with triumph there in the fading light. *Sea Star!* That was what he would call her! He had turned hundreds of names over in his mind and rejected them, and now she had settled her own identity in the very place of her imminent creation, the first hint of the spirit and character that every vessel made individually her own. There would be no changing it. No changing it when he had had Nicolette pressing in upon his thoughts when the decision was made. She was his star. She was his aim. One day he would tell her. One day he would tell her many things.

The great doors of the barn thudded as he closed one and then the other before leaving. He decided not to return home to Easthampton House by way of the five-barred gate through which he had come, but turned instead to take a shortcut across the meadowland long prohibited to trespassers, thinking that when he reached Hoe Lane, which ran parallel to the sea into the center of the resort, he would follow it and find friends at the club for a game of billiards. The grass was high about his feet, and in order to make easier progress he crossed over to reach the rutted track that ran by the high flint wall of the Honeybridge grounds, where once horses and carriages would have made their way up from the lane and swung into the yard to reach the coach houses and stables that were situated some distance away from the house.

Coming to the stable-yard gates, he stopped and looked through the rusty bars, still as intrigued as he had been in childhood by the silent, shuttered buildings that nobody entered, and where no horse stamped a restless hoof behind the closed doors. To his knowledge only one person had ever attempted to break into the house itself, and the punishment had been severe, for the villain had been sent to the House of Correction at Coldbath Fields, where the dreaded treadmill had still been in use, and the sentence had acted as a serious deterrent to anybody else with a mind to try his luck. Those boys who out of mischief had managed to get into the stable yard always found themselves unable to get out again due to the canting inward of the spikes that Daniel had had specially set in along the tops of the walls, and when released had received a dose of the birch for trespassing. Nobody trespassed a second time. Daniel had always known how to protect his property. He had once gathered together a host of his fellow pugilists to deal unmercifully with a gang of thugs hired to set fire to all that was being built in the first stages of Easthampton's development from hamlet into resort. Locally it was said that all the gentry living in the surrounding estates at the time had conspired in the plot, the grand families having been against the Warwyck venture in the beginning, but Daniel always named his old enemy, the late Alexander Radcliffe, as the instigator of that attempted arson and other crimes propagated against him then and later.

Tom left the gates and continued on down the rutted track by the wall, dodging the branches of neglected apple trees overhanging it from the section of the old orchard within the walls. Penetrating the grounds of Radcliffe Hall had always offered more sport than any attempt to get into Honeybridge as far as he was concerned, and he had never set foot there, but after what his father had told him about Kate Warwyck, he wondered whether she would have cared to have the house she loved barred to all life, dust and cobwebs settled in the rooms that had been dear to her. He had no way of knowing, but he did not think so.

He reached the lane from the track and turned into it. Beyond the tamarisk hedge at his right hand the sea lapped, a curious, opal color in the gathering darkness, almost giving light to the flints of Honeybridge House, which faced it squarely, solid as the great rocks embedded in the shore's sands. Again he paused to peer through a gate into Honeybridge territory. Once the garden gate had been low enough to look over, but after the attempted break-in it had been replaced by another, tall and stoutly made with a grille like a prison door, with a padlock on it to match, and through the grille he had a fine view of his late grandmother's first home in Easthampton. It was not a grand house—far from it; simply an unpretentious residence built of perfectly knapped flints over two centuries or more ago, a place of mellow charm and dignity, thickly thatched with Sussex reeds, the entrance porched, and the many windows presently shuttered from the outside, which in turn were veiled by the foliage of the gnarl-stemmed wisteria that spread itself across the whole frontage. He supposed the house would remain undisturbed until his grandfather died, but that was something he did not wish to contemplate, and hoped that it lay many years hence.

He decided as he strolled on that he must make some plan of action as to how he might see Nicolette again, for he could not and would not wait for capricious fate to bring about a meeting. It was highly unlikely that their social paths would cross anywhere by invitation, few people being tactless enough to ask Warwycks and Radcliffes to the same gathering. He must take matters into his own hands, but how? The simplest method would be to write her a letter with a request to meet her somewhere. Surely she would not refuse! But would that old dragon at the Hall intercept the girl's mail, querying any correspondence in an unfamiliar hand? Perhaps even opening it. He grimaced at the thought. No, a letter was out of the question unless it could be passed to Nicolette secretly. But by whom? He shared no close, mutual friend with the Radcliffe-Stuarts, and a servant from the Hall might accept a bribe and still give the game away. At all costs he must do nothing to invoke the widow's wrath against her granddaughter, or banishment to Scotland would result. There seemed nothing for it but to visit the grounds again by darkness, making sure of a moonless night this time, and seek Nicolette out in person. He knew where her bedroom window was situated, and could attract her attention with a little gravel-throwing at the panes. Scarcely any risk was involved since it was obvious from last time that the widow retired early in another wing of the house, and none of Nicolette's brothers and their crowd would expect him to be foolhardy enough to return to the precincts of the Hall, there being no reason that they knew of for him to venture there ever again after Laura's betrayal.

Laura. That gave him a nasty jolt. Would Nicolette resent his seeming to pursue her by night in a similar fashion to his previous exploit? The last thing he wanted was that she should think his longing to see her was anything akin to his lustful purpose toward Laura. He would have to keep the gravel-throwing as a last resort. In the meantime, there must be some other way to get in touch with her.

Deep in his reverie he had come to the end of Hoe Lane and turned his steps automatically down a street that would lead him to the club. He was certain that he knew now why Nicolette no longer took those early-morning rides along the sands that she had mentioned to him. She had been afraid of their meeting again, afraid of what she would feel, not wanting their relationship to continue in any way. It was highly likely that she had not abandoned those morning rides, but was taking them inland across the surrounding countryside instead. *That* was how he would find her! *That* was the way!

Much cheered by all he had resolved, he quite swaggered into the club with waistcoat outthrust and thumbs looped in its braid-edged pockets.

Chapter 6

At seven o'clock next morning Tom took the best horse from his grandfather's stable, saddled up himself, and was away through the woods that flanked the north side of the hillock on which Easthampton House stood, to reach the open countryside. Near the main gates of Radcliffe Hall he reined in under some trees and waited. Nothing happened, except that a faint drizzle damping the air turned suddenly into an unexpected downpour, chilling the morning, and the only time the gates opened was when the postman in his box hat and a dripping cape trudged through on foot to deliver the mail. Disgruntled and disappointed, his collar turned up against the heavy rain that did not ease, he turned homeward, where he changed his clothes and just had time to wolf down a quick and hearty breakfast before dashing off to get to the Pier by nine o'clock on his first morning as assistant manager.

The Pier had changed a great deal since it had first been built on ranks of iron-clad piles with an arched entrance and a simple promenading walk to a circular pavilion at the head of it, where in the past melodramas had been enacted for the enjoyment of summer visitors. The entrance to the Pier had been enlarged to encompass two shops on either side of it, one selling postcards and souvenirs, the other every kind of sweetmeat, toffee, and candy, some fashioned to look like highly colored pebbles from the beach, or babies' dummies, or false teeth, or any number of other, unattractive imitations, which had such a ready sale with those visiting the seaside. Most popular of all were the sticks of bright pink peppermint rock with the name of Easthampton imprinted throughout and revealing itself with every bite, and it was these that dominated the window to the west of the entrance with its green-painted turnstile. Once a modest, onion-shaped dome had crowned the archway through which the visitors passed after paying their tuppences, but in recent years that had been replaced by three of such size and proportions and gilded gaudiness that any one of them could have graced the Royal Pavilion at Brighton, the bizarre Arabian Nights architecture of which had influenced so much building at the seaside, associated as it was in everyone's mind with those riotous, bad old days of the Prince Regent. He had made going to the sea an excuse for highjinks and every kind of indulgence from wine bibbing to woman chasing. A song currently being sung nightly in the show at Easthampton's Music Hall, and echoed in roaring choruses by audiences, was called "Naughty but Nice at the Seaside," a typical example of how a long-dead prince had made his mark upon sea bathing and its attendant pleasures, making it impossible for the masses to dissociate the seaside from a slap-and-tickle atmosphere. The days when men like Daniel had tried to keep their resorts elegant and dignified were gone long since, only a few maintaining a reputation for being safe for one's maiden aunt's delicate sensibilities.

Tom entered a door at the side of the sweetshop and went down a short passageway into the pier manager's office to the rear of it. Mr. Beckworth, a squarely built, high-complexioned man with thin hair combed long across a balding pate, and a luxuriance of sandy-hued side whiskers, was already at his desk. Tough, astute, he had little imagination himself, but he could recognize potential in the ideas of others, and it was to his credit more than to anybody else's that in recent years the Pier had taken on a new lease of prosperity, competing successfully with other, newer piers along the coast. He hoped that one day

Easthampton Pier, which had been built in 1850, would be replaced by a grand edifice twice as long and twice as big, giving him
unlimited scope to make it the most talked-about pier in England,
but Sir Daniel was too old to launch such a heavy financial venture and had always dismissed any hint with a definite shake of
the head. Nevertheless, the old man couldn't live forever, and the
Warwyck money had to go somewhere, and he wouldn't mind
betting a pound to a penny that young Tom, who—unlike his
father—had an all-consuming interest in anything to do with
Easthampton, would come in for a whack of it. It was this belief
that had made him encourage Tom's company and willingness to
give a hand in the past, and had made him grab at the chance to
get that same Warwyck into a position of some authority on the
Pier's payroll. He welcomed Tom into the office with a hearty
handshake.

"Morning, Warwyck. You believe in punctuality like me. Well
done. Sit down. The roller-skating rink don't open for another
hour, and we'll go over these ideas of yours. I like 'em, as well as
the publicity you suggest. 'Ow about these Friday gala nights?"

"We'll make every third one a fancy-dress carnival, which
will allow for the regular change-over of holiday visitors in the
town."

Mr. Beckworth ticked a list he held. "These exhibition skaters
now. Think we can book any with the season well under way?"

"I've already made inquiries. There's a couple working at
Brighton who would come for grand carnival nights only, but
that's really all we want at the present time."

They talked on, and when Tom finally left the office he
emerged from another door onto the deck of the Pier itself, where
booths and other shops, much smaller than those by the entrance,
were built into the hollow arches of iron which ranked at intervals
along its full length. Although it was still raining, some visitors to
the resort, well wrapped in waterproofs, were already promenading the deck, and since the tide was in, anglers were taking
up favored positions, casting their lines down into the choppy
water. The fortune-teller, who had come out of her booth to hang

up her sign, greeted him when he went past, knowing him by name as did the rest who plied a summer trade upon the Pier.

He went into the circular pavilion at the head of it, passing through the foyer, where he exchanged another good-morning with the woman in charge of roller skates for hire, and entered the roller-skating rink itself. The building had been enlarged since its days as a theater, the stage dispensed with to give extra space, but the decor remained the same, all crimson plush and gilded cupids illuminated by gas lamps. The old seats had been utilized in rows against the walls, allowing skaters a place to rest, while the dress circle, still intact, offered accommodation to non-skaters who merely came to watch.

Tom surveyed the rink much as he had done the barn. Both were his domains now. The corners of his eyes crinkled in secret satisfaction. As part of the publicity campaign for his new gala nights, printed circulars in the form of an invitation were to be delivered over a wide area. He would make sure that there was a delivery to Radcliffe Hall. If Nicolette came just once with a party he was sure he would find some way to speak to her on her own. And, knowing the Radcliffe-Stuarts, he could not believe that the brothers would ignore any center of fun in the town. His mouth joined in with his eyes in an expression of pleasurable anticipation. In the meantime he would go daily to the gates of the Hall at an early hour and keep his vigil there.

Five more days passed before he had any kind of reward, and then it was not what he had expected. He was on the point of turning his horse away, waiting as usual until the last possible moment, which always made Aunt Donna fuss over the speed with which he gulped his breakfast, when the lodge keeper came out and began to open the gates. Both of them. Moments later there came the sounds of hooves on the gravel of the drive, and an open carriage bearing four passengers came into view, followed by another equipage carrying trunks and boxes bound and labeled. Through the screen of foliage he saw only Nicolette, fresh as the bright morning herself in something light and sprigged and cottony, a straw hat pinned to her glorious mass of hair, and he was

filled with such panic that she was departing from Easthampton
that he felt all color drain from his face, skin tautening over brow
and cheekbones in a way that was almost painful. He had his
hand raised spontaneously to bring the crop down on his horse to
gallop forward in some wild aim to stay her, when he realized in
the nick of time that it was Laura who was dressed for traveling.
He understood instantly that she was being taken to Easthampton railway station to catch a train, and it looked very much
as if the two young men also in the carriage, Bertie Radcliffe-
Stuart and another whom Tom recognized as one he had punched
in the eye during the fracas at the folly, were leaving too, their attire more formal than would be usual at the breakfast hour at the
seaside.

He felt enervated by relief. With mild amazement he saw that
his hand on the reins was shaking. God! What a terrible moment
that had been. He was about to leave the cover of the trees, the
two equipages being safely out of sight, when he drew his mount
back again, hearing the approach of another carriage. In this one
were seated no less than six of those who had joined in the attack
upon him, all laughing and talking, an air of departure about
them. Once through the gates the coachman whipped up the
horses to catch up with those ahead of him. Tom waited, but
nobody else came, and he rode homeward.

He totted up those who were left at the Hall. Hugh and the
twins and Lawrence Payne. The numbers of the enemy had been
severely reduced, but of them all he would have been best pleased
to see the back of the Payne fellow. He did not like the thought
of him hanging about Nicolette. The sooner he went, the better,
not that it would leave a clear field for him. Far bigger obstacles
divided him from Nicolette, but somehow and somewhere he
would find a way through to her.

He had almost reached home when he began to wonder why
Hugh had not gone along to escort Laura to the railway station.
Was it possible that the disclosure of the assignation in the folly
had caused such a rift between Laura and Hugh that there had
been no bridging it? That would most certainly have cooked
Hugh's goose for him. Anything Hugh had fancied from her

would have been denied him. Tom began to grin. He was still grinning when he went into the breakfast room at Easthampton House, and was deaf to the affectionate scolding that Aunt Donna gave him for leaving less time than ever between his morning ride and the hour for work.

On the platform of the railway station Nicolette waved to Bertie and the Hall's departing guests until the train was out of sight. Then she glanced at the clock above the waiting room. One minute past nine o'clock. She was alone and free for the first time since coming down from Scotland, and she was determined to make the most of it. With any luck her grandmother, who rarely made an appearance before lunchtime, would not learn she was in the resort without a chaperone until that hour, and by then it would be too late to do anything about it. In the station yard she dismissed the carriage that was waiting for her.

"Give word at the Hall that I have decided to stay in town to do some shopping," she instructed the coachman. "Return for me at the entrance to Lawton's Emporium at four o'clock this afternoon."

"Very good, miss."

She left the vicinity of the station and made for a footpath that would take her to the beach, passing on the way the old house known as Sea Cottage. She looked at it over the hedge with a sharp curiosity as she went by. It was neat and respectable enough now and was a boardinghouse with a sign stating "Vacancies" in one of the windows, but it was known locally to have been the haunt of smugglers in the days when brandy and lace and tobacco had been brought by night across the Channel from France. What was of more interest to her was that she knew this to be the house where Tom Warwyck's mother had lived as a girl before she had run away with Richard Warwyck and married him. Nicolette had heard her grandmother relate the tale with scorn many times, ridiculing Daniel Warwyck in her talk because his only son's wife had been the daughter of a common woman attendant at his own bathing machines, a widow of dubious reputation who had collapsed with apoplexy one day in the cold water shortly after the elopement, and had died without ever seeing her daughter again. Olivia's "Good riddance!" had always seemed singularly heartless to Nicolette, and even as a child she had wondered how her grandmother could be so kind and indulgent on one hand while being so utterly ruthless and unfeeling on the other. She had grown up in awe of her grandmother more than with love, in spite of the devotion and gifts Olivia had lavished upon her, and it was this long-held awareness of the vindictive streak in Olivia's character that had made Nicolette realize she could expect no mercy if ever she crossed the old lady's will.

She reached the beach by way of some ancient, seaweed-encrusted stone steps and ran down the shingle with a scattering of pebbles. The tide was coming in, wavelets stretching out to reach the ends of wooden groins. She did not slow her pace, her heels pitting the crisp sand in a trail behind her as she made for the water's edge, frills and ribbons fluttering into translucency in the sunlight, and a ripple almost touched the toes of her shoes when she came to a halt and flung wide her arms. Briefly she drew breath, feeling akin to the sea gulls that dipped and wheeled against the sky. How she had missed her moments of freedom and privacy in the open air, no longer able to take the morning gallops along the sands which she had so enjoyed as being part of the experience of being at the seaside, and even solitary rides into the countryside had been denied her since she had turned back one morning in a sudden, torrential downpour and spotted Tom Warwyck on horseback waiting under one of the trees in the lane. She had expected him to watch for her on the shore, but she had never imagined he would be bold enough to come to the very gates of the Hall. She had wheeled her horse around on the wet grass, too far away for him to hear any sound in the heavy rainstorm, and gone back into the grounds by a side gate. Anger and exultation and despair had racked her then and throughout the rest of the day, but gradually she drew strength from the certainty that eventually he would tire of her avoidance of him and look elsewhere. After all, he was a Warwyck, not to be relied upon in any way.

Her heartbeats slowed. Although nothing whatever could come about between them it was like a little death to think that the look in his eyes had been fickle and shallow and anything but true. Yet, as she reminded herself often enough, she must not forget that before their meeting in the conservatory he had been hot after Laura in much the same way, daring all to enter the grounds and keep the tryst. As before, that thought made her burn inside with something she knew to her shame to be jealousy.

Perversely her temper flamed against Tom as it did each time the thought of his dallying with Laura crossed her mind, bringing little spots of high color to her cheeks as she retrieved her folded parasol which she had thrown aside in her run down to the sea. She put it up with a sharp snap and rested it across one shoulder as she set off along the shore in the direction of the Pier, and she thought angrily that if only Tom Warwyck had not invaded her life she would have been enjoying a little summer flirtation with Lawrence, who had taken unwarranted encouragement from the single kiss she had allowed him and had become quite tedious in his attentions. She would be glad when he left the Hall, although when that would be she did not know, and considered it to be a pity he had not departed with the others that morning. There was one thing to be thankful for, which was that Laura's stay at the Hall had proved shorter than originally anticipated, the atmosphere between Hugh and her having become quite explosive, for contrary to her expectations she had failed to quell him and bring him totally to heel by flaunting her pursuit by his deadliest enemy; instead, he had taken an utter dislike to her and, being Hugh, had not hesitated to show it. The letter from India had come at a most opportune moment, Laura's mother wanting her to voyage out to Bombay without delay in the company of a returning officer's wife who would chaperone her. Laura confided to Nicolette that the young matron in question was much livelier than her mother realized and would be most jolly to travel with. A rush of arrangements had resulted, and it was sheer chance that the sojourn of Bertie and his friends should come to an end the same day. At least the Hall promised to be a deal more peaceful from now on.

She glanced from sea to land as she strolled leisurely, the whole of the day before her, and noted the thatched roof of the closed-up Honeybridge House above the tamarisk hedge that bordered the shore above the shingle, as well as the treetops of the woods that had been left to blend the countryside with the seaside, thus preserving a little of the resort's original setting. When she came level with the first of the hotels and terraces that faced the commencement of the promenade, she went up the slipway by the fishermen's huts where boats had been drawn up on the beach and nets hung out to dry since long before the first summer visitor had ever set foot in Easthampton. On the promenade itself, above their section of the beach, the fishermen had set up their stalls where they were selling lobsters, crabs, and prawns, as well as fresh fish caught offshore during the night.

"Lobsters for the pot! Fine 'addock! Only a bob for twenty-five juicy 'errings!" Their shouts rang out as they chopped off bright-gilled heads, gutted, fileted, and weighed up prawns ladled out with a metal scoop. A fishy aroma that pervaded the area came as much from the men themselves as their produce, their aprons sequined with scales. A groin or two nearer the Pier other fishermen plied a different trade for the day, adding their voices to the summer air.

"Any more for the *Skylark?* Still a few seats left on the *Mary Anne!* A trip round the bay at sixpence a 'ead and tuppence for the kiddies! Come along now! Just leaving!"

The *Skylark* and the *Mary Anne*, both large-sized sailing boats sporting flags much faded by previous summers' sun, waited in shallow water, wooden ramps on wheels giving dry-footed access for passengers, and although a number of people were already aboard there was far from a full load in either, and the promises of a speedy departure merely a lure to encourage others reluctant to wait. Seeing Nicolette pause by the railings to look toward the boats, a fisherman darted forward, his face weathered to the color of walnut.

"A ticket for you, miss? It's just the day for a lovely trip on the briny."

Why not? For once in her life her time was her own to do with as she pleased. She paid over her sixpence and returned to the sands by way of some wooden steps down from the promenade. A youth in a striped jersey on duty at the ramp helped her into the *Skylark*. She took her place on a thwart beside a young couple holding hands, the girl's wedding band very bright and new, their attention fixed entirely upon each other. Nicolette had heard that Easthampton had become a popular place in which to spend a honeymoon. On the other side of her was a family party, the little boys in their fashionable sailor suits much excited by the prospect of the expedition, the ribbons of their round straw hats whipping in the breeze as they clambered about in exploration until the arrival of more passengers made them take their seats to ensure not losing them. In less than a quarter of an hour a full complement of passengers had been gathered. A skipper came aboard, collected the tickets, and took the rudder, while his one-man crew ran up the sails, and with a thrust at the stern from the youth in the striped jersey the *Skylark* was fully seaborne, her bow smacking into the gentle roll of the waves.

Nicolette sat looking shoreward. The resort presented a pretty sight spread out like a skirt around the low hill on which Easthampton House stood, dominating the skyline, and along the promenade a confetti-colored stream of people flowed and mingled as they took morning constitutionals and breathed in the health-giving ozone. On the sands children were building sand castles with ramparts to stay for as long as possible the incoming tide, some with white-capped nannies in charge, and a small crowd had already gathered in front of the Punch and Judy show. A sand artist, working against time with a full hour before the tide swamped his work, had fashioned a mermaid with a large bosom veiled by curling locks and a huge, scaly fishtail, and pennies caught the sun as people leaned over the railings of the promenade to toss them down to him. Suddenly, down one of the slipways, there burst a sudden cascade of new arrivals from the first excursion trains of the day, their gleeful shouts, raucous and boisterous, marking them as the despised cheap day trippers in the eyes of the more well-to-do visitors. Shrieks and screams of another kind came from the direction of the ladies' bathing machines near the west side of the Pier, for even on this hot day the water struck chill to those taking the plunge, and the bathing women in attendance made it their duty to dip any bather who hesitated to go under. The machines, hub-deep in water, shone like a row of blue-and-white-striped sentry boxes on their huge, black-tarred wheels, and one of the docile cart horses, kept there daily for the purpose, was bringing another machine down the sands from the shingle to enable its hirer to enter the sea away from the stares of those on the beach. As the *Skylark* drew farther out into the bay it was possible to see the machines for gentlemen bathers to the east of the Pier where full-piece costumes were the rule, for the days had gone when male bathers were permitted to run naked into the sea.

As the *Skylark* sailed along, the skipper pointed out landmarks of interest on shore, gave a tale of a great sea storm that had flooded Easthampton a century or more ago, and indicated some rocks under the low cliffs where the last remains of a barnacled wreck could be seen when the tide was out. The trip lasted half an hour, which Nicolette thought good value for money, and she felt quite sorry when the *Skylark* turned shoreward again. She looked toward the Pier as they passed the head of it, thinking that whoever had designed it had been most skillful in giving it such fine and delicate lines that it appeared to be etched against the sparkle of sea and sky, the flag on top of the circular pavilion making a dancing arrow of red, white, and blue. All this she saw, but with the dazzling brightness of the sun in her eyes the people on the Pier were reduced to shapes and shadows, and her gaze passed distantly over them before she turned her head to face the spot on shore where the youth in the striped jersey was waiting to help the passengers alight.

But Tom had seen her. Standing in conversation with the Pier Manager by the pavilion entrance, he had glanced idly at the *Skylark* sailing by and become riveted by the sight of her sandwiched in with a typical boatload of holidaymakers. Whom was she with? Not Lawrence Payne or anyone he recognized. Could she possibly be on her own? Automatically he answered some question put to him. Mr. Beckworth jumped on it.

"What sort of a damn fool reply is that? *You think so!* Ain't you listening to me? It's either yes, there is—or no, there ain't.

Two seconds ago you was saying there would be no danger to the 'igh diver if 'e went off the end of the Pier on a bicycle, and when I express doubts you give me a shilly-shallying answer as if you don't know your own mind." The fact that Tom was a Warwyck never stilled the abrasive side of Mr. Beckworth's tongue whenever it was necessary, and in any case he had found that it created no ill feeling between them.

Tom wrenched his gaze away from the *Skylark*, which was bearing Nicolette away toward the distant ramp on the beach. "Er— of course I do." He spoke in a rush, eager to close the discussion. "The display would be perfectly safe. Mr. Samuels is an experienced diver and he is extremely keen to try his eye-catching stunt tomorrow at high tide."

"That's awright then. One of the pier 'ands can act as barker by the turnstile, and we'll draw in extra folk that way. Samuels is always a good attraction, but this'll pull in many more."

"I agree." Tom edged away with a few backward paces, impatient to get to the landing beach before Nicolette should leave it. Mr. Beckworth checked him.

"'Ere! 'Old on. What's the 'urry? I ain't finished all I've got to say yet. There's that matter of the posters."

"I'll go to each of the printers without delay and fix on the lowest price I can get," Tom offered promptly, welcoming the excuse to escape. "I'll ask for twenty-four-hour delivery, and in the meantime I can write up a couple of my own to stand by the turnstile."

It was agreed. Mr. Beckworth turned into the roller-skating rink, and failed to see the speed with which Tom dashed down the length of the Pier and leaped the turnstile, long legs flying. Outside the entrance he charged westward along the promenade, almost bumping into several people, and reached the landing beach to find new passengers filling up the *Skylark*. Of Nicolette there was no sign. He balled his fists in furious disappointment, barely able to restrain himself from snatching off his straw hat and whamming it to the ground in an explosion of wrath at missing her by minutes. With a sharp sigh he turned in the direction of the nearest printers, looking about him as he went, in search of a girl with dark red hair and deep, expressive eyes that threatened to haunt him for the rest of his life.

Nicolette window-gazed all the way to Lawton's Emporium, and once inside its classical portals she spent her time and some of her allowance most pleasurably, going from counter to counter and from floor to floor. She lunched at a damask-spread table for one on the roof terrace, shielded from the sun by a cool green awning, and afterward resumed her shopping. Altogether she made a number of purchases, all of which were to be taken to the Radcliffe carriage when it came to the entrance at four o'clock, and they included a small, round box of Pears complexion powder, an ivory glove stretcher to replace one she had broken, an ornamental comb for her hair, and a couple of hatpins with heads fashioned like tiny, gauze-winged butterflies. Later she added a pair of side-buttoned boots in cream French kid with Louis heels, and an evening shawl of silvery lace. But there was one purely extravagant purchase that she decided to take with her for use in that very same hour. She saw it displayed on one of the dressmaker dummies in the department of ladies' bathing apparel, and although she had swimming garments at the Hall, she knew she must buy this one. It was quite the prettiest costume for the sea that she had seen, being made of silk-trimmed flannel in a sapphire blue, the short overdress, which was sleeveless, having an open neckline, the trousers ending elegantly and a trifle daringly slightly below mid-calf. To wear with it, propped at an angle on the polished mahogany knob where a head should have been, was a most becoming cap to match. Not wishing to hire one of the towels at the bathing station, which were often only rinsed in the sea after use and laid out on the shingle to dry before being rolled up to serve the next customer, she bought a striped toweling cape at the same time to dry and to cover herself should the need arise.

The tide was receding again when she reached the promenade, and there was plenty of business for the bathing machines. She had given her ticket to a bathing attendant and was on the steps of the machine when somebody young and male called her name. She stiffened, but did not turn around. She would have known that voice, both longed for and dreaded, anywhere. With something close to panic she hastened into the machine and slammed the door after her. The horse, hearing the familiar sound, plodded forward, rolling the wheeled vehicle behind him into the sea, the tide-rippled sand under the open-slatted floor giving way to swirling water, the reflected light dancing over the white-painted interior like the sparkle from a thousand rings. She heard the bathing woman turning Tom off that section of the shore in no uncertain terms.

"No gentlemen allowed on this section of the beach! Do you hear me, sir? Are you deaf!? Stop him!" The words were repeated in a shriek, and to Nicolette's dismay she heard him take the steps at a leap and thump on the rear door through which she had entered.

"I must talk to you, Nicolette! Do come out! Please!"

"No! No!" she answered frantically. "Go away!"

The chains rattled as the horse was unhitched to return for the next load, and the sound of a scuffle followed as the man in charge of it answered the bathing woman's yell and tried to drag Tom off the steps. There was a thump and a grunt as Tom thrust the man from him with a wrathful retort.

"I'm leaving! I'm leaving!"

He clattered off the steps, and as if completely to reassure Nicolette of his departure the bathing woman rapped on the door. "He's gone, dearie."

Nicolette sank down onto the bench seat, suddenly aware that she was shaking from head to foot, her heart banging against her ribs. Was Tom mad? To create a public disturbance below a crowded promenade where any number of acquaintances made since her coming to Radcliffe Hall could report back to her grandmother! Perhaps it would be best to talk to him if he should accost her again, and explain once and for all that she wanted nothing whatever to do with him. But how to tell such a lie? How to hide the throbbing of her senses at his nearness, the wild excitement that she had experienced just hearing him call her name? Somehow she must do it. Quite apart from the misery that would await her should she be banished home to Scotland, there was the fact that she had come to love the Hall that was the seat of her

maternal forebears, and did not want to leave it. Slowly she un-
pinned her hat and hung it on a peg. Deep in her unhappy reverie
she began to unfasten the bodice of her dress, her fingers
unusually clumsy in their trembling state. Tom mustn't destroy
her life. It was bad enough not being able to let him into as much
as friendship with her, but she must not and would not let him—
however unwittingly he might do it—grind her down into an existence of despair from which there would be no escape.

The bathing woman's knuckles came again, but on the door
leading out to the sea this time. "Want any help, dearie?" she
called.

"No, thank you," Nicolette replied, busy loosening ribbons.
"I'll be out in a minute."

She put on the new bathing costume, tucked her hair well into
her cap, and the sunshine fell warm upon her as she went out
onto the wooden steps which had been hitched out from under
the front of the machine and lowered into the slapping waves in
readiness. The bathing woman would have given her a hand, but
Nicolette popped quickly into the water, the skirt of her costume
floating up about her like a water lily, and then, gasping a little at
the salty chill, she struck out strongly away from the machines
and the other women bobbing and dipping under the watchful
eye of the bathing woman toward a stretch of sea almost level
with the pierhead where she could swim and float undisturbed.
She and her brothers were all taught to swim at an early age, for
her mother, who had never had that accomplishment, had once as
a child been swept out of her depth on an ebbing tide, and had
never forgotten the horror of going under helplessly before being
rescued in the nick of time by a boathook.

For about ten minutes Nicolette swam and dived and floated,
and she was lying on her back, eyes closed and arms stretched out
as she drifted on the sea's current, when she felt a swish of water
as if some large fish had passed close to her. In alarm she folded
and began to tread water, terrified as to what alien creature had
penetrated these harmless currents, when to her anger and dismay
Tom's head broke the surface a few feet from her, his hair plas-
tered to his head and parted in the middle by the water running

from it. He grinned at her through the fronds, treading water himself, his shoulders clad in the short, black sleeves of his swimming costume.

"Nobody can chase me away here," he declared impudently, "unless they get a patrolling boat out as they used to in my father's day. But in any case we're too far from shore for anybody to see I'm in forbidden waters."

"You idiot!" she exploded heatedly. "You frightened me nearly to death. I thought there was a shark or an octopus or something else as horrid swimming near me."

He flung back his head and laughed, shaking the wet hair from his eyes. "Not in these waters. Sorry, Nicolette. I didn't mean to frighten you, but I dived in from the Pier and I thought if I shouted out you might head for shore before I reached you."

"You're right. And I'm going back there now."

He slid forward and with a little swish of foam came between the shore and her, his face only inches away above the shining green surface that was bright as glass. All laughter was gone from his expression, his eyes intensely serious as they searched hers.

"When and where can I see you again?"

She shook her head, making the sea drops fly sparkling from the frill of her cap. "We mustn't meet. We can't. You must realize that sooner or later word would reach our respective families. It's foolish of you to imagine that because I helped you when you were hurt you have any justification in pursuing me in this manner. I would have done the same for anybody in distress."

"I know." Simply. As if he had already come to know her as well as she knew herself. His eyes not leaving hers.

Indignation mounted in her. "Then leave me alone. Forget we ever met." Deliberately she hardened her voice with a scornful tone. "Your conceit is insufferable, Tom Warwyck. It hasn't occurred to you, I suppose, that I simply don't want our acquaintanceship to continue."

He spoke quietly. "Don't lie to me. Anything else, but don't lie."

Abruptly she turned and swam a few strokes, he immediately keeping pace with her, and then once again swimming around to see her face, which she had averted from him. She was not sure herself whether it was tears or the salt water stinging her eyes. She tried the scornful tone again, but it wavered and broke. "Just go away and leave me alone. Please."

"I can't." His whole heart was in his words.

She swallowed, her lashes blinking against the glitter on them. "I'd be sent away. We would never see each other again anyway. The consequences would most surely be as dire for you as they would be for me."

He could not deny it. His grandfather would withdraw the privilege of letting him use the barn for building his boat. Hab would be bribed to desert him. Everything he had intended would crumble about his ears and he would be set back in all his plans. But only if his meetings with Nicolette were discovered. "If we met only in places where nobody would recognize us, would you take the risk?"

"On the moon, perhaps?" she taunted wretchedly. "My grandmother knows people *everywhere*, and I've accompanied her to tea parties and in paying calls and have received guests with her at the Hall." She shook her head again. "Goodness knows how many people would know me by sight—and those who recognize me would know you, too. I'm getting cold. You must let me swim back to shore now. If I get cramp I could drown."

"No, I'd save you."

In the way he was looking at her it would have been as easy to drown in his eyes as in the sea. He came closer, his lids lowering slightly as he concentrated on her mouth. She could have withdrawn, could have swum away, but she remained where she was, and his lips came upon hers in a chilled, salty kiss that parted into a sweet warmth, and she closed her eyes against the sky and the gulls and the whole universe. But only for a matter of seconds. They both sank as he put his arms about her shoulders, the water closing over their heads, and they broke apart and splashed to the surface, cleaving back into the sunshine with shared and spontaneous laughter at their dousing, laughter that covered the great surge of inward joy that each had experienced in that brief contact of lips and limbs. Then almost at once laughter faded and reality was back in a deluge of another kind to beset them with unsolved difficulties.

"If you took to a morning ride along the sands again I could see you sometimes," he said, not pleading, merely setting out a possibility. "Nobody except the fishermen are around at an early hour."

She answered with a further suggestion. "The countryside around the derelict mill on Bambury Hill always seems deserted. I've never met anyone there yet."

"You see," he exulted softly. "There are places where we can meet."

She blinked, smiling a little. A smile with fear in it that made the corners of her lips tremble. Because she was afraid. Afraid and as happy as she dared be all at the same time. "How shall I let you know where I'll be?"

"You can write to me at Easthampton House. I'm living there for the time being."

She looked anxious. "Whatever you do, don't write to me. A letter could fall into the wrong hands."

He understood. It was as he had supposed. "I won't. Do you roller-skate?"

Her eyes widened at the apparent incongruity of the question. "Yes. Why?"

Briefly he explained his management of the roller-skating rink. "You can find me there any day of the week." He grinned widely. "If I don't get the boot for bathing in work hours."

"Then you had better delay no longer," she answered, amused, and she began to swim back to shore. "Goodbye, Tom."

"Come riding on the beach tomorrow morning," he called after her. "I'll be waiting for you."

She turned and gave a little wave in acknowledgment that she had heard before swimming on again. He watched her until she was a safe distance from shore, and then he struck out for the iron steps of the Pier from which he had dived.

Next morning he was on the beach before six o'clock. He waited and waited, but she did not come.

Chapter 7

From her bedroom window Donna watched Tom leave the house for work that morning, his step lacking its customary jauntiness, and she shook her head over him. There was a peculiar oscillation of his spirits that she could not understand; one day up in the air, and the next quite plainly despondent. Could the boy be in love? She remembered the barometric rise and fall of her own emotions in the days when she had been in love with the only young man who had ever courted her, everything depending on whether or not the beloved's letter came on the day expected, what he said when they did meet, and whether the second kiss in the garden had been as loving as the first. She sighed a trifle cynically, letting the lace curtain drop into place as Tom disappeared beyond Ring Park in the direction of the Pier. Thank God *she* was not young any more. The heart suffering of those days where the opposite sex was concerned was long gone, and the man she would have married no more than a tender ghost, rarely recalled.

But she had more to think about at the present time than her past. This afternoon she was to meet Constance Meredith at the railway station, and she hoped desperately that the woman would prove to be just the one to ease Richard's burden, and that Meg would take a liking to her. She had filled in all the information she had about Constance for her brother's benefit, and had visited the Grange several times to prepare Meg for Constance's coming. She took it as a good sign that after some initial argument which she had successfully overruled each time Meg had opened her mouth, there was no longer any show of hostility by her sister-in-law toward the idea of having a companion to look after her, although a certain slyness about Meg's expression had left her feeling a trifle uneasy, and she could not dismiss it.

When the three o'clock train from Victoria arrived at Easthampton station Donna was at the ticket gate, and she craned her neck to look through it in readiness to locate Constance. Smoke billowed from the locomotive, drifting around those alighting, but a momentary gap when some people moved away enabled her to glimpse Constance stepping out of a compartment some distance down the train and giving instructions about her baggage to the porter holding the door for her. Then the movement of passengers toward the ticket gate hid the woman once again. Donna pursed her mouth momentarily, a trifle surprised that Constance had traveled first-class, which seemed somewhat extravagant for someone still dependent on another's generosity. Naturally she did not begrudge what she had given the woman, and promptly made excuses for her, realizing that the train was crowded and of course Constance would want to arrive looking uncrushed and at her best to meet her future employer and the wife who was to be her charge.

Donna gave the ticket collector the platform ticket she had purchased and went through the gate just as Constance spotted her in turn. It crossed Donna's mind, not for the first time, that quite apart from the matter of traveling first-class, Constance would know how to spend money if ever it came her way, for she had taste and flair, giving a stylish look by her straight-backed bearing and neat walk to the simple traveling costume of gray check that she was wearing. She was tall and well shaped, and her features were quite high-boned and thin, bearing the stamp of the hard life she had known throughout her thirty-eight years in a sharpness of her grayish-blue eyes and in the compact line of the red-lipped mouth. But when she smiled—as she did at the sight of her benefactress approaching her from the gate—her face was transformed, not into beauty, but into something close to hand-someness, which was an entirely different attribute, being more powerful and less beguiling.

"Dear Miss Warwyck," she exclaimed with gushing relief as soon as she was within earshot. "How kind of you to be here. I must admit to being extremely nervous."

"There's no need for that, I'm sure," Donna replied with a wel-coming smile. "I have prepared Mrs. Warwyck for your arrival at the Grange today, and I see no reason why all should not go well. Let us go through the gate. I have a carriage waiting. Did you have a comfortable journey?"

"The compartment was over-full, but I was really too excited to pay any heed to being a little cramped for space."

Donna flicked an unnoticed sideways glance at Constance's animated profile. The inquiry had been made out of courtesy, and Constance's reply was such as to give, by accident or design, the impression that she had traveled third-class, for nobody could be cramped on a more expensive ticket where the seats were wide, with padded divisional armrests. Nevertheless Donna forgave the slip, accepting that Constance, who had not realized she had been seen through the gate, would be self-conscious about the extrava-gance, and she was moved with pity for her, thinking kindly and with satisfaction that a good home at the Grange would give Con-stance the security long denied her.

As they made their way out of the station building they met a number of departing travelers about to take the return journey on the train that had brought Constance to Easthampton. Among them Donna spotted the Radcliffe-Stuart twins, long-legged and tight-trousered, with gray bowlers at impudent angles, the sandy-haired one called Roger sporting a sparse moustache that looked like a cover-up for a barely healed lip that had been stitched not all that long ago. The more red-headed of the two, whose name was Oscar, had a front tooth missing. Had they been fighting each other, or sparring with another whose more powerful punch had rendered such unsightly results? She had heard that the twins had been commissioned into the Guards, and judging by the trunks and boxes being trundled along by a porter, they were bound for some military destination. Mentally she drew her skirts aside as she passed by these two with the hated name of Radcliffe. They were impudent young puppies in any case, and she thought with satisfaction that the army life should give them some much-needed discipline. One thing she did know, and that was the simple fact that Easthampton would be better off without them.

In the carriage she and Constance talked all the way to the Grange. Constance was able to give her some news of mutual friends and acquaintances among Donna's artists and sculptors, and in turn plied Donna with questions about Easthampton as they passed through it and left it behind. She had heard much about it when the post as companion had first been discussed, and now, seeing it, she wanted gaps about its history as a resort filled in for her.

All the time Constance was talking and questioning and listening her mind was storing away facts and details. She never liked to be at a disadvantage if she could help it, never liked to be caught off guard by not knowing how the land lay in any given situation, and just how and where she could best fit into it to suit her own ends. She had too much misery behind her to take life lightly, and having been given the chance to rise out of the squalor into which she had sunk through circumstances best forgotten, she did not intend to let it slip through her fingers. Donna Warwyck was compassionate, but she was no fool, and as far as Constance could judge from what she heard of the Warwyck family in general, they were business-minded and would expect value for money, which she was prepared to give. She would look after the wife put in her charge and do everything humanly possible to improve her condition and bring her back to a normal life. With a hollow lack of feeling Constance found herself compelled to recall how different it had been for her husband, whose addiction to opium as well as to the bottle had given her no chance to do anything except care for him as best she could. She had stayed with him because he had become utterly dependent upon her, and not from love as Donna Warwyck sentimentally imagined. There had been love once, before constant dissatisfaction with his own paintings and a sense of personal failure at being unable to attain the artistic heights for which he aimed had made him seek oblivion more and more in the palliatives of his choice, ravaging his health and bringing him to the dregs of existence, dragging her down with him. There was nothing she had not done to get food for their bellies and try to keep a roof over their heads. Her moral sensibilities had not been unduly offended, having been dulled from early youth, but she had dreaded the moving on by landlords for nonpayment of rent, as well as the moonlight flits to rooms worse than those before, loathing the increasing squalor of their lives amid slum streets littered with garbage, where often one filthy privy served a whole street, and she had come to hate the man whom she could not bring herself to abandon.

"We're coming to the Grange now," Donna said.

It was much larger and grander than Constance had expected, and she thought wryly that those who had always been used to money took wealth and possessions as a matter of course; it was those newly come to fortunes who wanted to flaunt and impress and would have let her know the size of the mansion in which she was to be employed. She drew a deep breath as her appreciative gaze took in all details. As Donna led her across the threshold into the Grange she was still more impressed by the gracious proportions of the hall and the sweep of the great staircase. On all sides there were huge paintings in gilded frames, and fine pieces of furniture with the mellow patina of time graced corners and arches and flanked recessed double doors. In a silk-paneled anteroom she barely had time to look around when Richard Warwyck appeared. Donna greeted him and made the introductions, after which she went to find Meg, leaving them alone together. Constance had not been prepared for such a splendid-looking man, and had to guard against staring.

"How do you do, Mrs. Meredith," he said, his deep voice pleasing to her ear. "Please be seated."

"Thank you, sir." She obeyed and smiled, well aware that her smiles attracted people to her, and she wanted desperately to make a good impression. He seated himself opposite her.

"You have been most highly recommended to me by my sister, and I understand all the facts have been put to you. I must warn you that there was some initial hostility on my wife's part upon hearing of your coming, but Miss Warwyck has done her best to smooth the path for you, and I hope all will go well."

"I'm sure it will," she replied confidently. "I believe that as soon as Mrs. Warwyck learns to trust me and to realize that I want to help her, everything will be on a different footing, but until that time I'm under no illusion as to how she may react toward me. Has she ever been violent?"

"She has attacked me several times in a fury and has been known to hurl objects at others in a temper, but always she has been in drink at the time with a resulting unsteadiness of balance that has made her easy to handle. Does the prospect of this aggressive behavior alarm you?"

"No," she answered in the same even tones. "I have had plenty of experience. Nothing that Mrs. Warwyck might do can compare with what I have known, and that did not break me. I'm here on a month's trial for either side, and I hope to have achieved enough in those four weeks for there to be no doubt on your part or mine as to whether or not my employment should be continued indefinitely."

He was impressed. He liked her quiet, capable air and her intelligent approach toward winning Meg's trust, which showed a full grasp of the circumstances. Moreover, he liked the look of her. He would have put up with the presence of an illiterate gorgon in the house if it should be for Meg's good and ultimate benefit, but it made everything much more agreeable that Constance Meredith was all that Donna had promised, a ladylike woman with her wits about her, who could be accepted at a limited level in company if Meg should improve enough in her charge to venture forth socially again. That Constance Meredith had another, age-old quality that men never failed to recognize he accepted with some part of his senses while disregarding it in his mind.

"I link my hopes with yours," he said gravely, pledging his support.

They discussed a few more points, and then she said, "There is just one more thing."

"Yes?"

"I would like a free hand in dealing with Mrs. Warwyck. I may have to indulge her weakness for a while before it becomes possible to direct her interests elsewhere. With my husband, as you have heard from Miss Warwyck, there was no such opportunity. He was set on self-destruction and too greatly addicted to drugs for me to do anything except get him what he needed, but with your wife it is a different matter."

"Provided you treat her with kindness at all times, you may have a free hand."

"Sometimes one has to be cruel to be kind, but I give you my solemn word that I shall work only for her good and yours. I suggest I make a daily report to you on all I have done, and then you will be able to check it all with me."

"An excellent suggestion, ma'am. I'll keep an hour free out of every day I am at home in which to see you for any discussion that might arise." He smiled. "Now you shall be shown to your rooms, and afterward the same servant will direct you to the East Drawing Room, where my wife and my sister will join us for tea."

Her quarters consisted of a sitting room and bedroom, from which a door opened into a bathroom with rose-patterned ware. She dismissed the maidservant, who would have unpacked her trunk for her, telling the girl to do the task later, and once on her own she kicked off her shoes to bury her stockinged toes in the softness of the carpeting, and moved about the rooms sitting on the chairs, feeling the bed linen, running her palms over the furniture, and handling the porcelain vases that ornamented the overmantel, the whole of her sensuous nature running riot amid such unaccustomed luxury. It had been the same when she had traveled down in the train, spending in a wild burst of extravagance the last of the allowance Donna had made her on a first-class ticket to have a whole compartment to herself. There she had gloried in the space and comfort, the crisp linen of the headrests, the faint aroma of expensive cigars left by a previous passenger. She had laughed then like a child, and she did it now, flinging herself full length upon the bed and stretching out luxuriantly. But she must not delay too long before going downstairs again. On this thought she swung her feet to the floor, found her shoes, ran a comb over the front of her hair, which she wore in a chignon at the nape of her neck, and with a quick flick at the lace at her throat and wrists she rang the bell to summon the return of the maidservant.

She was shown into a drawing room of considerable size, and although she had an overall impression of soft colors and still more paintings, her gaze went at once to Meg Warwyck, who sat on a yellow silk sofa behind the silver tray holding teapot, cream jug, and sugar basin, as befitted the lady of the house. Beside her sat Donna, watchful and alert, and Richard stood close at hand. No servants were present, a stand of cakes and tiny cucumber sandwiches set in readiness. Constance guessed that her employer and his sister had determined that should there be a scene, it was not to be witnessed by outsiders.

"Meg," Richard said, "allow me to present Mrs. Constance Meredith. Mrs. Meredith, this is my wife, Mrs. Warwyck."

Meg studied the woman carefully, saw that she said something, but did not bother to listen. She had taken a glass of brandy or two to fortify herself for this ordeal, determined to show Richard as well as Donna that she could conduct herself in a mannerly fashion whenever she chose, although in this case only as long as it suited her. She knew why she was to have a companion. Richard wanted to deprive her of all liquor, and this was his method of doing it, setting a jailer over her to watch her every move. Donna had tried to soft-talk her, denying that it was his aim, but she knew better. This Meredith woman looked a hard nut and had a whore's mouth. Nevertheless, it would be simple to get rid of her.

"Do you take tea, Mrs. Meredith?" she inquired, her speech only marginally slurred.

"Yes, please." Constance seated herself in the chair that Richard had pulled forward.

"Milk and sugar?"

"Both, thank you."

Meg poured the Georgian teapot. It was heavy, and her hands, which were never steady these days, shook, making the golden stream waver into the Dresden cup. Out of the corner of her eye she noticed Donna grow tense, ready to snatch up the teapot should it be in danger of being dropped. Meg tightened her grip on the silver handle, not wanting the duty of hostess taken from her; although she liked Donna she thought her an interfering busybody, and on this occasion she was looking forward to teaching her sister-in-law and Richard a lesson they wouldn't soon forget. She added the sugar to the cup with the engraved tongs.

Constance watched her. The drunken sot, she thought with cool contempt. Spruced up for the tea party, playacting the lady, but looking like the fishwife that birth and breeding had intended her to be, a fact Constance knew, for Donna had told her of the runaway marriage, believing that nothing should be left out if a way was to be found to help Meg. And following swiftly upon that feeling of contempt, Constance knew a sudden upsurge of envy and jealousy and exasperation at the unfairness of things. There sat that overweight, self-indulgent creature with bloodshot eyes, hair slipping from its pins, a gown spotted by some last-minute stains, and with nothing in her head except desire for the next drink, while at the same time possessing everything that any normal woman would have given her soul for, everything from a rich husband with a strong, virile look about him, to a beautiful home and three sons.

"Your tea, Mrs. Meredith." Meg held out the cup and saucer, and Constance, being within easy range, automatically reached out a hand to take it from her. Then Meg tossed it. The hot tea splashed all over Constance's skirt and she leaped up with a shriek, knocking the chair backward, the cup and saucer already in pieces at her feet. Confusion ruled, Richard and Donna springing forward to attend to Constance, who was more startled than scalded, the close weave of her traveling skirt and layers of petticoats having protected her, for the hot tea had been shaken off by the abruptness of her reaction before it could soak through to her. Only one hand and her left foot above her shoe showed a bright red mark.

Richard had been prepared for sulkiness and ill temper, but that Meg should set out deliberately to harm a perfect stranger was almost unbelievable. He spoke with fury, keeping himself under tight control, for he had never struck her and did not intend to start now, despising those who used violence against women. "If ever I needed proof that you can no longer conduct yourself in company it has happened now!"

Donna, who had snatched a smear of butter from a sandwich to apply immediate first aid to Constance's hand, endorsed his words. "How can you have been so churlish, Meg? Or so ungrateful! I'm totally out of patience with you!"

Meg's lips quivered. In truth, although she did not intend to show it, she was suddenly more than a little frightened by what she had done, being unused to her sister-in-law's displeasure, and she realized she could have caused a lasting breach between them. "I don't want that woman at the Grange," she mumbled mulishly, her eyes darting from one to the other of them. "I won't have her around me. I've made my intention clear."

Donna, usually able to keep calm at all times, almost stamped her foot in exasperation. "I searched high and low to find just the right companion for you. Do you think that I, who have always done whatever I could for you, would choose someone out of sympathy or lacking in understanding?"

Meg stuck to her guns, clenching her plump fists in her lap. "I don't need no keeper. I'm not a loony. I won't be watched over and denied all the comfort left to me in life." Self-pity overwhelmed her and, always lachrymose these days, the silent tears welled out of her eyes and trickled down her cheeks. The brandy she had imbibed earlier was taking its toll. "You're against me. Everybody's against me, 'cept my darling Jeremy. Tom can't get away from this house quick enough, and Lennox don't come to see his poor mother regular like a good son ought, and I've only set eyes twice on that stuck-up wife of his since the wedding. Just because she's the daughter of a bishop her mother-in-law ain't grand enough, and she's made being in the family way an excuse not to travel so often you'd think she had a dozen babies 'stead of only two—or is it three?" The tears rolled faster. "How would I know? I never gets to see 'em."

Constance, whose alarm that the employment was about to fall through was as great as the wrathful resentment at the thrown tea, gently brushed Donna aside and took a step toward Meg.

"I'll take *you* to see *them,* Mrs. Warwyck. My task is to bring you back to a full enjoyment of life again. None of your comforts shall be denied you. I'm here to serve you, not to set up barriers."

Meg blinked, lulled to a certain extent by the soft tones of the persuasive voice, and yet at the same time spurred by the instinct she had had when the woman had first come into the room: something was wrong somewhere. "I don't believe you," she declared, although on a slightly less forcible note than before, for she was feeling confused. "I never go nowhere no more." Her voice strengthened and took on a sarcastic edge. "My husband don't need his lawful wife, y'see. He has plenty of ladies willing enough to take my rightful place."

"Meg, Meg," Richard exclaimed wearily, turning away to go and stand by the window, drawing a tired hand over his eyes and face.

Outwardly Constance ignored the jibe directed against Richard, while inwardly storing it for future reference as she addressed Meg again as though without interruption. "The fact that you've had little social life over the past few years doesn't mean to say that it should continue like that indefinitely." She took a seat quickly beside Meg on the sofa. "Look at me, Mrs. Warwyck. Look me full in the eyes. Do I look like a woman who would fail easily in any task I had taken upon myself?" She had worded the question carefully. To have asked Meg if she would trust her would have brought a negative answer; Meg's distrust, which was plain enough, had replaced the initial determination to be rid of her at all costs, and that left room for maneuver.

Meg squinted at her, observed the hard determination in the steely eyes, and in spite of a sense of misgiving answered honestly. "No."

"Well then!" Constance swayed back from the waist triumphantly. "You know I'll do what I have promised, and to do that I must first carry through my trial period in this house. If at the end of those four weeks you want me to go, I'll go, no matter how much anybody else might wish me to stay. Is it agreed?"

Meg shifted uncomfortably, aware of being outsmarted in some way that she could not quite define. Yet images of how things could be under this powerful woman's control came to her in sparkling array: she could see herself visiting Lennox's home and taking a shawl-wrapped baby into her arms; there could be dinner parties again with Richard at one end of the table and herself at the other; perhaps even a ball big and important enough to make all the gentry in the district attend. Nobody would dare snub her with this gimlet-eyed creature preparing the way for her. Meg knew that it was sometimes boredom that made her drink, but mostly it was the wretchedness of her loveless existence that she most wanted to dull from her mind, so perhaps with something to look forward to, something to hope for, the nightmares of misery and loneliness could be abated by other means than that which left her with splitting headaches and the taste of ashes in her mouth and—worst of all—the disgust she read in her husband's eyes.

"Four weeks then," she agreed with some reluctance, a persistent doubt still niggling at the back of her mind, "and not a day longer."

Across the room Richard and Donna exchanged looks of thankfulness and relief. Constance smiled at Meg. "If you could send for another cup and pour me some tea to replace that which fell from your grasp I would be most grateful."

Meg nodded and looked toward the bellpull, which Donna promptly jerked before coming back to bend with concern toward Constance. "What about your hand and foot? Don't you think we should get those burns dressed without further delay?"

Constance shook her head. "They're not bad enough to blister, and there's really very little discomfort. I'll take tea first."

Again Richard and his sister looked at each other in mutual understanding of Constance's brave endurance in order not to remind Meg overmuch of the unpleasant occurrence, and as they seated themselves to drink the tea that Meg was pouring, another cup and saucer having been brought, they each congratulated themselves on a treasure having been brought into the house.

Constance's thoughts ran on other lines. She smiled, chatted, and acted as if nothing untoward had taken place, while inwardly seething against Meg for the stinging red patches on her hand and foot. The drunken bitch should pay for it. Sooner or later she should pay for it. Constance sipped her tea daintily, and none of the others present suspected how dearly she would have liked to hurl it into Meg's face in retaliation.

That evening at dinner she met Jeremy, whom she summed up in her descriptive thoughts as an attractive bastard, having met his type often enough in her checkered life, and she also made the acquaintance of Tom, who had come home to collect some books he needed from his room and stayed to dine with his parents. Meg, unpersuaded by Constance, who had decided to step warily for the first evening, came to the table, but she had imbibed again between teatime and the dining hour and sat slumped in her chair, eating practically nothing and drinking more wine than anybody else. Tom attempted some conversation with her, but Jeremy ignored his mother. Personally fastidious, always immaculate, he was nauseated by her slatternly habits, and it was doubtful whether he would ever have willingly gone near her had she not been good for a loan whenever he needed it, loans that she never remembered and he never bothered to repay.

"You will find Easthampton quite a change from the Metropolis, Mrs. Meredith," he said smoothly to Constance, giving her the full benefit of his Warwyck charm. He knew nothing of her recent background, which Richard and Donna had kept confidential. Constance knew that this was how it had been arranged and was thankful for it. She had endured enough scorn to last her the rest of her life.

"I daresay I shall, never having lived at the seaside before. However, I'm sure I shall settle down. The wonderful sea air is a tonic in itself."

"I really meant on the social side. There is plenty going on, but naturally at a slower pace than in London, not counting—of course—the vulgar pleasures aimed at visitors to the resort, which Tom knows all about." He looked sardonically across the table to where his brother sat at Constance's side.

"Jeremy is pulling my leg," Tom explained to her. "I'm in charge of the local roller-skating rink. It's harmless family entertainment. Everybody enjoys it. Why don't you come along one day?"

"I don't know how to roller-skate."

At the head of the table, Richard, knowing Tom's good nature, half expected to hear him offer to teach her, but his son merely said, "There is a balcony for those who just want to watch."

Had Tom liked her he would have offered, no matter if she had been three times his age, but there was something about the woman he could not quite take to, and although willing to be agreeable toward her, hoping as much as anybody else that she would prove to be the saving of his mother, he wanted without really thinking about it to keep a certain distance between them. His omission over the matter of lessons, which could have been made out of meaningless courtesy not meant to be taken up, had not been lost on Constance, who was still raw enough to be irrational about anything that could be remotely attributed to a slight, and although Tom had not intended any offense, it being the last thing in his mind, she stored it up against him.

Jeremy distracted her attention at that point with some question about her late husband having been an artist, and there followed a lively conversation that continued through three courses about current trends in art, Jeremy fancying himself as being knowledgeable on the subject, and Tom joining in now and again, often with some humorous quip that brought forth laughter from all but Meg, who was unable to follow anything that was going on.

Richard, whose tastes ran to Millais, Hunt, Rossetti and the rest of the Pre-Raphaelite school, listened and observed, and was interested and amused. He thought it delightful to have an intelligent woman discoursing at the table, which was a common enough occurrence at his London *pied-à-terre*, but with the exception of Donna's moderate contribution to any conversation on the rare occasions that she dined at the Grange, it was a long time since the ancient paneled walls of the dining hall had heard anything uttered in a feminine voice except the most mundane remarks and well-worn tirades proffered by Meg whenever she was sober enough to speak. He frowned, checking his uncharitable thoughts, and took a sip of wine before continuing with the succulent slices of roast duck upon the plate before him.

Constance, catching that slight furrowing of brows out of the corner of her eye, imagined that he considered that she was stepping out of place by being so talkative. After all, she was no more than a paid companion, and it was privilege enough to be allowed to be present at dinner, although it had been agreed that her position in the household should be of equal status with the family for Meg's benefit, and perhaps he wanted her to remember that the privilege did not extend to private, domestic occasions. Momentarily she was at a loss and stemmed the flow of her talk, merely answering Jeremy or Tom in monosyllables. Richard raised an inquiring eyebrow.

"What is the matter, Mrs. Meredith? Have my sons outflanked you?"

"Not at all." Proudly and with some defiance.

"Well then? Why the retreat? I must say that I was thoroughly enjoying your upholding of the opinion that blobs of paint tossed willy-nilly onto canvas makes a work of art."

"Not willy-nilly, Father," Jeremy countered. "Not at all. The art critics, as Mrs. Meredith said just now, always slay anything new."

Constance, who had been looking quite serious, smiled a trifle ruefully at Richard, the molding of her face lifted and softened by it in the candlelight. "I confess that in my pleasure at being at this table this evening I had quite forgotten my true position at the Grange. I had no right to monopolize so much of the conversation, and all I can say to excuse myself is that it is a subject dear to my heart, one that I have discussed even more exuberantly in the company of my late husband's fellow artists."

"You had every right to talk as you did," Richard reassured her emphatically. "I have never discouraged anyone from contributing to the conversation around this table, not even when the boys were young."

Tom exchanged a wink with his brother, who grinned into his wineglass. It was true that they had never been quelled in voicing their views, but discipline at table had been such that they had only been allowed to speak when spoken to. Only upon their reaching young manhood had the ban been lifted. They had certainly made up for lost time since then. During the crisis of Jeremy's bankruptcy there had been a strained silence again at the table for a while, and even that had passed.

"You are most kind, Mr. Warwyck." Constance's smile deepened and widened at Richard, the rosy lips moist, the teeth very white and pearl-like, the glimpse of tongue curled like a lily petal. Unexpectedly he felt himself dangerously roused, although there was no hint of it in the casualness of his reply.

"Not at all, Mrs. Meredith. Not at all."

In her seat at the opposite end of the table to him Meg took the stem of her wineglass and held it up. "More wine," she demanded thickly.

When dinner ended Constance went to Meg's chair and, speaking firmly and softly, said she would help her upstairs to her room. Meg acquiesced without complaint, not really knowing who was at her side, and allowed herself to be put to bed like a child. She snored immediately. Constance straightaway began a tour of Meg's suite, looking into drawers and cupboards and opening the doors of the wall-long wardrobe to glance through the garments hanging there, wrinkling her nose at the stale odor of sweat and lavishly used scent that emanated from them. It should all go into the washtub or be delicately laundered, and she would see to it in the morning. It seemed that everything Meg possessed was soiled in one way or another, and it had been the same with the gloves and shawls and other things in the drawers. Her jewelry was more interesting. There were some fine diamond brooches, creamy strands of pearls, bracelets and rings and lockets and fobs, all higgledy-piggledy on the crimson velvet trays, and the key to the box was missing. That should also be seen to without delay. In future it would be kept locked, and she would supervise the pieces that Meg wore, because she was not going to risk letting Meg get rid of her by an unjust accusation over a mislaid piece of jewelry. And she intended to stay by making herself indispensable to this household where every luxury would be hers until such time as she could better her position in any way.

Seated in front of Meg's dressing table as she tried on a pair of sapphire eardrops, she saw her own face set deeper into the determination of her mood. Never would she slip back into hard times. Never again should there be squalor, and men not of her own pleasure, and penny pinching, and rags upon her back and her bed. Had she never known some degree of comfort, those last, terrible years would probably have been easier to bear, but she had been born one of five daughters to a hard-working grocer, her mother a woman with pretentious aims above their station in life, who had refused to live over the shop and had spread gentility throughout the neat terrace house where they had resided, always seeing to it that there was good food upon the table, a fire in the grate, and fine linen on the beds; moreover, she had made the girls walk five miles every day to and from a school that had better teachers than the one in the vicinity of their home, having dreams that they would wed into a higher social scale than the strata that she suffered; a bank clerk, perhaps, or a curate, in fact anyone who could boast of a profession instead of a trade. None of Constance's sisters made the grade, each in turn marrying a carpenter, a draper, a bookie, and a traveling salesman, only Constance breaking the pattern by marrying an artist who was something of a gentleman, but her mother never knew about that, because it happened long after she had got into bad company and left home for London, breaking all ties with the past.

Constance removed the eardrops and replaced them in the box. One of the first presents Gerald had ever given her had been a pair of eardrops. They had been pawned more times than she could remember before they finally went with everything else of value that she and Gerald possessed. There had been some happy and riotous times, particularly in the early days when he had been full of hope and ambition and the certainty that he would achieve a greatness in his work that would satisfy a craving within him and bring with it recognition and fame and fortune. That fulfillment was never his. In the end she had watched him die, no longer knowing her, and she had laid him out herself for his pauper's funeral in a sack. A couple of loyal friends and a model who had once been in love with him had stood at the graveside with her, but others who had enjoyed the affluent periods when wine had flowed and parties crammed his studio, had made themselves scarce long since. Gerald had not been a very likable fellow, and fair-weather friends had only put up with his moods and unpredictable insults for as long as he was still able to sell a painting now and again, for he knew how to spend money when he had it, and from him she had learned how to let it slip gloriously through her fingers, a lesson that had come back to her within the realms of Donna's generosity.

She closed the lid of the jewel box and rose from the seat of the dressing table. In the bed Meg continued to snore and did not hear the door shut as Constance went out of the room. Making her way back to her own quarters, Constance thought that had she been married to Richard Warwyck she would have seen to it that she did not sleep alone. And, judging him through her long experience as the type of man she believed him to be, he would not have let her.

Downstairs Tom took a second armful of books out to the dogcart and stacked them in carefully. Now he had more or less all he wanted for the time being. He stepped up into the seat and took the reins.

"Tom! Wait!" It was Jeremy running down the steps of the Grange. "Be a good chap and give me a lift into town. I'm going to the club, and I thought I would nip into Easthampton House first for a word with Grandfather. Can't let the old boy think I'm neglecting him."

Tom removed some of the books from the seat to make room for his brother. He supposed Jeremy was going to cadge a fiver or two from Daniel, which was the usual reason for a call at Easthampton House. "Get in," he said.

As he drove out of the gates he looked in the direction of Radcliffe Hall. Jeremy was talking on about a weekend house party at an old friend's country seat in Berkshire where he had stayed the previous weekend, but Tom did not listen, rapt in his own particular problems. Where was Nicolette? Why hadn't she written? What had happened to prevent her getting in touch with him? She was never out of his thoughts, and anxiety was gradually giving way to an angry fear that she had changed her mind and was spurning him after all. He would give her just so long and no longer before he sought her out at the Hall, which meant risking her being reminded of his pursuit of Laura, something he had hoped to avoid. Nevertheless, it would have to be done. There was no other way. No sooner had he reached this conclusion than a hefty dig in the ribs from Jeremy's elbow compelled his attention.

"Have you lost your hearing?" his brother demanded impatiently. "Here am I giving you the most momentous news and you retain a stony silence with a most stupid glaze over your countenance."

"Er—sorry," Tom said automatically. "I have things on my mind. You had a good time in Berkshire, did you?"

"That's what I've been telling you," Jeremy replied with a heavy groan. "I met this damned pretty woman there."

"Oh, yes." Tom's tone was bored. Sometimes Jeremy's conquests were worth listening to, but at the moment he was not in the mood.

"No, it's not what you think. This was different. My behavior was impeccable. It had to be. I think she's the one I'm going to marry."

Tom glanced at him cynically. "Is she as rich as all that?"

Jeremy glowered. "You cheeky young cuss. I ought to belt you out of that seat."

"Try it." Tom's grin was dangerous.

"Don't be an oaf." Jeremy dismissed the challenge with a lordly air and returned to the subject that was engrossing him. "I always forget that you haven't a scrap of finer feelings in you. It didn't occur to you, I suppose, that I could be falling in love with her?"

"No, it didn't," Tom agreed with cheerful bluntness. "Are you?"

"As a matter of fact, I am."

"Good for you. How rich is she?"

Jeremy gave an exasperated sigh and threw up his hands. "All right. She is very rich, I admit it. How could I afford to fall in love with her otherwise?"

"How indeed," Tom remarked laconically.

"But here's the odd thing about it all." Jeremy twisted in his seat toward his brother, leaning forward in his enthusiasm. "She's one of the Yorkshire Edenfields."

"Oh, yes." Tom rolled up his eyes in exaggerated non-interest. Jeremy's circles were not his.

"Use your loaf, Tom, for God's sake!" Jeremy exclaimed impatiently. "Doesn't the name of Edenfield mean anything to you? It should do. You're the one who's always taken more interest in Grandfather's past career as a pugilist than anyone else among us."

Tom looked at him with interest for the first time. "I know it was a Sir Geoffrey Edenfield who was Grandfather's patron and backer in his championship days."

"That's it." Jeremy gave him an approving clap on the shoulder. "Helen is his great-granddaughter, and from what I was able to find out, she and her invalid sister have quite a fortune between them, which has come down to them from the old gentleman himself. That's why I'm going to see Grandfather this evening. He'll be really interested to know that I've met one of the family."

"You're right, he will." Tom gave an apologetic chuckle. "I did you an injustice. I thought you were going to touch him for a fiver."

"I am," Jeremy admitted blatantly. "Although on the strength of this information I'm hoping to get it up to twenty." He ignored the look that his brother gave him and leaned back in his seat again, looking upward at the stars. "Helen is well named. A face to launch a thousand ships and a fortune to go with it. If only that wretched legacy from Aunt Jassy would come through I could get on with my courtship." His voice became thoughtful. "You don't suppose Daniel could be persuaded to cough up a hundred or two on the strength of my aim there, do you?"

"I couldn't say. That's between the two of you," Tom said flatly, turning the horses into the road that covered the last lap into Easthampton. "What's the point anyway? If the lady lives in Yorkshire you can't keep traveling up there to see her every five minutes on the strength of a weekend's meeting at a house party."

"I know that." Jeremy resented the common sense of the

remark, being already aware of it. "I must content myself with letters for the time being, although I would have liked to visit her home city of York in some style and take her out to dine and dance and for drives in the countryside. It's a hell of a time to wait until the autumn comes."

"Good Lord! I hope the legacy comes through before then," Tom exclaimed with some concern. "I'll be needing it very soon."

"I wasn't talking about the legacy. That could turn up tomorrow, if it comes to that. No, it's in the autumn that Helen plans to take a house by the sea and bring her sister to Easthampton for the winter. Apparently Beatrice Edenfield's health has declined over recent months, making a trip abroad to a milder clime too tiring for her, and Helen has chosen our resort instead."

"Due to your persuasion, I suppose?"

"Fortunately she brought the subject up herself. That's how we started talking in the first place. Of course I praised up Easthampton with its mild and salubrious air and all that, but she knew a great deal about the resort already. Apparently the Edenfields used to have a summer residence at Easthampton in the days when Grandfather was fighting to be champion of the prize ring, but it was sold many years ago now, which is why Helen has never been to this part of the south coast. I've promised to show her all the local beauty spots."

"In other words, the lady is as good as yours."

"I like to think so." Jeremy laughed softly, sticking his thumbs in his waistcoat armholes and playing his fingers against his chest as he narrowed his eyes lasciviously. "Wait until you see her, Tom. If ever a woman was made for loving, she was."

The lamps on the gateposts of Easthampton House showed the way through to the drive, and when they reached the entrance Jeremy was first out of the equipage and indoors without a word of thanks for the ride. Tom carried his books upstairs to his room and set them in place upon the shelves. When he came down again Jeremy was strutting through the hall, looking jubilant. He patted his pocket to indicate the success of his visit.

"I've had the most tremendous slice of luck, don't you know. A cool hundred guineas for myself, and Grandfather is going to write himself and offer the hospitality of his home to Helen and her sister for as long as they wish to stay. He says it is the least he can do for the great-granddaughter of the man who backed him to the Championship of England."

"They'll certainly have every comfort here."

"And I can be in and out of the house whenever I wish. You'll be seeing a great deal more of me when the autumn comes than you have done for years, young brother."

Tom set his hands on his hips. "If they accept," he pointed out.

Jeremy did not seem to have any doubt about it, departing with a spring in his step. Tom gave a sigh. He did not envy his brother, but he thought it would have been pleasant to have his path to Nicolette paved with equal ease. Then he reminded himself that the course of true love never did run smooth. It was small consolation.

Chapter 8

Nicolette was in disgrace. Her grandmother had been furious with her for taking a day on her own in Easthampton, and she had been forbidden even to go for her morning rides.

"Suppose something had happened to you!" Olivia had exclaimed, lifting lace-mittened hands in horror at the thought. "What on earth should I have said to your Papa!"

Nicolette thought it a ridiculous argument. "But nothing did—and nothing would. Things have changed since you were young, Grandmother. Girls are not chaperoned everywhere they go any more."

"*Respectable* girls are," Olivia retorted. "It is well known that at the seaside young men take liberties they would never dream of doing at home. What would you have done if one of them had started to bother you with his company?"

Nicolette lowered her lashes and kept her smile to herself. What would her grandmother say if she replied: *one did, and I let him kiss me.* Instead, she said, "I can look after myself."

It was an argument that could have gone on indefinitely, and Olivia was already exhausted by it, finding she tired easily under any strain. The truth was that she loved her young granddaughter more than she had loved her own child, which she believed not to be an unusual state of affairs, and yet it gave her a curious satisfaction to discipline the girl and exercise control over her. It was then that she forbade any outing whatever for an unstated period without her own personal chaperonage, and thus was the riding peremptorily curtailed.

Nicolette passed the time as best she could. Either by design or by coincidence it happened that Olivia made no outings and paid no calls during the fortnight that followed, which prevented Nicolette getting a glimpse of the outside world beyond the gates of the Hall. Some visitors called, all Olivia's elderly contemporaries, who made dull company for a young girl compelled to sit in at the stiff taking of tea and formal exchange of news, and lack of correspondence from acquaintances of her own age group enabled Nicolette to guess that her grandmother was opening all invitations addressed to her and refusing them on her behalf.

The injustice of the whole situation made her fret, although Hugh and Lawrence did what they could to brighten the days for her. There was croquet on the lawn, tennis singles with one or other of them, shuttlecock and battledore at the high net, and cards or some other game of chance in the evenings whenever the two young men chose not to go out. In fine weather she had plenty of opportunities for endless walks by herself through the grounds, exploring every copse and rose garden and box-hedged path while she thought of Tom and the extraordinary bond forming between them against the most tremendous odds. It was a great worry to her as to how he would have reacted to her not coming to the beach, and she tried to tell herself that he would understand that something unforeseen had prevented her. Had she been able to post a letter to him it would have helped, but the one she had written with a full explanation remained unposted in a locked drawer in her room, awaiting the first chance she had to get it on its way to him. Sometimes her brother and Lawrence joined her on her wanderings through the grounds, although their time was much taken up with local cricket matches, swimming in the sea, and driving as far as the Brighton racecourse. She did not discourage their company, the time being long and made longer by her growing resentment at the continuing restriction on any social activity beyond the grounds. It was when Lawrence came on his own to join her that she made some excuse to cut a walk short, because he always wanted to hold her hand or put his arm about her waist, which made her increasingly impatient with him. It came to a confrontation between them when he suggested one day that they take a look inside the folly, a place she had avoided assiduously since the night of the attack on Tom, not wanting to be reminded in any way as to the reason why he had been in the grounds that night, jealousy being a torment to her no matter that whatever had been between Laura and him had fizzled out and been long gone.

"No," she said sharply, pulling away from him. "It's a silly, gloomy place. I hate anything that is sham."

There was a gardener weeding on the other side of the lake, and Lawrence lowered his voice in case the water was carrying their conversation. "You've never been in there, have you?"

"Laura and I took a look at it the second or third day after we arrived at the Hall. That was enough for me."

He did not give up, obviously believing that once they were truly unobserved, away from possible intrusion of any kind, she would let him kiss her as she had done in the conservatory, for his next words revealed an association in his thoughts with that moment. "Wouldn't you like to see where we felled Tom Warwyck? That was quite an event in the history of your family."

Her eyes blazed at him. "Don't use that hideous night as bait to me! I never want to hear it mentioned again—or anything at all that happened during it."

He was put firmly in his place, no illusions left that the kiss between them had had any promise to it, and she stalked off along the path away from him, continuing the walk he had interrupted. Seconds afterward he caught her up. "All right," he said with a light shrug, "but we can still be on good terms, can't we?"

"Yes," she said, much relieved. "I don't like quarreling with anyone."

"There's one thing I must add before we close the subject. You have every right to be angry that Warwyck got away after what he did to the rest of us in one way or another, but Hugh will get even with him in the end, have no doubts about that. In the meantime, that London dentist recommended to your grandmother will fix the twin's missing tooth so that no one will ever see the difference, and scars that were suffered by others will fade with time."

She was saved making any comment by his hasty switch to another topic on more neutral ground, and throughout the rest of the walk he kept level with her, but made no attempt at any physical contact. She cheered up. It looked as if she had solved one problem.

Another week crawled by, Olivia using the indisposition of a slight cold as an excuse to continue to keep Nicolette within bounds, when Hugh, annoyed on his sister's behalf, approached her with the suggestion that at least he could take Nicolette somewhere to break the monotony. He looked glum as he reported his failure, and Nicolette, struggling with her disappointment, gave him a hug and thanked him for trying.

When she first heard that her father was arriving from Scotland she thought with panic-stricken dismay that her grandmother had decided after all that a single day's truancy warranted her being packed off back to Edinburgh and James Stuart was coming to fetch her; fortunately that did not prove to be the case after all. It turned out that it was Hugh who was involved, and at once both he and Nicolette were able to guess what was afoot.

"Grandmother is going to make you her heir, Hugh," Nicolette exclaimed excitedly. "If she said to you that it was something important enough to make our father's presence necessary, there can be no other reason."

"I hope so. God! I trust you're right." He paced the floor of the conservatory, where he had come to join Nicolette and Lawrence, who were having iced lemonade after a game of tennis together, their racquets beside them on a chair.

"Congratulations, old fellow," Lawrence said, raising his glass in a toast. "I envy your good fortune, but how has it happened that you have been picked out for the honor? You're not the eldest Radcliffe-Stuart by any means."

Hugh made a quietening-down gesture with hands in front of

him. "We mustn't count our chickens before they're hatched, Lawrence, but my being the sixth son has nothing to do with it. Grandmother has always said I'm most like my grandfather, Alexander, although he died long before I was born, so I've no idea myself. What's more important to her, I should think, is that I'm the only one who has ever shown any real interest in the estate, and there's never been any pretense about that, because for as long as I can remember, whenever I came to the Hall I was here, there, and everywhere to see the cattle and find out about the crops and the forestry. I never knew that Grandmother was taking note and putting it all to my credit."

"Aren't your older brothers going to be annoyed about it?"

"Why should they? My eldest brother inherited an estate from my father's side, and the rest have married into land or money or both." Hugh chuckled on a note of jubilation that he could not crush down. "Radcliffe Hall—mine. All its land—mine. I hardly dare think about it."

Nicolette sprang up from her chair and hugged him exuberantly. "Dear Hugh! You'll make a wonderful lord of the manor—" She bit off the words, remembering how he had treated Tom. Admittedly Tom was a member of the Warwyck family, but would Hugh deal any less harshly with anybody else who trespassed or committed some mild breach against his property?

"What is it, Lettie?" Hugh questioned jovially, calling her by her old nursery name as he held her back from him by the arms. "You're looking extremely serious all of a sudden."

"Landowners aren't very kind to poachers and people who don't pay their rent and all that. You won't be unjust, will you, Hugh? When the responsibility is yours you will temper justice with mercy, won't you? Promise me!"

"I promise," he answered glibly, laughing at her. She heard Lawrence join in his laughter and knew she had wasted her breath so far. Before she could remonstrate further with her brother he remembered a message he had to deliver, which he announced with dramatic emphasis, knowing what it would mean to her. "At long last you are to have a taste of liberty, my dear sister. The matter slipped my mind while I allowed myself to be carried away by all this speculation. Grandmother has decided to go for a drive now that her cold has quite gone, and you are to accompany her. How's that for a riotous end to virtual imprisonment?"

Nicolette did not wait to reply to his banter. Even after such a long time it was not so much eagerness to accompany the old lady that spurred her to a skirt-billowing, bow-flying run up the stairs and made her change into an outing costume with such haste, but that at last a long-awaited chance had come to post her letter to Tom explaining why she had had to stay within the grounds.

Once out in the carriage she announced that she had a letter to post, and displayed an envelope addressed to a friend in Scotland, not adding that there was a second letter tucked into her pocket, which would be delivered to a destination less than two miles away. Olivia noted that the letter held out for inspection was going to a female, and at the first postbox she halted the coachman, allowing Nicolette to get out. With her back to her grandmother she whipped out the second envelope and shot both into the scarlet aperture. There was a spring in her step and a smile on her lips as she took her place again.

James Stuart arrived that same evening. He was tired by the journey, which he had made by train, and would not willingly have come south at the command of his mother-in-law, for whom he had much respect and little liking, if it had not been made plain that his son was about to benefit munificently from the old lady if certain conditions were met. He knew it to be his parental duty to bear witness to it, and so answered the summons with promptitude after reading a timetable to see how quickly he might get home again.

Nicolette came running to meet him in the entrance hall, and he greeted her warmly. He realized how much he had missed her without being aware of it, for at home his young wife with her capricious whims and demands for attention kept every moment occupied. Yet he reveled in his second marriage, his carnal pleasure in Felicity excelling anything he had ever known with his first wife, who had been dutiful and fruitful and little else, and although that pleasure had been curtailed at the present time due to Felicity's condition he was as besotted as ever and did not wish to be away from her for an hour longer than was necessary.

"You're looking bonny, Nicolette," he said, glad to see a sparkle in her eyes once more and a return of the impish vivacity in her face that had been missing during those last, tempestuous months at home. Not particularly perceptive where his own children were concerned, he saw no other change in her, and to him she was still the rebellious child in the girl's body who had tilted her head proudly upon departure and refused to look out of the window at those waving goodbye.

"I have a matter of great urgency to discuss with you, Papa," she insisted, falling into step with him across the hall. "It's about my chaperonage. I have less freedom here than in Edinburgh." She could no longer bring herself to call the old house home. "I'm not allowed to go shopping on my own any more. Isn't that quite ridiculous in these days? A word from you to Grandmother—"

"We'll see." He patted her on the shoulder and she thought it might just as well have been on top of her head for all the notice he had taken. She had hoped to secure his support before her grandmother brought the subject up, which was almost certain, and it had been in vain. She slowed her pace to a standstill, letting him go on ahead to greet Olivia, who had appeared with her claw-like little hand in the crook of Hugh's arm for support.

It proved to be an evening full of tension. James and Olivia dined alone, obviously to begin discussing everything at once since he had made it clear to her from the outset that he wished to start for home in the morning, while Nicolette and Lawrence had to put up with Hugh's increasing restlessness and his impatience to know what was being decided. Eventually he was summoned to his grandmother's favorite drawing room, and a quarter of an hour later Nicolette, to her consternation and surprise, was asked to present herself there as well.

She saw at once from Hugh's face that he was getting all he had hoped for, but her father looked less pleased, his brow wrinkled, and he looked at her uncertainly. Olivia waved her to a chair and then looked expectantly at her son-in-law. "Now, James. Let Nicolette hear what you have to say."

He cleared his throat twice. "Your grandmother has most kindly made Hugh her heir. Radcliffe Hall and all its lands will be his, and from tomorrow he will be under instruction as to its management, taking the reins completely as soon as he is able enough. There is one condition. Through legal channels he has to drop the name of Stuart from his surname and become known as Hugh Radcliffe."

Nicolette was not surprised that there had been no opposition from her brother there. She believed he would have sold his soul for the estate. Nevertheless her sympathies were with her father, who had given in years ago to pressure that he should let his firstborn and all other offspring bear the double-barreled surname, never dreaming the true purpose behind it. There was no doubt that Olivia was as cunning as she had been foresighted: only a true Radcliffe was to inherit the Hall and all that went with it. "I congratulate Hugh on his future inheritance," she said neutrally.

"Now we come to you," her father said after clearing his throat again. "There will be a handsome dowry and your own income for life if and when you marry with my full consent as well as your grandmother's. Should you not marry, one section of Radcliffe Hall will be yours to live in throughout your lifetime, the monies that would have made up your dowry added to your income. Is that not generous?"

It was generous indeed, and yet how insidiously the condition involved in the munificence had been slipped in: her grandmother intended to govern her choice of husband, having a half-say in the matter with her father. Did they imagine she would care anything about money where love could be involved? She tilted her chin.

"In one way it is generous, but money is not important to me. I would want any consent to come solely from you, Papa."

There was a second or two of stunned silence. Hugh covered his mouth quickly to hide a grin at such defiance, unnoticed by the others. Olivia, outraged, thumped one lace-mittened fist on the damask arm of her chair. "You ungrateful minx! Money is important enough to prospective suitors and could weigh the scales in getting you the husband of your choice. You're no beauty, you know. Think about that for a moment, miss!"

Nicolette colored at the cruel barb, but only tilted her chin still higher. James, whose eyes had softened briefly at the declaration she had made to him, frowned and became stern again, reminding himself that Nicolette had always been a source of trouble and he could not expect her to be any different now. "I have already agreed to your grandmother's proposal. You're too young yet to know your own mind about anything, and neither she nor I would wish you to throw away security for the rest of your life through a present folly over which you have no control. The matter is quite settled."

Her shock at his betrayal showed in her face. Of course he would agree to anything her grandmother suggested, for it was as much for his good as her own: he did not want her turfed out of the Hall and sent home again any more than she wanted to go, but she would not have surrendered upon such a vital issue and he knew it, spiking her guns before she had even entered the room. She found her voice again.

"After I'm twenty-one I can marry without even your consent, Papa."

Olivia snorted, wanting perversely to hurt the very one she most loved. "Most girls are on the shelf by then."

For the first time since the interview started James did not acknowledge that his mother-in-law had spoken, and replied solely to his daughter's remark. "Aye," he agreed uncomfortably, "but not, I trust, without the full approval of your grandmother and myself. Neither she nor I would be able to reconcile ourselves to such a flagrant disregard of our wishes. You would find yourself left quite outside the family."

The threat was unmistakable. It said that she might not care about the money, which would not be forthcoming in the face of such rebellion, but she did care about the family and James would see to it her connection with it was severed. She stared at him bleakly, hurt and angry. Surely her brothers would not listen to him in such an event? No, she *knew* her brothers loved her. Swiftly she looked toward Hugh in mute appeal, but he was studying his fingernails as if he had never seen them before, and she realized that for the present moment at least he was going to do nothing that might jeopardize all he had won for himself. It registered with her that she would never be able to forget that he had failed her when she had most needed a brother's support.

Olivia, benign now that she believed the little contretemps was over, voiced the most used platitudes that never failed to infuriate the young. "It is all for your own good. You'll thank us for it one day. Now give me a kiss and run along. Hugh may go with you. I want to talk with your father a little longer and hear the latest news of my other grandchildren as well as my great-grandchildren. There has been no time yet."

Olivia had expected Nicolette to come forward, but instead the girl whirled about, snatched open the door and rushed out, leaving it swinging behind her. They heard her footsteps vanish into the distance.

"Temper, temper," Olivia commented, not at all irked. The girl would be over it in the morning and begin to think what a fortune would mean to her life: beautiful dresses, a carriage and a pair of her own, jewels, furs, and everything else she could possibly wish for. Olivia glanced toward her grandson. "Go after your sister, Hugh. Try to calm her down." As the door closed after him she looked again toward her son-in-law. "Nicolette really is a highly strung little miss. As you said, James, we must excuse her. At that age girls are too foolish to know whether they are coming or going. Those who let them go unchaperoned are asking for trouble—we all know how that ends up."

Her words reminded him of something. Then he recalled Nicolette's appeal to him upon his arrival. He gave some thought to it while his mother-in-law continued to decry the follies of present-day society.

Hugh knocked on Nicolette's bedroom door, but she refused to open it. He could tell she was crying.

"Go away! I've nothing to say to you, you traitor."

He tried to make amends. "Oh, don't make a fuss, Lettie. You know I'd never let Father or Grandmother or anybody else set up barriers between us. We've always been good friends. I was pleased as Punch when they said those rooms in the west wing were to be kept for you to live in."

With his head bent toward the door he heard her scramble off the bed, where she had flung herself, and then he drew back sharply and involuntarily as an indignant thump from her fist on the other side of the panel resounded loudly. "So you think I'll end up an old maid, do you? You think it's just what Grandmother said—I'm too ugly to marry."

He half laughed in his exasperation with her. "Of course I don't. You're just silly to upset yourself over something that's purely hypothetical anyway. I'll wager my last penny that you'll end up marrying someone whom everybody approves of and you'll both live in luxury on Grandmother's loot for the rest of your days."

Inside the room she rested her tear-stained cheek on the door as her weight sagged against it. "I suppose I will," she conceded wretchedly.

He took it to mean that she had listened to his sensible reasoning, and after adding a few more encouraging adages he went off downstairs to find Lawrence and a bottle of fine port from the cellar.

Nicolette returned to the bed and lay back on it again, gazing up at the ceiling, one arm under her head. All the time she had been listening to Olivia and her father it was as if her heart had already selected Tom, and all unwittingly they were setting everything in motion against him as if his being a Warwyck was not a positive cul-de-sac against hope in that direction. It was that which had caused the pain within her, the desperate knowledge that life would be barren with anyone else. In spite of her brief agreement with Hugh through the door she could visualize herself growing old and gray and withered in a bed in the west wing room while Tom married someone else and forgot all about her. She rolled over in the bed and buried her face in the pillow, not crying any more, merely weltering in a limbo of despair.

When something pattered against her window she thought it was starting to rain until there came a silence afterward, to be followed by another pattering, a piece of gravel dancing in across the floor. Roused by curiosity, she slid from the bed and went across to the open window, holding the curtain back. She could see nothing in the darkness below, for there was no moon that night, but Tom's wrathful, sibilant question reached her clearly enough.

"What happened to you? You said you'd write. I've heard nothing."

She almost exclaimed with joy, undisturbed by his furious attitude, and all imagery of his faithlessness forgotten. "Go to the conservatory. I'll meet you there." Without waiting for any reply she dashed across to her door, opened it cautiously, and peeped out. Nobody about. She removed the key from the door and locked it on the outside. Anybody who tried the handle would think she had fallen asleep while still upset.

Coming from the lighted corridor into the blackness of the conservatory, she was still unable to see him, and yet she knew unerringly where he was. Only the hostility emanating from him checked her from flying to seek his arms. The angry, pain-racked accusation tore out from the heart of him.

"I suppose Payne has been engaging all your time! Turning your head with his flattery, perhaps? Is there no way in which you can manage to keep your word?"

So he was jealous. Bitterly jealous and hurt beyond measure with it. She could feel his torment within herself, so sensitive was she toward him physically and mentally, and a reaction of indignation that would have been normal to her at any other time was lost in an empathetic comprehension of his pain. She made no pretense.

"There is nothing between Lawrence Payne and me. There never has been, except a single kiss that was more to keep him away from finding you in hiding than for any pleasure it gave me, although to be perfectly truthful I didn't quite realize it at the time. He will soon be leaving. Hugh has liked having his old friend at the Hall, but from now on everything will be changed. In future I'm sure we shall only be seeing my brother at mealtimes, because he's going to be busy from morning until night. And now that the twins have left to join the Guards and the others have gone to the Continent, Lawrence will soon get bored with his own company since he has already tired of mine." She thought she had mollified Tom somewhat, but if she had set his mind at rest on one point, he was still desperately raw on another, quite unappeased and frantic.

"You could have *written!* Pen and paper and ink are simple enough to acquire!"

"I did write," she answered simply. "Straightaway. The only thing was that I had no chance to post the letter until this very afternoon." Quietly she explained the circumstances, and he, listening, became very still, letting the reassuring words soothe his jangled nerves, not saying anything. He was no longer overly concerned about the letter in itself. It was enough for him that she had kept her promise. Then, tentatively, not at all sure how she would receive him after his unjust abuse, he reached out his hands. She did not hesitate. With eyes now accustomed to the darkness she swept lightly forward and slipped her fingers into his outstretched clasp. All around them the foliage, disturbed anew by her swiftness, whispered and swayed, some of the larger leaves rising and falling like giant fans, stirring the exotic blossoms wafting their perfume out upon the aromatic air.

"You shouldn't be here," she declared fervently with a shake of her head, beginning to be aghast at his recklessness while at the same time glorying exultantly in it, her pulse racing.

"I couldn't stay away any longer." He caressed her hands as he held them with the touch of his thumbs and with sensual pressure, her intense excitement conveying itself through the tremor in her fingertips and her quick, soft breathing. He longed to put his lips against the place of her wildly beating heart. "I waited and watched for you everywhere I could, and you never came." He drew her down with him onto a cushioned seat beneath a canopy of palm fronds.

"Nor can I," she answered him, "until I'm released from the bondage of going everywhere with my grandmother. I'll have to think of *something*."

"Until you do, I'll come here."

"No!" She was terrified for his safety. "If Hugh as much as suspected there was an intruder in the grounds again, even if he had no idea it was you, he would have the game wardens alerted with guns and shot."

"Would he have the authority for that?"

"He would now." She explained what had been arranged for her brother that evening, although she made no mention of the conditions governing herself. After all, it was a state of affairs that could never concern him, however much she might wish it otherwise if this extraordinary feeling that she had for him proved to be impossible to quell or let fade away, a prospect not to be contemplated for the time being.

He was interested in what she told him, simply because it meant that if he managed to establish his boatyard eventually he and Hugh were destined to be neighbors for the rest of their lives, but more important at the present time was being with Nicolette. He drew her into the circle of his arm and she did not stiffen away from him as he had feared, merely coming with some slowness to nestle against him, her head on his shoulder, her hand resting lightly on his chest. The softness of her, the delicate scent of her skin and the butterfly touch of tendrils of her hair against his cheek intoxicated him with a new wonderment as if he had never embraced a girl before, making him long to cherish her, to deal with her tenderly and ardently and never to let her go.

"Nicolette." His throat strangled her name lovingly as he touched his lips to her eyes, finding them closed in quivering anticipation. He lowered his head until, almost in homecoming, his mouth came down in the forceful abandonment of passion upon hers. He felt her initial shock, knew she had never been kissed thus before, and then she yielded with a kind of innocent ecstasy, her arm sliding about his neck, bringing her arched body even closer to him. He held her until he dared hold her no longer. Putting an agony of temptation from him, which took all his strength of will, he eased his embrace to let her draw back a little from him, still within his encompassing arm.

"Lovely, lovely Nicolette," he murmured endearingly. "How I wish we had met abroad somewhere with no one to throw the names of Warwyck and Radcliffe at us."

"Better still to have been born Smith and Jones without the inheritance of other people's old quarrels," she said seriously.

He chuckled, smiling again into her face, this time his expres-

sion holding no mysterious quality to set her at a loss. "I think the
name of Tom Smith would suit me very well. What is your opinion, Miss Jones?"

She laughed delightedly with upraised chin, the beautiful
stretch of her long neck gleaming at him. "Yes, yes. Why didn't
we think of that before? When we meet we'll leave our real selves
behind and be two ordinary people with nothing whatever standing between us."

"Not ordinary," he joked, laughing with her. "Nicolette Jones
could never be ordinary."

"Neither could Tom Smith," she interrupted happily. "We'll
be two special people instead. What a pity we can't find a special
little planet of our own where we could be together."

It was lovers' talk, but in her guilelessness she was unaware of
it. He gathered her hands into both of his own. "Maybe there is a
planet somewhere," he said thoughtfully, "if only we can locate
it."

She understood. "A meeting place where we could both go if
there was the remotest chance of the other turning up."

He nodded. "Bambury Mill would do if we could get into it.
You said yourself that you never saw anyone when you rode that
way. After all, your grandmother can't keep you tied to her side
indefinitely. There are bound to be chances when you'll be able to
get away."

"I hope so. Tell me where you watched and waited for me. Did
you come to the gates of the Hall in the early morning again?"

He was taken aback. "You knew I went there?"

She told him how she had avoided letting him see her, giving
her reasons. He shook his head that she should imagine he would
be so easily deterred, and there followed a loving little argument
about it until she admitted that she had not really believed that
he would stop trying to see her. "It was an attempt to end this
madness before it began," she explained helplessly.

"But it had begun. It was already too late for evasion tactics."
He went on to list the various places where he had watched for
her then and over the past few days. She was intrigued and darted
little questions at him, wanting to know about his time at the

roller-skating rink in between his searching for her, and what he thought of this or that, whether he cared for horses as much as she did, and what he wanted most to do with his life. It was then that he told her about the forthcoming creation of *Sea Star*.

She listened, enthralled, able to visualize through his eyes the first swift boat cutting across sparkling water, to be followed by others, each an advancement and a refinement on the one before, until eventually the fastest yacht in the world came from the Tom Warwyck boatyard. It was a beautiful dream, and she did not doubt its ultimate fulfillment.

"As long as *Sea Star* proves herself in design and maneuverability I can raise the financial backing to take the next step and then the next," he told her, more moved by her rapt response than she could possibly suspect, and explained why he had faced such opposition from his father. "Although we have recently resolved the matter of my future, he still has no idea how much sailing I have done, or the true extent of my knowledge of small yachts and their handling. Several summer holidays abroad with a school friend and his family were spent sailing day in and day out on a forty-foot yacht that he and I hired between us. I've also taken part in races with the same friend off Cowes and the Devon coast, but my father has never shown the slightest interest. I suppose he thought that if he ignored it all long enough I would come to accept the future he had planned for me."

"He will come to terms with it when the *Sea Star* is a success," she said confidently.

Her belief in him was intoxicating. He kissed her again with increased ardor and would have gone on kissing her in head-spinning desire if she had not been the first to hear voices some little distance away outside. It was her brother and Lawrence taking a stroll in the grounds, Hugh in high good spirits and the two of them guffawing together. She peered through the glass of the conservatory after them.

"They're going in the direction of the lake, so if you keep well to the west of it there'll be no risk of your running into them."

He was reluctant to leave, but she wanted him to depart while he knew his enemies' whereabouts and could avoid any trouble.

Promising to let him know as soon as there was any chance of their meeting again, she let him out of the conservatory door and watched him vanish into the darkness.

She was halfway across the hall when her father came out of the library. To her relief he did not question why she was there or where she had been, his tiredness at the end of a long day of some tension giving a drawn look to his features, and although she expected a reprimand for her abrupt departure from her grandmother's presence, it was not forthcoming.

"I have been giving thought to your chaperonage," he said thoughtfully, falling into step with her up the stairs on his way to bed. "I'm going to send Beth Macdonald down from Edinburgh to take charge of you."

"Beth to come here!" Nicolette paused on tiptoe with delight. "But how can you spare her? Isn't she to look after the new baby when it is born?"

"Er—no. As a matter of fact, my wife has chosen her own nursemaids, and all the rest of the household staff is being replaced by servants of her own choosing."

So Felicity would have nobody in the house who had served her husband's first wife. The new broom was sweeping cleaner all the time, and it was impossible to have regrets about it on this occasion when it meant that Beth would be coming to the Hall.

"Is Grandmother in agreement?" Nicolette asked in sudden trepidation.

"Aye. She remembers Beth from her visits, and was always impressed with her firm handling of you and her keen sense of responsibility. There'll be no more running astray with Beth to keep an eye on you."

Nicolette linked her arm through her father's and kissed him on the cheek. "Thank you, Papa. Oh, thank you. It's going to make all the difference to my life at the Hall."

Safely in her room, she danced a little jig of excitement, catching hold of the bedpost and whirling herself about on it to land with a thump of knees on the bed in a far different mood from her tearful collapse at an earlier hour. Beth had been the youngest nursemaid and newly come to the household on the day the only daughter in the family was born. Nicolette's mother soon discovered that she had a prize in Beth, who rose to a position of responsibility in the household and was as loved as she was respected by those children young enough still to be in her charge. When Nicolette's mother had fallen ill it was Beth's devoted nursing that had eased her weeks of suffering and made less hard her final hour. Nicolette had no illusions of leniency with Beth in the matter of her chaperonage, but Beth had always been understanding, and surely where love was concerned she would deal kindly with her, at least allowing her to talk and walk with Tom under a watchful eye and yet out of earshot. Nicolette hugged her arms in a rush of hopeful anticipation.

Chapter 9

In amiable mood next morning Nicolette did as her father requested before his departure: she apologized to Olivia for a disrespectful loss of temper, but gave no conciliatory and belated kiss on principle, which fortunately went unnoticed, or else there could have been a further confrontation.

Beth arrived three days later. She was a plain, sensible Scotswoman with neat, dark hair and capable hands. She had only known love once in her life, and that had been a brief, heartcracking affair with a footman who had turned out to be a deceiver and a thief to boot, being dismissed by the Stuart household at a moment's notice. In the one moment of madness in her life she would have thrown up her own security and gone with him, but in the ugly resentment of dismissal he had snatched up his packed valise from his bed and uttered some home truths at her that had revealed all too clearly that he had never cared for her. It had suited his convenience to have a woman to hand. Nothing more. After that she had closed the door on love, not that any other opportunity had ever come her way, and instead had devoted herself to the family to whom she felt she belonged. At Radcliffe Hall, no sooner had she crossed the threshold of the servants' quarters than Nicolette came rushing to meet her. They embraced each other affectionately.

"I can't tell you how glad I am that you're here, dear Beth," Nicolette declared after the woman had been shown her quarters, a comfortable room on the same floor only two doors away from Nicolette's own. "I've been practically confined to these grounds and only allowed out in Grandmother's company. She is going to talk strictly to you, I'm sure. Never to let me out of sight and to protect me at all times from the young mashers on the promenade." Nicolette flung back her head in laughter and whirled about the room.

Beth, removing long pins from her hat, eyed her observantly. The lass was in a singularly buoyant mood, and she had the feeling that there was more to it than her own arrival. Well, she would wait and see. In the meantime she had old dragon Radcliffe to face, and the sooner that was over the better.

"Ye'd best take me tae your grandmother right away. Then I'll know what my duties are tae be and the extent of them. I wouldna want to appear tardy the furst day."

Somewhat to her surprise the interview went off better than she had expected. Mrs. Radcliffe made it quite clear that Nicolette had been disciplined for her own good, but now the ban on morning rides could be lifted provided Beth kept a close check on route and time, and the girl allowed her former liberty under chaperonage. It meant that Beth's position in the hierarchy of domestic service had also been improved: she would take her meals with the housekeeper and not in the servants' hall, have authority over whatever carriage was needed for her charge, and her wages were to be considerably higher than those she had received at the Edinburgh household, plus an increase every six months provided all went well and there was no trouble of any kind. The money aspect was important to Beth. All her life she had saved whatever she could, having dreams, first of a home of her own one day with a husband and children, and later, when that dream appeared to be no longer viable, of getting a small shop for herself selling candy and provisions and no longer being at anyone else's beck and call. Fond as she was of Nicolette, she would make sure that her charge did nothing to jeopardize her own chance of eventual independence. That evening Nicolette set out the immediate program.

"First of all, I want you to come roller-skating with me," she said. "I must get some practice in. There's going to be a carnival night at the Pier Pavilion at the end of the week, and Hugh is organizing a party to go to it, so I don't want to be falling about on the rink all the time. You must also help me with my costume for it. I've done nothing about it, because I didn't know how long Grandmother was going to keep me in custody, and never thought she would relent so soon. Papa must have put her into a good mood by agreeing with all her plans." She had already told Beth of the conditions laid down.

In the morning the two of them set out in a wagonette for Easthampton, Nicolette holding the reins. They went first to Lawton's Emporium, where the material was chosen for Nicolette's carnival costume. She had decided to go officially as *Summer Night* in sapphire-blue satin with a swathed bustle of tulle a-shower with silver stars, but secretly she saw herself as *Sea Star* and hoped that Tom would guess the significance of the ornamentation. With a shop assistant carrying the selected materials in their wake, she and Beth went through to the dressmaking department, where in a curtained cubicle she was duly measured, and all details for the garment written down. A querulous voice sounded from the next one.

"This color don't suit me. It's drab. I want something brighter. A nice magenta or that orangy satin I saw in the window."

"This myrtle-green silk is the very latest from Paris, Mrs. Warwyck," an assistant in attendance replied.

Nicolette, a tape measure about her waist marking a satisfactory eighteen inches, stiffened slightly with a thump of the heart. Could that be Tom's mother on the other side of the curtain? As far as she knew there was no other Mrs. Warwyck in the district. Then there came a third voice, firm and persuasive, but with an undertone of authority.

"It's in perfect taste and a most elegant garment, Mrs. Warwyck. That soft shade takes away from your high coloring, and it has a slimming effect."

That seemed to settle the matter, for there was no more argument although there was some discussion over the size of a bow on the bustle. Nicolette could hardly contain her curiosity. She delayed in the cubicle as long as she could, emerging with a quick conclusion on all points as soon as she heard sounds of leaving from Mrs. Warwyck and whoever was with her.

She came almost face to face with Meg, gaining an impression of a stout, ruddy-cheeked woman of middle age freshly come from a hairdresser's ministrations, not a curl out of place under a pretty new hat. The woman with her must be the companion whom Tom had mentioned when he had talked about his home during the account of the differences he had had with his family over his aim to build boats. In spite of her hard face, Mrs. Meredith was being considerate toward Tom's mother, asking her if she would like to rest for a while over morning coffee before they continued with their shopping.

"Yes, I would. My feet are killing me in these new shoes," came the reply. As Nicolette and Beth left the dressmaking department Meg and her companion turned in the direction of the restaurant, where amid the potted palms a quartet was playing, the melodious strains of a violin drifting out to meet them.

Meg settled herself in the gilded, high-backed chair and looked about her. Most of the tables were occupied and she recognized several people. To her delight two ladies at a neighboring table inclined their heads politely and smiled, albeit a trifle distantly, but that was not important. By one of the marble pillars three more turned their heads in her direction and nodded.

"Did you see that?" Meg said in an awed voice to Constance, who had given their order to a waitress. "Five of the local nobs nodded to me first. It must be these new togs I'm wearing."

"You are looking very elegant this morning, and we are only at the start," Constance answered. "It's going to be as I promised you." But it was also going to be a long, hard struggle, she added silently to herself. Already she had done battle with Meg a dozen times, starting from the first day by getting a control that she did not intend to relinquish, the velvet glove covering the iron hand that was not going to release its grip by one iota. It had begun on the first morning by turfing Meg out of her rumpled bed by nine-thirty and, after giving her a special headache powder to ease the pain left from too much liquor the evening before, she had plunged her into a bath, scrubbing and soaping and shampooing while thinking all the time that it was like having an ill-tempered, overweight baby of appalling dimensions squalling protest and wallowing about in the lavender-scented water.

During the scenes and tantrums of that first day Constance had learned a great deal. Out it had come in an orgy of self-pity from Meg that was awash with the torment of loving a man who no longer came to the marital bed. In the early years there had been the children to keep Meg busy, but later, although she had long realized that his real love had been Lucy, his own half sister, it had come as a dreadful blow to her self-esteem to discover that he had taken other women into his life. She, who had never cared much for drink, found that if she took more than one glass it helped to deaden the jealousy that gave her no respite. Gradually a third and even a fourth glass quite calmed her down, and she no longer suffered the pangs that made her wonder how she found the strength of will to go on living. Constance was not denying her the drink she had become accustomed to, but reducing four glasses to three, sometimes two with special success, and diverting Meg with some other interest such as an outing to buy a new dress or hat to cut down the number of times drink was taken in a day. Constance discovered that she had one great advantage on her side, which was that in her heart of hearts Meg genuinely wanted to try to win back her husband to her. Meg had felt able to fight a ghost from the past, but real live women had defeated her, her own shortcomings educationally and socially handicapping her in her own eyes, vanquishing her before she could even start. Now Constance was going to change all that. So Meg hoped; a thin, sweet hope that had come when it had seemed to her that not as much as a last straw floated above her head as she drowned in her own wretchedness of spirit.

"No cream buns?" she exclaimed in disappointment when only the pot of coffee and cups were set down upon the table.

"You are going to bring your weight down," Constance reminded her, pouring the coffee black. "And no sugar either," she added, deftly removing the sugar bowl from Meg's reach. "Don't grimace. It's not genteel."

Meg swallowed her retort, crooked her little finger as she sipped her cup, and made up her mind to take a stiff drink to restore herself as soon as she got home again.

At the Pier Pavilion, Beth waited while Nicolette hired a pair of roller-skating boots in the foyer, and then went up to the spectator's gallery. Nicolette, carrying her boots, entered the rink. It was not very busy. Not more than half a dozen couples were going around the rink together, and a few people, including some children, skated individually, the rollers on their boots making a hollow rumble. Seeing no sign of Tom, she sat down on one of the chairs that encircled the arena to put on her boots. She had one laced up and was about to lace the second when suddenly there was Tom on one knee beside her foot.

"Allow me, Miss Racliffe-Stuart," he said, his eyes twinkling at her.

She gave a little gasp of surprise. "Where were you? I didn't see you when I came in."

"But I saw you from my office. It's up there." He nodded over his shoulder toward what had once been a box in the pavilion's decades as a theater, but which had been filled in, leaving a small window. Amid the gilded cherubs a W for Warwyck still ornamented the fascia. "Are you alone?"

She was reminded of Beth and glanced upward, but the overhang of the gallery was above, making it impossible for them to be seen from there. He listened while he laced her boot as she told him of Beth's coming and of the lifting of certain restrictions already. "I haven't told her about you yet," she said as he helped her to her feet, "but I shall as soon as I can be sure that she will help and not hinder us in meeting. Now I had better start skating or she'll come down looking for me."

She moved onto the rink. Although it was quite a while since she had last skated it was as if it were yesterday, and she came into the sway and rhythm of it almost immediately. In the front row of the gallery above, Beth waved to her and she waved back.

Tom watched her every movement, leaning his arms on the wooden barrier that circumferenced the wide rink, and followed her with his gaze; each time she came around again her eyes would meet his and would hold until her speed broke the contact and took her on past him.

She skated for a quarter of an hour. "I'm coming to the carnival evening," she said as Tom helped her unlace her boots again.

"Good. In the meantime, let's meet tomorrow morning early at Bambury Mill."

"I'll be there," she promised.

That evening Tom made a call at the Grange to see his mother as he had promised. He found her in the drawing room. She was far from sober, but coherent, and although indifferent toward him she seemed quite pleased to have a visitor, telling him at length about the day she had had until he realized she must be confusing the previous day with it as well, but he heard her out patiently, poured himself a madeira to drink with her, and was thankful to see her looking less slovenly, her hair quite prettily dressed.

"Your pa and I dined alone this evening," she said proudly. "Mrs. Mered-d-" The name stumbled on her tongue, and she changed it. "Constance thought it would be nice for us."

Tom had a mental picture of his parents attempting to find common ground in their talk across the dining table, his mother garrulous as she was at times, his father polite and strained. He pitied them both. "Where is Mrs. Meredith now?" he asked, for something to say.

She looked vaguely about, trying to remember. "Downstairs, I think. Yes, that's it. You'll probably meet her on your way out." Her gaze came to rest on his cravat. "Why aren't you properly dressed when you come to see your mother? You know I can't abide that check cravat. It's vulgar. Not what a gentleman would wear. You'd never see your father in one like that."

"It's new. You haven't seen this one before."

She frowned, all the old irritation with him gathering itself together. "You've money to fritter away, have you? Earn tuppence and spend thruppence. You'll never make anything of yourself in life with that policy."

It was time for him to go. She was about to begin one of her old tirades against him, all her good humor dispersing. He made to take his leave. "I'll be getting along."

"You can pour me another drink before you go."

He was not sure what new rules had been laid down, and at his almost imperceptible hesitation her face congested and, reaching out, she snatched at the neck of the decanter herself.

"Don't bother," she snarled sarcastically. "I know that doing anything for me is always too much trouble." She refilled her own glass, ignored his good-night, and did not look up as he went from the room.

He did meet Constance on his way out. He saw her for a few revealing seconds before she noticed him coming down the curve of the staircase. She had just closed the door of his father's study and she leaned against it for a moment or two, a curious expression of satisfaction and excitement upon her face. Then she took a couple of leisurely steps that brought her level with one of the pier glasses on the wall, where she smiled enigmatically at her own reflection, touching her hair with spread fingers of feminine affectation and not through any need to tidy it. Her lashes flickered as she sighted him in the mirror, and instantly her expression became composed, almost bland. Tom felt his initial dislike of her harden within him.

"Good evening, Tom." From the first evening his youth and her elevated position had eliminated her use of any prefix to his name. "You have been to see your mother, I suppose. I hope you did not upset her." Conscious of having been caught at a slight disadvantage, she was turning to attack before defense.

"Yes, I did." He made no excuses and gave no reason, merely answering her question.

She showed an exaggerated display of concern. "Oh, dear. That's the last thing we want now. I never thought I should get through her hostility during those first few days, and although I must expect setbacks I don't want those that can be avoided."

He made no comment. "Good night, Mrs. Meredith."

She looked after him out of the corner of her eye as he went out of the house, always able to tell when someone did not like her. She had had plenty of experience in facing enmity in one form or another. Well, what Tom thought about her did not matter. She had only to get Meg completely dependent upon her, and then she would be more in control of this house and this family than anyone else could ever imagine. Already she had the goodwill of Donna, Jeremy, and—most important of all—Richard.

Richard. As she went up the stairs in the direction of the drawing room she let her thoughts dwell almost sensuously on the half hour she had spent in his study. She knew he was beginning to look forward to her daily reports, which were fast becoming a bright session for him in the routine of life at the Grange. Like all men who had devoted their lives to business, he was quickly bored by too much leisure on his hands, and she was intent on providing the diversion he needed. He was an extremely interesting man, a trifle serious, almost solemn at times, and she counted it a triumph when she could make him smile and even laugh. Yet she was watching her every step in that direction. Nothing must be rushed. At the present time she was keeping securely within her role as companion to his wife, treating him with the outward respect that befitted his position as her employer, while at the same time revealing in little snatched glimpses the other woman beneath the façade, the woman whom with time he would want to know and discover for himself. Never had she played a game with more skill and care than this one in the Warwyck household.

It began to rain as Tom drove back to Easthampton House. In the morning the gray downpour continued, a rough wind adding to the discomfort of the day, and although he rode as arranged to Bambury Mill he wondered whether Nicolette would be allowed to venture forth in such weather. But she came. Riding up the hill from the woods, the raindrops dancing off the hard top of her hat, a cape about her soaked to darkness upon her shoulders and into soggy folds around her skirt. Already dismounted, he ran to seize her by the waist and pull her down to him. They kissed, clinging to each other, heedless of the rain, and then he hastened her with him into the inadequate shelter of the recessed doorway of the old mill, where they kissed again until, breathless, she leaned back from him against the ancient door. Her lovely face was dewy with raindrops, and her hair wet beneath the brim of her hat. He saw that she was shivering.

"Are you cold?" he asked with concern, moving close again to protect her as best he could from the relentless rain.

"A little," she answered in an understatement, and ran a gloved hand over the blackened oak of the door. "Is there no way into this old place?"

He had already investigated. "It would take a battering-ram to get through that lock on the outside, but I think I can get through one of the windows and open it from the inside." Stepping out of the doorway, he looked up. All the windows were high up, but if he climbed one of the sails, which had been braked long ago into a stationary position, he could reach a first-floor aperture where the panes were broken, as they were in most of the other windows.

She was alarmed, coming to peer upward with him. "Those sails don't look safe. Lots of the struts are cracked."

"They'll take my weight." He used his horse to get high enough to grab a sail and manage a foothold, Nicolette holding the bridle. Then he was climbing upward, the wind whirling his coattails and tearing at his hair, the rain beating on his head and trickling down his collar. It was more difficult than he had anticipated, the sails having more play on them in the buffeting wind than was apparent from the ground, but he had climbed enough masts in his time to know what he was doing, and he tested each strut before putting his weight on it.

Watching him, Nicolette became aware of the size and width of the sails, which was not easy to appreciate from below until someone like Tom was crazy enough to climb them. She wished she had stopped him, but it was too late for that now, and she did not dare to call out for fear that she would break his concentration. There! He was reaching for the window and it was just out of his reach. She held her breath, saw him secure another hold and swing himself out again. This time he was able to get a hand inside a broken pane to the latch, and seconds later he was pulling the window open. She saw him clamber from the sail through the window and vanish inside. Several moments later, her ear to the oaken panels, she heard him prizing away with something metallic at the lock within. She huddled close, eager to get inside into the dry, and when the lock broke with a clang she was poised in readiness as he swung the door wide.

"Come in, dear young lady," he invited in a stage villain's voice, grinning broadly as he twirled the imaginary end of a moustachio in the best traditions of melodrama.

"Thank you, kind sir." She skipped in, laughing. A musty smell of corn and flour and straw pervaded the air, and the mealy dust billowed up about her feet. She looked about her excitedly. They had found a sanctuary where they could be together and no one would find them. "Let's explore, Tom," she implored eagerly, throwing off her wet cape.

He hung it on a nail for her and she added her hat while he stripped off his own wet coat. Hand in hand they scampered up the wooden flights of steps that linked the floors, their footsteps echoing hollowly, and the boards creaked as they inspected the silent machinery, she exclaiming in awe at the sight of great millstones. He would have liked to set the old sails rotating, and had it not been for the certainty that someone would spy them going around and come to investigate, he would have done it. Nevertheless he teased her with the threat of it, gripping the old lever through its coating of cobwebs and pretending to exert his strength while she became more and more agitated.

"No, Tom! Bambury Mill can be seen for miles around! Somebody would come! Think what that would mean!"

He was enjoying himself. Her pretty, flustered state excited him, and she had her arms looped about his neck from behind, trying to pull him away. Turning his head over his shoulder, he looked with amusement into her anxious face. "What will you give me not to set the sails turning?"

Then she knew he was teasing her, the pucker vanishing from her brow as she withdrew her arms until only her fingertips rested on his shoulders. "A kiss," she offered, sharing his amusement and yet shy with it.

He held his breath for a second. "Not enough," he said, low-voiced and bold, his eyes looking hard into hers.

Her color flowed, but she gave him back as good as he had given. "Turn the sails then," she challenged, throwing up her hands carelessly, "but I'll not stay to watch them. Good day to you, sir."

She darted away and he after her. There followed a hilarious chase around the empty bins and the sacks of moldy corn, up and down the steps and around the wheels until eventually he caught her, bringing her tumbling down with him onto some piled straw. Then the laughter melted from them and they saw only each other's eyes, warm and glowing, conveying so much that neither had yet put into words. Her riding jacket was wide-revered to reveal a waistcoat and high-collared shirt of pleated silk, and when he slid his hand under the waistcoat's satin lining to come upon her breast, the silk rippled against his palm like tiny waves, dividing him from the firm young flesh beneath. Whether she would have pulled away from him then he was never to know, for barely had he touched her when she sat bolt upright, looking above him, her face transfixed between terror and aversion as she screamed out.

"Look! Oh, look!"

It was a rat, large and gray, scuttling along a beam only a few feet overhead. In the same instant there was a rustling in the straw nearby, and over by the moldy corn sacks another showed itself, the long tail slewing behind it. She was already on her feet, white-faced and panic-stricken, and she bolted for the steps leading to the ground floor, beating at her skirts as if she feared one of the loathsome rodents might be clinging to it. He threw himself after her, desperately afraid that she might lose her footing on the steep flight in her panic, but she reached the ground safely and rushed to wrench open the heavy door without a glance behind her.

"Wait!"

She did not or would not hear him. He snatched their outdoor garments from the nail and ran out after her. He caught her up before she reached their tethered horses and pulled her into the comfort of his arms. She was sobbing, her head bowed against him.

"Those horrible rats! They were all around us!"

"I should have known there would have been the odd one lurking there, but I would never have expected to find it overrun."

"Why didn't they show themselves before?"

"They were probably scared by the noise we were making as we chased around, and came out as soon as it was quieter."

A violent shudder went through her, making her catch her breath. "I've never been more frightened in all my life. I thought that big rat was going to jump down on us." She raised her wet, dilated eyes to his. "I can never set foot in there again, Tom. The mill cannot be our meeting place."

"I know that now," he said gently, putting her cape about her shoulders and fastening it for her. "Somehow and somewhere we'll find another place."

She nodded, putting on her hat, and he helped her back into the saddle. If there had been no risk of their being observed he would have ridden away with her, but he had to let her go alone. She was still weeping. He knew it was as much for the loss of their promising hideaway as it was the aftermath of the fright she had received. The dismal curtain of rain soon closed off his sight of her as she rode off through the woods.

Chapter 10

Daniel finished reading the two letters that had come with the afternoon post. The first had been a charming letter from Helen Edenfield, accepting his hospitality until she was able to find a suitable seaside residence for herself and her sister, and the other letter made him look grave as he folded it away again, leaning back in his chair. His daughter, Lucy, was coming to see him; one of those quick, dutiful visits that caused pain to them both. She kept up a pretense that his increasing withdrawal from her caused her no anguish, but he knew otherwise. How could he not, when there was a deep and natural bond between them that was somehow stronger than with Donna, offspring of his lawful wife. Why did it happen that a man could feel more for his by-blow, begotten out of fornication and lust, than for the daughter born of the woman whom he had adored passionately beyond all reason? Was there no measure to the quirks of human nature?

He stirred restlessly, unease settling upon him as it always did when a single thought of his dearest Kate slipped past the barriers he had put up against her in his mind. His loss was as raw this day as it had been in the blackest moment in his life, when she had gone from him forever while he still held her in his arms. He passed a shaking hand over his forehead, recognizing the symptoms of his own personal torture that no effort of concentration and strength of will was going to keep back on this occasion. In days gone by he had managed it most of the time, but with the passing of the years it became more and more difficult, and the simple explanation was that to those of his age the days that were gone long since were more easily recalled than what had happened yesterday. He steeled himself, feeling the darkness descend, seeping through his brain into the very core of his being and taking him down with it into an abyss of wretchedness, all brought about inadvertently by the letter from Lucy with its consequential news of her family affairs and the announcement that she was coming to see him.

He got out of his chair, taking his stick, which he resented but which had become necessary most of the time, and Barley, who had been lying at his feet, sprang up in tail-wagging excitement. "Yes, boy," he said as if the dog had spoken. "We're going for a walk."

He used no leash for Barley. The dog was intelligent and well trained, and after an initial prancing about down the length of the drive it settled to a happy trot at Daniel's heels. They did not go along the promenade, which was usual, Daniel always liking to view both the full width of the bay and the resort in its daily pattern of color and weather; instead he took the shortcut that his grandson followed to the Tudor barn, taking first the narrow side streets, and afterward the lane that led to the five-barred gate opening into the meadow where the barn stood. Beyond the distant copse of trees and the foliage of the old orchard was Honeybridge House, and Daniel deliberately set his eyes away from its direction, concentrating on opening the gate, which set Barley bounding through in a wild search for rabbits or anything else that was chaseable in the tall grass a-shimmer with meadow-sweet, blossoming nettles, the spears of sorrel and pink willow herb.

A track was worn from the gate to the barn, the old ruts made from the wheels of wagons that had borne the loads of slates and bricks from the time when the seam in the brickfield had still run rich and deep. More recent indentations showed where the timber for Tom's boat had been hauled in across the earth that had been made moist by rain, already hard in the return of the July sun. The doors of the barn were open, and Daniel made for them. While swallows, nesting in the rafters, swooped in and out of the barn over his head, he took a step or two across the threshold, amazed to see the interior completely cleared of rubbish, measured chalk marks showing the place where the building board for the yacht was to be set up. The atmosphere was quite aromatic; the sound smell of good, seasoned timber came from the stacked supplies at the far end of the barn, where his grandson and Hab Burns were in deep discussion, the latter taking a pencil from behind one ear to check off a list they were studying between them. They probably would not have noticed Daniel for several minutes if Barley had not raced down the length of the barn with ears and tail flying, to greet Tom exuberantly. Not for the first time Daniel wondered if Barley recognized some likeness between the young Warwyck and the old one, for Barley never shared such a greeting, reserved for his master, with anyone else except Tom.

"Hello, Barley! Where have you come from?" Tom crouched down to rough-handle the dog affectionately and then looked toward the doorway. "I'm pleased to see you here, Grandfather. It looks different now, doesn't it? Hab has done a fine job in clearing the decks."

"G'day, Sir Daniel." Hab stuck the pencil back behind his ear. "Weren't 'alf a lot of junk to chuck out, I can tell you."

"I'm sure there was," Daniel remarked a trifle drily. He did not doubt that Hab had found a market for whatever could be disposed of without questions being asked.

If Hab noticed the dryness in Daniel's tone he made no sign, merely ducking his head amiably in acknowledgment of what he outwardly took to be praise. Baptized Albert after the Queen's late consort thirty-five years ago, his name was abbreviated to Hab before the celebratory booze-up in his father's fisherman's cottage was over, and he had been called by it ever since. He had small, dark eyes, but they were very bright and twinkling, not unlike jet beads set in his rugged face, and beneath the surface there was always a look of devilment as if he were never far from laughter at himself and others, except in a rage or in his cups, when those who knew him gave him a wide berth. Straw-haired, a heavy-shouldered man of average height, he had little to commend him visually beyond his fine physique, but women found him attractive and he had never married, saying that he had no need when he could have the pick of the barrel whenever it suited him. Not, Daniel thought, the ideal company for his grandson, but as a hard worker Hab was beyond reproach.

"Let me show you around," Tom said to his grandfather. "You couldn't have come at a better time to see how we have planned everything. There's another load of timber to come yet, and a host of other materials, but at least I can show you the layout."

As the two Warwycks began to amble from point to point in the barn, Hab noticed a scrap of slate on the flagstones that had previously escaped his eye, from a pile he had moved out. He picked it up, moving to the open doors to chuck it out into the meadow grass, much as if tossing a pebble on the surface of the sea, his gait lively in spite of being somewhat uneven on his peg leg, for he used no crutch except when the ground was icy in winter or conditions otherwise unfavorable. It meant that he suffered more falls than he would have done with a prop under his arm, but he hated the encumbrance as much as Daniel detested his stick, and took his chance. It was the small, unexpected hazards like the overlooked slate fragment that could topple him, which was why he had been quick to get rid of it.

It had been more than missing a leg that had lost him his employment at several boatyards; sometimes it had been through fighting with his fellow workers; once he had blacked a foreman's eye; there were also times when he had thought it provident to leave before missing materials had to be accounted for, being one of those who believed that anything that belonged to the rich should be shared out with the poor, although his definition of *the poor* was simply himself when his pockets were empty. He knew that at the present time Tom did not have two pennies to rub together, everything going into materials for *Sea Star*, but in any case he earned enough from fishing to carry him through the summer, so he was looking upon Tom's venture from a long-term angle. If Tom made a success of it there would be plenty of rich perks for himself as well as steady wages as a foreman, because there was an unspoken agreement on that point. In return Tom would receive all the skill and mastery that he had in his brain and his fingertips with regard to boatbuilding, for it was impossible for him not to take a pride in his work, because he loved boats and everything to do with them, and it would be no fault of his if *Sea Star* did not turn out to be the finest little yacht afloat. He looked across at the two Warwycks. Sir Daniels was a wily old fellow and had been on to him about what he had sold to his advantage out of the old stores in the barn, even a rag-and-bone man shelling out for the last of the rubbish. No doubt young Tom had also guessed, because the two of them were as alike as two peas in a pod in spite of the span of sixty-odd years between them, and would not begrudge him his meager reward for all the hard work involved in shifting the stuff. The Warwycks had never been tightfisted. They would have value for money, but they could be generous when it was needful.

"How is it that you're able to be here at this time of day?" Daniel inquired of his grandson as they moved on after he had been shown the steaming box in working order and where the drawings were to be spread out. "Should you not be on the Pier?"

"I'm well organized. Mr. Beckworth knows I put in far more hours at the roller-skating rink than anybody else would, because I haven't taken a day off yet, as you know. So he's agreeable about my being absent for an hour or two when I need the time, provided he is on the Pier to cover any emergency while I'm away, and vice versa. I combined the ordering of the timber at Merrelton with a check on the publicity I have organized for the first Grand Carnival evening."

"When is it to be?"

"Next Saturday." And Nicolette will be there, Tom added to himself. He had not seen her since they had parted by the old mill, although she had written to him and he had read and reread this letter, keeping it in his inside pocket with the first one that she had penned to him. He kept wondering if the realization had come to her after her fright and distress had finally subsided that he had dared to touch her more intimately than ever before, chaste enough though the caress had been, there being such a hasty end to it, because it struck him that there was a hint of wariness in her letter, a kind of uncertainty as if something had happened to portend a change in their relationship and she was left in limbo, not sure about going forward, and yet finding it impossible to turn back. He longed to reassure her.

Daniel broke into his thoughts. "Saturday, eh? That's the day your Aunt Lucy comes to stay at Easthampton House."

"Is she staying long?"

"No, only until Monday morning."

"What about Uncle Josh? Isn't he coming with her?"

"He's abroad on railway business. I imagine she is doing a round of visits while he's away. With all the traveling he does, her husband likes to stay at home when he is there. I don't blame him. There's no place like it."

The tour of the barn came to an end after an inspection of some of the timber, Daniel having a special knowledge of the quality of various woods from his property-building days. Before leaving the barn he swung his stick and made a sweeping gesture with it to encompass the entire site.

"Are you going to invite your father to come along and take a look as your boat begins to take shape here?"

"I think it would be salt in the wound," Tom replied thoughtfully.

"It may be, but he'll not hold that against you. I know Richard. With all his faults he's a fair-minded man and, having given you the chance to mold your own future, he would appreciate being invited to view *Sea Star* in all its stages. It would not go amiss to show him around now as you have shown me. He wouldn't recognize the old barn, never having seen it in this pristine state. By the time he was born I had been using it as a warehouse for many years."

"He's welcome to come any time."

"Good." Daniel looked pleased and he clapped a hand on his

grandson's shoulder. "Tell him that, boy. You and your father have been at loggerheads for too many years. It's high time things were changed for the better."

"Yes, sir," Tom replied without optimism. He had no illusions. His father had not given in before his determination not to go into the Warwyck business empire, only stepped aside temporarily. The promise extracted from him at the close of their discussion together about his future had revealed that. Richard was biding his time. One failure, one setback, and then pressure would be brought to bear again.

Tom walked his grandfather to the five-barred gate and called to Barley, who had been trying in vain to find the piece of slate that Hab had tossed into the grass, no doubt imagining it to have been cast out for a game of retrievement. Giving up the search, Barley sprang after his master, and the two of them went through the gate together. Tom noticed that Daniel did not as much as glance in the direction of Honeybridge, and it was said that he had not set foot in Hoe Lane or been near the house since Kate's death way back in the past.

Back at Easthampton House, Daniel found tea about to be served in the Green Drawing Room, where Donna, in the company of a visitor, was awaiting his return. It was Constance Meredith, whom he had met several times, for Donna encouraged her to come there whenever she had a little time off duty, not wanting the woman to be lonely. For himself, he neither liked nor disliked the widow, merely hoping that she would be of some benefit to Meg, which—according to all accounts that he had heard from Donna and from Richard—she was managing promisingly so far. He greeted her, inquired conventionally after her health, and seated himself.

He contributed nothing to the conversation during tea, allowing his daughter and Constance to talk uninterrupted, for he had not read the latest novel they were discussing, and had not the least interest in whether bustles would become even more pronounced in the autumn. He had decided that when the widow left for the Grange again he would tell Donna about Lucy's coming, and in the meantime he was content to enjoy the scones with new-made strawberry jam and a slice of plum cake. Pleasures, he thought laconically, became much reduced with age.

"Don't you think that would be a good idea, Papa?"

He looked at his daughter blankly. That damned deafness in his ear combined with a lack of attention had made him miss whatever remark had been made previously. If he had got in a heavier punch to that opponent in the prize ring all those years ago, smashed home more decisively to the fellow's ribs, he would have avoided the right and left to his own head, which had dealt him the damage to an eardrum. Many a time he had refought that fight within the rounds of memory, and little good it did him; here he was, caught out just as neatly in another realm.

"Hmm? Er—" It went against the fierceness of his pride to admit to not having heard.

Donna rescued him. "Perhaps I should put it another way. Meg must be encouraged to widen her interests in all directions and be shown that she can mix socially again. She had a bad day yesterday, Constance told me earlier, but we cannot hope for miracles, and this is something we must expect from time to time. I have suggested—and Constance agrees with me—that you and I should invite Meg and Richard to dine with us one evening. As a matter of fact, next Saturday would fit in very well with my arrangements. It would be Meg's first step back into circulation, and we can cushion it for her in surroundings that are familiar to her. What do you say?"

"I'm agreeable to an invitation being extended," he replied carefully, "but whether Saturday would be the best evening is another matter. I have not had the chance to tell you yet that I heard from Lucy today. She plans to visit us at the weekend."

Donna held her breath for a second, momentarily taken aback. She had felt it necessary, unbeknown to her father, to explain Lucy's delicate position in the family circle to Constance, only to discover that Meg had already blurted it out to her in a violent, drunken mood together with confessions and recriminations that had made Donna thankful that she could trust Constance to keep it all to herself. However, it did not seem right to let Daniel know that a hired companion was in possession of the facts of a matter that was not even discussed among themselves, a skeleton in the cupboard that, for Richard's sake more than for Daniel's, Donna never wanted to rattle.

"In that case—" Donna began.

Constance interrupted quickly. "I'm aware that Mrs. Warwyck, for some reason known only to herself, does not care very much for Mrs. Lucy Barton"—the lie to cover her own knowledge from Daniel came smoothly off her tongue, accompanied by an apologetic sideways glance for it in Donna's direction—"and this, I think, makes Saturday such a good choice. The dinner party will be extended to include someone a little outside Mrs. Warwyck's circle, and she will have to exert herself to be on her best possible behavior more than might otherwise be expected of her."

Donna nodded, trying to keep back an unbidden observation on how easily deceit in small matters came to Constance. "I agree with that. What do you think, Papa?"

"Very well. Write the invitation and let Mrs. Meredith take it back to the Grange with her. Make sure that Meg knows we are ready to welcome her."

Constance delivered the invitation into Meg's hands. It was read and hurled aside. "I'm not going there to sit at the same table with that Lucy Barton! It's an insult! A damned insult." Meg's face was crimson with outrage.

Constance went on quietly tidying up some ladies' magazines that Meg had left scattered about. "If you don't go, I shall leave. My month's trial is up tomorrow, or have you forgotten?"

Meg banged down the glass she was drinking from and sprang up from her chair in agitation. "You can't leave! I won't let you!" She reeled unsteadily and would have fallen if she had not grabbed hold of Constance's arm. "I haven't begun to do half the things you promised I should do—visit London and hold a ball and everything else."

Constance turned her face to avoid Meg's brandy-laden breath and carefully disengaged the gripping hold of the plump fingers. "None of that can be achieved in one month, especially when we remember how often you have disobeyed me, taking drinks behind my back and pretending that someone else had been at the decanter."

Meg's lower lip trembled moistly, and her face crinkled with self-pity. "I couldn't help it. I've been under a great strain, going shopping and being seen by people and all that. My nerves couldn't have withstood it all otherwise. You don't know what an ordeal it has been for me." She put the heel of her hand against her bowed forehead quite unconsciously in the classic pose of despair and abjection. "I have tried. God knows I've tried."

Yes, she had, Constance thought. Meg's yearning to win her husband back to her ran deeper and stronger than anyone else, even Richard himself, could possibly suspect. Without that yearning Constance knew she would have stood little chance of doing anything with the woman in her charge, and once again she determined to use that knowledge to make Meg conform to her will.

"And now you are going to give in," she taunted crisply. "As soon as the chance comes to show Mr. Warwyck you can behave with grace and dignity in the presence of his half sister, whom he knows you dislike and about whom you have never ceased to plague him, you are going to back down and make yourself conspicuous by your absence. You realize what your folly means, don't you? Once again he will be free to admire whatever it is he does admire in Mrs. Lucy Barton, and you will not be there to counteract it in any way. Can you wonder that I have lost patience with you and have decided to hand in my notice without delay?"

"No!" Meg gave a great wail and flung herself down onto her knees at Constance's feet, clutching at her skirts. "If you go, all that I've gained will be lost again. Richard has spent more time with me since you came than he has done for years. But don't ask me to go to Easthampton House, because I can't. Don't you see? I can't endure to look upon them together and know that he still loves her." She gave herself up to noisy, sniffling sobs, her head bent to her knees as she groveled before Constance, who looked down on her completely without pity, her face hard with distaste.

"How stupid you are. He doesn't still love her. I know men. True and everlasting devotion is something completely alien to the male sex."

Meg raised her tear-blotched face, irritated by the gibe, and tetchy with it. "You don't know nothing about the Warwyck men or you wouldn't say that," she snapped. "Look at my father-in-law, for example. He hasn't had his wife's name mentioned in that house of his since she died—all because he can't get over his grief at losing her."

Constance was unimpressed. "Fiddlesticks. He wasn't faithful to her, was he? Lucy Barton is living proof of that. More like a guilty conscience if you ask me."

Meg sat back on her heels, wagging her head from side to side in a reluctance to accept the argument, while not denying the possible truth of it. "That's as may be, but I don't think his conscience would trouble him that much. After all, he had over twenty years married to Kate Warwyck after Lucy's mother was dead and gone. He didn't sulk around in them days." A wistfulness revealed itself in her eyes, showing that she wanted to set her hopes on what Constance's emphatic statement meant to her, and yet not daring to. "What makes you think that Richard or any other Warwyck might not be as snared in the past as they seem to be?"

"For the reason that I stated before, which is that I know men for what they're worth. I'm not denying that possibly your husband does harbor a sentimental attachment for his half sister, but, believe me, that's all it can be after this length of time. Has he ever told you that it's more than that?"

Meg's mouth became thin-lipped with bitterness. "His precious Lucy was always too special to discuss with me. He would never let me bring it out into the open. Always shut up like a clam whenever I tried."

"I'm still convinced that you have nothing to worry about there." Brutally Constance rammed home the real issue. "You're only afraid of Lucy Barton because she represents all the other women your husband has fancied in his time. Unless you face up to her you'll never stand a chance of winning him away from the rest of them."

Meg flung her arms over her head and rocked violently in her misery. "I can't! I can't! What's the good? I thought when I married Richard that I could make him forget Lucy, and I failed good and proper. Why should it be any better now?" Swinging herself about, she crawled a couple of paces on her knees to snatch down the glass from the table where she had left it, spilling some of the contents, and she downed what remained in a single gulp.

Constance watched her, letting the magazines she had collected up slide back from her clasp onto the floor in an untidy mass about her feet. "Then I'm leaving tomorrow. Your husband shall have my notice as from this very minute. I can't help you when you refuse my counsel and insist on going your own headstrong way." She picked a path over the scattered pile of journals, making for the door.

"No! No!" Meg scrambled up and went down again as her foot slipped on one of the magazines, landing with a thump, but she did not seem to notice, intent only on getting up again as fast as she could to stop Constance before she could leave the room. "Don't desert me now! If you do, nobody else will ever lift a finger to help me again."

Constance, who had opened the door a gap, held it against Meg's pressure to close it again, looking at her with narrowed eyes. "Your spinelessness is sickening. Somehow or other you secured for yourself a husband who must have always had a full choice of women, and yet you have chosen to give in and go under instead of fighting to keep alive whatever it was he first saw in you."

"You don't know what it's been like all these years! Always that shut-in, shut-away look in his eyes. I haven't known how to bear it."

"Well, somehow or other you must find the strength to go on bearing it, because that's how it will be now for the rest of your days. Goodbye, Meg." Constance jerked the door open wide to get through.

Meg let out an agonizing shriek. "Stop! Wait! I'll go to that cursed dinner party! I'll do anything you say! Only don't go. For mercy's sake just don't go."

Constance's eyes gleamed. The little crisis was over and she had gained the upper hand. It had all happened exactly as she had planned since she had first entered the Grange. From now on she would be able to use the thumbscrews whenever it suited her. If Meg could not do without her, then neither could anyone else in the house. Maliciously and with relish she gave Meg moments of agonized suspense. "I don't know." She bit her lip and shook her head hesitantly. "How can I be sure that you won't back out at the last minute, either on Saturday evening or any other time when I have advised you in your best interests?"

"I'll always do whatever you say. I swear it! Just so long as I know you're there to give me the support that I need!" Meg was frantic, her eyes unfocused with panic. "I'll give you anything you want. You can have the pick of my jewel case and my furs—my new sable cape is yours! The one you admired when you saw it in the winter wardrobe! Only stay!"

Constance swallowed a gasp of avaricious delight. Better and better. She had looked for some reward and had mentally selected a diamond brooch of value that Meg never wore, but the cape was something she had always longed to own and never imagined would ever come her way. Carefully she made a show of virtuous affront. "I happen to value being of help in this world far higher than any mercenary return for it. The offer of furs or anything else could never sway me."

"I know, dear Constance, I know," Meg shrieked. She had completely forgotten her first impression of her companion, not having been sober at the time, but if she had remembered, it would have made her less vulnerable to the hold that was closing in upon her. "I only want to show you what it'll mean to me if you stay. I've never worn it out anywhere—there was never anywhere I wanted to go in it—and although Richard paid for it, he can't stop me giving it to you, because it's mine to do with as I please." The suspense proved too much for her and she clasped her hands together in supplication. "Don't be angry with me—and stay."

Constance pursed her lips thoughtfully and then gave a slow, slightly reluctant nod. "Very well. I'll stay for as long as it takes you to win your husband back to you again, because after that you will have no need of anyone else." And that will never be, she added pithily to herself, for she had observed Richard carefully whenever he was in his wife's company and could tell that nothing would ever bring back the desires of his youth in that direction. Meg had seen the truth of it in his eyes and had not recognized the bleakness for what it was: physical revulsion.

"Thank you! Oh, thank you." Meg was bubbling over with joyous relief, and Constance suffered a tear-wet cheek pressed against hers in gratitude. "You'll never regret it. Never. No matter what you say, you shall have my cape. I'll fetch it." She went stumbling off, catching at a chair here and there for support on the way out of the room. Constance, triumphant and gleeful, managed to keep a calm demeanor as she followed her.

When the hour came for Constance to present herself in Richard's study for her daily report on her duties and how Meg had been that day, he stood on the terrace beyond the glass doors opening out from his study, finishing a cigar in the quiet evening air. He was experiencing the usual anticipatory sharpening of his senses at her coming, which was not unpleasurable, but which was unwise; never before had he found himself attracted to another woman in such home circumstances, and it confounded his ethics on the matter. Had he had a current mistress elsewhere to divert his needs it would have been different, but he had tired of a certain lady in London before adjourning to Easthampton for the summer, and had thought to spend the time at the Grange in resigned celibacy, a state of affairs that rested uneasily upon one of a deeply sensual nature. Out of consideration for Meg, who would have had to face the resulting gossip, always rife in the resort, he had never dallied locally and did not intend to start, all of which was combining to make him more keenly aware of Constance Meredith's physical attributes than he might otherwise have been. The attraction was mutual, he harbored no doubts about that; the respectful air of employee toward employer which she adopted during their evening hour together was a cloak that was thin in places, and he knew full well that each smile breaking through her reserve, each unexpected sparkling glance, each soft laugh, and all the rest of her little tricks, were as deliberate and as well planned as if she had worked them all out on paper before coming into his presence. Yet she did it cleverly, and he gave her credit for that, not decrying a sharpness of wits in a woman. Constance Meredith knew her way about the world in spite of the hard times that had befallen her in recent years, and she had the liquid eyes in that thin-boned face of hers that had stamped the sexually knowledgeable woman down through the centuries. In more desperate circumstances those same eyes gazed out from street corners as they had done from time immemorial.

Meditatively he stubbed out the butt of his cigar in an ashtray on a terrace table. He considered it ill-mannered to smoke in the presence of ladies, and although Constance did not come into that category he was not one to make social distinctions where courtesy was concerned. The month's trial was up, and he would hear this evening whether or not she would be staying on. Without doubt she had by some means of her own brought about a slight change for the better in Meg; at the present time it was little more than a new cleanliness and neatness of appearance plus some minor outings of little importance with no other people involved, and he was thankful even for that small improvement. Whether it could ever be anything more than that he did not know, the bad days and the lapses outnumbering those that Constance had classed as good ones, but he hoped for Meg's sake that she would stay on to maintain the fraction that had been achieved. Long before Lucy had come into his life, when he had been little more than a schoolboy with no thought in his head of ever marrying the fisher-girl who gave herself to him so freely in a beach hut, in long grass, under a bower of roses, as well as other places that he had long since forgotten, he had found Meg's pungent young animal warmth a sexual intoxication that had been beyond all limits. Never had he imagined, in the fondness he had had for her at the time, that what had once been charming disarray could become slatternliness over the years, or that the habit of a sea-water dip instead of a tin bath in a cottage kitchen could deteriorate into a lazy disinclination to bathe at all.

The sound of footsteps in the study made him turn. Constance had come into the room without his hearing her, and although she had already sighted him on the terrace beyond the open doors, she did not come forward to join him and sit out there as she had done on other occasions when the evening weather had permitted. He saw with some surprise that she was carrying his wife's sable cape, her expression anxious and distressed, and he had the extraordinary feeling of looking in upon a small, lighted stage from the dusk outside, Constance a lone figure and tall in her wine-colored gown, the fur holding a sheen in the gaslight. It went through his mind that Meg had slashed the cape in one of her tantrums, although why she should pick on her furs at this season of the year seemed beyond explanation.

"What are you doing with Meg's cape?" he inquired, taking a step or two forward into the rectangle of light falling out upon the terrace. She did not answer him, letting the cape slide quickly from her arm into both hands, and she clutched it to her, its softness nestling her chin, the rich folds flowing against her, while apprehension continued to show on her features. He became convinced that Meg had done some damage to the expensive fur and Constance was blaming herself for it. He sought to reassure her. "I can see you are upset. Come out onto the terrace and sit down. Whatever has happened there is no need for you to be afraid to tell me."

It was not the first time he had to give comfort after she had had some traumatic experience with Meg, whose behavior was always unpredictable during a drunken spate. Usually his calm words had an immediate effect, but this evening, in spite of coming with slow steps out onto the terrace, she remained taut and bolt-straight, shaking her head as if she found the words of what she should say impossible to form. He took hold of her arm above the elbow, both to guide her to the nearest basket chair on the terrace and to give further reassurance. It was a mistake. In her distress she swayed against him, and almost of its own volition his other arm went up to support her, even though he was certain that her swaying had not been accidental. A tremor went through her and he was intensely aware of it, the scent of her filling his nostrils, but at once she moved quickly away from him to seat herself, the sweep of the sable cape coming to rest on the chair arm and over her lap.

"I'm giving you my notice," she said throatily, her voice choked. "I must go tomorrow."

He swung another basket chair forward and set it beside her, where he promptly sat down, leaning forward with elbows on his knees to try to peer into the downward tilt of her face. "What has happened? Until I know what has occurred I cannot accept your decision to depart. Has Meg taken scissors to this sable cape? It would not be the first time she has destroyed something of value in an alcoholic rage, so hold nothing back."

She raised her head sharply in surprise. "No, it's not that. In fact, I truly see it as something much worse. Mrs. Warwyck wants me to stay—she has begged me to stay, and when I agreed to carry on if she promised to cooperate, a simple ploy to make her set more store by my advice, she insisted on presenting her sable cape to me." Her hands spread wide in an uncharacteristic gesture of helplessness and indecision. "I cannot accept it, and a rejection of it, which I made immediately, brought her to such a state of hysteria that she could show me no kindness in her turn, that I was forced to an acceptance of the gift simply to bring her to her senses."

He sat back against the cushions of the chair, the basketwork creaking. Inwardly he was wryly amused, his face giving nothing away. He would wager his last shilling that Constance would sell her soul for such a cape, and the artful manner in which she had got around to admitting to an acceptance of it only confirmed his defined opinion of her. He noticed that her fingers were playing sensuously with the fur, running into its softness, and guessed how desperately important the next few minutes were going to be for her. By what he said she would rise or fall, possession of the sable cape depending entirely upon his whim.

"How has this unlooked-for generosity in my wife necessitated your leaving?" he asked levelly, playing along with her game.

"Surely you must see why," she exclaimed. "If her gift had been a bottle of scent or a silk scarf or some such item all would have been well, but a costly cape puts my staying out of the question. It must have cost hundreds of pounds."

"It did," he remarked laconically.

"There! You see!" She sprang up restlessly and took a few swift paces along the terrace, taking the cape with her, an involuntary action that spoke to him of a very real fear of losing it.

"I have always heard that the value of a gift did not matter, it being the thought behind it that counts," he said, watching her closely.

She spun about to face him, a flow of silk from the bustled drapery of her gown swishing the flagstones. "That is said when the giver presents little more than a token—not a gift like this one!" Again she clutched the fur to her.

"In my opinion it is an adage that can work either way." He rose to his feet without haste. "Take the cape. It's yours. Meg has given it to you. Count it as a bonus for the unpleasant tasks you have to perform for her, and let us hear no more of a handing in of your notice."

Her mouth dropped in a little gape. He could tell that she was overwhelmed by obtaining what she wanted with such ease. So keenly was he observing her that he caught the exultant flash in her eyes before she hastily dropped her lids, looking down at the fur.

"There is still a barrier," she protested fervently, strength in her voice.

Whatever that barrier was he could tell she felt secure in the knowledge that he as a gentleman would never go back on a word given, and he had told her she could keep her trophy. "Yes?"

"I hesitate to speak of it." She folded the cape and put it across the back of one of the chairs, able to release it now that it was hers. "You will think me impertinent."

"Surely not. Speak your mind, ma'am." He was interested to know what was coming and had a good idea what it might be.

She advanced across the distance between them, the light from the study highlighting the swell of her bosom and hips, her measured pace seductive, her lids still lowered as if she could not do as he had bidden her if she must meet his eyes, and with renewed force his desire was roused. Had they been in any other place than his home territory, and had their association not been what it was, he would have put aside restraint and acted very differently.

When she was no more than a pace away from him she came to a standstill and raised her eyes to his. "If I am seen wearing such a luxurious garment locally there could be—gossip."

It was as he had expected. "For what reason?" he questioned without expression, eyes narrowed, not giving her an inch. The atmosphere seemed to crackle about them, each intensely and physically aware of the other's lure.

She said it. Boldly and quietly she said it. "I'm known now in the neighborhood to be the companion in this house, little more than a servant in most people's eyes, and since Mrs. Warwyck has never appeared socially in the sable cape that you gave her last Christmas I can't help believing that to the uncharitably minded it would appear to be far more likely that the fur was donated to me by the head of the household, not the wife." Her gaze on him did not waver. "Mud sticks, Mr. Warwyck. I have no wish to give any cause for blackening my name or yours."

"Most commendable of you," he replied drily, "and so unselfish. However, I think I see a way out of that problem."

"Yes?" Her lips pinched together anxiously. Did she think he would recommend putting the fur into a box with mothballs? He smiled slowly at her.

"Just continue the excellent work you are doing, and bring my wife back into a social round where you will be seen to be both friend and companion to her, which in itself should prevent the kind of malicious speculation that you fear. As if that were not enough, there is something else that should weigh the balance, something that you appear not to have discovered for yourself before this evening."

"What is that?" She tilted her head at him curiously.

"A quality in Meg that the years have not changed. During our daily discussions about her failings and weaknesses at length, perhaps I have been remiss in not pointing out that she has always been exceptionally generous by nature, always wanting to give to those who have mattered most to her, and never, to my knowledge, when in control of her faculties, did she ever turn away a charitable appeal for a good cause. This quality of hers is well known by many people, and so the gift of the cape will not appear as outlandish as you have been anticipating." He picked up the cape for her and she turned to let him put it about her shoulders.

"In any case, by the time the weather is cold enough for you to wear furs I'll be spending some time in London again, and my absence from the Grange will only aid the innocence of the case."

"If you are sure—?" She let the sentence trail off into a murmur as with both hands she fondled the fur covering her arms, with a look close to ecstasy on her face. Then the significance of what he had said dawned on her, and she spun toward him again. "I thought you told me one day that your eldest son was ready to step into your shoes as head of all your concerns."

"So he is," he replied, "but as there are only twenty-three years between us I'm not ready yet to relinquish my control completely." Another reason, which he did not intend to disclose to her, or anyone else for that matter, was that he wanted to make sure that Tom received the best chances going when the lad had got the boatbuilding dreams out of his system, which he reckoned would take two or three years at the most. It was not that he thought Lennox would deal unfairly with Tom, far from it, but it would smooth out all manner of problems if the father of both of them still held the casting vote. It was his experience that on the whole youth became sane at the age of twenty-one, no matter what follies and indiscretions had occurred beforehand, and he had every hope that in the end Tom would conform and realize on which side his bread was really buttered. He became aware that Constance was answering him.

"No, of course you are far too young to retire." She spoke with emphasis and some eye play, not wanting him to imagine for one second that she thought he looked older than his fifty-three years. Indeed, he looked much less, and could have outshone any number of men in their forties, for there was no jowliness to the strong chin line, no sagging or the high color of debauch to mar the well-cut features, and his waistcoat fitted smoothly with no wrinkling over an unsightly paunch. If she had been in Meg's shoes, what a fine couple they would have made together, her taller-than-average height complementing his splendid tallness, and she dressing to do credit to him, not owning one secondhand sable cape, but a wardrobe of soft furs and all the dresses to go with them. Everything, in fact, that was presently being wasted on that sluttish Meg. She gave a sigh.

"What is the matter?"

"I was wondering how I should manage without having you to talk to in the evenings when some special problem arises."

"I have every confidence in your ability to cope alone by then. However, London is not far, and I will be home from time to time, although I expect to make lengthy business trips abroad when the winter comes. In all fairness I must allow Lennox to become accustomed to leadership, which is impossible for him when I am there."

She preceded him back into the house with leisurely steps. "Nevertheless, I shall miss your presence when you are not here."

"Will you?" He gave her a sideways glance as he closed the glass doors after them. "You gave no thought to me in your flurry to be gone yourself less than half an hour ago."

She gave a little laugh, appreciating the fact that for all his serious mien he had allowed himself to be drawn by her as near as he had ever come to flirting with her. "That was different. Everything was different then." Her mood was merry and lighthearted. She swung the cape from her like a matador in a ring and struck a Spanish pose, one arm upflung as if she clattered castanets. "*Olé!*"

The sudden gaiety of her mood was infectious. There had been little enough laughter in the house for him over many years. His eyes twinkled and he applauded her as if she had indeed danced for him with castanets at their own private fiesta. "Most charming," he said with pleasure.

"I'm acting foolishly," she declared, not with any self-consciousness, her smile showing that she did not really believe what she had said, and she lowered her arm to her side.

"Not at all." He did not take his penetrating gaze from her. "I wanted you to be happy while you were here. Now it seems that you are."

Her nostrils quivered slightly as if she could actually scent the force of the attraction that she had for him. "I am," she admitted huskily. "Coming to the Grange has changed my whole life."

A silence fell between them. Their eyes held. It was a moment of dangerous temptation for him. She had put her own interpretation on his allowing her to keep the cape, and there was nothing she would not do to show her gratitude. He had only to reach for her and she would be in his arms, probably tearing off her own clothes in a bursting forth of pale breasts and quivering thighs. The eroticism of the thought brought forth other lightning images and it was all he could do not to shake his head to rid himself of them. Instead, he drew on his own reserves of self-discipline and made a surface remark to bridge the terrible intimacy of those moments of silence.

"I feel we should drink to that happiness," he said casually. "What may I offer you? A glass of champagne perhaps?" He jerked a tapestry bellpull. "We'll have it served in the drawing room."

She felt angry and snubbed, but did not show it, blaming herself for having rushed things a little too much. Yet it was a long time since she had had a lover to her liking, and she had been overcome by yearnings that had racked her through, leaving her as taut and frustrated as if every nerve end had been stretched to screaming point. She was close to hating him at that second for his rejection of her.

They had not been in the drawing room for five minutes before Meg appeared, Donna's letter of invitation in her hand. Already inebriated, having been left an extra tot or two by Constance to keep her quiet and out of the way, her flushed face lit up at the sight of the champagne, and she guzzled down the whole glass at Richard's toast to Constance's continued happiness and employment at the Grange.

"I like champagne," she confided unnecessarily, wiping her mouth on the back of her hand, and she held out her glass for more. "It's all them lovely bubbles." For some reason she found her own remark funny and giggled helplessly.

Richard, who had taken the glass from her to refill it, thought that Meg would not have giggled if she had been aware of her own grammatical lapse, for when sober she always strove to keep up the best front she could, and it was her own personal tragedy that she had gradually become more and more like the coarse, ill-spoken mother whom she had both loved and despised, a woman who had also striven vainly after gentility to cover a past of a less savory kind. As he handed the glass back to Meg he recognized his sister's writing on the letter in her lap.

"I see you have heard from Donna," he said, still standing.

Meg's cheeks bulged over a gulp of champagne before she swallowed it. "Tha's right. We're invit— invit— bid to dinner on Saturday evening. Didn't my dear friend, Constance, tell you?" She slapped an affectionate hand over Constance's, which rested on the sofa beside her. "She's agreed to come with us."

Constance escaped the sweaty clasp and folded her hands in her lap. "It will do Mrs. Warwyck good to attend. Your sister made it clear that I was included in the invitation." She gave that explanation more for Meg's benefit than for his, because it had been tactically agreed between them with Donna from the start that she should not let Meg go anywhere without her.

"I'm delighted to hear it." He took a sip of champagne, somewhat preoccupied. He wondered what Donna had in mind and hoped she was not under the illusion that Meg was ready to mix with company other than the family. It was far too soon. Unwittingly Meg answered his questioning thoughts, adding a barb of her own.

"It's jus' a li'l family party, but posh." Her head was unsteady on her neck as she addressed Constance with a sarcasm directed at Richard. "The Warwycks are frigh'fully posh, don' y'know." Her good humor had ebbed on the memory of old slights, real and imaginary. "But I'll show 'em. I'll be as grand as any of 'em on Saturday night, 'specially *her*." She saw her husband's glance jerk toward her and she adopted a jeering note. "Yes, *her* whose name don' cross my lips when I can help it. Your father's by-blow. She's staying for the weekend at Easthampton House."

Constance saw the muscles in his jaw clench. Pain, she thought. Not love on thoughts of Lucy, but pain. What a fool Meg was to antagonize him, although his patience with her seemed to be limitless. Another man in his place would have struck her from the sofa to the floor.

"The champagne is finished," Constance said, rising up and seeking to put an end to the evening quickly. "Let you and I go upstairs now, Meg. I admit I'm quite tired."

Meg set her mouth stubbornly and did not stir. "We'll have another bottle." She thrust out her empty glass toward Richard.

"Not this time," Constance said firmly, putting out a hand to help her up from the sofa.

Meg ignored her, repeating her demand, eyes set angrily upon her husband. "Another bottle. A magnum this time."

He answered her forcefully, patience strained to its limits, although he did not raise his voice. "No!"

Meg let forth a scream of temper. "Skinflint! Miser!" She smashed her glass to the floor. "Getting anything out of you is like getting blood ou' of a stone. And tha's what you've got for a heart. Jus' a cold stone!"

Constance caught hold of her and turned her authoritatively around in the direction of the door, speaking to her in a soothing, toneless voice. "Never mind about the champagne. Never mind about anything. You and I have made plans for the future and we're not going to let them be spoiled by any foolishness now, are we? That's it. Come along. You look pretty in that dress, you know. The color suits you. What shall we wear on Saturday evening? Would you like a new dress for it?"

The sound of her voice seemed to have an almost hypnotic effect upon Meg, who stumbled along obediently until she reached the door, which she grasped by the edge, setting her strength against it to prevent Constance drawing her through. Looking over her shoulder at Richard, her expression showed something of the appalling realization dawning on her that once again she had undermined the little that had become better between them.

"I do like champagne," she mumbled moistly in slurred, apologetic tones. "I tasted it the firs' time at our wedding breakfast. Jus' the two of us in tha' hotel."

He let fall the hand he had put to his brow and nodded toward her. "I know, Meg," he said gently, his face strained and haggard. "I remember."

She hesitated a few seconds longer as if there were more she would like to say if only she knew how to express her feelings, but Constance was prizing her fingers from the door and she submitted without protest. She went staggering out of the room, Constance's arm about her waist in support, and she began to weep copiously. Her sobbing and the low, continuous murmur of her companion's voice faded away up the stairs. Richard was left alone with his thoughts. He took a cigar from a silver box on a side table and lit it, the match flaring its brightness as briefly as the hour that had been his before his heart had become stone-like. Poor Meg. Even on their wedding night he had taken her filled with longing for the woman who could never be his. The injustice he had done Meg by marrying her was little short of a crime. He should have left her to her boats and the other fisherfolk and the shore of Easthampton where she had always been laughing and free and content. But at the greatest crisis in his life she had been ready with her love and staunch support and her implicit belief that he could do no wrong. If she had stopped loving him over the years they might have made some sort of civilized life together, but from the start her possessiveness had smothered him, and her jealousy, all unfounded in the beginning, had created a hell for them both.

In the hall someone had entered the house. Richard thought it was Jeremy coming in until he heard Tom's voice.

"Where's my father, Hopkins?"

"In the West Drawing Room, Master Tom," came the servant's reply.

Richard turned as Tom came breezing into the room. For once Richard would have preferred not to have had his company. Scenes with Meg always left him on edge, which he supposed to be a reaction to the excess of patience needed to deal with her. Out of his frayed nerves all the irritations with his rebel son came perilously near the surface even as the lad greeted him.

"I hoped I'd find you at home, sir. I've just come from the Pier. It's been a long day." Tom flung himself down in a wing chair and swung his feet up on a footstool in front of him. "A load of timber has been delivered for the building of *Sea Star* and I'm hoping that Great-Aunt Jassy's legacy will be through by the time the second one is due."

"I warned you. If you get into debt, do not look to me," Richard said with undue harshness, all the old wounds inexplicably raw again.

Tom set his feet back on the floor and sat up. "I thought that was all settled between us. I didn't come home this evening to give hints in that direction, only to say that Grandfather came to have a look around the barn today and I wanted you to know that you could do the same if it's of any interest to you."

Richard gave a derisive snort. "You know my opinion on this waywardness of yours. Don't come looking for my stamp of approval."

Tom sprang up sharply from the chair, his face offended and angry. "That wasn't my intention! My God! I'll never mention my venture to you again, sir. Have no fear about that. Good night!"

Richard heard his youngest son slam his way out of the house, and his own anger burned. How dare Tom come to step upon his toes in that manner! The defiant young whippersnapper! He would not be at all surprised if Daniel had something to do with it. Well, he'd be damned before he set a foot in that barn. Thank God the subject of the yacht had been closed between them. Did ever a man have a more difficult and obstreperous son?

Tom, having much the same heated thoughts about his father, drove back to Easthampton House at a spanking pace. The rift between them had opened up immeasurably once again.

Chapter 11

Donna went into the dining room to check that all was ready for the family dinner party. White damask set off the gleaming silver, the napkins folded like water lilies, and garlands of roses had been skillfully looped between the tall candelabra down the length of the long table, their fragrance scenting the air. She had a word with the butler, rearranged one trailing piece of greenery, and was checking the seating in her mind when her half sister came into the room. Lucy had arrived that afternoon, although as yet she and Donna had had no chance to talk alone together, Daniel being present until she went up to her room to rest from her journey and change for dinner. She had never worn conventional colors with her burnished, red-gold hair, which was skillfully tinted to keep its youthful glow, and this evening her bustled gown was of shaded rose silk, paler than a blush at the bodice and deepening to the richest of nuances in the frills about the hem.

"How beautiful you look!" Donna exclaimed with genuine admiration.

Lucy acknowledged the praise with an absent little nod, the anxious contraction of her brows not smoothing away. "Is Father downstairs yet?"

"No." Donna went to her in a rippling flow of flower-patterned chiffon, and spoke in a lowered voice as she took Lucy's arm to lead her away from the dining room and out of earshot of the servants. "Is something wrong?"

"Nothing—and everything, which is usual when I come here."

In the Green Drawing Room, so called for its soft sea colors, Donna closed the door after them and faced her half sister. She could have liked Lucy, could have been close to her if circumstances had been different, but she could never forget the effect that Lucy, through no fault of her own, had had upon their lives, disrupting their whole existence when the truth of who had fathered her burst upon them. It had all happened so many years ago, and yet the aftermath lingered on. Worst of all was the memory of that terrible night when a blackmailer had been silenced forever, and she and her mother and Lucy had worked like conspirators together. But she must not think about that now, or one of those increasing spells of depression would sweep over her, bringing a splitting headache in its wake. She drew a deep breath.

"You have every right to visit your own father. I'm only sorry that Josh could not be with you this time. Have I done anything to make you feel unwelcome?"

"No, no. It's Father. Every time I come he seems more withdrawn, less pleased to see me, and yet I see sadness in his eyes whenever I leave."

Donna answered carefully. "He's an old man, and it's natural that any break in routine is upsetting to him."

Lucy's eyes flashed. "Don't try to fob me off with that nonsense! He isn't old. He'll never be old. He's too alert to all that's going on, and as to his routine, he told me himself that he has invited the great-granddaughters of his old patron to stay at Easthampton House during the autumn for as long as it suits them." Her frills rustled as she took a step toward Donna. "I love him dearly. You cannot possibly realize what it meant to me to discover that I had a father after growing up in a convent believing myself to be an orphan. I have never lost the wonder of it after all these years, but I must not come again. This must be my last visit."

"Why? I don't understand."

"It's Kate. She's finally come between us."

Donna bristled. "How dare you speak thus of my dear mamma's memory. In those last two years of her life, knowing she was dying, she did all she could to unite you and Papa as if the time of not knowing of each other's existence had never been."

"I know that." Lucy twisted her hands. "It's not her fault. To divide us is the last thing she would have wished, but it has come about because Father will not let her *die!*"

Donna blanched. She swallowed hard. "Mamma has been in her grave for thirty years. She lies beside the two daughters and the son she lost in their early childhood. I have never heard crueler words than those you have just uttered."

"Cruel because they are the truth?" Lucy shook her head despairingly. "If Kate were dead and at rest her portrait would still hang in this drawing room, and all the things she loved would be on show for the rest of us to touch or see and remember her with love or respect, according to how close we were to her. Instead, she has been locked away in Honeybridge House, and I swear if the grave were opened in the churchyard we should find it empty."

Donna gave a strangled cry and she struck her half sister hard across the face. The sound of the stinging blow seemed to hang in the silent room. Donna was unrepentant, breathing quickly, her own color coming and going. "Never, never say such a dreadful thing again."

Lucy, deeply shocked by the blow, straightened her shoulders and lifted her chin bravely, determined to say what had to be said. "The opportunity will not be mine since I'll not set foot in Easthampton House again until Kate is at peace, whenever that may be. To my sorrow I fear it will not be until our father releases her by his own death. All I do know is that whatever paternal love he has for me is overshadowed and tormented by all I represent to him these days. He sees me only as living proof of his infidelity to Kate. Each time I come the agony is worse both for him and for me. Because I love him I must stay away. He will be sad and he will miss me, in spite of himself, but that will be easier for him to bear than the torture of being reminded of the wretchedness he caused Kate through his unlawful coupling with my mother."

Donna gasped. She was aghast at such outspoken statements in her own home. "Stay away, then. If it were not that Papa would be more deeply distressed by my ordering you out of this house now I would do it, but I will not add to his sufferings. You and your late mother have caused him enough. You should never have come here in the first place all those years ago. You should have gone to your Aunt Olivia at Radcliffe Hall and lived there. I know your mother was only sister-in-law to Olivia's husband, Alexander Radcliffe, but by sheer association with that hateful family she was tainted by it, and I see that taint on you!"

"How strange that you should say that," Lucy said sadly. "It was because Olivia saw me tainted by my Warwyck blood that she would have nothing to do with me." She moved to a scroll-ended sofa and sat down wearily. "I never thought we should ever quarrel, Donna. How tragic life can be. I remember when you and I were so bound together in filial love for Daniel that we defied the law of the land to save him in his innocence of the crime he had committed."

"Don't speak of it!" Donna shot a glance nervously over her shoulder in the direction of the door as if she feared eavesdroppers. "From that day until this you and I have never mentioned that awful occasion. Why bring it up now?"

"Because after I leave Easthampton House this time it may be a long while before we see each other again—if ever. I have never admired anyone's courage more. It was a dreadful deed you had to do, riding off alone into the night to drag that body onto the railway line."

"Stop it!" Donna was ashen. She fluttered forward and sat down beside Lucy. "Does your conscience ever trouble you about that night?"

"No. We did what was best for Daniel and for Kate. He would never have been able to prove that Ben Thompson's death was accidental, and neither you nor I were prepared to let our father go to the gallows through a miscarriage of justice when we had it in our power to prevent it."

Donna shuddered and covered her face with her hands. "My conscience plagues me still."

Lucy put an arm about her shoulders and questioned her sympathetically. "Why, Donna? Ben Thompson was a dreadful, merciless man. It was the gallows that should have had him."

Donna gave a stifled groan. "I left his body there in the train's path without a prayer for his soul."

It was a macabre conversation and, unseen by Donna, Lucy closed her eyes tightly on the horror of it. When she had referred to the nightmare experience shared she had never expected it would lead to such a full discussion. She forced herself to speak calmly and in as much a matter-of-fact tone as she could muster. "Everything had to be done quickly inside the house and out of it. There was no time to think beyond the basic details of concealing all the evidence."

"I realize that, but the dreadful end of that man's remains will haunt me to the end of my days."

Lucy was filled with compassion for her. Never had she suspected how Donna had been suffering mentally over it all throughout the years. She hoped that by discussing it now some balm might be given to her, and she wished they had talked it out long ago, but she had always supposed that Donna had put the whole awful experience from her mind as resolutely as she had done from hers, being only thankful that Daniel had been spared, and never more so than when Kate had needed him so much in the last months of her life. Surely that period in itself should have been enough for Donna to see that all had been done for the best, for nothing could have brought Ben Thompson back to life. It had been the one time when Lucy had not been concerned with the rights or wrongs of a situation: people had mattered more. "If you had dallied by the body," she pointed out, "it could have meant discovery, and all our efforts would have come to naught. Try to think of it in that light."

Donna nodded, lowering her hands to her lap, the haunted look lingering on in her eyes. Outside there came the clop of horses' hooves and the jingle of a carriage drawing up. Lucy went to the window and looked out.

"Meg and Richard have arrived with Jeremy, and there's another lady with them."

"That will be Constance." Donna got up from the sofa stiffly, still in the grip of the ordeal she had been through, and forced herself to concentrate on the evening ahead of her. She hoped Meg would behave herself. At the present moment she felt that at the slightest sign of a scene she would have hysterics herself.

When the double doors were opened she saw that her father had come downstairs in time to greet the newcomers in the hall, his stick discarded for the evening, his well-groomed, silvery head as gleaming as his evening shirt front with its diamond studs. As the ladies' wraps were taken and Daniel turned with his guests in the direction of the elegant drawing room, where she waited with Lucy, Donna took refuge in a white-hot flare of anger against Constance, because she saw at once that at Jeremy's side Meg was walking with the exaggerated dignity of the very drunk. Surely Constance could have ensured Meg's sobriety on this of all evenings!

Constance, whose own impatience with Meg was at breaking point, saw Donna's mouth purse censoriously and answered the unspoken criticism in her own mind. How was she to know that Meg had a secret hiding place for a last-resort supply? She thought she had unearthed all the bottles tucked behind dresses in wardrobes and in top cupboards and behind the bedhead. It had been all she could do not to give vent to her temper when she had returned after changing her own clothes to find Meg, whom she had left dressed and ready, more than a little inebriated from a bottle she had never seen before. The old excuses of needing something to keep her spirits up had come tumbling forth, and with an iciness close to hatred Constance had taken the bottle into the adjoining bathroom and poured the remains of the whiskey down the rose-patterned porcelain pan of the water closet. Just when she had wanted to devote her whole attention to Richard and Lucy she would have to keep a constant eye on the drunken sot in her charge.

Pretending not to notice anything amiss, Constance smiled at Donna and made sure she observed Richard and Lucy closely as they greeted each other. There was no deep look of reunion, no lingering touch of hands, nothing more than the normal friendliness and familiarity of people who have known and liked each other for a long time. Constance breathed freely. It was as she had believed: Meg had nothing to worry about there, and—something far more important—neither had she! She had been gradually readjusting her first outlook on how things should be for her at the Grange, ever since she had sensed the sexual rapport between Richard and herself, and in the light of the recent development over the sable cape a far better state of affairs was beginning to present itself in her mind. She was convinced there was a hidden promise in his readiness to let her keep it. No man would let his wife give away anything so costly unless he had an ulterior motive of his own. Richard was a complex man, difficult to understand, but he was still a man like all men and he desired her. On that plane she had no equal. It was home ground and she tingled with anticipation. Her smile as she was introduced to Lucy was dulcet and charming, while in her own mind she labeled Richard's half sister as having all the complacent signs of a woman well satisfied with her marriage and all appertaining to it: an enviable state of affairs, and she disliked her intensely for it. Still smiling, Constance tossed a casual remark to Richard as Lucy went to speak to Meg, aware that he was as attuned as she to the suspense of what would happen between his half sister and his wife within the next few seconds.

"How are you, Meg?" Lucy said in greeting.

Meg eyed her, the enemy, and—after this evening—the vanquished. "Nicely, thank you. Are you well? And your husband and your daughters?" There! It was done. She had shown good manners, and all must have noticed. Without listening to Lucy's reply she glanced toward Constance for a nod of approval. It was not forthcoming. Constance was talking to Richard and neither was looking in her direction. She felt piqued. As Lucy moved on to speak to Jeremy, Meg looked about searchingly. "Where's Tom?" she demanded touchily.

Daniel answered his daughter-in-law. "He cannot be with us

this evening. The first of the gala skating carnivals is being held at the Pier Pavilion."

"He ought to be here." Meg was annoyed. This was her big evening, and at the very least Tom should have been present for her arrival. She had had her darling Jeremy to give her his arm, but that did not excuse her youngest son, who always seemed to go out of his way to cause her some dissatisfaction. His grandfather had spoiled him, that was the trouble. It was all the old man's fault. She fixed Daniel with her gaze, wanting to hold him steady in her vision, which was playing tricks with her. "Send for him."

The room went quiet. All looked toward Meg, who stood stout and dumpy in her elaborate new gown of stiff oyster satin, an angry color flushing her throat, her white-gloved fingers twitching. Daniel, always at ease, had full control of the situation.

"That would ruin the surprise I have planned for you and for him."

"What's that?" Her tone was suspicious.

"There are seats specially reserved for us in the spectators' gallery at the carnival this evening. I thought we should all go on there after we have dined."

His announcement caused no little sensation. It was entirely his own idea, and he had said nothing to Donna, who might have opposed it, or to Tom, who was not to be distracted from his managerial duties by watching out for the arrival of a family party. And, to be honest with himself, he had wanted to see something of his grandson's success with the gala, and thought it would do no harm to let Richard witness it too.

Meg stared at him. She did not want to go traipsing the length of a windy pier in her new gown, and she certainly was not going to show Tom favor by appearing there. "That's no place for ladies and gentlemen of quality," she stated coldly. "I'll not be seen at a common people's carnival."

Daniel was taken aback. He had forgotten Meg's snobbery, for in his time he had bridged all classes from the prize ring to a drawing room at Buckingham Palace, and never gave such matters a thought. He liked to think he had brought up his children with the same broad-minded outlook, and at least Tom had followed in his footsteps even if his other grandchildren had not been so fortunate, through no fault of their own.

"Well, now. Dear me. If you do not wish to go, then we'll say no more about it." He gave no indication of his own disappointment. "We shall not be lacking in good entertainment here, because I'm sure we can persuade Lucy to play the piano for us. We know that the musicians at the carnival would not be able to match her exceptional talent." He looked toward Lucy and did not notice the strained expression still hollowing her eyes from the earlier part of the evening, and she gave him a graceful half curtsy in acknowledgment of his praise before addressing Meg.

"What would you like me to play? Have you a favorite piece of music? Or a song?"

In her heart Meg had her favorite songs, the shanties of the sea that she and the other fishermen used to sing a long time ago. Gone. All gone. "Nothing sad," she replied tightly. "I don't like nothing sad."

The crisis of the moment had passed. On the other side of the room Constance breathed a sigh of relief. The prospect of getting Meg through a truly public appearance that evening had been daunting, the dinner party being quite enough. Richard was of the same opinion, although he did not voice it. Some other guests arrived just then, two married couples of middle age whom the Warwycks had known for many years and who could be counted upon to help Meg through the evening, as well as turn a blind eye if things should not go as planned.

It was as well. Meg's wineglass was empty as soon as it was filled. She ate little and contributed nothing to the conversation. In the middle of the fourth course, with a sudden, dreadful noise of retching, she vomited violently and unexpectedly before she could rise from the table. For a few stunned and horrified seconds nobody moved, host, family, guests, and the servants in attendance all seemingly transfixed, and then Constance and Donna sprang up simultaneously, rushing around the table with snatched-up napkins to where Meg sat gazing blankly down at her ruined gown and the obnoxious state of the spattered damask cloth in front of her. Only Jeremy spoke.

"Mother!" he exclaimed in low tones of total disgust.

She looked at him pitifully as servants turned her chair about, her companion and sister-in-law mopping her up as best as they could before helping her to rise. "It musta been the trout. Not fresh. Funny fish, trout."

Richard had pushed back his chair and risen to his feet, but Constance shook her head to indicate that he should offer no assistance. Between them, she and Donna took Meg from the room. Daniel stood up.

"I suggest we adjourn to the drawing room, ladies and gentlemen."

As soon as the company had left the dining room the butler flung wide all the windows and summoned kitchen maids with buckets to wash the carpet, while two footmen gathered up the soiled tablecloth. It was the most calamitous dinner party that he had ever witnessed.

Opposite to the entrance to the Pier the Radcliffe carriages were drawing up, Hugh having invited a number of local friends to join in the outing to the roller-skating carnival. All were masked and in costume; even Beth, who had been instructed by Olivia not to let Nicolette out of her sight, was arrayed as an Eastern lady in flowing robes and a yashmak. Nicolette herself had been acclaimed as the belle of the occasion in her blue spangled costume with sequined stars sparkling on the ribbons entwined Greek fashion in her hair. She had new, high-laced boots of white leather with roller skates attached, and when she had alighted she and Hugh and two others similarly prepared began to skate across the promenade to show tickets at the turnstile and continue up the deck of the Pier, racing each other, wheels spinning and rumbling in the direction of the pavilion ahead, which glowed with colored lamps and from which music drifted out on the summer night. Hugh, dressed as a cavalier, the plumes flowing out from his hat, took the lead almost immediately. A sheik, who was Lawrence, and Henry VIII were hot on his heels, outdistancing Nicolette, while the rest, who were on foot, lay far behind, with Beth trudging up in the rear.

In the foyer Nicolette, eager to catch a glimpse of Tom, left her brother and his friends breathlessly congratulating each other on

the speed they had attained, while they awaited the rest of the
party, and she went on through the doorway that led by way of an
aisle to the rink. She blinked at the brilliance of the scene after
the starlit night outside. Overhead a canopy of Chinese lanterns
created myriad patterns of red and gold and dragon green, while
the rink itself was a whirlpool of color that spilled over into the
seats where skaters were resting, and was echoed in the spectators'
gallery. Some of the costumes, such as those Hugh and Lawrence
were wearing, were obviously from a well-stocked charade wardrobe, but others were truly magnificent in the application of innumerable glass jewels. Still more bore witness to the amazing inven-
tiveness of the wearers, which included a number that must have
been decidedly uncomfortable to be clad in, such as the papier-
mâché jar encasing a man representing one of the Forty Thieves,
only his head and legs visible, and the girl, her skirt hem aswirl
with green velvet shamrocks, who sported a yacht in full sail on
her head, which bore the name *Irish Lady* on its side. She held
her head stiffly as if fearful of disaster.

"Not a patch on *Sea Star*," Tom whispered close to Nicolette's
ear, his hand capturing hers. He was masked like everybody else,
but being on duty, his white tie and evening clothes gave him the
status of one in authority amid the hurly-burly of the scene.
"Come on. This way."

He led her around the rink, held back a crimson door curtain,
and took her out through an emergency exit onto the gallery that
circumferenced the rear of the pavilion. It was deserted. There
was nothing between them and the sea except the railings, with
France lying somewhere over the horizon in the darkness, lost in
stars. He pushed his mask up onto his hair and loosened the ribbon ties of hers in order to draw it down from her face until it
rested against her like a necklace. After that he did not seem to
dare to touch her, his hands hovering as if the irradiating of the
spangles on her hair and costume held some force to keep him at
bay.

"I've missed you," he said huskily in little more than a whisper.
She nodded, choked. "I haven't known how to bear it."
"Is anyone else with you this evening?"

"Yes, a whole crowd, including Beth. They'll come looking for me if I'm out here for long."

"Let them!" he challenged recklessly. He had had enough of subterfuge. He wanted everyone in the world to see him with Nicolette and know that he loved her.

"Then this would be our last meeting for at least three years."

"Why three years?"

"Because I'd have to wait until I was twenty-one and free to do as I wished before I could get from Scotland to see you again."

Three years. He could hardly endure three minutes without the sight of her. His mood changed to one of angry despair and he rammed a fist down on the top rail, making it ring. "I thought you were to have more freedom when Beth came."

She could tell that in his pent-up feelings he was on the edge of quarreling with her. "It's not working out like that. Beth is carrying out my grandmother's instructions to the letter. When I dropped a few hints about her turning a blind eye she said in her blunt Scottish way that it would not be worth her while. The closer watch she keeps on me, the better the remuneration she will receive from my grandmother."

He straightened up, his expression changing thoughtfully. "She said that, did she?"

"I'm afraid so."

"I'd like to meet Beth."

"Why?"

"Maybe I could offer her a better deal than anything Mrs. Radcliffe is prepared to give her."

She was awed, her eyes wide. "You mean *bribe* her?"

"It's worth a try."

"Suppose she should go straight to my grandmother and report it?"

"She needn't know my name is Warwyck." He grinned widely. "I'll call myself Mr. Smith. Not even your grandmother would send you back to Scotland for being pursued by a Mr. Smith. It's one of the hazards of the seaside."

Nicolette laughed and flung her arms about his neck. It was the contact that he had longed for and feared from the moment they had come out into the night together. All restraint went from him. His mouth bored into hers and there was no assuaging his hunger for her in the kisses that he could not stop. In silence they clung to each other as though parting forever had come upon them, she as frantic in her kissing as he, lost in a kind of whirlwind of passion that dazed her with its force. Finally it was she who broke from him, pushing her hands against his chest when his opened mouth would have taken hers again in a further frenzy from which she would not want to escape.

"I must go back inside the rink," she protested breathlessly, exerting her strength against him. "When you have found a place where we can meet I'll arrange for Beth to come and see you. Until then there is no point."

He still held her about the waist, crushed to him. "I know somewhere. It may take a little time to get a key to it, but once I have obtained possession of it no one will ever find us there."

"Let me know when you have the key." She took his face between her hands. "I wish I did not have to leave you now. I wish many things, Tom."

She broke from him and darted away to the door of the emergency exit through which they had come, but it had closed of its own accord, and she sped on to re-enter the pavilion by way of the main entrance, retying the ribbons of her mask as she went. He leaned back against the wall of the pavilion, wishing that he did not have to go back to the festivities within. He would have liked to stay out there quietly, thinking of Nicolette and the haven he planned to get for her. How he would manage it he did not know, but locks and bolts and bars were not going to keep him out of it.

Lowering the mask back over his eyes, he moved along the circular deck until he reached the west side of the pavilion, where he could see Easthampton stretched out in a carpet of twinkling lights. It was dark in the area of Hoe Lane where the woods still clustered and Honeybridge House stood closed and silent. As soon as he and Hab started work on *Sea Star* in the barn nobody would question his presence in the vicinity of the house. Somehow he would find a way into the grounds and then into Honeybridge itself. It had been a place of love once, in Kate's time. Why shouldn't it be so again?

Chapter 12

At Easthampton House the disastrous party was dragging through to the hour when it would be permissible for the guests to take their leave. Donna had returned to the drawing room to announce that Constance had taken Meg home. It would have been distasteful to suggest returning to the dining room for the two courses that had not been taken, and a compromise was reached by a *croque-embouche* being served buffet style in the Green Drawing Room, followed by coffee. Everybody talked, but it was difficult to keep up the illusion that all was well, and Richard was acutely and uncomfortably aware of the sympathy directed toward him. It was Meg who needed the sympathy, not he. Only Lucy seemed to recognize this fact, but then Lucy had always been more understanding than most other people, and it was his misfortune in life that he had never met another woman like her. He watched her as she played the piano for the company, and was touched that the final piece was something she had played for him alone a long time ago when they had been young and had not yet discovered the true relationship between them. It conveyed her goodwill and her hope for him in the time of his trouble. When her fingers came to rest on the last notes he did not applaud with everybody else. There was no need. Lucy looked across at him, and the serenity of her face was like a promise to him of a light somewhere in the darkness ahead. If he should find it he would remember these moments, which were like the words of goodbye.

The party finally broke up. Jeremy, wondering why he had allowed himself to be drawn into a family gathering in the first place, decided he needed some *divertissement* to rid himself of the evening's unpleasantness before going home, and he made some excuse to slip away on his own. Richard talked a little about Meg to his father and Donna, Lucy listening in silence, and then he bade them good night. Lucy went with him to the steps outside.

"I'll not be coming back to Easthampton House ever again."

"So I was right." It was as he had known it when she had played that final piece before closing the piano.

"You alone need no explanations, Richard."

He took hold of her by the arms. "Father will miss you. We'll all miss you, but there will be less pain for him than for me."

She shook her head. "Not for you after all these years."

He would not burden her with the truth. "No. I was thinking back to first meetings."

"That was a long time ago. We're different people now."

"We are indeed. However, this is not a final break. I'll hear news of you when you write to Father, and if ever you are in London you must allow me to take you out to luncheon."

"That is kind of you," she said, but it was a refusal and he did not expect it to be otherwise.

"Goodbye, Lucy." He kissed her on the cheek.

"Goodbye, Richard." She embraced him quickly and went back indoors. He descended the steps. The Warwyck brougham was waiting, the groom holding the door open, but he dismissed it, saying that he felt like taking a walk and the coachman should wait by Ring Park until he was ready to go home. Like Jeremy, he needed to have some time to recover from the evening before retiring, although in his case it was not to forget poor Meg's pathetic lapse, but to adjust to a final parting with Lucy.

When he reached the promenade it was as if every visitor to

the resort was abroad on that warm, early August night. As he turned eastward people everywhere were strolling in groups with linked arms or in pairs, young lovers wandered along with heads together, and older folk paraded at a similar, leisurely pace, shadows crossing and recrossing in the glow of the gas lamps that sentineled the mile-long stretch of the promenade. The tide was out, and on the sands Pierrots were performing on a small, brightly illuminated tented stage that had been set up. In another groin a band of minstrels with polka-dot bow ties and blackened faces was singing Negro songs of the American South. The hour being late, there were few children to be seen, but donkey rides were still taking place along the sands. Young blades and their girls held races in the bobbing saddles, to shouts and shrieks of merriment and a flurry of petticoats revealing ankles and occasionally the lace frills of cambric drawers to those watching from the rails of the promenade.

It was all so familiar to Richard. He had grown up in that same seaside atmosphere, although it had been less bawdy in his youth, only the well-to-do able to afford holidays by the sea in those days. The coming of the railways had changed everything, bringing the ordinary folk to the seashore, and the Pier had been built as an added attraction for their enjoyment. He paused to gaze along the lamplit stretch of it to the pavilion at the head, whence came the distant rumble of roller skates and the thump of music heard clearly in the night air. It was time that the Pier was replaced by a new one, although an annual inspection by an engineer declared it to be safe enough. Nevertheless, the buildings on it had all been enlarged in recent years and since the south coast often took quite a lashing when tides were high and a storm blew, he would not want to see it in use after another decade at the most.

He reached the end of the promenade, where in the darkness beyond the gas lamps the rising cliffs formed the eastern curve of the bay, and he turned inland through some narrow streets faced by ancient flint cottages left standing from the days when only fishermen and other humble folk had inhabited Easthampton. Twice on the way he was accosted by painted women lingering in shadowed doorways, and he thought wryly that half a century ago Meg's mother had been one of that ilk.

The streets led him to a square where the Warwyck Theater, which had once known grander days, now housed a music hall. In days gone by he had been there many times, particularly when the boys were young and he had taken them to the annual panto-mime, treating them to a box and supper afterward as if they were already grown up and young men of the world. Tom, being the youngest, frequently fell asleep before supper was over, having worn himself out joining in the songs and rolling off his seat with laughter at the dame in her striped stockings; many a time Rich-ard had lifted his sleeping son onto his shoulder and, when home again, carried him up to bed, chocolate and ice cream still besmearing his face.

Releasing a sovereign from the gold fob on his watch chain, Richard put it down in front of the cashier in the theater's box office. The second house was half over, but this was no deterrent to latecomers drawn to the long bar at the back of the circle where they could drink while watching the performance through the windows set in the wall, or drift out onto a promenading gallery to join in the rousing choruses of the performers' songs whenever it suited them. Some had been doing this when he arrived, and were cheering the buxom young woman in bustled scarlet satin who was blowing kisses as she curtsied to their ovation. He or-dered a brandy, lit a cigar, and taking the glass with him, he went out onto the red-carpeted gallery. A troupe of tumblers in sugar-pink tights and sequined fringes had taken over the stage and were bouncing and leaping like rubber balls, bursting through paper hoops and jumping from seesaws onto each other's shoul-ders. The audience, which was like any other music-hall audience in being noisy and involved with whatever was taking place behind the flaring footlights, whistled and stamped its appreci-ation of the feats. When at last a human pyramid of bright pink-clad limbs and breathless, heaving bodies fanned outward, thun-derous applause broke out and the velvet curtains swung together. The tumblers were taking a bow, strung out hand in hand across the closed curtains, when the double doors behind Richard opened and a bunch of late arrivals poured from the stairs onto the gallery, presenting a more bizarre appearance than anything that had been seen on the stage. All were in costume, some carrying the masks that they had discarded, and Richard guessed that they had come from Tom's carnival at the roller-skating rink.

As they streamed past him on their way to occupy one of the empty boxes he recognized Hugh Radcliffe-Stuart, or—as he was now known locally—merely Radcliffe these days since becoming the acknowledged lord of the manor there. An older woman, dressed in an Eastern costume, looked harassed as she shepherded the girls along, and several of the young men dropped back to go into the bar, money and bottles changing hands before they caught up with the rest of the party and went into the box.

Normally these days he had so little contact with Radcliffe Hall that the old feud very rarely came to mind. But in his present, hollow mood, caused by the final parting with Lucy, which had set a terrible restlessness upon him, a rawness of nerves that neither a walk in the night air nor the cheerful atmosphere of the music hall had been able to alleviate, he felt the old hostility toward all Radcliffes, inherent in him, stir to the point of angry irritation at the presence of any one of them. Too many old hurts and wounds had been brought to the surface for him this evening, and he wanted no more reminders of them.

The dark red hair of a young girl in blue gleamed in the box where she sat. Variations of that color ran through Olivia Radcliffe's side of the family. When he had been young, Olivia's hair had still held tawny streaks, and that of her daughter, Sophie, had been a harsher shade of Lucy's handsome, red-gold mane. It was said that Olivia's sister, Claudine, whose adulterous affair with Daniel had brought Lucy into the world, had hair that had dazzled all who had looked upon it, making her appear to be a great beauty when in reality her features had been unremarkable and faintly feline. All that was hearsay, for he had never seen a portrait of the woman, who had died young, and neither had anyone else he knew; not even Lucy had ever seen a likeness of her own mother. If Olivia had had one it would have been destroyed long since, for she had never forgiven the liaison with a Warwyck, and it was said that a kind of madness had come upon her when she heard that her sister was dead, for she had laughed and screamed until she had fallen down in a faint.

Richard took a handful of change out of his pocket and selected a sixpence, which he dropped into a slot, enabling him to take a small pair of opera glasses out of a brass container, and he put them to his eyes, looking in the direction of the box. The face of the girl with the rich-colored hair was in profile to him, the glow of the stage putting highlights to her brow and cheekbones. She was very young, with the delicate bloom of a virgin and all the promise of becoming an extremely beautiful woman. The family likeness was unmistakable, and he had no doubt in his mind that this was Sophie's daughter. What was her name? Ninette? Nina? No, Nicolette. And a Radcliffe. He pitied her misfortune. Allied to that brood she could not help but be contaminated by the tricks and sharp dealings that had made the family notorious. Not the type of young woman he would ever want to join his family circle, and thank the Lord there was no chance of it.

He dropped the opera glasses back into the container, put down his emptied brandy glass, and left the gallery, not wanting to stay any longer. Roars of laughter from the audience at the jokes of a comedian boomed out from behind the closed doors as he went back into the night. At Ring Park his brougham was waiting, and with every turn of the wheels he knew why he was returning home instead of trying the conviviality of his club in one last effort to lift the heaviness of his spirits. As if it had been written out for him he knew what would come of it.

From the drive he saw there was a lamp alight in his study. He gave his silk hat and gloves to the servant in the hall, asked if Jeremy was home, and upon hearing that he was, gave instructions for the house to be locked up for the night. Adjusting a cuff into place, he passed by the wide staircase without haste and went down the thickly carpeted corridor until he reached his study.

Constance swung around from holding back one of the drawn curtains at the window as he entered. She was wearing a full silk robe with velvet ribbons over her nightgown, her hair hanging loose about her shoulders. "I thought you would be anxious about Mrs. Warwyck," she began. Then her voice trailed away, a pulse leaping in her throat as she saw the dark way he was looking at her. Her lips moved in a barely audible whisper. "I have been waiting for you."

In the silence of the room the key clicked as he turned it, shutting the two of them away from the rest of the house. Her eyes gleamed, triumphant and exultant, and he took her robe in both hands and tore it from her. The nightgown fell in ripped folds about her feet and he knew hard nipples and soft flesh, and through a violent lovemaking he experienced an erotic release from the past that left old ghosts banished and gone.

Chapter 13

In the barn Tom, a frown of concentration in his face, stepped back from the keel and framed assembly of *Sea Star*. He and Hab had worked hard every spare minute they could get since they had made a start on the craft, and in a short time they had accomplished a great deal. Hab, wiping a forearm across his sweating brow, came and stood at Tom's side. Around them the barn no longer had a barren appearance, tools for the task in hand having turned it into a giant workshop, only a single stretch of space down one side of it bearing witness to a second load of timber awaiting order.

"That's it. The first step," Hab remarked with satisfaction. "She looks much more advanced than she really is at this stage."

He was right. The lead keel, which had been cast on the spot by the two of them, was wedged into the building board set solidly upon thick timber legs. The stem rose clear and clean, bearing one end of the plumb line that stretched to the transom and which had been the guide to setting up the frames true on the center line of the backbone, resulting in an illusion of width and form. The graceful overhangs, which would give her such length, seemed to shimmer there.

"She's beautiful already," Tom endorsed quietly.

A shadow fell across the flagstones in the slanting rays of the sun as Jeremy entered the barn in time to hear what his brother had said. "Too skinny for my taste," he commented mockingly as he approached at a saunter. "Fortunately I have brought you something to put some flesh on her."

Tom looked at him with ill-concealed impatience. "What the devil are you talking about?"

"This letter." Jeremy drew it out of his pocket and proffered it. "It was delivered at home with the midafternoon post. I thought you'd like to have it without delay. I received one from the same source, so I know what news it contains."

Tom's face was transformed as he took it. "Is it the legacy?"

Jeremy nodded. "It's come through at last and worth waiting for, although these American lawyers certainly know how to take their time, don't they?"

Tom ripped the envelope open and read the contents. He gave a spontaneous shout of laughter and made the prize-ring fist of triumph. "It's Merrelton for you tomorrow morning, Hab! You can order immediate delivery of the rest of everything we need for *Sea Star*. This calls for a celebration. Drinks on me at the Crown."

He reached for his jacket, which was hanging on a nail, and as he swung it out to shove his arms into it an ancient ring of rusty keys shot out of his pocket and landed on the flagstones at his brother's feet. Jeremy picked them up. "Where are these from?"

Tom took them quickly and thrust them back into his pocket. "I'm collecting every key I can find these days. There are some drawers in the side benches here that have lost the original ones and can't be locked."

No more was said. The three of them made their way to the Crown, which had been dispensing ale to the local inhabitants since long before a Warwyck had set foot in Easthampton. It still catered mainly for a local trade, being in a lane away from the main part of town and not gaudy or bright enough to attract visitors away from the flashier saloons with mirrors and brass fittings and opaque designs on the windows. In the taproom, where the floor was covered with sawdust and the low ceiling was stained ocher-colored by age and tobacco smoke, Tom bent his head to avoid the low beams as he brought three foaming tankards of ale from the bar to an oaken table between settle seats where his brother and Hab had settled down. There the celebration continued with further rounds until Jeremy, who had not offered to pay once, became bored with the boat talk between Hab and his brother and broke up the festive occasion by announcing he was ready to take his leave.

"One for the road," Hab invited exuberantly, having insisted on taking his turn in paying throughout the evening. Jeremy declined and departed. Tom allowed himself to be persuaded, and then he and Hab parted company outside the alehouse to go their separate ways.

When Tom reached the five-barred gate that led into the meadow where the barn stood, he climbed over it and entered the building only long enough to take a lantern and light it. Keeping it closed to avoid the gleam of light being seen, he went around the outside of the barn and trudged on through the long grass until he reached the padlocked gates that led into the grounds of Honeybridge House. There he allowed himself some light, knowing that the trees shielded him, and with his hands through the bars he tried each of the keys on the ring that he had taken out of his pocket. Until he found a means of unlocking this rear entrance into the grounds he could make no further plans to meet Nicolette there, because too many people passed along Hoe Lane for either of them to come and go at the front of the house.

To his exasperation each key failed him in its turn. He had lost count of the number he had tried, and had come to see that it was no ordinary padlock that his grandfather had put upon the gate. There was nothing for it but to file through the chain held together by the padlock, which was what he had hoped to avoid. With the tool he had brought with him from the barn he began the slow and laborious task.

It took a long time before the link was severed completely and the padlock fell with a thud on the inside of the gates. Quickly he drew the chain through the bars and, having found two weeks ago a large key to fit the more commonplace lock of the gates themselves, which he had oiled in advance, he inserted it, and with a grinding snap the grounds of Honeybridge were opened up to him. In spite of himself he knew a sense of awe as he went through, pushing against the thorns and other weeds that had grown up like a second barrier, for he was entering a period of family history that had been closed long before he was born.

As soon as he was a good distance inside the gates he breathed more easily. His eyes had accustomed themselves to the dark, and he allowed himself a ray of lamplight only when there was any-thing to which he wanted to give closer inspection. Everything was far more overgrown than he had realized, clumps of tall grass growing up between the cobbles of the stable yard, creeper cover-ing doors and windows of the coach houses, and the stone mount-ing blocks were green with moss where once Kate must have stepped up to take the sidesaddle of a horse she had owned called Bonnie. So much was coming back to him from the jigsaw scraps of information that he had been told or overheard in the years of childhood and later. He pulled back some creeper from one of the coach-house windows, and the fingers of lamplight showed him a carriage of some size covered with tarpaulins gray with dust and dirt. He would have liked to investigate, but it was not the out-buildings of Honeybridge to which he had to gain access, and he left the area of the stable yard to push his way along an overgrown path through what had once been a kitchen garden. Once he paused. The very air breathed the perfume of sweet herbs, and he guessed that somewhere in the vicinity Kate's herb garden had run riot in its own way, still producing the seeds and roots and sprigs that she had used in her task of caring for the sick, and the healing of cuts and burns and other injuries suffered during the course of their work by men in Daniel's employ. Tom thought it strange that he should continue to think of Kate by her Christian name and not in her role as his grandmother, albeit he and she had never known each other, but perhaps that was be-cause he could not associate her with the advanced age of a grand-parent when she had been little more than forty at the time of her death.

He found himself by the back door of the house, a thick web of brambles filling the porch and entwined about the supports. He had used an old fence strut that had come to hand to slash back the dense bushes and make a way for himself, but the brambles needed cutting down and the penknife he carried would not be adequate. He turned his attention to what appeared to be a pantry window; it was shuttered from the outside, as were all the windows, extra protection added at the time when the house had been shut up, but when he pulled at the ivy that covered it, the wood proved to have become rotten over the years, and it broke away at the same time, leaving the window exposed. His penknife came into use, sliding through a gap to release the catch within. He pulled at the frame and out it swung. Seconds later he was in the room-sized pantry of Honeybridge House.

All the shelves were bare, nothing hung from the hooks across the ceiling, and the huge flour bin was empty with the circular lid propped against its side, and yet it seemed to him that the smell of smoked hams and preserves lingered there still. He brushed down festoons of cobwebs with his arms as he crossed the stone floor to the door that led into the kitchen. His lamp showed him the black range and the dresser and the long wooden table, but he did not linger, and went through a baize-lined door into the hall. Here furniture as well as mirrors and pictures on the walls were covered by dust sheets, and it was the same in each room when he looked in. Upstairs were four-poster beds with hangings drawn and doubly shrouded by vast dust sheets that billowed faintly in the draft that he had caused by opening doors, as if some sleeper had been disturbed by his intrusion and had rolled over into the pillows again.

Downstairs the shape of one shrouded object showed that it was a tall, long case clock. He pulled the dust sheet from it and looked up at its finely painted face. The hands stood at five minutes past the hour of two. He took his watch out of his waistcoat pocket and snapped it open. His own merrily ticking timepiece matched that of the clock that had stood silent for over thirty years. An eerie feeling descended upon him. He felt his scalp prickle and it went through his mind that such clocks often stopped at the hour when the owner of the house died. It was highly likely that Kate had slipped from life at such a time, for it was often in the small hours that a last breath was drawn.

He dropped his watch back into its pocket and looked for the key to the long case clock. It was tucked in by one of the carved columns that ornamented it. After immobilizing the striking mechanism, for he could not risk a booming of the hours to resound beyond the walls of Honeybridge, he wound up the clock until its strong, slow tick came clearly into the quiet hall, the pendulum swinging. To Tom it was as if he had set the heartbeat of Honeybridge going again. Before the clock needed winding again he would bring Nicolette to this haven where he felt he belonged. And why shouldn't he feel part of Honeybridge? Kate's blood ran through his veins as much as Daniel's and that of his own father who had been born within these very walls. Although he could see little enough of the house by lamplight he could understand already why Kate had wanted to keep Honeybridge for her own even after she had moved into Easthampton House on the hill, for this old house, with its oak-paneled walls, black-beamed ceilings, and mellow floors, had a special atmosphere about it, something warm and safe and secure that he could neither identify nor explain, but it was there. The thought of sharing it with Nicolette made his pulse race. Here he would be tender and loving to her in a privacy that had never been theirs before.

Before he left the house he looked in the kitchen for a rack on which keys were hung, and he found what he was looking for. Whether it was the right key for the back door or not did not matter, because he found one that fitted. Pocketing it, he left by the same route as that by which he had entered, and after locking the outside gates he secured them with their own chain, to which he fastened a padlock of his own brought along in readiness. As he turned homeward to Easthampton House he was jubilant in the knowledge that he had accomplished everything he had set out to do.

All that remained was to get word to Nicolette, and that could be done. He had seen her several times since the evening of the carnival, sometimes to speak to, at others only to view her from a

distance, waiting for the moment when he could catch her eye, and then for a few brief seconds they would say more to each other from a distance than they had dared yet put into words. When she had failed to come to the second carnival evening he had been racked by jealousy until he learned that a farewell party for Lawrence at the Hall had prevented her coming, although even then his feelings were mixed. His reluctance to accept that anything should have kept her away was combined with an elation at the departure of the detestable fellow who had dared to kiss Nicolette within his sight and hearing, it being no excuse that Lawrence had not known he was lying bruised and battered and bleeding within inches of them in the conservatory. A truculent misery returned when she did not appear at the third and last carnival of the season, for in order to be able to skate with her he had adopted the disguise of a clown, not even Beckworth able to recognize him beneath the white paint and the huge scarlet mouth that gave a permanent smile to lips that became more and more compressed as the evening went by with no sign of Nicolette. Recklessly he had gone to the Hall in search of her when the carnival came to an end, only to find that a birthday ball for Olivia Radcliffe was in progress, and he had skulked about in the darkness, going from window to window to peer in at the festivities, savage to see that Nicolette was much in demand for the dancing, and scarcely able to hold himself back from bursting in and snatching her away from everybody there. Had the night not turned to a chill drizzle, a sharp reminder that summer was fading fast, he might have managed a word or two with her in the grounds, but the dampness kept everyone indoors, and he was forced to wait until the last carriage had gone and a light appeared in her window before he could make his presence known. He had forgotten in his wretchedness that he had failed to remove the clown paint from his face, and it had not helped his mood that she had burst into laughter at the sight of him, which had spurred him into quarreling with her, an outlet for his thwarted feelings, and that night there had been no sweet kisses to heal the breach: she had flown back into the house with her color high, and the light in her window had been extinguished a few minutes later, showing that she wanted no more to do with him that night no matter how much more gravel he showered at her window. Not that he did anything but turn his back on the Hall, the grotesque, painted grin on his face at war with the wrathful despair in his eyes. He had not seen her since. All he could hope for was that she had recovered from the quarrel as quickly as he had done and that she would not turn aside from the prearranged signal that they had planned together.

It was early morning when he rose at Easthampton House. Taking a horse from the stables, he rode to the tree near the gates of the Hall where once Nicolette had spotted him waiting for her. There he knotted a length of blue silk ribbon to one of the branches, a piece that Nicolette had given him some time ago for that very purpose, and after a glance through the gates in the faint hope of seeing her, a hope dashed by the sight of the deserted drive, he cantered away again. Had there been the slightest chance of Nicolette coming out alone on horseback he would have waited, but Beth, who had been country bred, could ride staunchly if not elegantly, and since her coming to the Hall she always accompanied Nicolette on all morning gallops whether on the shore or out into the countryside.

All that day, although he realized there was little chance of Nicolette letting him know immediately that she had seen the ribbon, he looked for a message from her, refusing to believe that she would let the quarrel come between them. The following morning he went through the letters on the tray in the hall before they could be brought to the breakfast table, and was sharply disappointed to find nothing from her. The pattern was repeated the next day, and even though she was constantly on his mind as each hour went by, he was nevertheless taken by surprise when proof came to him that she had put the quarrel from her as he had done. He had come from one of the small souvenir shops on the Pier, having settled some query about whether there should be a sale of present stock before it closed up for the winter, when a woman, waiting near the entrance of the roller-skating rink, came forward into his path.

"Good afternoon, Mr. Warwyck."

It was Beth, stern-faced and soberly dressed, who had addressed him. He was taken aback that she should know his true identity and seek him out there, which could mean she had come to warn him off Nicolette, a disastrous state of affairs. He hid his qualms.

"Good afternoon to you, Miss Macdonald. We can't talk here. Come with me to my office."

In the narrow confines of the tiny office that had once been a theater box she took the chair he offered and sat primly and stiff-backed, holding her tartan purse vertically on her lap, gloved fingers bent over the clasp. He leaned back in his own chair, trying to appear relaxed and at ease.

"Well, now," he said. "There must be a very good reason for you to come here. I'd like to hear it."

She eyed him astutely. She had seen him several times at the roller-skating rink, but this was the first time she had had the chance to study him close at hand. It was easy to see why Nicolette was infatuated. Although she herself was more than twice his age, that did not prevent her summing him up as a disturbingly handsome young man who had the height and leanness to set off the good clothes that he wore, and in spite of a boyish fullness lingering in the lips of the well-cut mouth there was a mature determination to the nose and chin, denoting a strength of will that stretched beyond his years. She had decided, before she came, to lay her cards on the table, which was in keeping with her practical nature, and she could tell he would prefer it to be that way.

"When Miss Nicolette furst dropped hints tae me that she had an admirer I told her it wouldna be worth my while tae risk losing my employment by letting her have more freedom than that tae which she is entitled." She jerked her head up. "I have come tae see whether ye're prepared tae make it worth my while, Mr. Warwyck."

Her bluntness made him sit forward in his chair, and he folded his hands on the desk in front of him. "I think we could come to some arrangement, Miss Macdonald. Tell me, how did you learn that I was the admirer in question?"

Her thick brows twitched together cynically. "I'm a canny creature. I soon spotted how Miss Nicolette always looked for ye when we came to the roller-skating rink. I have seen the expression on her bonny face when ye have come to watch her skate, or stroll oh so casually down the aisle when she took a wee rest. I found out who ye were, and then I understood why ye couldna come a-calling at the Hall like any other respectable young man with honorable intentions."

He sucked in the corners of his mouth and frowned. "I had not realized we had made our feelings for each other so transparent."

"Not to anyone else, have no fear of that. Ye must remember that I have known Miss Nicolette since she was a wee bairn, and in any case I was already alerted to the fact of her being attracted tae someone of whom her grandmother wouldna approve. I'll not ask how ye intend finally tae resolve the situation, because it isna my place tae ask or question, but if I'm tae be expected tae look the other way tae allow the two of ye tae meet, I must secure my ain future." Her expression was grim. "I'm not a sentimental woman, Mr. Warwyck. Life taught me the foolishness of that many years ago. I carried out my duties in the Stuart household tae the best of my ability, simply because I valued the position I held and didna want tae lose it. Good domestic posts are hard tae come by anywhere, and times have always been very hard in Scotland. There'll be no easy return tae employment there for me when my present post as chaperone comes tae an end. For a long while now I've been saving every penny tae buy myself a wee shop and finish being at the beck and call of others. That's my ambition, Mr. Warwyck. How far are ye prepared tae see me taewards that aim?"

He decided that it must have been a hard school that had taught Beth to be so set toward her own ends, but at least she had made no pretense about it. "What figure did you have in mind?"

She answered promptly. "Two hundred pounds in cash now. Another hundred if I should be dismissed for failing tae keep my charge under my eye day and night. Mrs. Radcliffe is a real tartar, y'ken, more than a mite touched in the head it seems tae me, and if she gave me the sack I could expect tae find myself put outside the gates of the Hall with my belongings, and my wages stopped and no letter of reference tae secure another post. The same arrangement for payment must apply if and when ye and Miss Nicolette part company, which has tae be taken into consideration, because I'll remind ye that she isna nineteen until the twelfth day of January next, and I want full compensation for the risks that I'll have taken, risks that could still come out when it's all over and earn me my dismissal."

He was thinking that it was a lot of money that she had asked for, but he did not intend to quibble over it, merely thankful for Great-Aunt Jassy's legacy that would enable him to pay the sum. As for ever parting from Nicolette, he could not foresee such an incredible happening taking place on his part, and he would not contemplate any on hers. "And in return?" he queried in a businesslike manner.

"I'll ask no questions and I'll not notice if Miss Nicolette goes off on her own sometimes. Tae me this feud between the Warwyck and the Radcliffe families is like those between the clans at home. It will no be the first time that two young people have braved the wrath of their elders tae meet, nor will it be the last."

"I'll have the money for you tomorrow."

She stood up. "I'll call for it in the afternoon about this time, and if ye want tae accompany Miss Nicolette on her morning ride tomorrow, I'll bide behind." For the first time her expression softened slightly. "I'll do my best for both of ye. If my circumstances were different I wouldna have put a price on my aid, because, as I said, I've known Miss Nicolette for a long time and naturally I'm fond of the lass and wish her only the best in life, but the thirty pounds a year I receive in wages from her grandmother wouldna get me that wee shop this side of my sixtieth birthday. Your money will."

As she stepped it out down the scarlet flock-papered corridor she almost laughed aloud at the meager bonus Mrs. Radcliffe had promised her for taking good care of Nicolette. Tomorrow she would have the price of the shop in her hands, and later Tom Warwyck, being a gentleman and thus to be trusted to keep his word, would give her the rest that would set her up in stock to sell in it and still leave a bit for the bank. It meant that, for her own financial settlement, the sooner the love affair was over the better, and she could not see it being of long duration for the very reason that she had given to the young man, who was himself at an age when one pretty face could turn his head as quickly as another. Ungrudgingly she wished them joy of their love while it lasted. Everyone should throw a bonnet over the windmill just once in life. With hindsight she did not regret hers. It had comprised the sweetest moments she had ever known.

Tom did not go on horseback to meet Nicolette next morning. He would not have Beth dictating when and where they should meet, however well-meaning her intention had been. Before anything else they had a quarrel to patch up between them, and he would wait for Nicolette to set the time and place for that when it suited her. When Beth came for her money in the afternoon she looked askance at him, but made no reference to his non-appearance earlier that day, simply pushing the money into her purse and going again, scarcely a word passing between them. He had the feeling that Nicolette had not gone riding for the same reason, although that he would not know until he saw her.

A restless anticipation filled him. Now, whenever they were together, there should not be that tenseness of preparation for flight about her, for they would know just how long they could spend in each other's company without fear of untimely interruption or discovery. When she came at last to seek him out it was in the one place he had least expected and where he most wanted her to be. He was on his own in the barn, having gone there to put in some work planing a stack of timber while Hab was out fishing, and when he happened to glance up, a sixth sense telling him he was no longer alone, he saw her through the bare frames of *Sea Star*, watching him. Against the fading daylight of the half-open barn door behind her, her fine-boned face held a luminous pallor, her eyes seemed larger and darker, and a rich-toned nimbus of the last sun rays was held in the escaping tendrils of her hair. She carried her hat and her gloves as if she had discarded the conventional part of her before venturing into the barn, and he was vaguely aware that the soft pattern of the dress and shoulder cape that she wore seemed to blend with the mellow hues of their surroundings, making her look at one with the beginnings of the craft by which she stood. Slowly he straightened up, putting the plane down on a side bench. She let what she was carrying drop into the wood shavings about her feet, and her hands lifted wing-like from her wrists as if she were poised for his arms where she stood. Yet both knew that the foolish, unnecessary quarrel still hung between them like an invisible mist. Both wanted it dispersed, and broke the silence of her coming simultaneously.

"I'm sorry I lost my temper—"

"I shouldn't have laughed when you were rain-soaked and cold—"

It was enough. All was healed. He skirted *Sea Star* to reach her, and she came running to him with outstretched hands, which he grasped, scooping them toward his chest and bringing her close to him so that they stood in intense awareness of each other's nearness, stunned a little from the renewed explosion of love in their hearts, which seemed to have left speech solely to their eyes. He bent his head and kissed her upraised lips tenderly and cherishingly. To her the world held still.

"I love you, my darling." It was the first time he had voiced the words that he had conveyed to her in silence a thousand times. He had not been conscious of waiting until the right moment, but this was it, when all he wanted from life was with him in this girl whom he loved and the boat that he would sail. Such perfection of circumstances was akin to paradise, and as he slid his arms about her slenderness and held her to him in a long embrace, she laid her head against his shoulder in her own utter contentment.

"I love you, Tom," she murmured blissfully. "For ever and ever."

"For ever and ever," he repeated in promise, kissing her hair. "Nobody shall part us, not your family or mine. Somehow and somewhere we shall marry, and if *Sea Star* is the only home I can offer you for the time being, will you bear with me?"

She arched herself from the waist away from him to link her hands behind his neck and look into his face, her own aglow with soft wonderment, and it was as if their love flowed between them, joining their heartbeats, absorbing each into the other. "I would live in the open air with you if that was how it had to be," she declared fervently. "You are offering me a palace. Show me how *Sea Star* will be. Tell me how she will look when that day comes."

He kissed her again, fiercely this time out of the joy within him, and she responded adoringly, straining against him in innocent amorousness, until out of consideration for her he forced himself to break the gentle lock of her loving arms. Still murmuring of his love for her, punctuating his words with kisses, he drew her from a source of wonder and delight more compelling than the subject of *Sea Star* to tell her what she wanted to know. He moved around the beginnings of the yacht, slapping a hand with casual pride against the stem or the transom while he described how the planking would be fastened, pointed out the gussets and the hanging trees that would secure the deck beams, and demonstrated how high the cabin roof would come. He tried not to be too technical, but by the questions she asked she revealed an intelligent grasp of the fundamentals, and when he talked of priming and caulking, brasswork and paintwork and measurements, masts and spars and rigging, she listened intently all the time, her very attention a further expression of her love for him. When he came to the end of all he could tell her for the time being he smiled a trifle self-consciously at her, thinking that perhaps his enthusiasm had run away with him.

"There. I've talked too much and too long about the other girl in my life, haven't I?"

She laughed quietly, shaking her head, and came to him with swift steps to kiss him with great warmth. "I want to see *Sea Star* grow and be launched and take sail. Don't leave me out of any of it."

He chuckled, pleased and proud, and pulled her to him in the crook of his arm. "I promise. You'll not be far from her whenever we meet from now on. Nowhere could be better, because few people come along the barn lane since it leads only to this meadow, and the trees shield the stable gates of Honeybridge on all sides."

Her eyes widened in consternation. "Honeybridge? It's derelict, isn't it?"

He guessed she was remembering the mill and feared it would be the same. "The grounds are overgrown, and the house is dusty with everything covered in sheets, but there's no sign that I could see of mildew or damp or anything else to spoil it for us." He went on to describe how he got in there, and explained how Daniel had made a gift of it to Kate because she had never wanted to relinquish their first home together.

"How many times have you been in there?" she asked.

"Only twice. The first time was to have a quick look around, and the second time I left matches and candles ready in the kitchen, because the house is shuttered inside and out. I did spend several hours clearing away some of the undergrowth to make a pathway that can't be seen by anyone passing the gates."

"Do people go past often?"

"Hardly ever, as far as I know. The meadow is out of bounds to trespassers, and the fines imposed have been heavy in the past. I'll try to get at least one room to rights before I take you there."

"No, don't." Her eyes were entranced. "Let's do that together, Tom. It must be a very special place if your grandmother held it so dear. It mustn't be blundered into and treated like any ordinary house."

"It isn't an ordinary house. Far from it."

Something in his voice made her look at him keenly. "What haven't you told me?"

"It is that everything that would have reminded my grandfather of Kate was put into Honeybridge after she died. I don't know what is there. I didn't have time to look. All I do know is that there'll be a portrait of her somewhere. It used to hang in the Green Drawing Room at Easthampton House, but my grandfather's grief at losing his wife has never left him, and for that reason the portrait remains with all else that was hers at Honeybridge. Shall you mind so much of the past being there?"

She considered carefully. "No. It's sad and romantic. I've heard many harsh tales about Daniel Warwyck, but I never knew of this side to his character."

"The Warwycks are not as black as they've been painted to you."

"Neither are the Radcliffes as you believe them to be," she countered quickly and defensively.

He wanted no friction between them to mar these moments, and he traced the curve of her face with his fingertips. "There'll be time to talk about the feud and anything else we want to discuss or sort out between us at Honeybridge."

She relaxed again and caught his hand to her lips, kissing each knuckle fervently. "We'll never quarrel about anything again, the feud least of all."

He had made the same resolve, in spite of being less optimistic than she, realizing only too well how deep-rooted were their individual loyalties, but he was convinced that he could make her forget all else in his loving of her, and in time she would sever all ties without a backward glance. His question came with eagerness. "How soon may I take you to Honeybridge?"

She answered him radiantly. "On Thursday next we can have the whole evening together. There's a magic lantern show on Ancient Egypt at the Assembly Rooms, the first in a whole winter's course of lectures on civilizations of the world, and Beth gained permission from my grandmother to take me." She chuckled deliciously. "Nobody thought to ask me personally if I intended to go or if I wanted to attend! Beth can go on her own. I'll be free to be with you."

He was rendered almost speechless by the prospect, having wondered sometimes how he would be able to synchronize time off from work at the Pier with the hours when she would be able to get away. Now he would simply make every Thursday evening his night off from the roller-skating rink, and all other meetings would be a bonus. "That's wonderful." He shook his head at the miracle she had achieved. "Really wonderful."

They kissed in such jubilant passion that he could no longer hold back from thrusting open the little silken loops that fastened the buttons down the front of her bodice, and amid lace and cambric he cupped the warm firmness of her high, young breast in his sensitive, seeking hand. She started at the alien touch and stiffened in his embrace, her breathing quickening to match the panic-racing of her heart, but he tightened the arm that held her and went on kissing and caressing her with such tender exploration that the tenseness melted from her, leaving such a trembling in its place that it seemed to pass into his own body, her love flowing with it, and had he had any doubt at all of the strength of her feeling for him it would have been swept away.

When he released her she was quick to turn her back to him, shy and fearful that he would look upon what he had made his own with his caresses, dazed by the sensations he set throbbing within her. As she fumbled with shaking hands to refasten the button loops, a blush seeped up her throat to burst like fire into her cheeks at the full realization of what she had permitted and what he had done.

He saw the color dyeing her cheek as she struggled with the buttons, and loved her for it. From behind her as she fastened the last one he lowered his head to kiss her neck, which made her respond involuntarily with an ecstatic shiver, setting her close to panic again, her movements agitated. When he took hold of her by the shoulders to draw her back against him she resisted, moving instead a couple of paces forward out of his range and, still turned from him, spoke in a tremulous voice. "I'm afraid of Honeybridge."

If she had said she was afraid of him or of herself he would have been less surprised. He supposed her to have made some lightning reconsideration of the house's shrine-like condition. Did she imagine it would cast some gloomy spell over the splendor of their loving? "There's nothing to frighten you there. On the contrary, it has a welcoming atmosphere."

"It is exactly that I now fear."

He understood then what filled her with trepidation. He had also first thought of it as a place of love, but only as a fit setting for the two of them to be together. "No harm shall come to you at Honeybridge," he vowed intently, a new meaning to his previous words.

He meant it. He loved her, he longed with all the heights and depths of his sensual nature to make love to her, but he had no intention of seducing her. She was not Laura or any of the others in the past with whom he had had his way. She was the girl he was going to marry, not to be treated lightly or selfishly, and everything in his upbringing and in his station in life had geared him to this respect for the gently reared young woman of his choice.

Nicolette was wiser. She realized that however high his motives, however staunch his intentions, their courtship must inevitably continue to follow a different pattern than was usual, and the seclusion of Honeybridge would set traps for them that normal circumstances would never have allowed. Until a few minutes ago she had not thought beyond an exchange of kisses in the sanctuary he had found for them. Now she was at a loss, needing courage to go forward, knowing there was no retreat. The time for retreating had been months ago on the night she had found Tom bruised and blood-spattered on the floor of the conservatory. Scarcely able out of her new shyness to meet his ardent, watchful gaze, she spoke over her shoulder to him, her own eyes awash with emotion, the clear hazel of the irises as full of shadows as the rock pools off Easthampton, and to him just as intriguing and mysterious.

"How shall I find my way to Honeybridge?"

"I'll show you now." He linked his fingers with hers, paused while she stooped to pick up the hat and gloves she had dropped, and led her out of the barn and through the shelter of the trees, holding aside low branches for her, until they came to the gates of the stable yard. She peered through uncertainly, just able to discern the distant chimney pots in the gathering dusk.

"How overgrown it is. Shall I ever find the pathway?"

"I'll be waiting by the gates for you. A locksmith has duplicated the keys for me and I'll give you yours tomorrow evening." His face was serious and full of yearning. "Every hour will be like a day until the time comes."

She said nothing, only looked at him in a gush of loving that overwhelmed all else. In that dark, secret house they would come to know each other truly, and it was foolish to harbor misgivings about how that knowledge might come about. They belonged to each other, and together all problems and anxieties and mysteries could be solved. Abruptly she threw herself forward against his chest and flung her arms about his neck, entangling him in her hat ribbons as she kissed him full on the lips.

"Good night, dear Tom."

She swung away and hurried at a little darting run in and out of the trees back the way they had come, ramming on her hat as she went. He followed as far as the barn, and was in time to see a bright flicker of taffeta ribbons disappearing at a point down the lane where Beth waited alone for her in a wagonette.

After he had locked the barn he set off for the Pier. Business had fallen off somewhat since the season had come to a close and the visitors had departed, but such was the craze for roller-skating that a good crowd of local enthusiasts showed up every evening, although these were expected to diminish sharply in number when the new roller-skating rink in Merrelton had its grand opening in two weeks' time. Neither Tom nor the manager could wonder at this switch of patronage when the facilities offered there would outweigh anything the somewhat dilapidated Pier Pavilion could provide, to say nothing of the long, windswept walk up the deck to it in the colder autumn weather. Nevertheless it had been a profitable season, and there was nothing to complain about. Tom knew his hours at the Pier would soon be sharply reduced, but this suited him, for it would release as much time as he needed to work with Hab on *Sea Star*, and now there would be the additional bonus of being able to come and go freely at Honeybridge.

Because it was a weekday none of the patrons stayed until the last minute, and Tom was able to lock up and go home by ten o'clock. He had forgotten completely that Helen Edenfield and her invalid sister had been due to arrive at Easthampton House that day, and was momentarily surprised when he entered the hall to see a total stranger coming down the stairs.

"You must be Tom," she said in a warm, undulating voice. "I'm Helen Edenfield."

It struck him at once that here was a woman self-assured and completely at ease with herself, a woman able to deal with life competently without the need for male protection and guidance. Perhaps it came from the responsibility of looking after an invalid sister for many years, but whatever the reason, even he could feel her independence as a challenge, and he could see well enough why Jeremy was eager to wed and bed her, quite apart from the fortune she possessed. She was swift and graceful in her movements, her step light as she came down the last of the stairs, and her figure all that any man could desire. Her hair was black and glossy, dressed into a heavy chignon, and her dark eyes were lively and sparkling in an oval face enhanced by a very fine complexion. Tom looked at her and liked her, and thought his brother a lucky fellow if he could get her.

"How do you do, Miss Edenfield."

"Call me Helen, please," she insisted, smiling at him. "In that manner you'll be following Jeremy's example. I dislike unnecessary formality, and kind-hearted Sir Daniel and Donna have already made Beatrice and me feel like members of the family."

"I'm glad to hear it, Helen."

"That's much better." She nodded approvingly. "I was looking forward to meeting you. Jeremy was here to greet us when we arrived, and he's waiting in the drawing room now with your grandfather and your aunt."

So Jeremy was losing no time. "How is your sister?" Tom asked.

"Very tired from the traveling, I'm afraid. Everything exhausts her. I have just seen her into bed and there she must stay for two or three days at least. After that I hope she will be rested enough to come downstairs and start to enjoy her surroundings and benefit from the marvelous sea air of Easthampton." She turned in the direction of the Green Drawing Room, and as he fell into step at her side she looked up and around at the elegant proportions of the hall that was lighted by day through the circular, glazed lantern in the high ceiling, and in the night hours by a crystal gasolier, which was sending shadows softly across the floor. "My sister and I are both quite enchanted by this beautiful sea dream of a house."

It was a beautiful house. He thought it observant of her to have noticed how its muted golds and blues and greens combined to echo the hues of the sea and shore of Easthampton, for not everybody was sensitive to it. In many ways the house was old-fashioned, the furniture and decor unchanged since his grandfather had built it during the reign of George IV, but that was its charm, linking it with that royal patron of the prize ring and the seaside, and only the elegant furniture of that period would ever look at home in Easthampton House. Tom commented on this fact as he went in front of Helen to open the double doors for her.

"I agree entirely," she replied with a little nod that sent a gleam running across her rich, black hair. "Thank heaven nobody in this house has a penchant for horsehair sofas and Gothic chairs and skirts around any shapely piano leg."

Tom exploded into laughter and she joined in with him, her merriment full of lilting cadences, while the opening doors revealed them as if in a frame to all who were in the drawing room. Then with a start she saw that three newcomers had arrived since she had taken her sister up to bed. It was not hard to guess whom they were, there being a likeness to Jeremy across the eyes of the florid-faced woman with a tremor to the fidgety hands that were playing with a silver mesh reticule on her lap. Sitting beside Donna on a sofa was the quite fashionably dressed person who must be Mrs. Warwyck's companion, and standing tall by the fireplace was Richard Warwyck, the broadly built man who had fathered the Warwyck boys. Helen became extremely conscious of his piercing blue eyes fixed upon her in a faintly incredulous stare as if the sight of her had shattered the darkness of an incalculable number of years. She found it disturbing and electrifying, the man's powerful personality seeming to swamp the room uncomfortably for her, and in escape she looked thankfully and with a very real gladness at Jeremy, who had sprung to his feet at her entrance.

"Allow me to present you to my parents, Helen. It's most opportune that they should call in on their way home from a concert at the Assembly Rooms."

Tom, whose spirits had flagged at the unexpected sight of his father in the drawing room, watched as Richard's gaze shifted and changed to rest stonily upon him. They had not met since the night of the quarrel, although out of a sense of duty Tom had visited his mother at the Grange several times. The bitter words that had been exchanged lay like a desert between them, nothing resolved or changed, but he would not let common courtesy go by the board in his grandfather's house. "Good evening, sir," he said stiffly. The greeting was returned with a curt nod, and then Tom was ignored again as his brother presented Helen Edenfield.

Meg, who was craving for a drink, every nerve end screaming, forced herself to a show of some interest when faced with the young woman whom her dear Jeremy had wanted her to meet. "How do you do, Miss Edenfield," she said in the special voice she had cultivated for genteel company. "I'm sorry to have missed your sister, I'm sure. She's poorly in health, I believe. I hope you'll bring her to take tea with me soon. I'm at home every Wednesday afternoon."

"Thank you, Mrs. Warwyck. We'll look forward to calling on you."

Jeremy spoke up, tucking Helen's hand into the crook of his elbow. "You'll be seeing Helen often at the Grange, Mother, if I have anything to do with it."

Meg's eyes were blank, her own private desperation taking over, and she was no longer listening. She had done what her son had required of her, and all she wanted now was to get home as quickly as possible. Constance always allowed her a good measure as a nightcap, and tonight, as a reward for sitting through that boring concert in full view of many of the local gentry, she deserved half a bottle at the very least, and would demand it.

Helen, able at close quarters to recognize signs in Meg of the alcoholism that had sent her own father to an early grave, promptly understood the reason for the constant companion, and her heart stirred with compassion for both the unfortunate wife and the husband caught up in circumstances that blighted all aspects of family life and brought every kind of misery in its wake. All earlier confusion forgotten, she regarded Richard Warwyck levelly, no longer thrown by the tempestuous forcefulness of an unhappy man. To aid her, no trace remained of that flash-point stare that had caught them both unawares. On the contrary, he showed a bland politeness well suited to the occasion of meeting a prospective daughter-in-law for the first time.

"My Aunt Anna sent her kindest regards to you," she said easily. "I believe you used to attend card parties at her house years ago when she lived in Easthampton before she was married."

He answered her graciously. "I did indeed. I well remember the elderly Miss Edenfield who chaperoned her and the rest of the young ladies present on those occasions."

"That was my great-aunt. She was quite a dragon, I believe."

"Aren't all chaperones?" he remarked drily.

Her eyes twinkled at him. "Don't say that, Mr. Warwyck. I have chaperoned my brother's schoolgirl daughters from time to time."

"All I can say is that they were very fortunate," he said with gallantry. She returned his smile.

Meg, seeing Helen move on to speak to Constance, wondered how much longer it would be before she was released from the purgatory of not having a glass in her hand. She was sorely tempted to cut short this impromptu reception for Miss Edenfield by announcing that she was ready to depart, but any lapse of behavior resulted in Constance being stricter about her drinking than Richard had ever been, withdrawing those extra tots that were so welcome when the stress and strain of longer and longer periods of abstinence from alcohol became all too much for her. Vaguely she realized that Constance had set an iron hand upon her, although exactly how and when it had come about she was not quite sure; all she did know was that on the credit side Constance was gathering together some semblance of life for her as lady of the house, and although it was only Donna and a few other close friends of the Warwyck family who came when she was *at home*, Constance had promised that eventually all the local ladies would call, and she believed her. In the meantime, her throat was parched and she hoped and prayed that the silver-topped brandy flask that she had hidden down the side of the upholstered seat in the landau that was waiting to convey them home again had not been discovered. She blinked. Tom had drawn up a chair beside her.

"How are you, Mother?"

"No better for your inquiry," she snapped repetitiously.

He recognized her mood. "Did you enjoy the concert?" he inquired tolerantly.

She sniffed disdainfully. "There wasn't nothing but violins screeching and cymbals clashing loud enough to take off the top of my poor head."

"I'm surprised you went," he said. "I know you don't care for classical music."

"Constance wanted to go, and I asked your pa to get tickets." Her silver-mesh reticule jingled as she twisted it to and fro in her increasing tension. "God! I must get out of this house soon or I'll go crazy."

He knew the reason for her wild despair and put a comforting hand on her arm. "I'll tell Father you're ready to leave."

"No!" Her high-pitched note would have drawn attention if everybody else had not been engaged in conversation. "Constance don't allow that. She likes to be in company, and if we're on our own she decides when to leave, but if your pa is with us she says I must always defer to his wishes. He'll decide when it's time to go."

Tom had noticed with increasing disquiet the iron dominance that Constance was exerting over his mother. Admittedly there seemed to be a marginal improvement in her condition, which could have come about anyway with the right kind of supervision, but he was certain that his mother was becoming more than a little afraid of her companion. For himself, he had come actively to dislike the woman, who forever seemed to be lurking about when he visited the Grange, giving him the feeling that she listened at doors whenever the opportunity arose. Unfortunately there was nothing he could pinpoint to give grounds for definite complaint. Had he and his father been on speaking terms it could have been discussed between them, but in the present state of hostility it was out of the question. Instead, he would talk to Aunt Donna, who had always been close to his father and could bring the situation out into the open. In the meantime he felt compelled to speak his mind.

"Have you told Father about this rule?"

Meg shrugged irritably. "It ain't a rule. Just part of the pattern of getting things back to normal."

He could tell she was quoting her companion's words, and his anxiety increased. "Do remember that you must tell Father if there is anything in Constance's attitude toward you that you consider to be cruel or unjust or simply unkind," he urged with emphasis.

Her wrought nerves snapped, her high color congesting to a dark crimson in her cheeks. "Don't you *dare* to tell your mother what she should or should not do! And—worse!—cast aspersions on my dear friend." She was confused in her wrath, subconsciously aware that somehow Tom had probed into a dread that she did not want to think about or examine. "You've been a troublemaker all your life, a worry and a nuisance since the day you were born." All else was forgotten in a need to punish Tom for what he had done. "Don't you come near the Grange again. I don't want you there and neither does your pa." She sprang to her feet and shouted at her husband across the room. "Richard! Ain't that true? Didn't you say that Tom had no place at the Grange except on his bended knees?"

A dreadful silence fell. With a stricken expression Richard rose from where he was sitting and looked from the blazing face of his wife to the ashen visage of his son, who had also risen to his feet. Before he could speak Tom burst out the awful question.

"Did you say that?"

It had been said weeks ago in a spate of temper against Tom's rebellion. The old adage of the one who had offended coming on bended knees before a reconciliation could be made had been uttered without thought and without true meaning in the heat of the moment. Richard had even forgotten it until this minute. He went on looking at the dearest of all his sons and saw the gulf widening as if the very floor between them had cracked and was sweeping them apart at an incalculable speed, but he could only answer with truth.

"I said it," he stated austerely.

Helen, acutely conscious of being the only outsider present, saw

what was happening and longed to cry out to the father and son
not to go on knifing each other in the estrangement that Jeremy
had told her about. Their personal agony was almost palpable,
their anguish visible to all but the loud-mouthed woman who
screeched triumphantly, rounding on the lad.

"Now you know! You're no son of ours no more."

In the background Donna gave a stifled moan, and Daniel, who
had not moved from his chair, closed his eyes and shook his head.
After one last, tearing exchange of looks with Richard, Tom spun
on his heel and went from the room, leaving the doors swinging.
Helen saw that Richard had been on the point of saying something conciliatory and had left it too late. She wanted to cry out
that he should go after Tom before such a rift proved irrevocable,
but she had no right to interfere, for she was the stranger in their
midst.

"We'll be our way now," Richard said to the room at large, and
he made a bow to Helen. "Good night, Miss Edenfield."

Constance also bade her good night, and only Meg was dumb,
her buoyancy ebbing away as a realization of the scene she had
created took over. Her pleading eyes darted everywhere like those
of a child seeking a friendly face after committing some wrongdo-
ing, only to find it was in vain. Constance hurried her out, and
Meg, suddenly released toward the source of her salvation,
snatched her own cape from a servant and rushed out ahead
into the landau. Constance followed swiftly, suspicion aroused.
By the time she reached the landau Meg was gulping down the
contents of a brandy flask, her head thrown back, a dark stain
across the front of her magenta bodice where she had splashed
herself in her haste when snatching off the silver top.

In the drawing room Jeremy and Helen were left momentarily
alone, Donna and Daniel having both followed the others out to
see them off. "I'm dashed sorry about all that," he muttered.

"Please don't apologize," Helen replied reassuringly. "Nobody
can predict a family quarrel."

"At least you have glimpsed the harsh side of the Warwycks,"
he said with a rueful sigh, exerting his considerable charm while

seething inwardly at what had taken place. "So you'll be able to judge me in every kind of light."

Her face was serious. "That is how it should be. All that stands out in my mind is the Warwyck kindness I have received and the pleasurable moments spent already in Warwyck company that will always far outweigh anything else."

Her words had been intended to encompass the few times that she and Jeremy had been together since their first meeting, but she found herself thinking of Richard instead, and how he had looked at her as if he had been suddenly reborn.

Along the sands in the starry night Tom walked off his temper at a furious pace, kicking aside pebbles and driftwood and anything else that lay in his path. That was it! The last straw! He would not go near the Grange again whatever happened. His mother was less to blame than his father, for drink had blunted her ability to reason, but there was no excuse for Richard Warwyck, who appeared set on driving his youngest son as far from him as possible. Well, if that was the way they wanted it, Tom told himself, it was all right with him!

He went such a distance around the bay that it suddenly dawned on him that his parents wouldn't have a youngest son at all if he did not beat a hasty retreat from the incoming tide. Swinging back on his heel, he broke into a run along the shingle under the cliffs and skirted the old wreck through shallow waves with his shoes in his hand and his trouser legs rolled up, just in time to avoid getting cut off and stranded beyond help. The escape from danger in the nick of time had a sobering effect, and by the time he re-entered Easthampton House he had calmed down, although his resolution not to set foot again in the Grange until invited remained unchanged. He was less than pleased to find his Aunt Donna waiting up for him, for he was now dog-tired and ready for bed. In addition, there was nothing more irritating than to recover one's own equilibrium after a spot of trouble to find that somebody else had not. He could not remember having seen her look so annoyed with him before.

"How could you have criticized Constance to your mother?"

she began, wringing her hands in the distress of it. "I found out the details before they went home. Meg was so upset that she took to brandy in the carriage, undoing all the good the evening's outing had done her in the first place. It's taken Constance all these weeks to build up Meg's trust, and now you have set out to undermine it." Donna threw out her hands in an appeal for an explanation. "Why? What on earth had got into you? Tell me why."

His jaw set as he stood facing her in the drawing room, and he thrust his hands deep into the pockets of his evening jacket. "I don't trust Mrs. Meredith. I had made up my mind to speak to you about her. If Father and I had been on civil terms I would have put my misgivings to him, and you can be sure that he wouldn't have rested until everything was sorted out."

"You are being ridiculous." Donna bristled with indignation. "She has done wonders for Meg. When was your father last able to take your mother to a public social function as he did tonight? It must be several years at least. Constance is mending Meg's life where everybody else has failed, to say nothing of putting your parents' marriage together again as an outcome of that success. You should be as grateful as the rest of us. Let me hear what grounds you have for your distrust."

"The woman is sly. I can never be sure if she is speaking the truth or not."

Donna paced up and down in distress, her aesthetic garments flowing. "That is merely your own personal opinion of Constance, and I'm sorry to say it is also an adverse reflection upon my good judgment in appointing her." She was determined to take umbrage at everything he said, which warred painfully with her deep affection for her nephew and exacerbated her sense of outrage. "Let me have some proof from you of Constance's mismanagement."

"I have none, but I'm still sure Father would have been willing to follow through on my opinion where you are not. I truly believe that my mother has begun to go in fear of her."

"Nonsense!" Donna rounded on him. "Meg respects her authority, which is an entirely different matter."

"All I know is that I wouldn't let someone like Constance Meredith within a mile of my boat, and I consider that to be a good enough criterion for the far more important issue of wishing to protect my own mother from her evil influence."

"Strong words, Tom! Strong words indeed." She was visibly shaken that he should speak out so forcibly, and he seized the opportunity to quieten her down.

"Come on, Aunt Donna," he coaxed, putting an arm about her shoulders. "Stop being angry with me and consider what I have said. You're the only one in a position to judge whether or not there's any foundation for my unease about the woman. The Grange is barred to me now by both my parents, but that doesn't mean I have ceased to be concerned about either of them, and I should esteem it an enormous favor if you would make it your business to go often to my home to keep an eye on things, if only to prove me wrong."

"I shall prove you wrong," she retaliated sharply.

"Good. There's nothing that could please me more." His tone showed he did not expect to be easily won over. "Now if you will excuse me I'll be off to bed." At the door he stopped and looked back at her, his expression extremely grave. "Don't delay in going to the Grange, will you?"

"I have your mother's interests at heart," she reminded him touchily. "If I have the slightest doubt about anything I promise you it shall be put right."

He looked relieved, knowing that he could trust her. If she discovered she had made a mistake about Constance she would admit it and be true to her word.

The next day Donna visited the Grange, taking Helen with her. They found Meg sober, well dressed, and neatly coiffured, no sign of nervousness about her beyond the intense strain usual to her when on her best behavior, and Constance was smiling and attentive. The atmosphere was congenial, no reference being made to the disastrous events of the previous evening, and Jeremy joined them for tea. Just before they left, Richard came in, and somehow he and Helen began to discuss trees, whereupon he suggested that Jeremy show her the arboretum, which was a feature of the grounds. The young couple was gone some time, and when they returned Donna noticed that Helen looked immediately for Richard, obviously wishing to comment on the trees she had found most interesting, but he had absented himself again.

A good visit, Donna concluded to herself on the way home. Nothing at all to worry about with Meg and Constance. If there had been, it would most certainly have shown up today after yesterday's little contretemps. Whatever had made Tom think things were amiss? She would tell him how well everything had gone on this occasion, and reassure him from time to time to keep his mind at rest. Only one thing had struck her as a little odd, and it was not worth mentioning since it only emphasized the harmony between the two women: Meg had invited Constance to pour the tea. Anyone coming upon the scene by chance would have thought that Constance was the lady of the house.

Helen, seated in the carriage beside Donna, had her thoughts running along an entirely different line. In the arboretum Jeremy had kissed her, thus making his intentions toward her perfectly clear. They had come through the dark, mysterious shadows of many rare evergreen trees into a glade canopied by amber-hued foliage, the diffused light as golden as if each leaf were a miniature Chinese paper lantern. It was quiet, not a rustle beyond their own movements to disturb the silence, and she had been struck by the beauty of the scene.

"It's perfect here," she said in a hushed voice. "Just like being in the eye of a hurricane, a place of utter stillness while beyond these trees life goes teeming on."

"This is the middle of the arboretum, the very heart of it," he said, coming close to her as she leaned back against a gnarled trunk, marveling at the colors overhead. Her gaze lowered from the spread branches to rest upon him. Desire had tightened his features, his eyes dark and blazing, and she could not help but be stirred to excitement by the strength of passion directed toward her. All along he had attracted her, and yet she cherished no illusions about him. She had been sought after for her money before, and could tell a fortune-hunter as soon as she met one. Jeremy was no exception, and she would have known what he was about even if she had not heard of his ill-starred gaming ways and his commercial failures from others before they were actually introduced. She would have dismissed him as lightly as all the rest who had thought to court her if it had not been for an elusive, undefinable something about him that had made her reluctant to dismiss him out of hand. Just for once she had felt compelled to look beyond a man's mercenary attitude to the marriage that she knew he would offer her. She believed herself to be old enough and wise enough to have survived the early wildness of the heart common to the young, and understood sensibly her own yearning for physical fulfillment and the bearing of children. Her decision to bring Beatrice to Easthampton instead of Brighton or Bournemouth had not been swayed only by Sir Daniel's welcome offer of hospitality, but by the need to get to know Jeremy on his home ground and to discover whether they could build up a relationship that would survive the odds set unquestionably against it. To make a first decisive step in discovering the strength of her own feelings she had surrendered her lips willingly to Jeremy's kiss in the glade.

On the memory of that amorous encounter Helen passed a hand across her eyes. Donna, noticing it, leaned forward in the carriage seat. "Have you a headache?" she inquired kindly. "I thought when you came back from the arboretum that you looked a little drawn."

Helen shook her head, which was as much an attempt to clear her mind as it was to reassure Donna. "No, I'm quite well. It's been a busy day."

As soon as they reached Easthampton House, Helen went straight upstairs to see how Beatrice had fared during her absence, although the two maidservants they had brought with them, both middle-aged and reliable, alternated their duties to allow one or the other to be on call night and day. She found her sister sitting up in bed against the lace-edged pillows, a good fire blazing in the grate, and the curtains drawn against the dusk. As always Beatrice greeted her with a smile, put aside a book, and patted the coverlet with one thin hand for Helen to take a seat.

"Did you have a nice time?" she asked. Although only a year older than Helen she looked much more, the nature of her illness having pinched her features by suffering. There were premature gray streaks in her brown hair which presently lay loose about her shoulders, and her dark-lashed, amber eyes had the artificial brightness that comes from ill health. High spots of color tinted her cheeks. She had ailed from early childhood and had long since resigned herself to being a spectator of life more than a participant. She saw no virtue in her attitude, but Helen and all who knew her never ceased to wonder at her courage and amiable disposition. It was difficult at times to remember she was the invalid when she commiserated with someone who had a sniffy cold or concerned herself with another's cut finger, forever turning aside inquiries about her own state of health.

"Yes, it was most pleasant," Helen replied, sitting on the bed. "Did I seem long away?"

"Not at all." Beatrice chuckled proudly. "I had two visitors to my room. Sir Daniel brought Tom to meet me, and I found him a most agreeable young man. Tom brought me this book on the Sussex countryside that I have been reading, and a selection of those new picture postcards showing views of Easthampton, which I shall send to all our nieces and nephews. Now tell me about your afternoon at the Grange."

It was customary for Helen to give as interesting an account as she could of any social event she attended when Beatrice was unable to accompany her. "Richard Warwyck was there for a little while," she began. "He inquired after you and hopes to meet you soon."

"That was kind."

Helen went on to describe the Grange and to recount some of the conversation that had taken place over the teacups, but her thoughts returned again and again to what had happened in the arboretum that afternoon. Jeremy's kiss should have dominated all else for her, but remaining with her was the disquieting sense of disappointment that she had experienced when they had returned to the Grange together to find that Richard had gone off elsewhere in their absense.

Chapter 14

All through the day Nicolette had waited with a nervous impatience for the evening to come. Never had she known the hours to drag by so tediously. Then, almost without warning, the time to set out was upon her. She went to say good night to her grandmother, who would have retired by the time she returned home again, and was on the point of leaving the Hall with Beth in her wake when Hugh came in from the darkness outside. He was splashed with mud and reeked of the byre where he had handled a difficult calving, his ill-tempered expression showing that all had not ended well.

"Hello. Where are you off to?" he inquired of his sister, snatching off his coat and throwing it at a waiting servant.

"I thought you knew," Nicolette replied. "Grandmother has given me permission to attend a course of magic-lantern slide lectures."

"Oh? What's the subject?" If the entertainment promised to be amusing he would go with her, needing something to distract his mind from the blunder he had made. He had been so sure that he knew better than the cowman and the others there who had warned against too much haste. He felt he had made himself look a fool in front of his inferiors, the calf dead and a valuable cow on the point of expiring. Tomorrow he would instruct the steward to pay off the men who were present and see that they and their families were out of the tithe cottages on the estate by the end of the week. He made a grimace as Nicolette answered his question. "It sounds heavy going. I wouldn't have thought it was your cup of tea."

"I'm looking forward to my evening," she replied airily. "Come along, Beth. I don't want to be late."

Beth dropped her near the meadow gate and continued on to the Assembly Rooms. It was dark and chill, and the barn loomed black as she skirted it to make for the stable gates of Honeybridge, her dress and petticoats hitched up to avoid soiling the hems in the wet grass and fallen leaves. Beyond the hedges and Hoe Lane the sea sucked noisily at the shingle and spat it back again in breaking waves, but to her it was not as loud as her own hammering heart, and her breathing was fast and light.

"Tom," she whispered. "Are you there?"

He loomed up so quickly on the other side of the gates that she gave an involuntary gasp of alarm, and in his eagerness he reached through the bars to take the pale, oval face and bring it forward to meet his, kissing her with excitement and relief. "I nearly came looking for you, only I was afraid of missing you somewhere in the dark. I'll just get these gates open. They still screech a bit. I'll oil them again tomorrow."

As he opened them to pull her through she was caught up by his excitement, wildly in love and showing it in the way she leaned rapturously against him when he put an arm about her to show her the path he had cut through the undergrowth to Honeybridge. He had left the door open, and briefly they were in pitch darkness until a match spluttered and the wick of one candle and then three more in a four-branched candlestick leaped with flame to show her the white wood and copper of the great kitchen. She swiveled around looking at it all as she unfastened her cape and Tom took it from her, hanging it on a peg beside his own inside the doorway.

"Does it mind?" she said in a low voice, more to herself than to him.

"What do you mean?"

Her eyes were wide and uncertain. "Honeybridge. Do you feel any resentment at our intrusion?"

He smiled indulgently, hugging her to him. "You funny little thing. No, I don't. Why? Do you?"

"I'm not sure of anything yet. I won't be until I've seen all over it." She spun to look about her as if she might find in her immediate surroundings some hint of what would come. "Let's look in every room, explore each nook and cranny, and then after we have decided which room we like best we'll cover up the rest of the house again and lock it away."

"We're going to disturb a lot of dust. Didn't you bring anything to protect your clothing?"

She clapped her fingers to her cheeks in dismay. "I never thought about that. I should have brought the smock I wear when painting watercolors."

He had been about to move toward the dresser and he paused. "You paint, do you?" There was so much he had to learn about her, so much to know.

"A little," she said modestly.

His dwelling look praised her as if she had admitted to the talents of Manet and Degas and Renoir all rolled into one. Then he crouched down to pull out the bottom drawer of the dresser, where he scooped out a pile of starched aprons, much yellowed by storage, and dumped them on the kitchen table with a chuckle. "I'm sure there's something among all these to fit you."

She laughed. "Splendid! What fun! How clever of you to discover them."

"I took a look around in here while waiting for you. These aprons must have been used by the servants who came in weekly to clean Honeybridge all the time my grandmother used it as a retreat from Easthampton House."

"How did you find that out?" She had put on a large housemaid's apron with a bib, and she turned her back, holding the straps and ties for him to fasten it for her.

"My Aunt Donna is a source of information once she gets started." He tied a tight bow at the back of her waist, and immediately she swung about to set her hands on his shoulders, looking earnestly into his face.

"I want you to tell me all you can remember about the history of Honeybridge, and what you know of Kate Warwyck."

"I will," he promised, and kissed the tip of her nose. "Now I'll show you over the house." He picked up the candlestick and took her hand into his. "I did as you said, and haven't touched anything. We'll unveil Honeybridge together."

Their shadows fell behind them as they went through the baize-lined door into the hall where the long case clock ticked languorously and doors opened off into rooms that led into each other. It was a long house, facing south, quite unpretentious and simple in design. For her sake he had earlier brushed aside cobwebs all over the house and made sure there were no mouseholes anywhere; otherwise Honeybridge was as it had been since the shutters had been closed inside and out, which meant there was no danger of any crack of candle glow being seen beyond the house. He lit lamps and sconces as they went, flooding one room after another with light and bringing forth the mellow tones of hand-blocked wallpaper and the richness of old wood paneling. Nicolette was in realms of delight, pulling the sheets from chairs and tables and sideboards and cabinets amid clouds of billowing dust, taking to the house and all she found in it. He was as happy as she, smiling as he watched her skipping and darting about, bright as a butterfly in her yellow woolen dress, her apron flapping, and her hair in pretty disarray, gleaming bronze in the soft lights.

In the dining room she was distressed to find that part of the huge open fireplace had collapsed, bricks crumbled over the hearth, the dog irons standing up like sentinels amid the debris. Tom knelt to examine the damage while she hovered anxiously.

"Could you repair it, Tom? Would it be difficult?"

He reached up and examined a beam that had dislodged through lack of support, which in turn had caused the ancient salt box set in the wall above the hearth to split open, the little door lying askew on brass hinges. "I could do it if I brought in cement and more bricks. It's not a major job at the moment, but for the sake of the chimney it should be done."

"Then you'll do it? It will be a token to Honeybridge for letting us be here."

He sat back on his heels and looked up at her. "You're set on appeasing Honeybridge, aren't you? There's no need, you know."

"I'm not sure about that yet," she said gravely.

He shook his head smilingly at her and returned to examining the damage, wanting to estimate the full extent of it. His probing disturbed some lodged rubble and it descended in a cloud of choking dust, making him draw back quickly, coughing and wiping grit from one eye with the back of his hand. Something glinted in the rubbish that had fallen, and she pointed to it.

"What's that? Over there."

He picked out the object and rubbed it in his handkerchief to clean away the dust. "It's a button," he exclaimed with surprise. "A silver button. Where the devil did that come from?" He handed it to her and then peered under the beam again to try to locate the place that had released it. "It looks to me as if it came from the back of the old salt box." He rose quickly to his feet and opened the little door above the hearth still wider to dive his hand into the recesses of the aperture. "There's nothing else. The back is broken right away. Oh! Yes, there is something." He drew out his hand again and rolled into his open palm another button. Like the first, it was badly tarnished and dented where the wood had shifted against it, but by a lucky chance the silver loop on each for sewing by thread was undamaged.

She had folded her fingers around the one she held and she looked at him wonderingly. "Who could have put them there? And why?"

"I expect they were good-luck tokens or something like that. I know old shoes are sometimes built into a cottage wall to bring good fortune to a country abode."

"They must be very old."

"I'm sure they are. Do you want to know what I think?"

"Yes, Tom."

"I think they're a gift from Honeybridge to us. One for you and one for me. Tokens of goodwill to safeguard us from the outside world."

Such sweet pleasure melted into her face that his heart contracted with love for her, and he ached to bring a sharper, richer fulfillment of joy to her in a totally different sphere, while she, all unknowing, took the second button from him and held them side by side. "I'm sure you're right," she agreed, her lightheartedness quite restored. "I'll polish them until they're as bright as the day those unknown hands put them in the back of the salt box, and we'll wear them on silver chains around our necks."

When the buttons had been put in a safe place they continued the tour of the house, Nicolette having already decided that the dining room should be their quarters.

Upstairs they made a lighthearted tour of the rooms, she continuing her joyful stripping away of covers from the furnishings, he grinning happily as he set sconces ablaze for her. Then in one bedroom she uncovered a large wing chair; its leather cracked and much worn, with a plaid rug folded over one arm and a footstool by it.

"That must be old Jem Pierce's chair!" he exclaimed. "I've always heard that toward the end of his life he couldn't get downstairs and used to sit for hours by the window."

"Who was Jem Pierce?" she asked.

"Grandfather's trainer—the one who saw him through from his first fight in the prize ring to the championship. Kate let him have Honeybridge for his retirement. After he died nobody else ever lived in it. She kept the house for herself and visited it whenever she felt like it, sometimes for a day, often only for an hour or two."

Nicolette slipped both her arms around the crook of his elbow and smiled up into his face as she leaned against him. "Like us, and how it will be for us. I believe Honeybridge will become as dear to me as it was to her."

They went from Jem's bedroom into another, which was much larger and dominated by a ceiling-high, rectangular shape that was the four-poster, and he helped her pull the dust sheets from it. It was an exceptionally wide bed, the bulbous posts and canopy ornately carved by craftsmen gone to dust for three hundred years or more. Tom imagined that Daniel would have bought it for a matter of a few pounds in the days when he had furnished

Honeybridge, for bargains would have been all-important to a young prizefighter with no money running spare in his pockets, and the bed and other old pieces in the house would not have been any more fashionable then than they were now, when a totally different kind of heavy furniture was in vogue. Maybe that was why Honeybridge had such a comfortable atmosphere, the furnishings being weathered to its own age, all that was more elegant or more valuable having been removed to Easthampton House when that was built. He was about to say as much to Nicolette when he saw she had discovered a lily-patterned hip bath set beside a stack of brass-cornered wooden chests. Amused, she kicked off her shoes and stepped into it. He, joining in the game, snatched up a copper jug to pour imaginary water over her feet, not expecting the descent of a large spider which fell out with a plop to scuttle about her stockinged toes. She shrieked and stumbled over her skirts as she tried to get out, and he lifted her up in laughter, staggered as his heel slipped, and together they fell across the nearby bed, its timbers creaking under the impact, the velvet hangings bursting loose from rotting cords and swirling over and around them.

He flicked back some covering from which she was trying to free herself, and leaned over her laughing face, his own mirth ebbing before the exquisite awareness of lying body to body with her, their limbs entangled, and he saw her expression subdue and change, reflecting his own new seriousness. With gentle fingertips he stroked back her tumbled hair from her brow, and she watched his gaze traveling over her face as though he could never satiate his looking at her.

"I love you," he whispered, as if it did not show in his eyes or throb in his voice or reveal itself in the tenderness of his touch. "Dear, beautiful Nicolette."

Her eyelids closed in a sweep of lashes as his lips descended, not to take her mouth, but to kiss with delicious prevarication every other part of her face, which became a revelation to her. Never had she imagined the earlobes to be so sensitive to a lover's tongue or the throat capable of absorbing such vibrant sensations, and she felt the little hollow at its base must hold the kiss he placed there as a shell holds a pearl forevermore. The effect was wonderfully paralyzing, all will melted, all thought gone beyond the wandering of his loving lips, and yet, when his mouth came down on hers in sudden, blazing passion, she was instantly a-leap with love, responding to him with equal wildness, burying her hands in his hair and running them down the back of his neck to spread them like fans upon his shoulders, holding him to her.

Still locked in kissing he arched her back, releasing the hooks of her dress that followed the length of her spine, and when he had uncovered her breasts she was lost in a delirium of delight under the sensuous exploration of his mouth and caressing hands until somewhere in the subconscious regions of her mind the primeval clang of a warning bell made her break with a pain akin to dying from the ecstatic realms he had created. Almost in desperation she sat up, clutching back her crumpled bodice to her, the loosened ribbons and lace of her chemise in complete disarray about her breasts, and her lips were soft and moist in her appeal.

"Not yet. Please not yet."

His senses returned. He had been as lost as she, and it was not what he had intended at all, but he was off his head with love for her and had forgotten all his fine resolves in the heat of his desire. He nodded, trying to find the voice to answer her. "Not yet," he echoed throatily. "It's just that I love you so much."

"I know."

"Have I made you afraid of me?"

She shook her head, dazzling him with the upsurge of love in her face. "No. And I could never be afraid of anything with you."

"Then—?"

She rolled her face away from him, not knowing how to phrase what she had to say, being as yet unable to overcome her inherent modesty, all innocence in the belief that the ultimate intimacy led to only one result. Had not her mother had a baby, a miscarriage, or a stillborn child every year of her married life! Her answer came in such quiet, whispered tones that he had to bend his ear to catch what she said. "I'm only frightened of the consequences that would make them take me away from you."

He knew that behind her few simple words lay all the disgrace and shame that the outside world could muster, the upbraiding and the banishment, and the authoritative farming out forever of the evidence that one sweet girl had lain in love with the one man whom others would do everything in their power to prevent her meeting ever again. He wondered that his heart did not burst with all he felt for her. He wanted to reassure her, to let her know that what she feared would not come about through his lack of care for her, but he did not know the extent of her knowledge, for well-bred girls were brought up in such prudish ignorance that they knew little about their own bodies and often nothing at all about a man's. The way she had phrased her appeal had shown that she was aware that sooner or later the consummation of their love was inevitable, although that was no indication that she understood how and where and the whyfors of it. He would exercise patience and lead her to him with such adoration and tenderness that when the day came for no more turning back, she would come joyously and without restraint to give as he would give, worshipping her with his body as he did with his heart.

"We're together," he said gently. "That's all that matters now. It's enough to be with you."

She lay back again and drew his head to rest against her half-covered breasts. He slid his arms about her waist, and thus they stayed in loving and quiet embrace, murmuring endearments to each other, trying as lovers will to solve the mystery of the miracle that has befallen them, knowing that none else had ever shared such a passion as theirs.

It was she who finally reminded him with a kiss on the brow that their time together for the present was drawing to a close. He raised himself on his elbows, smiling down at her. "Whatever you say, my darling. Let me tie your ribbons and fasten your dress."

When the pleasant task was done Nicolette began to wander slowly around the room, taking careful note of everything. "Do you know," she said thoughtfully. "I believe this must have been Kate's bedroom."

"It's certainly the largest upstairs room," he commented.

She shook her head, her eyes pensive. "It's more than that. Nowhere else in the house is there any disorder, and yet in this room there are those chests and other things set down at random. Suppose they are Kate's personal effects brought from Easthampton House? Isn't it to be expected that they would be placed in the room that was once hers?"

"I should think you're right," he agreed. Then he saw her give a start as an ancient floorboard creaked underfoot, although she had taken no notice of the old house's quiet stirrings anywhere else. To him her whole attitude seemed suddenly tuned to the listening to anything that the room might manage to convey to her.

"There's no need to be nervous," he said reassuringly, although as soon as he had spoken he saw it was not nervousness that had taken possession of her; instead it was more a yearning to be in harmony with the room and the nature of the woman who had once slept there. She crossed to the nearest of the three shuttered windows and set a hand lightly against it, speaking as much to herself as to him.

"Kate would have had a magnificent view of the sea when she went to bed at night and rose again in the morning." Turning again, she went back to the side of the bed and smoothed the disorder of it, carefully pulling the patchwork quilt back into place before running a hand over its many colors faded to the delicate hues of a meadow full of wildflowers. She did not doubt that Kate had sewn this quilt for the marriage bed. It should be her love bed too when the time came. Lifting her gaze from the fine needlework, she met Tom's eyes across the great width of the bed, finding them to be as eloquent as her own. Not for the first time she marveled at the empathy that so often made speech unnecessary between her and the man she loved.

Together they uncovered the rest of the furniture in the room, exchanging smiles with each other's reflection in the little dressing glass when she brushed a layer of dust from its surface, and they were murmuring happily to each other, her waist in the crook of his arm, when she reached out to twitch the sheet from a large painting propped against the wall. Taken by surprise, they stared at the portrait that had been revealed. Nicolette did not have to be told the identity of the woman in her late twenties whose face shone out at them.

"So she was here all the time," she breathed.

Tom's arm tightened about her. "This must be the portrait of Kate that was removed to Honeybridge from Easthampton House on the day she died."

"She's beautiful," Nicolette said with a catch in her voice. She moved closer to the painting, scrutinizing it wonderingly, and made an eager gesture. "Do fetch the candles over here, Tom. I want to study every detail."

He did as she bade him and brought them forward, holding the candles where the light could fall full upon the portrait. Kate Warwyck was beautiful, and yet it was not porcelain perfection that was held within the gilded frame; the deep qualities of her character revealed in the oval face showed that she was no stranger to joy or to sorrow. Dressed in a gown of oyster silk with the dropped shoulder line and balloon-like sleeves of the 1830s, she wore her moon-colored hair drawn back from her high brow into a coil at the nape of her neck, her features classical and fine-boned, the gaze of the light blue eyes direct and straightforward, the artist having captured them in such a way that the beholder was forever held by them from whichever angle the portrait was viewed, and her chin was undeniably determined in its angle. She looked strong and courageous, a woman capable of fathomless love and inestimable tenderness, a Warwyck wife to surpass all others.

"She is holding the championship colors," Tom said on a note of respect, putting the candlestick down in order to point to the flow of a blue silken neckerchief and another of green silk in the poised hands resting lightly on Kate's lap.

"What are they?" Nicolette questioned with avid interest.

"In the old prize-ring days each bare-knuckle pugilist had his own color which he wore about his neck until he stripped off in the ring. Then the seconds would tie the two neckerchiefs to one of the four stakes, and when the mill was over the winner claimed the loser's color. Grandfather's color was that particular sky blue, and the emerald one is that of Ned Barley, the great fighter whom he defeated in his last mill when he won the title of Champion of England. That fight went down in the annals of boxing, and it is said that to this day there has never been another to match it in skill and courage and good sportsmanship."

"I suppose your grandfather wanted something of himself to be in her portrait."

"I doubt if he had any say in that, because the colors were hers anyway. He had given them to her on the day he became Champion of England. My father told me the tale years ago. You see, the greatest compliment a fighter could pay was to present his victorious colors. It was rarely done, for they were trophies to keep. However, Kate was at the ringside by the special invitation of Daniel's patron, because it was as rare for a lady to be at a fight then as it would be now. After the championship had been won Daniel stepped down from the ring and presented her with the colors in full view of over thirty thousand people. They say the cheers were heard for miles around."

Nicolette was enchanted by such gallantry and could not tear her gaze from the portrait, thinking what a romantic and treasured moment it must have been for Kate. "Have you ever seen the colors?"

"No. They were buried with Kate. It was her last wish."

All Nicolette's elation drained from her. She turned a face to Tom so wrenched by sadness that he gave an exclamation of concern and gathered her to him, holding her soft and warm and sorrowful within his encircling embrace. Her voice came muffled against his shoulder.

"How dreadful for her. She declared her everlasting love in that portrait, and it has been shut away all these years and denied by the one man for whom it was painted."

He stroked her hair comfortingly. "There's nothing we can do about Daniel's decision, but the portrait is here for us. It's no longer shut away. I'm Kate's grandson and you're going to be her granddaughter by marriage, so we'll give it the homage it deserves."

She drew her head back to look at him, her spirits soothed by his thoughtfulness. "When you have repaired the fireplace downstairs, let us hang the portrait above it in the place of honor. Kate shall grace that lovely old room again."

He agreed that it should be done. Then both realized that the time had come for Nicolette to go back to the lane where Beth would be due to arrive at any moment. When she had collected the buttons they had found, saying she would polish them up and put them on silver chains by the time they met again, he locked up the house, and together they made their way back down the path until they reached the stable-yard gates. There he made sure she was able to use the key to them without any difficulty, and showed her where he had hidden a lantern in case she should ever reach their meeting place before him. He went with her right to the lane and watched while she hurried toward the lamps of the hooded conveyance that Beth had brought to a standstill by the verge. Nicolette waved to him, climbed in, and then the lamplight wheeled as Beth drove her away.

Chapter 15

Constance wished she could feel less resentful toward Meg, but she supposed it was a form of jealousy she was unable to suppress. This very afternoon she had been at snapping point, finding herself uttering an abusive tirade soundlessly under her breath while Meg dithered over accepting an invitation from Donna that had been delivered by hand. It was for an afternoon drive and tea afterward. Once Meg blinked at her.

"Did you say something?"

Constance's eyes widened with a false innocence. "I only said an outing with your sister-in-law should prove extremely pleasant." No mention of inaudibly calling Meg a number of names no lady would use. "You could wear your new hat with the Parma violets under the brim." A glorious hat, wasted on that moon face.

Finally Meg was gone. Constance, free at last, took up a hand mirror and enhanced her appearance skillfully with a touch of paint and powder. An artful tousling of her hair followed, and after unbuttoning a few inches of the braid-bound trimming at her throat she went in search of Richard, whom she knew to be in the grounds.

She sighted him discussing the rose garden with the head gardener, and she stopped in the shadows of a tree some distance away. But he had seen her. She had made sure of that. His gaze came to her again and again as the discussion continued. Languidly she leaned against the sloping trunk of the tree, stretching her arms sensuously as if in worship of the sun and the warmth and Richard himself, a pretense of private longing for him to come to her. If she had her way there would not be a night when she did not share a bed with him, but he came to her when the decision was his and she had to be content with that. Once, half wild with desire, she had gone to his bedroom, and his anger that she should trespass on his domain had truly frightened her and she had not dared to risk his displeasure again.

Now the gardener had been dismissed and he was approaching her, the set of mouth and chin being one she recognized and welcomed. He took her by the wrist and pulled her into a rhododendron arbor, out of sight.

"Meg has gone out with your sister," she told him softly, "for hours and hours."

He drove his fingers into her hair and crushed her mouth with his, kissing her cruelly as if to erase Meg's name from her lips. His lovemaking matched his kisses. She thought him incapable of physical tenderness.

That evening Nicolette arrived early at Honeybridge House with the silver buttons, which she had taken to a jeweler, having found them too dented to shine up as she would have wished. The work had been done well, the concave surfaces restored and the intricate pattern of the rims revealed, although the initials that the buttons had once borne had been obliterated by damage, only the stem of one letter still visible. With Tom not being due for another quarter of an hour, she had time to thread each button onto its own silver chain, and was sitting in lamplight at the kitchen table admiring the results when he arrived. She sprang up to throw herself joyously into his arms. They could not stop kissing each other. It was as if they had been parted a year instead of a mere seven days. They kissed with wild passion and with tenderness and with laughter, swaying together in one embrace and then another, the flickering lamplight casting their shadows about the kitchen in a dance of love. Her hair fell from its tortoiseshell comb and she lost a shoe, which gave them fresh cause for amorous mirth, and when finally they sat down together on the bench, breathless and exhilarated and totally happy, their arms were still about each other. It took some time before they were able to turn their attention at last to the silver buttons on the table.

"This one is yours," she said, taking up the chain with one hand and letting the button rest on her other palm to enable him to see it at its best. "It shows the single stem of what remains of the initials that were on it. The jeweler could not tell what they had been. Do you know what I would like to think?"

He smiled into her eyes. "K for Kate. But they're a man's coat buttons."

She was not discouraged. "That's not important. I believe it was her hand that put the buttons in that damp-free cupboard."

"It was an odd place to store them."

"Not necessarily. She may have put them there until they could be sewn onto a coat or waistcoat, not wanting to leave them around in a needlework box."

It was as good an explanation as any, and he was content to accept it. She spread the chain and he lowered his head to let her loop it around his neck. The button hung like a shining round globe of minuscule size against his chest. Then he took the other one by its chain and slipped it over her head.

"Now we are linked," he said softly. "Next time it will be by rings."

She did not know how it could be as he promised, and neither did he. It was as if Honeybridge had spread a protective wing over them and all things were possible within its ancient walls.

She had come prepared to be practical that evening, for they were to cover up again the rooms they were not going to use, and after changing her dress she tied up her hair and once more put on the big apron that she had worn before. "It's like putting part of Honeybridge back to sleep again," she said as he stood on a stepladder, draping a dust sheet over a tall cupboard.

As each room was re-enveloped they closed and locked the door. Upstairs Jem's chair was covered up once more and the bedrooms resumed their shrouded, ghost-like appearance before being left to silence again. When finally they came to the threshold of Kate's bedroom he set an arm across the door to delay their entry there.

"Let's not shut this room up again," he said very quietly.

She saw the reason in his eyes and read it in her heart. In acquiescence she slid her arms about his neck and laid her head against his shoulder. They would make Kate's room completely their own. One day in Kate's bed she would become his. One day.

As always when they were together, time melted away. Before they parted after leaving Honeybridge he took her into the barn and by lantern light showed her the work that had been done on *Sea Star*, setting the pattern for how their evenings were always to end, for she wanted to keep abreast with the building of it and to miss nothing of the yacht's development. Daily it was taking on character, weight, and substance, and she lingered longer than she should have done to look at it all, risking Beth's nervous impatience that would greet any delay. He was glad of the extra moments she was spending there with him. Loath to part from her, he would have gone right to the hooded carriage waiting in the lane, but she stopped him as she had done before, wanting their last good-nights to be said privately and with kisses that were not for her chaperone's eyes.

For Nicolette nothing counted any more except the Thursday evenings when she met Tom. They thought up little surprises for each other in the form of a bottle of wine and meat pies as well as fruit and chocolates for picnics by candlelight. He had discovered an old concertina on a cupboard shelf, and sometimes they sang together or in turn while he squeezed music from it. After Kate's bedroom had been cleaned and put to rights, he having taken the chairs and hangings and rugs outside into the night air to brush and beat them as his share of the work, Nicolette brought some potpourri which she placed in containers upstairs and down, filling Honeybridge with a summer fragrance. At times it was to her like the childhood game of playing house, but at others there was a full adult meaning to her growing intimacy with Tom.

It was impossible to put the dining room completely in order until he had finished repairing the fireplace, and he took time whenever he could to work there on his own. He had discovered that it was a false wall that had collapsed, for at some time in the past oaken settles within an inglenook on either side had been bricked up. He had no qualms about restoring it to its original state since his grandfather was still comparatively hale and hearty, which meant it would be many a long day before the property was inspected for probate, and none would question the pristine state of a long-forgotten inglenook.

He and Nicolette had shared several Thursday meetings when she arrived one starry November evening to find that he had finished the task, the woodwork smelling of new polish and gleaming in the white-hot glow of a charcoal fire in a brazier that he had set between the dog irons, it being impossible to risk a coal or wood fire for fear of smoke being seen coming out of the chimney. Nicolette was full of admiration for what he had done, and held out her hands to the welcoming warmth.

"How clever you are! How cozy this room will be now."

He beamed at her praise. Later that same evening they carried Kate's portrait downstairs from the room above and hung it in its full glory above the reopened hearth. The painted eyes were so clear and lifelike that Nicolette was glad that she and Tom had the inglenook settles on which to nestle and kiss out of range. Much as she had come to revere Kate, it would have been like having a third person present to embrace within that lady's steady gaze.

Inspired by the success of the hearth, Tom began to seek out other defects in the house caused by long neglect, for he was developing a proprietory interest in Honeybridge without really being aware of it. A bad crack in the kitchen chimney breast would have to be made good, some floorboards were rotten, needing to be replaced, and he must get into the attic to make sure that it was watertight. Progress on *Sea Star* was fortunately ahead of schedule due to his having more time on his hands, since the opening hours of the roller-skating rink had been reduced to Saturday evenings until the summer season came around again.

On the whole he lived entirely in his own private world of Nicolette, *Sea Star*, and Honeybridge, with intermittent periods spent at the Pier Pavilion when he was needed. Those at Easthampton House saw him at mealtimes whenever he happened to be at home, but otherwise it was not often that he sat around at leisure. Therefore it could not be said that whenever Richard called in that his son went out of his way to avoid him, but if Tom heard his father's voice in any one of the rooms he did not enter there, and hoped to find him gone by the time it was necessary to do so. If Richard had not departed Tom received a frosty acknowledgment of his presence, and was afterward ignored as if he were no longer visible.

Helen thought it a great shame that Richard and his likable, hard-working son, with whom she had struck up a cheerful friendship, should be at loggerheads, and she did her best to talk to them both impartially, keeping conversation on a safe plane whenever they were together in the same room, which was as much for their benefit as for whoever else was present at the same time. Sometimes she wished Richard was a less frequent visitor to the house, for her sake as much as Tom's, although she knew from what Daniel had told her that it was Richard's custom to call in as often as he did whenever he was in residence at the Grange, which seemed to have reached a semi-permanent state since Lennox had proved himself capable of holding full control in his father's absence. There were times when Richard did go to London to exert the upper hand, and it dismayed her to find herself waiting for the sight of him again. She made all manner of excuses to herself over it, deciding it was because he was such interesting company, a man who had done much and traveled widely, and with whom one could have entertaining discussions and discourse; what was more, she was grateful that he had proved himself exceptionally kind to Beatrice, never sparing of the time he sat at her bedside on days when she was not well enough to rise, or by her couch downstairs when she was feeling stronger again. Richard also took Beatrice for drives, it being considered by her doctors that she should get as much sea air as was possible on the milder days, which left Helen with more free time to spend with Jeremy, who was ever on the spot.

He had not proposed as she had anticipated, and it was a profound relief, for she knew her mind was far from made up, and it went against her straightforward nature to keep a man dangling in uncertainty. In the meantime she found him a most dashing escort, saw through his flattery and was amused by it, and generally let things take their own course, coming to realize that his conceit would make him hold back from a proposal until he was sure of a definite acceptance. At least he could be certain that there were no other contestants for her hand, for she was senior to most of the young women in the local marriage market, and among the older men who did show interest in her there was not one who could compete with that Warwyck charm, and she found them dull company.

She had always enjoyed walking and made a point of getting some exercise every day, usually when Jeremy was elsewhere. Although he rode well and she had seen how accurate his aim was when she accompanied him on a shoot, he was not over-fond of being energetic, his natural setting more that of a club or gaming room or elegant dinner table than the blustering, windswept foreshore or the tranquillity of the wintry woods near Honeybridge and on the outskirts of the town. Yet she was rarely alone on these walks. To everybody's surprise, Sir Daniel's spaniel had taken to her and eagerly accompanied her when the increasingly cold weather kept his master indoors with aching joints. Another unexpected companion at times was Constance Meredith, who had encouraged Meg to take hot sea-water baths and massage for her health and figure's sake, and during these sessions, which were conducted under the supervision of a qualified person, Constance had two hours or more to while away. Since Meg's appointments were regular and at the same hour each time, Helen dropped into the habit of meeting Constance to walk together if the weather permitted, and to chat in a tearoom or the newly opened winter gardens under glass if it proved too inclement. Occasionally they would look over a house for sale when Helen had received details of one that sounded remotely suitable, because although she and Beatrice were perfectly happy at Easthampton House, they could not take advantage of Sir Daniel's generous hospitality indefinitely, and Helen was most anxious to see her sister comfortably established in a home of their own.

Always Helen turned to Daniel for advice when she received details from the estate agent of any house that it was thought would suit her requirements. In most cases he was able to tell her all she wanted to know, the property often dating back to the days when he had first laid out Easthampton in the early stages of its becoming a bathing resort. The houses would long since have been sold to others, but they were still houses of charm and elegance that he was proud to say he had built. With an invalid to consider, Helen needed to give special thought to the location and facilities of a property, and one after another of the houses was viewed and rejected.

She was coming across the hall of Easthampton House one December afternoon when a maid brought her a long envelope that had just been delivered. Opening it, Helen discovered details from the estate agent of a residence for sale that had come onto the market only that day. Glancing through the description she went into the drawing room, where Beatrice, propped up against cushions on the sofa, was being read to by Donna. Daniel, who was supposed to be listening as well, stirred in his chair and straightened up to show he was not dozing when the reading stopped and the book was lowered. Helen announced that she believed the right house had come her way at last.

"I know this property," she said, still scanning the details. "I have seen workmen busy there whenever I have walked westward along the sands with Barley." At his name the dog, lying in his favorite place at his master's feet, cocked his ears and sat up, but when no signs of a walk were forthcoming, the spaniel settled down again. Only Daniel and his daughter remained alert, Beatrice showing mild interest.

"Not Sea Cottage, is it?" Daniel boomed in distrust. "The tenant died a few weeks ago. I heard it was being renovated." He never went that far along the beach, not even when active enough, for it meant passing Honeybridge House, which could be clearly seen in its wooded isolation, and to him the sight of it was yet another reminder of Kate to be avoided at all cost.

"Yes, surely not that place," Donna exclaimed tartly. "As a

matter of fact, it was Meg's childhood home. She grew up there. It's also the place where Lucy had an apartment when she first came to Easthampton."

Helen raised her eyebrows with a smile. "It is obvious you are both far more familiar with the property than I."

"It is Olivia Radcliffe's property," Daniel growled.

The Edenfield sisters knew all about the feud and exchanged glances before Helen answered him. "In this case it is her grandson, Mr. Hugh Radcliffe, who is named as the vendor."

"It seems she has handed most of her business into his charge as well as the running of the estate," Donna observed coolly. "I believe she dotes almost as much on him as she does on her spoiled granddaughter. Fortunately for her he is proving himself by bringing everything up to date, replacing the old agricultural machinery with new, and putting everything she owns to rights. Unfortunately for some of their long-established tenants he is turfing out many who cannot afford the higher rents he has imposed, causing a great deal of hardship among the poorer folk dependent on the Radcliffe estate for their livelihood."

"Sea Cottage was empty and in this case he is prepared to sell," Helen pointed out.

Daniel snorted. "I can tell you the reason why he and his grandmother want to get rid of Sea Cottage. It is the only house they own that is flanked by Warwyck territory, and as far as they are concerned it has been a white elephant for years."

"I would strongly advise you not to have anything to do with it, Helen," Donna interposed. "It has most probably received a shoddy covering up of damp and dry rot and all sorts of other mishaps that have befallen the house. *Never trust a Radcliffe* has always been a saying with us Warwycks and it holds good today as it did all those years ago when Alexander Radcliffe, Olivia's husband, narrowly escaped going to trial for inveigling a plot against Papa on the very eve of the championship fight. His trainer, good old Jem Pierce, was stabbed by the villains and suffered from the wound for the rest of his life, and had Papa not awakened in the nick of time his legs would have been smashed to a pulp by a club where he lay."

Beatrice went pale. "How dreadful!" She looked anxiously at her sister. "I think you should put the details of Sea Cottage into the fire, and we'll wait for something else to turn up."

Donna continued to press home her point. "The planned assault was only one incident in a long record of knavery against us and anybody else who stepped into their path. When I was still a girl Olivia tricked Papa over a matter of land for the building of the railway, and later, when my nephews were young, the Radcliffe grandsons of similar age resorted to the most unsportsmanlike behavior when they all clashed in fisticuffs, which was a fairly frequent occurrence as each Radcliffe became old enough in turn to join his brothers on visits to their grandmother in school holidays." Her expression became one of grim satisfaction. "I once knocked two Radcliffe heads together when Lennox was being brutally kicked on the ground."

"Come, come, Donna," Daniel chided a trifle sharply. "The issue at point is whether or not Helen should consider Sea Cottage as a future home. Naturally you and I would have nothing to do with it, but let us give her the chance at least to tell us whether she has any intention of going to view it in the first place."

"I must admit that I have," Helen replied determinedly. "With all due respect to you both, my sister and I cannot take advantage of your kind hospitality indefinitely."

"Yes, yes, but there's no need to rush into things." Donna sprang to her feet at the sound of a voice in the hall. "I hear Richard! What luck! Now he can add his persuasions against the house to ours."

As always, Helen felt the same shock of pleasure at Richard's nearness when he came into the room. It was as if her whole being was drawn instantly in some way to his, as fire followed flammable vapor, totally independent of the rigid discipline of thought and behavior that ruled her at all times. The look he had given her at their first meeting had never been repeated, his gaze on her always calm, slightly impersonal, occasionally quite distant. The madness was entirely hers, and madness it was indeed. Gradually, over the past weeks she had been forced to come to terms with the fact that for the second time in her life she had fallen in love disastrously, the first time having been many years before when the man she loved had jilted her most cruelly on the eve of their wedding day, a traumatic experience that had shattered her and made her wary of emotional entanglements ever since. Only Jeremy had succeeded in capturing her interest where other men had failed, and the tragedy was that the Warwyck attraction that had drawn her to him was the stronger by a thousandfold in his father, who even now had turned from hearing Donna out to set that same, coolly benign gaze upon her.

"What is it about Sea Cottage that specially commends it to you?" he inquired.

She had seated herself beside Beatrice, whose worried expression had not lifted, and taken her sister's thin hand reassuringly into her own as she gave him her reply. "It is right on the edge of the shore, where Beatrice would gain the maximum benefit of the sea air, a private road is being laid out to give easy access to the west end of town and the railway station, and the garden is secluded, well screened by woods on either side."

Beatrice, feeling compelled to support Helen against all others, tried to be helpful. "If we should purchase Sea Cottage we could give it a new name and sever its last link with the Radcliffe family."

Helen received the suggestion approvingly. "That's a splendid idea."

Richard nodded. "I must say, it would be pleasant to have the Radcliffe influence removed from that part of the shore. Don't you agree, Father?"

Daniel answered without expression. "It would have happened years ago if I had been able to do anything about it at the time."

Richard explained the cryptic statement to Helen. "Father owns the woods where the footpath runs through from Hoe Lane to Sea Cottage as well as the woods beyond it, and neither Alexander Radcliffe nor his widow after his demise would sell an inch of Radcliffe land to a Warwyck whether it was wanted or not. It would be a good thing for us to have that particular property pass out of enemy hands, because it would put an end once and for all to endless legal tussles and disputes over Radcliffe rights-of-way put forth to keep the feud raw and very much alive."

"Then I can only hope that the interior of the house will live up to the promise of its exterior," Helen replied.

Donna, who had been swung over from her original opinion by her brother's words, no longer offered any opposition, merely giving Helen a further warning. "Just be sure that you get the property properly surveyed before making a move toward any decision. As a start, you couldn't do better than take Richard with you for a preliminary inspection. There's nothing he doesn't know about building and property."

Helen glanced at Richard uncertainly. "It would be an imposition."

"Not at all," he replied. "What about going now? It's the only chance I'll have for a time. As a matter of fact, I dropped in now because I'm catching a late-afternoon train to London and have no idea at the moment when I'll be coming back."

Donna intervened. "You'll be home for Christmas, won't you?"

He smiled at her. "Naturally. Have I ever missed spending Christmas at the Grange?"

No, Donna thought, and small comfort he had had there since the children had grown up and Meg had ceased to be any sort of wife to him. But it was no time to dwell on the dismal side of her brother's life. Beatrice had decided to go upstairs for a little while and Helen was assisting her, intending to fetch hat and coat at the same time. Over by the fireside Richard was promising to make some purchase on his father's behalf when in the Metropolis. The peaceful atmosphere that had existed earlier had been quite disrupted.

As Richard and Helen went off down the drive Donna held back the drape of the curtain and watched them go. They had decided to walk since the weather was fine and Sea Cottage lay no great distance away. It was also an opportunity to give Barley a run, and he had gone with them exuberantly, only to be kept on a leash until they were away from traffic. Donna expressed a slight feeling of disappointment.

"I would have gone with them if they had asked me."

Daniel sighed to himself, taking his pipe from its rack and filling it from his tobacco jar. Donna had never been able to see what was under her nose until it was pointed out to her. His fifty-three-year-old son and that twenty-eight-year-old young woman deserved to have a short time alone together whether they admitted the pleasure of it to themselves or not. Nothing could come of it. Nothing would come of it, but the attraction was there. Daniel, far from being in his dotage, quietly observed more than anyone else around him realized, and he had seen the sunshine flicker into Helen's expressive face even at the mention of Richard's name. It was a great pity that the years between them were not fewer and that Richard was tied inexorably to an ill-tempered, alcoholic shrew. It was Helen's particular misfortune that with all her amiable tolerance of Jeremy's ardor, she preferred the company of the father to that of the son.

At the estate agent's office Richard and Helen collected the keys to Sea Cottage, declined the agent's offer to accompany them, and continued on their way. The tide being in and splashing over the promenade, they chose to go by Hoe Lane, which was one of Helen's favorite routes to the woods, a country area of the old Easthampton that had been left unspoiled while the rest of the resort had grown up and spread out and around it. Ahead of them as they talked together, Barley, who had been freed from the leash, trotted happily, sniffing in the grass verge and keeping a lookout for rabbits. It was not until they drew near Honeybridge House that the spaniel changed the pattern of his walking, suddenly breaking into a wild barking at the closed front gate.

"Come along, Barley," Richard called. "There's nothing there."

"It's most odd," Helen remarked. "He did that one day when I came this way with Constance."

"Did he? Perhaps I had better check to make sure there has been no break-in."

Richard caught Barley by the collar and refastened the leash, which he handed over to Helen. Then he tested the front gate, found it securely bolted, and went down the old track by the side wall until he reached the double gates that led into the stable

yard to the rear. They were securely padlocked. Within the
grounds nothing had been disturbed. He returned to where Helen
was waiting for him in the lane, saying that everything was in
order, and they continued on along the lane to reach the path
through the woods and follow it to Sea Cottage. Up in the
Honeybridge attic Tom paused in his repair work on a rafter and
listened. He could have sworn he had heard Barley's bark, but all
was quiet again. With a shake of his head he went back to the
work in hand.

Richard was agreeably surprised by the improvements made to
Sea Cottage since he had last seen it. Wrought-iron gates replaced
the wicker one that had screeched on its hinges, and new windows
of gracious size were set gleaming into pink-washed walls. Indoors
the rooms had been enlarged, ceilings raised, and elegant marble
fireplaces filled every one of the old open hearths and mean
grates. He had to admit that Hugh Radcliffe had made the con-
version with taste and, as far as he could judge from a preliminary
inspection, had used good craftsmen to carry it out. He followed
Helen as she went from room to room, and could see she was fa-
vorably impressed by what she saw.

He was not a sentimental man and did not let his thoughts
dwell on the fact that a young and carefree Meg had grown up in
the house, but upstairs, where once Lucy had rented rooms from
Meg's mother, he did pause on the threshold of what had been his
half sister's drawing room, remembering when he had come with
a nosegay in the first stages of his courtship of her, not knowing
then that there was a blood tie between them. He had loved un-
wisely then, albeit in ignorance of the truth, but there was no excuse for a similar folly now. Twenty-five years lay between him, a
worldly, middle-aged man who had experienced most things in
life, and a lovely young woman who was viewing a house she
would probably never live in since his own son intended to take
her to wife. Jealousy, white-hot, searing, mind-stunning, seized
him like a convulsion, and he shuddered away from the threshold
without entering and went to stand by a landing window, staring
out at the full gray tide thundering about the rocks at the end of
the long garden. Helen had haunted him from his first sight of

her, and no amount of reasoning and common sense had altered by one iota this new dawning in his autumn years. He had never thought to find love a second time, never thought to desire any other woman as deeply and passionately and blindly as once in vain he had desired Lucy, but when it was too late for any kind of fresh beginning, Helen had come into his life with all the brightness and beauty of a spring morning, making all else dust and ashes to him.

Helen, finding herself alone in the room, went to look for him. His big frame with his back to her was silhouetted against the narrow window and took much of the light from the landing. Something about his whole stance emitted dejection, and she was puzzled by it.

"Is something wrong?" she asked. He turned his head and she saw that all guard had fallen away from his tormented features, his eyes holding such a blazing love for her that all the breath seemed to go from her body.

"Are you going to marry my son?" he demanded harshly.

She found her voice. "He has not asked me."

"He will. You know he will. Do you love him?"

"I'm fond of him."

"Fond!" The word came self-derisively. "Never wed one of whom you are merely fond, Helen. On mere fondness neither partner can weather the other's faults and failings. Love, on the other hand, is astonishingly resilient, and in some curious way is strengthened by the troubles and difficulties along its path. Learn to love my son, and some measure of happiness could be yours."

She leaned back against the wall by which she was standing, feeling in need of some support, for her pulse was pounding and all strength seemed drained from her. "How can you say that to me?" she asked shakily. "You know the one among these hard-headed, tempestuous Warwycks who is dearer to me than all the rest."

She thought she would never forget the stillness that followed her words. Neither of them seemed to breathe, their eyes dwelling in each other's, and beyond the silence of the house the waves boomed and dragged upon the shingle like sounds from another sphere. He spoke out of a terrible despair. "I have tried to think of you as my future daughter-in-law at all times."

"Just as I tried to keep my thoughts toward you on a similar plane," she answered emotionally, "but I failed."

His voice was low and troubled. "You are not alone in your failure."

She gave a sad little smile that was beautiful to him. "It appears we have played out a strange charade. You had me quite deceived. At least now we can be honest with each other."

His burning gaze on her intensified. "All I know is that over these past months you have been becoming part of me."

She closed her eyes briefly on the wonder and danger and glory of what he had said, and when she looked at him again her face reflected her whole heart.

Yet to his credit he made no move to touch her. In spite of all they had said to each other he would still have kept his distance, being more aware than she of the cataclysmic disaster they could bring down about themselves if either reached out for the other. Later she blamed herself entirely for igniting the moment between them. Drawn by some magnetism, unable to stop herself, she stepped forward quickly to rest her palms upon his chest and press her cheek against his shoulder in total subjugation to love. He uttered a groan between anguish and exultation and seized her to him, his mouth covering hers in the fiercest of kisses, his passion unleashed, his love for her completely overwhelming him.

How long they kissed on the landing she had no idea. Exactly when they found themselves lying together in one of the upper rooms she could not say, the silken lining of his spread coat cool beneath her naked back, his body a warm, protective canopy above her own that was afire from the kisses and caresses with which he had aroused her to a passion that matched his own. Her long-held virginity was surrendered with a rapture that banished pain, and he carried her with him to realms beyond her wildest imaginings and into a sharing of almost unbearable ecstasy.

For a long while afterward he held her close and softly breathing in his arms. They talked quietly together and then neither spoke any more, although from time to time they kissed lovingly.

Once she wept silently, and tenderly he brushed the trickling tears away with his fingertips until they stopped. Already the outside world was pressing back in on them and they were both aware of it, the pain of parting in their locked embrace. Finally he lifted himself away from her and gathered up his clothes. Out of respect he left her to dress in solitude. When she came downstairs he was waiting at the foot of the flight.

"Helen—" he began huskily.

She had reached the last tread and stopped there to take his face between her hands, her lustrous eyes on a level with his, and she shook her head to silence whatever he had been about to say. "My dearest, we cannot go back on the decision we have made. This afternoon must last us a lifetime. It was a beginning and an end, no matter how much we wish it could be otherwise. Let us help each other now. It is all that is left to us."

She stepped down and went before him out of the front door, where she unlooped Barley's leash from the brass foot scraper where he had been left to wait for them. Then, turning her back on the house that at first she had thought would be perfect for Beatrice and her, she walked with Richard to the railway station. His train was waiting to depart. He got into a first-class compartment and let down the window to rest his arms on it, looking out at her. The train began to move. Their gaze held in desperate farewell until the speed of the wheels increased, shattering the last tenuous link of contact between them, and she became no more than a glimmer of her crimson coat wreathed by the smoke that swirled far back over the platform. She would be gone when he returned to Easthampton. Helen, the only woman in his whole life whom he had found himself loving as totally and immeasurably as he was loved in return. There seemed to be no end to the cruelty and irony that fate directed against him. He never expected to see her again.

Chapter 16

With the lantern lectures coming to a close until after Christmas, Tom and Nicolette were forced to come to terms with a separation longer than the customary seven days' break between their meetings. In the barn, their last evening before the festive season at an end, they clung together, more reluctant than ever to part. Above them the graceful curve of the yacht's hull gleamed spectrally in the lantern light.

"I'm not going to enjoy Christmas at all this year," Nicolette declared fervently.

He tried to cheer her. "We'll see each other at the meet on Boxing Day."

Perversely she jerked herself away from him, not wanting to be comforted in the face of the barren time stretching ahead until the lectures began again in the middle of January. "What's the good of that? We'll not be able to talk or even look toward each other. It's cruel and unfair and I wish I were dead."

He felt an awful chill at her words and gathered her to him again almost desperately. "Don't say things like that. The four weeks will pass quickly, you'll see."

She clasped her arms frantically about his neck, her face close to his. "Don't go to the meet, Tom," she begged, "or to that wretched New Year's Eve ball at Denham House. I'll not know how to bear it to have you near and spend my time with others. I don't even know if I'd be able to stop giving myself away if by chance we should come face to face."

"You're making it difficult for me," he answered, cuddling her close, his cheek against hers. "Just seeing you from a distance was going to help me through this time apart, and I'd make sure I didn't suddenly appear in your path."

"But you can't be sure. Anything could happen. Oh, please stay away, Tom. I have to attend both occasions, because my grandmother will make me go with her. She's never missed seeing the Merrelton Hunt ride off on Boxing Day since she first came as a bride to Radcliffe Hall, or the other event where she always danced the New Year in with my grandfather. Although why she should bother I really don't know, because her face goes dreadfully hard and her lips thinner than ever whenever she mentions his name. It is as though she intends to carry on these traditions to renew hatred instead of fond memories. She is very strange and quite frightens me at times."

"I only want to please you," he assured her, not quite promising that he would do as she asked, being confident that nothing could go wrong if he should go. Fortunately she seemed to think the matter settled and gave herself up to kissing him, which prolonged their parting as each tried to assuage a hunger for the other that would plague them through the weeks ahead until they met again.

In the saloon bar of the Crown, Beth Macdonald glanced at her fob watch. Unbeknown to Nicolette she had taken to cutting short her attendance at the weekly lectures, finding that she nodded off through boredom anyway if she stayed until the end. Instead she stayed long enough to get some idea of what the lecture was about, saw three or four lantern slides, and then departed to spend the rest of the waiting time in the warm and comfortable atmosphere with a small tot of whiskey to keep out the cold when she did venture out into the night again, for she was careful always to be sitting in the carriage with her reins in her hands when Nicolette finally appeared. Usually she was alone when she took her whiskey, for the Crown was a common house and its patrons preferred the conviviality of the public bar, with its sawdust-spread floor and brass spittoons, to the narrow confines of the saloon bar with a single gas jet that spat and danced in a global shade. Those who did occasionally come in there were always lower working-class folk of only slightly better standing than those being noisy and raucous beyond the wooden partition in the other bar, so she had no fear of being recognized and questioned by anyone having social dealings at the Hall.

It was time she went. Even allowing for the young couple taking longer than ever to say good night before this Christmas separation she had best be getting back to the carriage. She rebuttoned the top of her coat, pulled the shawl she wore for extra warmth about her shoulders, and went out into the darkness.

When Nicolette climbed up into the carriage Beth shared the thick woolen rug over her knees, and then with a touch of the reins they started the homeward journey. As usual, Beth began a brief summary of what she had heard and seen at the lecture before she forgot any of it. Nicolette listened out of habit, but her thoughts remained with Tom and the haven of Honeybridge, where they would not meet again for four whole unendurable weeks.

Helen was another who was secretly dreading the festive season, for it would bring Richard back to Easthampton, and her plans to be gone before he returned had come to naught. She had neither expected nor allowed for a refusal to leave Easthampton House from Beatrice. Like many gentle-tempered, placid people, Beatrice could dig in her heels and become totally stubborn when faced with a situation that appeared unjust, inflamed to a rare loss of temper that left even those of normal health upset and discommoded for several days afterward. In Beatrice's case it had a far more dangerous result.

Alone with Helen in her boudoir, Beatrice, lying on a chaise longue, had heard her sister out, her illness-shadowed eyes widening incredulously at the suggestion that they should accept belatedly their brother's invitation to spend Christmas and New Year with him and his wife and family in Somerset.

"What are you saying, Helen?" she expostulated, clenching her thin hands agitatedly on the crocheted coverlet spread over her. "I don't want to go there. Last time we went our sister-in-law made it perfectly plain that she considered it a trial to have an invalid in the house, and I have never felt more uncomfortable or more unwelcome."

"Our brother is hospitable enough to make up for his wife's failings. There is nothing he would like more than that we should go."

Beatrice, who had turned chalk-white from the moment the proposal had been put to her, shook her head with a firmness that normally was not natural to her. "I love him dearly, but I'll not be the cause of his having to endure his wife's nagging tongue throughout Christmas because of my presence in his home." She sank back against the cushions. "In any case, what could be more wonderful than to celebrate our blessed Savior's birth in this house among the dear friends who live in it?"

Helen turned restlessly from the fireplace by which she was standing. She dared not divulge the true reason for wishing to get away, for the doctors insisted that Beatrice was not to be worried unnecessarily since anxiety about those dear to her was wont to play upon her mind. "I admit it would be exceedingly pleasant, but we should forgo it and visit Somerset instead."

Beatrice's whole frame tautened again. "Apart from anything else, how can you think of subjecting me in wintertime to such a long journey there and back again?"

Helen took a deep breath. "We would not be coming back. As I told you, I decided against Sea Cottage after all, and I feel I have exhausted the properties in Easthampton and we must try another resort."

"No! You shall not uproot me from this lovely place." Beatrice gave way to sobs on the eruption of anger that consumed her. "I have felt better and more content at Easthampton than anywhere else since my illness first brought me permanently to a couch and bath chair." Her voice rose to the high pitch that presages hysteria. "Do you want to kill me?"

Helen went pale, alarmed by her sister's unexpected reaction, and rushing to the chaise longue, she sought to capture the frantic hands that beat upon the coverlet. "Be calm, darling. Don't distress yourself in this manner. Nothing has been arranged, nothing promised."

But Beatrice would not be still, rocking to and fro, more distraught than her sister could remember, the sobs having brought on a coughing fit which punctuated all she was crying out about never wanting to live anywhere else but Easthampton. Then Helen began to sense the fear behind the desperate anger and realized Beatrice was afraid of ending her days in an alien place among strangers. She put her arms around her sister and knew the decision to depart from Easthampton had been taken away from her. "It's all right," she cried soothingly, her own tears flowing. "We'll stay. I promise you we'll not leave Easthampton unless you wish it."

It was doubtful if Beatrice heard all that was said. She began to make dreadful choking noises and coughed blood into the handkerchief that Helen snatched up and held to her mouth.

For several days afterward Beatrice remained in bed, but as she began to recover again the doctor agreed that she could be carried downstairs on Christmas Eve, which did more to restore her than the physic that she took at his directions. Helen did not know who wrote to Richard to tell him of Beatrice's relapse, but she was the only one who was not surprised when she heard he would not be coming home for Christmas after all. He had written to his father and to Meg that in order to save Lennox a journey to the Continent away from his wife, who was *enceinte* again, he had decided to go instead to Germany in an attempt to secure for the Warwyck horseless carriage enterprise a young German engineer who was well ahead in the same field, staying with old friends in Paris afterward until the New Year.

The generous sum he deposited in Meg's bank account, which would have covered the most extravagant of celebrations at the Grange, did little to console his wife for his absence. However, Meg was able to give vent to some of her displeasure on Tom by instructing Constance to let him know that she wanted no visit from him or attempt at reconciliation in the spirit of the season, for she was done with him and there was an end to it. It gave

Constance great satisfaction to perform this duty, although Tom received the message with dignity and without surprise, making no comment. Only the tightening of skin over the cheekbones showed his reaction to this further endorsement of unremitting maternal enmity.

Meg turned down the invitation that came from Sir Daniel and Donna to join the gathering at Easthampton House, and remained stolidly at the Grange, much to Constance's annoyance, for there were few callers except for the waifs singing carols, and no opportunities to join in parties such as would have come her way had they been at Sir Daniel's residence. Jeremy, who had been lavished with gifts from his mother, did have the grace to take Christmas dinner with the two of them, but otherwise he was conspicuous by his absence, spending all his time in a round of social occasions as lively and bright as the candles on the Christmas trees, Helen included in the invitations with him, and invariably Tom was a guest as well.

Tom had refrained from going to the Merrelton meet, trying to abide by Nicolette's wishes, but by New Year's Eve he could go no longer without sight of her, and accompanied his brother and Helen to Denham House. Generations of Denhams had held the annual ball, and there was every reason to believe the tradition would be carried on in the future since there were four sons in the present family. Tom had been at school with the youngest son, who was his own age, and they were good friends still, although that was not the reason why he and Jeremy had been invited, for the Denham host and hostess had always held a neutral line, inviting both Radcliffes and Warwycks to the ball among the rest of established local families, past experience having shown that with six hundred guests under their roof old enemies could always avoid each other. To date, no unpleasantness had ever occurred there, and Tom had no intention of offending hospitality or of letting his good name down. All he wanted was a glimpse of Nicolette, and then he would leave.

He strolled about for a while and could not see her in the ballroom or any of the drawing rooms where people were chatting together. To pass the time of waiting for her to arrive he danced with girls whom he knew and a pretty one whom he had never set eyes on before with dimples and round, bouncing breasts. He could tell she was quite taken with him, and when he asked her to partner him a second time in a quadrille he knew very well that she crossed out somebody else's name on her dance card. He drew her with him to join other couples as the orchestra struck an opening chord, and suddenly he saw Nicolette in a sprigged white dress with ribbons in her hair coming hand in hand with a partner from the opposite side of the ballroom. Such a longing to be near her came over him that he hustled the surprised girl with him across the breadth of the floor to make up the fourth couple with those already lining up with Nicolette and the young man with her. When she saw him surprise filled her face with an expression of love, to be followed almost instantly by shades of consternation and unease. The dance began.

He tried not to look too much at her and was pleased with how well he could watch her out of the corner of his eye, but when it was his turn to take her hands in the rotation of partners he made secret love to her with his gaze, in his clasp on her fingers, and in a tightening of pressure about her waist in the swinging steps before he released her again to her own partner. Her slight breathlessness could have been from the exertion of the lively dance, but he was well aware that it sprang from excitement and the danger and a sweet terror that he had managed to convey all kinds of loving messages under the unsuspecting scrutiny of many pairs of eyes, for they had been observed from all sides. A Warwyck and a Radcliffe dancing together! The whispers gathered momentum, rustling around the ballroom walls among those who had come to watch or chaperone or were resting between dances. Heads began to turn, seeking out the presence of Olivia Radcliffe in order to witness her reaction to this hitherto unknown spectacle, many with malicious amusement, for she was little liked in the community with her acid tongue and haughty, condescending manner, but the dumpy figure in black with a sparkle of the Radcliffe diamonds did not appear to be present.

Yet Olivia was there. Assisted by her grandson, she was coming down a flight of stairs at the far end of the ballroom, and while still hidden by the curve of the stone balustrade from general view they were able to see the section of dancers just at the moment when Tom reached out to take Nicolette's fingers into his. Olivia jerked to a standstill, muttering fiercely to herself. Hugh, less restrained, gave a furious exclamation and bunched his fists, ready to rush down and intervene, but Olivia's gloved hand gripped his arm.

"No," she grated. "Let the quadrille end. Let there be no scene. I will not have mockery directed at either of us over your sister's behavior. There is nothing people like better than to laugh behind one's back. We shall ignore the whole incident until the evening is over."

Hugh was unappeased. "The damned impudence of the fellow! He must have pushed into that particular group of dancers to make a laughingstock of us. As for Nicolette, I'll wring her blasted neck for not having the wit to turn her back on him and leave the floor. What if he should try to get her to dance with him again?"

Olivia's profile was hard as granite. "Nicolette shall sit by me for the rest of the evening. There will be no more dancing for her at this ball or any other for a long time to come."

The quadrille came to an end and the dancers began to stroll from the floor. Olivia put her hand in the crook of her grandson's arm and with her head high, her face immobile, she made a grand entrance. In spite of her age she managed the small, graceful steps that she had been taught in her youth, appearing to glide over to the alcove with its blue velvet chairs where Nicolette awaited her, flushed and nervous. For the benefit of those watching, Olivia gave her granddaughter a little smile, no others being able to see the ice in her glance as she settled herself on a chair just as the orchestra struck up a waltz. As movement swirled back onto the floor again she reached out to twitch away the dance card that Nicolette held and pop it into her jet-encrusted reticule. Nicolette swallowed hard. At that moment her partner for the waltz bowed to her. He was one of their host's sons, but Olivia shook her head at him.

"My granddaughter will not be dancing again this evening, Mr. Denham."

The rest of the ball was a nightmare for Nicolette. Her grandmother had neatly reduced her to the status of a child allowed one dance at a grown-ups' party, and she thought she would never recover from her humiliation as one partner after another was turned away. If Tom had still been there to strengthen her with his presense she might have found it more endurable, but after creating the havoc of dancing with her he had departed in all innocence, not knowing what she was going through.

At supper she sat with her grandmother and several other old ladies while all around her the young folk were having a merry time together. The food on her plate remained untouched and she took no more than a sip of champagne. When midnight came she was the only young person not dancing the New Year in.

Waving her ivory fan slowly to and fro, Olivia sat watching the dancers, her back as ramrod straight as in her nursery days when she had had to sit for hours with a board strapped to her to teach her perfect posture, but it was not quite so far back in time that her thoughts were dwelling. She was recalling a night of New Year in this very place when she was left sitting alone while her husband took her own sister onto the floor instead. She could see them now. Claudine's bright head as red as fire in the light of the chandeliers, and Alexander holding her too close and too intimately for propriety. It was then that Olivia had been forced to face the truth of the situation. Later she had come to hate them both with equal intensity, but then she had only known sorrow and despair.

Claudine. Flirt, lover, or whore? Which was she, and who could say now that she had been dead these many years? Daniel Warwyck perhaps? Olivia's lips thinned still further to a mere line. By his lust, which had made a rival of Alexander and created the feud between them, Daniel had kept Claudine chained to Easthampton instead of letting her fly free of him, and when finally she did go, never to return, Alexander had shut himself away and wept, not caring that his marriage had been destroyed, for his wife's nervous breakdown over the affair had made it impossible for her to feel anything but loathing for him ever again. And all Daniel Warwyck's fault. The feud was a glorious outlet for all the hatred that still festered in Olivia's breast, and each year she took a masochistic satisfaction in renewing savage memories at the Denham House ball.

This night Daniel Warwyck's grandson had exacerbated her feelings to a blinding pitch by daring to put his contaminated touch on the only precious possession that was exclusively hers: her beautiful granddaughter. It crossed Olivia's mind that if she had suffered a heart attack there on the stairs it would not have been surprising, but she was strong for all her small frame, and hatred was the most stimulating of all emotions. All she had to do was to ensure that nothing like that incident ever occurred again.

The last notes of the waltz were coming to an end. It was the New Year of 1884. There was cheering and clapping and kissing. Champagne corks were popping. Some Scotsmen burst into "Auld Lang Syne" and everybody was taking it up. It was the moment when Olivia always chose to leave, and she turned to Nicolette.

"We shall go home now, child."

As she glided ahead of Nicolette, Olivia's face was almost in spasm from the inward violence of her emotions, and the hand that held the closed ivory fan clenched it with a steely grip.

To Nicolette it was a relief to be going home. Hugh, who had ignored her out of hostility the whole evening, was staying on with many other young people for the breakfast that would be served at dawn, something that Nicolette would have been allowed to do had she not been in disgrace. She took a seat opposite her grandmother in the homeward carriage, bracing herself for whatever rebuke would be forthcoming, never dreaming of the form it would take. No sooner were they on the move than unexpectedly Olivia leaned sharply forward and, swinging out her arm and using all her strength, dealt Nicolette a searing blow across the side of her face with the ivory fan.

"How dare you tolerate the insolence of a Warwyck!" Olivia's voice came in a kind of demented roar from the depths of her throat.

Too shocked to cry out, Nicolette put a hand disbelievingly to her stinging cheek, and when she lowered it again she saw by the passing light of gas lamps on the Denham House gateposts that there were dark stains on her glove tips. The edge of the fan had cut like a knife. She raised her gaze to the pale oval of her grandmother's face, the play of light and shade giving it the look of an evil mask, the muscles a-twitch, the eyes glittering alarmingly. Fear rose and gripped her hard. It was the first time that terrible vindictiveness in her grandmother's nature had been directed with full force against herself, but her spirit was strong and she would not be browbeaten.

"It would have been more to my shame if I had turned my back on him," she retorted fiercely. "Would you have it said that the Radcliffes were bereft of courtesy?"

"Be silent!" Olivia was beside herself. "You should have withdrawn from the floor immediately he appeared, thus retaining your dignity and proving once again that a Radcliffe does not consider it fitting to breathe the same air as a Warwyck. By joining the same set in the quadrille he was making sport at your expense."

"That's not true!"

"Hold your tongue! How dare you answer me back! I will not have it. That young blackguard was spoiling for trouble, and he would have engaged it if I had not restrained your brother. The wretch should be tarred and feathered."

Nicolette beat her fists upon her knees. "I won't let you talk so wickedly about someone whom you only know by name!" All caution was gone in the defense of the one she loved, and later she was to wonder what truths she might have blurted out if Olivia had not struck her with the fan again, across the mouth this time, causing her to clap hands over her lips to cup the agonizing pain. In reaction to this second shock of onslaught sobs began to rack her, born out of her outrage, the injustice, and a longing for Tom's arms to snatch her away from this terrible situation and the dreadful old woman whose main intent was to break her will.

Olivia put a different interpretation on the sobbing. She saw it as an expression of contrite submission and was triumphant in a sense of omnipotence once again. Composing herself, she settled back against the plush upholstery and continued to harangue her granddaughter in less heated, but equally stern tones, more to drive home the lesson that the girl had learned than because any further trouble was expected. "You will not forget this evening in a hurry, I know. I have taught you once and for all that the high standards of the Radcliffe family must never be lowered in any circumstances whatever to accommodate socially the brashness of a Warwyck."

Nicolette was beyond speech, too taken up with pain and a panic-stricken concern as to whether her face and lips had been disfigured for life, but she did hear what was being said to her and her skin crawled in the conviction that her grandmother was quite dangerously insane in that obsessional loathing of all Warwycks.

Upon their arrival at the Hall she flew indoors and up the stairs, holding her wrap about her face to hide her injuries from the servants, and did not look into a mirror until she reached the sanctuary of her own room. Her scream as she saw her reflection awakened the maidservant nodding in a corner while awaiting her return, and brought Beth at a run from her own quarters. Both of them reached Nicolette's doorway at the same time.

"Saints preserve us!" shrieked the maid. "Is she done for?"

Beth, ever practical in an emergency, turned and slapped the silliness from the creature. "Fetch me some lint, bandages, and a bowl of water. Hurry!" Then, as the maid rushed off to do as she had been told, Beth went to Nicolette, who stood as though transfixed before her reflection, her teeth chattering violently, blood running from the deep cut on her cheek and gushing from the split and swollen lip. Beth tilted the girl's face to the light.

The slash on the cheek could have been made by a cutthroat razor, and whatever weapon had been used, some part of it had narrowly escaped the eye, proof of which was in a bruise already closing it. "Who did this, and where and why?" she demanded. At the high-pitched, stammered answer she frowned incredulously. "Your grandmother? The auld loonie is mair off her heid than I thocht she was. Dinna fret now. Ye'll be as bonnie as ever ye were when the cuts heal up and disappear." When they do, she added to herself, thinking it would take a long time for the scars to fade. She cleaned and dressed the wounds, helped Nicolette disrobe, dispatched the maid with the blood-spattered evening gown to get it out of the girl's sight, and then saw her into bed with hot milk dashed with brandy to drink and a stone hot-water bottle wrapped in flannelette at her feet.

In spite of the warmth within and without Nicolette could not sleep. The cuts throbbed painfully, but it was more than that keeping sleep from her. She was thinking that if only Tom had done as she asked and stayed away from Denham House, none of this would have happened, and now, instead of meeting again on the evening of the renewal of the lantern lectures, she had become too hideous for him to look upon, and there was no telling when she would be able to return to Honeybridge. She must write to him and say there would be a delay, but at all costs she must not tell him what had happened, or else he would simply risk coming to the Hall to see her, injuries or no. She had discovered that evening just how self-willed he could be, and since he had ignored her wishes once he would do it again. Somehow she had to keep him at bay until she was ready to see him. It would not be easy, but she must find a way to do it. On this unsolved dilemma she finally slept.

At Denham House a gargantuan breakfast was being served. Hugh, keeping to champagne, ate little, and half an hour later he was still far from sober in the bitter, snow-flecked wind that beat against him, billowing his cape, as he staggered alone across the meadow to the old Tudor barn near Honeybridge. Weeks ago he had heard about the yacht that Tom Warwyck was building there, and a chance remark by someone at the breakfast table had reminded him of it. At once he had seen a means of extracting payment for Tom Warwyck's temerity in dancing with Nicolette. The memory made his gall rise. *His* sister, damn it! In his hand he swung an iron stake that he had torn out of some railings nearby.

The barn doors were stout and the padlock held, but he found a window that he was able to prize open without much difficulty. He climbed through, fell to his knees, and then reeled upright

again, blinking with some amazement at the sweep of the hull
that seemed to take on immense proportions as it glimmered in
the darkness.

"Dam' fine boat," he muttered. "Dam' fine. Won' be much
longer." He looked about for what he needed on the nearest tool
bench. Taking up a hammer, he clenched the stake and went to
wreak the damage he had planned. As the hammer crashed home
and wood began to splinter, spitting fastenings, Hugh tried to recall what it was that had induced a particular unease in his mind
at the time of seeing Nicolette and her partner line up in the
same set with Tom Warwyck, but he was too hazy with champagne to give serious thought to anything except the work of de-
struction in hand. He managed a leverage again on the stake and,
using all his strength, he swung his not inconsiderable weight on
it. When he had done all there was time to do he left the barn by
the way he had come, and just managed to escape being seen by a
fisherman going down to the beach. Upon his return to the Hall
he went straight to bed and fell asleep, still with some indefinable
query about Nicolette niggling at the back of his mind.

It was Hab who discovered the damage. He was whistling merrily as he unlocked the barn, for life had never been better for
him. He had a beautiful boat to work on by day and a new
woman of comparable charms to pleasure him by night. The
heavy doors swung open and he entered. The whistling stopped as
abruptly as if a sack had been jerked down over his head. Then he
rushed forward to examine the wanton damage, swearing and
cussing in a dangerous monotone that committed the wrecker of
Sea Star to every kind of imaginable fate. Had he caught the van-
dal red-handed it was doubtful whether he would have been able
to restrain himself from murder, for his rage was molten and
seared white-hot through his veins.

He fell twice on the icy lane as he went with all the haste he
could command to break the news to Tom, his peg leg sliding
away from him as it never did when he was on a sloping boat
deck at sea. He grabbed a stout stick from the hedgerow to help
him get along. When he reached Easthampton House he pushed

aside the servant who opened the door and charged in, ignoring protests.

"Mr. Tom!" he bawled, thumping the stick to aid attention. "It's Hab! Mr. Tom-m-m!"

The din of his voice, which boomed against the glass of the lantern holding the wintry hue of the morning high in the hall ceiling above him, reached the dining room, where Tom was breakfasting with his grandfather. Tom leaped up, napkin still in hand, and hurried to the hall.

"Hab! What's wrong?"

"It's *Sea Star!* 'Er planking 'as been stove in!"

Tom would have rushed from the house into the cold outside without any top clothing to protect him from the weather if the servant had not had the wit to run forward with overcoat and scarf. Tom thrust his arms into the sleeves as he ran. From the window Daniel watched him disappear through the gates with Hab stumping far to the rear in his tracks left in the light powdering of snow.

Later that morning Daniel, accompanied by his dog, drove with Donna and Helen to view the damage that had been done. Unbeknown to the others he had sent a steward to inspect the walls and gates of Honeybridge in order to make sure that the vandalism had not been more widespread, and was thankful when the report came back that the walls were unbreached and all securely padlocked. As he made his way along the meadow path in the wake of the two women he avoided looking toward his old home, knowing that when the orchard trees were threadbare at this time of year the rooftop and chimneys could be glimpsed through a network of branches. Heaven alone knew how many times in his pugilistic days he had come jogging this way home under the critical eye of his trainer to see Kate's lovely face watching for him at upper windows now blank and shuttered. The past had no right to remain so vividly with him when all he wanted was peace from the torment of too many bittersweet memories.

He shook his head in dismay at the damage done to the yacht. Helen also stood dumb, having no words to convey her deep distress at the sight of the gaping hole near the bow, and there were splinters everywhere, which Hab was sweeping up. Donna was decidedly more vocal, making herself heard above Barley's barking as he greeted Tom as if they had been separated by a long absence instead of a few short hours since breakfast time.

"Who *dared* to do this?" Donna stamped her foot on the thought that anyone should commit such a mischief against her beloved nephew's boat. "What did the police say? Have they caught him yet?"

Tom smiled ruefully and shoved his hands onto his hips. "A constable was here and took down details, but there is no clue as to who might have done it. Since nothing was stolen, and the rest of the barn is undisturbed, he thinks it was the work of someone bearing a personal grudge."

Daniel's chin jerked up. "Any idea who that might be, my boy?"

Tom exchanged a long look with him. "No more than you might have, sir. I seem to remember hearing that damage of this sort was instigated against property of yours many years ago."

Donna saw no need to keep names unspoken. "Do you think Olivia Radcliffe is behind this? It was her husband who once set thugs to try to burn down Honeybridge."

Tom gave a shake of his head. "I hardly think it was Mrs. Radcliffe. Alexander Radcliffe was trying to destroy Grandfather's building of the resort and drive him from it, but she can have no possible reason to wish to keep my boat from the water. If a Radcliffe is involved I would look more to my own generation. Hugh and I have an unsettled score, although I would have expected a more personal confrontation than this sending in of a bumbling menial to do less than could have been done to *Sea Star*."

Donna looked puzzled. "What do you mean?"

"The damage looks a great deal worse than it is. Fortunately the wrecker missed all the main frames except one, otherwise we would have had to start more or less from scratch again. That is what I find puzzling."

After some further talk during which Tom explained how the

repair work would be done, the visitors left the barn, although Helen had gone no more than a few steps when she came back again.

"It has just struck me," she said to Tom. "Suppose the one who did this damage was not a clumsy fool, but a person in his cups."

"That's possible. What made you think of that?"

"Well, Jeremy and I stayed on to breakfast after the ball, and Hugh Radcliffe was extremely drunk. He left the house on foot shortly before us, because we overtook him in our carriage. It's no great distance from Denham House to the barn. At that hour nobody would have seen him enter it or leave again."

Tom pondered over what she had said. "It's an idea, but why on earth should he have picked such a time to do it? I saw him at the ball, but as usual we both looked the other way."

"You did dance with his sister in the quadrille. I'm afraid Jeremy frowned on your bravado and thought it a foolish thing to do when you could have joined any other of the sets lining up." To her surprise she saw that Tom looked decidedly uncomfortable, and he shrugged with affected nonchalance.

"I daresay Hugh Radcliffe did object," he agreed. "His grandmother wouldn't have been too pleased either, but it would have been more in his nature to take me to task outside in the grounds there and then. Frankly, I would have welcomed it. A spar between the two of us is long overdue."

"Thank goodness it did not come to that," Helen declared, "and I must say I did feel sorry for the Radcliffe girl even if she is lined up as an enemy with the rest of her family. I noticed she did not dance again after the quadrille, but sat by her grandmother's side for the rest of the evening."

"She did?" Tom looked so concerned that Helen was touched that he should feel compassion for the girl.

"Jeremy thought it was because she did not snub you as any other Radcliffe would have done in a similar kind of circumstances. I had heard that old Mrs. Radcliffe is quite a tartar, and she certainly looked it to me."

For the rest of the day Tom worried about Nicolette and berated himself for not thinking of the consequences of his action for her. He made up his mind to go to Radcliffe Hall that night, but he was thwarted by the snow that fell heavily during the day, making it impossible for him not to leave a telltale track of footprints to the spot beneath her window.

The snow, renewed by falls, lay for three weeks. He and Hab worked long hours on *Sea Star*, and by the end of that time the hull had been made good again and only a different shading in the planking showed where the damage had been done. He received a letter from Nicolette that only made him all the more anxious to see her and find out what was happening at the Hall. She wrote simply that she was indisposed and spending all her time in her room, but he was not to worry, and she would explain everything when they met again, although when that would be she could not say. She loved him and missed him, and she was ever his devoted Nicolette.

The thaw came at last, banishing the snow to banks and hollows. That night he stole into the grounds of Radcliffe Hall and threw gravel at her window. It was in darkness like the rest of the house, but he knew she was a light sleeper and would wake as she had done before when he had signaled to her. But this time the curtains did not stir. Finally he was forced to give up the attempt and go home again.

He returned the following night with as little success. The third time a lamp was burning in her room, and it was promptly extinguished as the first handful of gravel hit the panes. He waited in vain, alternately angry and in despair, completely bewildered as to why she should be shunning him. Short of bursting into the house and demanding to see her there was nothing he could do to find out what was wrong. Then another note came.

Dearest Tom. Please be patient for a little while longer. I love you. Your own Nicolette.

He was sick and tired of being patient, and his anxiety had not lifted. What were they doing to her at the Hall? Keeping her a prisoner for dancing with a Warwyck? Olivia Radcliffe was a weird old woman, but he could not believe she would go to those lengths.

With *Sea Star* whole again there was no need to keep midnight hours working on her as he and Hab had done ever since New Year's Day, and he decided to finish off whatever still needed doing at Honeybridge whenever he had some spare time. It would keep him busy until Nicolette ceased her mysterious withdrawal and came back into his arms again.

Chapter 17

Helen sat alone in her room with her fingertips pressed to dry eyes as she came to terms with what she must do. In no way had Beatrice changed her mind about wanting to stay on at Easthampton and, equally important, the doctor, who had just left after one of his regular calls, had made it clear that Beatrice must have no exertion or demands on her strength of any kind.

"You mentioned moving from Easthampton House to me," he had said to Helen. "On no account must a journey of any length be undertaken. At the present time a simple drive to another local place of residence is all I would advise. Find accommodation that opens onto the sea, with a garden or balcony where she can get maximum benefit from the salt air on balmy days. In that manner we may hope to extend her days; otherwise"—here he became extremely grave—"I cannot see more than the shortest of spans left to our invalid."

"I understand, Doctor," she had answered quietly, "and I have seen such a place. It is Sea Cottage."

Sea Cottage. Helen rose from where she was sitting on the edge of her bed and went to take her hat and coat from the wardrobe. All her own feelings on the matter must be shelved. She would go to the estate agent without further delay and make an offer for the property, which was still up for sale.

The business did not take long. Upon her return to Easthampton House she told the others the news. Beatrice was overjoyed, and the color came too bright in her cheeks. "Now I need never leave this charming resort, and all our old friends can come from far away and visit us by the sea."

That evening Jeremy received the information that Helen was buying Sea Cottage with a certain amount of private satisfaction, being convinced that she thought it was high time he proposed and was bringing him up to scratch—to use the old prize-ring patter—with this pretense of wanting to move into a poky little house no bigger by his standards than a rabbit hutch. He decided to play along with her little game for a week or two longer, letting her continue to feel a trifle uncertain about him, which would make her all the keener to accept him and fall in with his wishes when he did ask her to be his wife. He had concluded some time ago that, having reached the age of twenty-eight, she must have woken up to the fact that not only was time running out for her, but it was not every man who would be prepared to accept the continuous presence of an invalid sister-in-law to whom Helen was inordinately devoted and attentive. That was one of the reasons why he planned on using her money to buy a really large house where one wing could be set aside for Beatrice, with a qualified nurse to replace Helen's ministrations.

Sitting opposite her at dinner in his grandfather's house, he was in high good humor, noticing how reluctant she was to talk about Sea Cottage, which made it even more obvious to him how little her heart was really set on it. Cheerfully he radiated his Warwyck charm, paying compliments, being witty, fully aware of his dashing looks, which were being reflected in the looking glass above the long sideboard. Daniel's worldly eye watched his grandson cynically, for he was being reminded of his own late brother, Harry, who also had had the gift of that special charm, although in his case it had been combined with the tenacious sense of responsibility that was the more worthwhile trait of the Warwyck character, possessed to its limits by Richard, but completely lacking in this profligate grandson.

It was hard for Helen to return to Sea Cottage, but it had to be done. She went in and out of the empty rooms, trying to keep at bay the memory of a certain wintry afternoon when love had had complete reign there, but she was defeated, and went away again with no decisions made about such mundane matters as carpets and other furnishings.

The next time she made firm arrangements with a seamstress to meet her there and measure the windows for curtains. When she set off, taking Barley with her as usual, she was not sorry at the prospect of extra company when she met Constance Meredith near Ring Park.

"I was on my way to see you," Constance greeted her. "May I join you on your walk?"

"Come along by all means. I have news for you. After all the houses we looked at together I have finally found one, and the sale is already going through. That is where I'm going now."

Constance was extremely interested and inquired about it as they continued on together, taking the shortest route through side streets to reach Sea Cottage.

"Have you left Mrs. Warwyck at the hot sea-water baths?" Helen asked when they were almost at their destination. She did not want Constance to be late in collecting Meg, for she had noticed a certain carelessness in that direction and did not care for it.

Constance grimaced. "Not today. I'm afraid I have a little rebellion to deal with there. Mrs. Warwyck has started to think up every kind of excuse to avoid going to the salon."

"It can't be easy to face coming out of that heated place into a cold carriage on these winter days," Helen pointed out, "no matter how many furs and wraps await her."

Constance's tone held an unguarded note of utter contempt. "It's not just that. She simply lacks the stamina to keep to any kind of diet or treatment or exercise for her health's sake. I have a constant battle on my hands."

Helen felt herself freeze inside. She did not like to think of

Meg since the clandestine afternoon with Richard, but she liked even less to hear her spoken of with something close to cruelty. Suddenly she wished that she had not let Constance accompany her, but it was too late for that now, and the seamstress, who had arrived in good time, was waiting by the gate.

In the gloomy weather the daylight faded quickly, and a lamplighter was already about his rounds when they had completed their work and Helen locked the front door again. She would have liked to go straight back to Easthampton House, where Sir Daniel and Donna and Beatrice would be enjoying tea by a blazing fire and waiting to welcome her into the circle, but Constance had already invited her to take tea at the Royal Hotel and she had felt obliged to accept. They set off along the path through the woods and came into Hoe Lane. Barley, who was off the leash, had been snuffling contentedly among the leaves, but now he pricked up his ears and was instantly off at a run, making with all speed for Honeybridge House.

"Barley! Come back!" Helen's call went unheeded and she saw him vanish into the dusk. "Oh, dear. I had quite forgotten. Barley has started to behave most disobediently whenever I bring him near Honeybridge House. He will go and bark at it."

"I can't hear him barking now," Constance remarked, listening.

"I'll have to go and find him. Perhaps he has gone through the far hedge to the barn. Wait here. It will be muddy underfoot and you'll spoil your smart button boots."

She jumped the ditch that bordered the lane at that point, and held up her hems as she hurried as best she could through the long grass, calling to Barley as she went. Then she saw the high flint garden wall of Honeybridge looming near and remembered that an ancient track followed it somewhere to the rear. The going was easier there, and when she paused to take breath she could discern a pair of tall gates ahead, one of which looked as if it were a few inches ajar. Surely her eyes were deceiving her? She approached it warily. The padlock had been released and the gate was just wide enough for a dog to have squeezed through.

"Barley!" she called again, thinking she must report that the gates were no longer locked. From the lane Constance heard the distant call and sighed impatiently. She was snug enough in her sable cape, but her feet were getting cold. She began to pace up and down as she waited.

Helen, stepping inside the gates, was certain she had caught a single muffled bark. Alarmed, she thought of wells with age-rotten lids and other dangerous hazards that could trap a lively, inquisitive dog in this deserted place. She pushed her way through undergrowth and found herself in a yard. The coach house and stables as well as several outhouses loomed darkly up around her. There were any number of stout doors that could have closed behind Barley. With ever-increasing anxiety she began to search, calling Barley all the time. So far she could see no well, and each door as she pulled on its ring was securely fastened, but she remained convinced that he was somewhere near at hand.

Unexpectedly one latch responded to her touch, swinging outward silently on oiled hinges, and there wafted out a pungent aroma blended of builders' sand and cement and straw. Deep in the velvet darkness Barley whined in his throat and she went rigid, sensing that he was not alone.

"Who's there?" she demanded with a bravado she did not feel.

To her complete astonishment Tom's voice answered her in low and urgent tones. "Come in and shut the door, Helen. Are you alone?"

"Yes." Automatically she obeyed his instructions, drawing herself into the blackness. "At least, to be accurate, Mrs. Meredith is waiting for me in the lane."

There was a metallic click as the shutter of a lantern hanging from a rafter was opened. In its pale gleam she saw Tom holding Barley in his arms and muzzling the dog with one hand. "Is she likely to follow you?" he questioned keenly.

"I shouldn't think so." Helen continued to regard him with bewilderment. "What on earth are you doing here, Tom? Isn't it forbidden territory?"

His mouth twisted in a wry grin. "It is as far as my grandfather is concerned." He reached out to take the leash she was holding, and after clipping it to the spaniel's collar he returned him into her charge. "Whoever thought that Barley would find me out and that you would be hot on his heels."

"You've been here before today, haven't you?"

His eyes narrowed warily. "Why do you suppose that?"

"Simply because Barley has barked at Honeybridge House on other occasions when I've brought him this way." She looked about her at the pile of yellow sand, the sack of cement, and the stack of russet-colored bricks. "What are you rebuilding?"

"The chimney breast in the Honeybridge kitchen is crumbling away." He answered the unspoken lift of her eyebrows. "Yes, I have a key to the house too. Are you going to give me away?" His engaging smile showed that he did not imagine such a possibility.

The Warwyck charm, she thought to herself. They all have it in different ways. Even old Sir Daniel still retained a glance able to make a woman feel beautiful beyond all others. Warmly, she smiled in return. "Of course I'll not betray you in these circumstances. All along I've thought it a great shame that such a picturesque house should be shut up all these years, and I'm glad to know that it is being looked after by a member of the family. You had better not leave the gates unlocked again. Somebody other than Barley could discover you."

"Normally I lock them after me each time, but I've been carrying bricks over from the barn for the past half an hour, and nobody ever comes near the stable-yard gates at the best of times. Visitors on such a dark, late afternoon were the last thing I expected."

She was reminded of Constance Meredith waiting for her. "I must go. It would never do for—" She broke off, hearing the faint scrape of a footstep a little distance away through the opening door. The woman had come looking for her! Swiftly she put a finger to her lips, giving warning to Tom, and he shuttered the lantern in the same instant.

Coming out into the yard, she was in time to catch a faint glimpse of a female figure going in the direction of the house. The dusk was deceiving, but she was convinced it was not Constance. Who had taken advantage of the open gate to prowl? All her protective instincts toward Tom were aroused. Nobody else must suspect his comings and goings at Honeybridge. Purposefully she set off after the intruder, winding another loop of Barley's leash about her hand to prevent any further chance of his bolting back to Tom, and found a well-traveled path through the undergrowth quite easy to follow. Skirting an overgrown bush, she came upon the back porch of the house as a slender girl was hastening up the steps.

"Wait! What are you doing here?" Helen demanded authoritatively.

The girl, not having realized she was being followed, gave a frightened gasp and shot half a glance over her shoulder before darting into the darkest corner of the porch. With her back turned, she pulled her collar up about her face, huddling into it.

"Who are you?" Helen advanced swiftly and seized the girl by the arm, swinging her around and causing a key to spin from inside the girl's muff and fall with a clatter to the floor between them. For Helen there was instant recognition of the pale features before her. Her grip slackened almost in disbelief and fell away. It was the young Radcliffe girl.

"Oh, my dear God." Helen's whisper sounded loud to her own ears, full comprehension coming home to her. The pretty little thing remained silent, swallowing convulsively, the huge eyes half blind with fright. Momentarily Helen was at a loss to know what to say or do. A Warwyck and a Radcliffe. She realized she had the young couple's whole world at her mercy and wished she were anywhere but there. Yet a decision had to be made, and she would make it as she judged best whether it should prove to be for better or for worse.

"Tom is not in the house," she said tremulously, the depths of her compassionate nature stirred. "You will find him in the stables." Then she spun about quickly, dragging Barley with her, and half walked, half ran back to the gates without looking behind her.

In the lane Constance had grown tired of waiting. Where on earth had Helen got to? It was really too bad to be kept kicking her heels while that blasted dog led Helen a chase through the undergrowth. She peered up the track that followed the Honey-bridge wall and called out tentatively.

"Miss Edenfield! Any sign of him?"

The deepening darkness gave back no reply. Constance wandered up and down for a while longer, and then complete exasperation took over. With mud sucking at her heels she began to stalk up the track, intent on requesting an end to the search. The dog had probably made its own way home or would do soon since it was familiar enough with the district. She slowed her pace when she heard a faint clang of gates. Gates? Although she had never explored this area she assumed there would be a rear entrance in the Honeybridge grounds somewhere, but as she understood it, locks and bars prevented any coming or going. Helen's voice murmured somewhere ahead, and Constance came to a standstill, able to tell that Barley was safely on the leash again. As Helen drew near she took a step forward to meet her.

"Where did you find him?" she asked curiously.

Helen, preoccupied with her thoughts, more than a little upset by what she had come across at Honeybridge, gave a violent start at finding Constance suddenly in her path instead of some distance away in the lane where she had expected her to be. "Er—not as far afield as the barn after all. Have you been looking for me?"

"I was beginning to wonder if the earth had swallowed you up," Constance replied. "I couldn't hear you calling Barley any more."

"Couldn't you? Shall we go and have that pot of tea now? I'm sure we're both more than ready for it."

The Royal Hotel was warm and comfortable after the sharp cold outside. They were shown to a table in a flock-papered alcove. No sooner had Constance given the order for tea, buttered crumpets, and assorted pastries than she frowned disapprovingly down at Barley.

"That dog has brought yellow sand in across the carpet. Look at him. His paws are caked with it and there's some clinging to his coat." She had leaned slightly sideways in her chair to look down at the spaniel, and her gaze traveled surreptitiously to Helen's boots. They were the same. Yellow sand had stuck to the mud on them. Constance glanced at her own. No sand there. Helen was answering her.

"He must have run through it somewhere. I'll give him a good brushing when I get him back to Easthampton House."

Throughout the tea conversation continued normally, although it seemed to Constance that Helen was careful to keep it flowing constantly, allowing no pauses. It was almost as if she wanted to ensure that no opening occurred for any reference to be made again to Barley's disappearance. Outside the hotel they parted company and went homeward by their separate ways.

Nicolette was already home. Her minutes with Tom had been brief, snatched at risk after a visit to the Easthampton library, her first public outing since New Year's Eve. Terrified that, in spite of Miss Edenfield's gasping out where Tom was to be found, they were to be betrayed, she had rushed to the stables and thrown herself weeping into his arms.

It had taken nearly all their short time together for him to banish her fears, explaining that if Helen had reacted as she did it meant that their secret would be safe. After all, she had already condoned his presence at Honeybridge, and he knew she was to be trusted. He turned questions then to anxieties of his own.

"Why didn't you come down to the conservatory when I threw gravel at your window? What was all the mystery? I nearly went out of my mind!"

"I couldn't let you see me. You would never have loved me again. I injured my face after the ball at Denham House and I looked like a monster with a black eye and swollen lips."

"It wouldn't have made any difference! Surely you must have known that?"

Nicolette was still clinging to him, continuing to need the reassurance of his hard, young strength and the closeness of his embrace as a physical endorsement of what he had said about Helen Edenfield not giving them away. "I knew that was what you would say, but you have no idea what a gruesome sight I was. Beth dressed the cuts for me, but the next day the doctor had to come and put two stitches in my cheek."

"How did it happen?" He wanted to look into her face, but she kept her head buried against his neck.

"It was just a little accident. I've missed you so much, Tom."

He was not to be diverted from finding out what he wanted to know. In the end he got it out of her and was distraught to think that indirectly he had been the cause of her pain. He made her turn her face toward the lantern light and when he saw the scars, which were still discernible against her fair complexion, he traced them with his lips as if to erase all sign of that abominable violence from her face. She left soon afterward on the promise that they would meet again on the following Thursday evening when Beth would attend the lantern-slide lecture on her behalf once more.

At home again, she removed her velvet pillbox hat and unbuttoned her coat, and noticed that there was yellow sand on her heels. Quickly she gave them to a maid to clean, and they were returned ten minutes later with no telltale evidence of a swift reunion in a lantern-lit stable.

At the Grange, Meg became sharply envious upon hearing that Constance had visited Sea Cottage. Although as a rule she did not care to be reminded of her humble beginnings, she experienced a wave of nostalgia as she remembered the good times she had had in that house. In retrospect it all appeared a deal better than it had been, but she saw it as a real home, something that the Grange had never been to her, and she was filled with longing to see inside it once again before somebody else became the owner-occupier. She adopted a casual attitude, pulling at the fringe ornamenting her cuffs.

"I've a mind to write Miss Edenfield a note telling her I was born at Sea Cottage and ask if she would mind if I had a look at the place before she moves her traps in."

Constance, tidying the pages of the newspaper that Meg had spread all over the sofa, answered her idly. "I'm sure she'll invite you to take tea once she's in residence."

Meg pouted. "No, it's now I want to see it before she covers the old floors with fancy carpets and the walls with pictures. I want to see the old house as it was."

About to reply with a touch of malice that it was already past recognition as Meg would know it, Constance changed her mind quickly on a thought that had come to her. "Don't bother to write. I should think I could take you there tomorrow. We'll go into Easthampton in the afternoon. You can have your hot sea bath and I'll call at Easthampton House to ask if we might have loan of the key for an hour or two. In fact, I'm certain Miss Edenfield would be more than willing to come with us."

Meg bit her lip. Those hateful baths. She was sure Constance only pushed her into going there in order to have more free time without her. She had told Constance again and again that the hot salt water did her no good at all, because she felt quite nauseated afterward, but her complaints had fallen on deaf ears. That was why she was beginning to make a stand against going to the salon, although already her resolution was crumbling, because she was very much afraid that if she did not take the bath tomorrow Constance would see to it that she did not get a visit to Sea Cottage until Helen Edenfield was well and truly installed.

"Very well," she submitted with ill-concealed resentment, and then muttered self-pityingly: "The pill before the jam as usual."

Constance pretended not to have heard. Everything seemed to have been whittled down recently to a constant tug-of-war between Meg and her, and in spite of there being no serious threat to her absolute authority, it was getting on her nerves. As if that were not enough to put up with, she had a physical need of Richard that ravaged her by night and shortened her temper during the day, so that she blamed herself in no small part for having less patience with Meg and being careless enough to show it at times. She had not seen Richard since that early December afternoon when he had left the Grange to see his father and sister before catching a train to London. He had not written to her during his absence and she did not expect him to, although Meg had received some correspondence from him. That was the worst of being a mistress instead of a wife. One always took second place unless one was fortunate enough to secure a real hold on the man concerned, and she was aiming in that direction, determined to bring it about for his sake as well as hers. When they had become lovers there had been a new beginning for her, and in some unexplained way it had been the same for him as well; all her experience of men had enabled her to judge that. In sexual matters he was powerful and uninhibited and he used her without tenderness, but she exulted in the violence of their copulating, using all the arts and skills she had ever learned to give him back the same rich degree of carnal pleasure that he gave her. She thought they were perfectly matched, each having a desperate need of the other, and she saw herself as the balm and even the panacea to all that had destroyed his happiness within his own home. She wanted the affair to last, to become a permanent relationship, because although she did not love him in the romantic sense of the word and cherished no illusions about his feelings toward her, she desired all that he could ultimately give her and was resolved that he should never harbor any regrets over it. She knew that if she could get him to commit himself to her with some vow of protection he would never desert her any more than he would turn his lawful wife out to fend for herself. She would be provided for until the end of her days, never to fear the future again. To fulfill her aim she had to bring Meg to a level of improvement in her alcoholic condition that would convince Richard that any other competent woman could then be left in charge of his wife. That would snap the shackles of her employment at the Grange, leaving her free to move out. She had come to want more than a niche in this great house. She wanted Richard to establish her in a home of her own. She fancied living at Brighton, which was a lively place all the year round, and it was within easy enough distance of Easthampton as well as London to enable him to visit her whenever he wished. All this she hoped for and planned, confident that she could bring it about. She allowed herself a twitch of a smile on the thought of it.

Although the following day was the last in the month of January it was bright and sunny with a crispness that was welcome after the bone-chilling dampness that had melted the snows. Constance was encouraged to wear her new green coat, and tucking her hands into her velvet muff, she set out in the brougham with Meg and left her at the bathing salon. At Easthampton House she saw Helen, who was not able, or perhaps not willing, to accompany them to Sea Cottage, but she loaned the keys after only fractional hesitation, and said that Meg was to take all the time she needed to look around the property.

When she saw Sea Cottage, Meg's mouth dropped open at the transformation of the old house where she had first seen the light of day in such humble circumstances as daughter of a bathing attendant, and with father unknown. Indoors she gasped at the classical pillars framing an archway where once a doorway had led to the lodgers' hall, and a curved staircase with gilded banisters replaced a narrow one that had gone straight up and down.

Constance glanced at the pretty fob watch that had been a gift from Meg at Christmas. "I'll leave you to look at the house on your own for a while. I'm sure you would prefer it. I'll be back before long."

As soon as she was out of the house again Constance took the path through the woods that brought her into Hoe Lane. There she hurried toward Honeybridge House and, glancing right and left to make sure the lane was as deserted as it usually was, she turned aside up the ancient track that followed the flint wall. She reached the stable-yard entrance and tried the padlock. It was locked, and the chain held in spite of the hard shaking that she gave the gates.

Defeated, she stepped back, breathing heavily, and being unable to dismiss the certainty that the gates had been unlocked the previous day, she turned her attention to the ground at her feet. The mud had hardened since the damp cold of yesterday, and stooping down, she peered closely among the grass tufts, where she was able to discern footprints and the small indentations made by a dog's paws, held as though baked in potter's clay. These were inside the gates as well as outside, some holding grains of yellow sand as though gold glinted there.

Constance straightened up. She was not pleased by her discovery and had hoped to prove herself wrong in her suspicion that Helen had been on Honeybridge land yesterday, because at the time she had felt that in some indefinable way she was being made a fool of. Now she knew she had not been wrong. Helen had chosen to withhold the facts of Barley's recapture, and it showed Constance more clearly than anything else could have done that the friendship she had hoped for was never to develop. She was not trusted.

In a far from agreeable mood she returned to Sea Cottage, her state of mind not aided by the fact that she was shivering with the cold. With the early going of the sun the temperature had fallen considerably and, as with most empty houses, the cold, if anything, seemed intensified within Sea Cottage's walls. She had expected to find Meg ready and waiting to depart, but instead her footsteps were still wandering slowly about upstairs.

"I'm back," Constance called out sharply from the foot of the stairs. "Let us go now."

Meg made some answer, but failed to appear. Constance's mood did not improve. With all patience gone she rapped her knuckles loudly on the newel-post and called out again on a rasping note that boded ill for her charge if she was not obeyed. Reluctantly Meg came to the head of the stairs. Ever since she had been left on her own she had been reliving the good times she had had in the house, times that had had nothing to do with money, for there had always been little enough of that; it was more the laughs she had had with her old ma, the roasting of chestnuts by the hearth in winter, the hiss of a red-hot poker in a mug of ale when she came in from a bleak night's fishing in her boat, and the raucous, cheerfully vulgar company of her fellow fishermen when they gathered about an old timber table downstairs to join in some celebration, such as the time she had become betrothed to one of them, not knowing then that she was to desert him for Richard one wild, despairing day in the future. Memories had been revived for her at Sea Cottage that afternoon in a manner that she had never expected, and images of faces long gone had flooded before her.

Halfway down the stairs the prospect of leaving the house again overcame her. She gave a long, sad wail. "If only my poor old ma could see this home of hers now."

Constance curled her lip at such maudlin sentimentality. "Well, she can't, and you have, and it's time we left. The light is fading and it will be dark soon."

Meg did not appear to hear her, lost in her own reverie, sinking down to sit on one of the stairs and resting her forehead against the banisters. "The house had a bad name when she took it over," she said in a faraway voice. "It were odd how she wanted to live in a place where she'd been no better than she should be in her young days. Maybe she thought that if she could make Sea Cottage respectable it would clear her from the past at the same time. She had a hard struggle turning it into a boardinghouse fit for decent folk. It would have made her real glad to know that one day it were going to look like a palace."

Constance had had enough. "For goodness' sake, move yourself. You can wallow in your memories as much as you like when we get back to the Grange."

Meg raised her head and looked at her bleakly. "You've no heart, have you? Just a stone."

Constance stiffened ominously. "Don't adopt that tone to me, or you know what will happen. Straighten your hat. You have knocked it askew against the banisters and you look ridiculous. Now do as I say. I'm freezing to death in this empty place."

Meg continued to stare her companion out. It was as if something of the girl she had once been had entered into her from contact again with her former home, for Meg was reminding herself that no outsider would have dared to order her about in the days when she had lived under this roof and been strong and bold and unafraid, quite as ready to box the ears of any fisherman who took unwanted liberties with her as she had been to risk her own life in dragging back aboard those same men swept off their vessels in an angry sea. "You should have worn *my* sable cape," she retorted pithily. "That would have kept you warm while waiting until the one what employs you as her paid servant is ready to leave."

Constance's cheeks flared and her neck went blotchy with temper. With great difficulty she controlled herself from leaping forward and striking that plain, bloated face that bore such a newly defiant expression. "All right, you fat bitch," she said through her teeth. "I'll teach you a lesson for insolence that you won't forget. No extra tots for a week, and I'll see you don't get a drop down your gizzard tonight." Her face flashed with malevo-

lence. "I'm going out to the carriage, and I give you one minute
to follow me, otherwise you can stay here and rot for all I care."
She gave a last shout over her shoulder as she stalked off down the
hall. "Shut the door behind you. It wouldn't do to let other
riffraff in!"

Left alone on the darkening stairs, Meg looked with mild
amazement at her hands; the tremulousness that was normal to
them these days had been replaced by a violent shaking that
seemed to spread from her wrists and up her arms to enter her
whole body. Even her teeth were chattering. She had done it. She
had spoken out against the tyrant who turned the visage of a saint
to others and who had long since dropped any pretense with her.
Constance hated her with a virulent hatred that took an outlet in
endless small acts of cruelty by treating her as if she were some
kind of trained animal that must beg for an extra tot of brandy,
grovel for the alcohol that had become her very lifeblood, and
give back in extravagant gifts for the privileged supply of extra
bottles drunk in the privacy of her rooms unbeknown to her husband or the rest of the household. Constance was careful to hide
the alcoholic indulgences she allowed, and guessing that after
Tom's accusation some investigation might be forthcoming, Constance had kept her on black coffee half the night and subjected
her head to dippings in ice-cold water in order to have her sober
and restrained by the time Donna arrived with Helen Edenfield
the next day. For the promise of alcoholic reward as soon as they
had departed Meg had surrendered the pouring of the tea and
known Constance had demanded the privilege to show her who
was in command.

In the midst of her shaking and shivering Meg moaned. Constance had taken her dignity from her. She knew herself to be
degraded and debased more by Constance's contemptuous treatment of her than by the alcohol itself. But she had struck a blow
for freedom. Why then did she feel cold in her stomach? It was
nothing to do with the chill of the new-plastered, new-painted
house. Meg knew the answer even as she faced the question. It
was fear of Constance that put ice in her veins. Somehow she
must find an ally to stand by her. She would speak to her darling

Jeremy. He would protect her, the dear boy. He would find a way to break Constance's domination and get the detestable woman banished from the Grange. Gaining courage from this thought, she took out the silver pocket flask that she had concealed in her own muff, took a long, gulping swig from it, replaced the cap, and hid it again. Then she rose from her seat on the stairs, straightened her hat, and went from the house, leaving the door open behind her. The groom who waited to hand her into the brougham was the one who locked the door of Sea Cottage and secured it.

On the drive back to the Grange, while Constance maintained a hostile silence, Meg worked out an immediate plan. She could not face the torments of going without her drink through the long night hours, and on this occasion she was resolved not to go groveling and pleading with Constance in one of those awful and all too frequent scenes that it shamed her in her present, half-sober mood to remember. Yet only too painfully she knew her own weakness and what would be the result if she did not act quickly. It was fortunate that she knew exactly where to lay her hands on a source of liquor that she had never touched before, enough to last her until Jeremy had taken charge and put everything right for her. Had Constance not been looking out of the window, keeping her gaze averted with haughty disdain, her suspicions would have been aroused by the expression of cunning satisfaction on Meg's face.

Upon their arrival back at the Grange, still without exchanging a word, the two women went upstairs and divided off to their own rooms. Meg knew Constance would have tea served in her own sitting room, not deigning to share a cup with her whenever she was considered to be in a state of disgrace, which would give her exactly the opportunity she wanted. Meg listened at her door until she heard the clink of china on a tray as a manservant carried the tea past on his way to Constance's sitting room. Quickly Meg darted out and went swiftly across the landing and down one of the long, carpeted corridors, her feet making no sound, the ribbons fluttering on the pink satin laundry bag that she carried. Breathless, she arrived at Richard's study, thankful that he was still in London and would not miss his liquor until he returned, by which time Jeremy would have everything under control. Opening a rosewood cupboard, she knelt down and began to fill the empty bottles she had brought with her from the decanters, careful to do the pouring within the cupboard where the spilled port and sherry and brandy would not stain the carpet and give the game away to the housemaids who polished and dusted there.

The laundry bag bulged and sagged with its heavy load when she closed the cupboard again, and she had two unopened bottles of Napoleon brandy under her arms. She was tempted to take the tantalus that stood on the cupboard, but the housekeeper could start making inquiries if it was missing, and she dared not risk it.

When she left the study she did not return immediately to her own quarters, but went instead to Richard's bedroom. It was a handsome room, all dark mahogany with green and gold furnishings and a richly patterned carpet. It was a long time since she had last entered there, and sadly she surveyed it, inhaling that fragrant, masculine aroma of good cigars and clean linen and the spirit that he splashed on a new-shaven chin. A sob rose in her throat. Constance had promised that Richard would come back to her, and he was as far removed from her as ever, never more the darkly passionate man who had transported her to ecstasies that haunted her to this day in memories of paradise lost.

The sob broke noisily and ended in a snort. She had set down the laundry bag and the bottles, and she fumbled for a handkerchief. Failing to find her own, she went to the bow-fronted chest of drawers and took one of Richard's from it, unfolding it and pressing it to her eyes to dry and keep back further tears. She had no time to weep now, no matter that her anguish was knifing her to the depths of her soul. There was too much to do before Constance finished tea and went to her room to check on her. She had to find good hiding places for the bottles, and this was the one area where Constance would never think of searching for secret supplies.

She took the first bottle and hid it in the pocket of a tennis jacket hanging in the huge wardrobe, knowing that at this time of the year Richard's valet would not disturb the garment, and two more went behind straw boaters on a shelf. The bathroom offered no hiding place for all its spacious size and comfortable furniture, but in the dressing room she found secure places for all but two of the bottles, which she kept in the laundry bag and took with her when she left the bedroom to hurry off to her own room, meeting no one on the way. She was in such a highly nervous state that she would have started in upon a bottle without delay and drained it, had not the overpowering thought remained with her that she must speak with a fairly clear head to Jeremy, so she had to content herself with what remained in the silver pocket flask.

Soon after six o'clock the lady's maid, a hard-faced creature who had been appointed by Constance and was quite unbribable, came to lay out a dinner gown and all to go with it in the daily pretense that Meg's day was like that of any other lady married to a wealthy business magnate. During Constance's first weeks, and under her encouragement, which had since proved to be utterly false, Meg had changed her garments and appeared downstairs each evening, but recently she had begun to slide back into her old habits. This evening must be different.

"I'll change now," she announced thickly, putting a hand against the wall for support as she came from the drawing room into her adjoining bedroom.

The lady's maid was past surprise at anything good or bad that went on in this house. "Very well, madam."

"Do my hair nice too. Real nice. It's important."

Constance came in during the procedure, noticeably without the decanter in which she usually brought the ration her charge was allowed during the early part of the evening. She looked askance at Meg having her hair dressed, but said nothing and departed as she had come, in silence. Meg well understood that the threatened punishment had begun. Had she not known of her own, safe supply it would have sent her half crazy with worry as to how she would endure the long, dark hours until morning.

When the lady's maid left the rooms, her tasks done, she went straight to Constance. "Mrs. Warwyck is going out, I think. She wanted pains taken with her appearance."

"Mrs. Warwyck goes nowhere without me," Constance answered harshly. "Those are her husband's orders. Tell the servants to send word to me at once if she should attempt to leave the house."

At her window Meg was watching for Jeremy. She knew he had to come home and change before he went anywhere, and she intended to put her case to him during that leisurely half an hour he allowed for a cigar and the evening newspaper before going upstairs to get ready. But this evening of all evenings he was singularly late.

In her anxiety Meg filled a glass from one bottle and swallowed it down before hurrying back to the window. Although the waiting seemed interminable, it appeared to be in no time at all that the bottle was empty, and she stared at it stupidly, scarcely able to accept that the contents were gone. Then she heard Jeremy's voice somewhere in the house and realized he must have returned during one of the times when she had broken her vigil to refill her glass.

"Jeremy!" She stumbled across the room and went out into the corridor. He was coming at a leaping run up the stairs in great haste, and when she sought to block his path on the landing he made to dodge around her.

"Can't stop, Mamma. I'm in a great rush."

She snatched at him, grabbing at the lapels of his jacket. "You've gotta stop, my darlin' boy. You've gotta help me."

He tried to loosen her grasp, instantly irritable whenever he saw she was the worse for drink. In his childhood it had been a nightmare to him to find her turned into an unsteady, bumbling stranger with slurred speech and clumsy movements, although the occurrences had not been as frequent then as in more recent years. "You must ask Mrs. Meredith for whatever it is you want," he said, imagining she was about to pester him for a bottle of brandy from his own cupboard, for he had once hit her for helping herself in the past, an incident that fortunately for him had never reached the ears of his father, and she had not done it since.

"No, I can't!" Meg was frantic, trying to tug him toward the seclusion of her drawing room, but when he remained rock-firm, leaning back from her, she redoubled her efforts and her appeal. "We mustn't talk here where we could be overheard. It's secret, I tell you. Desperate secret."

He wanted to put his hand full in her red, bloated face and push her away from him. She was ruining his jacket, disgusting him with her winy breath, and delaying him from getting ready for what was most certainly going to be one of the most important evenings of his life. "I'll come and see you tomorrow morning." He wrested her grip from him with ungentle force. "We'll talk then."

"No!" She flung herself at him again even as he would have turned away, and clung to his arm with all her strength. "It's a matte' of life and death. I swear to God it is. You must listen to me now."

He could tell she would continue to make a scene until he complied with her idiotic request. Better to get her shoved back into her quarters and summon her companion afterward, or there would be no end to her nonsense. "Very well," he said in controlled exasperation. "I'll allow you two minutes, and no more."

She almost wept with gratitude. "Thank you, my own sweet boy." She did not doubt that when he heard what she had to say he would cancel all his plans for the evening, and she would never have cause to fear Constance again. She continued to hang on to his arm as he went with ill grace into her own quarters with her. There he sat her down, but remained standing himself.

"Let me hear it," he demanded uncompromisingly, looking at his watch. "What is this secret you wish to disclose?"

"It's 'bout Constance." Meg wished she had managed to abstain from drinking as she had intended, finding her tongue would not obey her clearly as it should. "Nobody but me knows the truth. I've found her out. She's a real wicked creature."

He thought he understood what was at the root of the trouble. "You mustn't take umbrage when Mrs. Meredith complies with your own wishes and Father's in helping you to cut down your drinking in every way she knows how. Naturally at times you must wish for more, but that's no excuse to turn on the woman so vindictively."

"It's not tha', and I ain't vindictive." She was unaware that she was kneading her hands as if demented. "I can do withou' liquor when I likes. Always have done and always will." It was an old boast made automatically whenever she was inebriated, but on this occasion she gave it new impetus. "No thanks to *her!*" She tossed her head in a curiously girlish way. "She don' care what happens to me."

"You are completely mistaken there," he argued. "Mrs. Meredith is dedicated to your well-being, and in my hearing she has always been full of praise for every advancement you have made in overcoming your particular problem."

"She don' mean a word of it. She's only dedicated to Constance Meredith. Self, self, self—that's her."

He was getting tired of his mother's drunken babbling. "What *is* it that you particularly wanted to tell me about?"

"That woman's hatred of me!" Meg sprang to her feet and took a reeling step forward. "I can't bear her near me no more. She has to go. Tonight!" Hope raised the pitch of her voice. "Send her away from your poor mamma, angel boy. Save your poor mamma from that two-faced wretch!"

His expression remained unmoved. "I'll remind you that you are talking about the person to whom you gave your sable cape and to whom you have given innumerable presents since." His tone took on an edge. "Your dear and wonderful friend, Mamma. Those were your own words." He had always been civil to his mother's companion, but he had not approved of a woman of inferior class being accepted into the family circle. If Constance Meredith had a real fault it was in stepping out of her allotted place as an employee, but because she was the only one who had managed to drag his mother back from the brink of total alcoholism she must be encouraged to stay. Just to see his mother this evening in a fashionable gown, with hair that had started out as being well dressed, the agitated movements of her head having since caused some pins to loosen her tresses untidily, was proof in itself of Constance Meredith's good influence, and credit must be given where credit was due. "If you have had a little tiff with Mrs. Meredith I'm sure she'll be the first to want to forget it and be friends with you again."

"Tiff!" She shrieked the word out, clasping her hands to her head and tearing at her hair. "I've tol' you. I thought she was my friend once, but now I know she's my enemy. Don' talk to me as if I was a half-wit!"

He had had enough. "Pull yourself together, Mamma, and stop behaving in this ridiculous manner. You're getting quite hysterical. I have to go now anyway."

She threw herself in front of him across the door, hitting her shoulder and being unaware of it as she spread out her arms, making a barrier of herself. "I'm afraid of Constance," she said piteously. "Make her leave. You're the master in this house with your pa away." The tears began to run down her face and drip from her chin. "Do this for me. I beg you."

He scowled, spoiling his handsome looks. "Be reasonable, for God's sake. Aunt Donna and Father and everybody else I know hold Mrs. Meredith in high regard. She has done you no end of good, whether you care to admit it or not. What's more, she is not a kitchen maid to be kicked out at a moment's notice, and you should know better than to suggest such a move. I want Mrs. Meredith to stay. Nobody ever had any peace of mind about you until she took charge. Now we all know that Aunt Donna secured a companion in a million for you, and I thank the Lord for it." He breathed heavily and flapped a hand at her. "Step aside, Mamma. You've made me late enough as it is."

She could not believe that he, her favorite son, her joy, her special boy, would desert her in her hour of need. "Don' go," she whimpered. "Stay with me this evenin'."

His face hardened dangerously. "I don't want to have to haul you away from that door."

Panic and despair re-erupted in her. With some befuddled notion of preventing his departure she clutched at the doorknob with both hands and hung on to it defensively, but immediately he dragged her aside and wrenched the door open. She screeched out pathetically and would have run after him, only to have the door slammed in her face. With her arms hanging limply at her sides she surrendered to helpless, noisy sobbing until, unable to face the pain of his heartlessness, she staggered into her adjoining bedroom to find the other bottle she had hidden beneath her pillow.

Constance, restless at the certainty that Meg was up to something, met Jeremy just as he was about to go out. "Take a look in at my mother, will you?" he requested. "She is upset in more than one sense of the word. I'd have stayed with her myself if I hadn't had an engagement this evening."

The liar, Constance thought to herself. She had seen enough of Jeremy Warwyck to know he did not put himself out for anyone. "Did Mrs. Warwyck say what had caused her distress?" she probed warily.

"To be frank, she's drunk herself into one of those orgies of self-pity when she thinks the whole world is against her, and this time you've been singled out as the cause. I know she'll have forgotten it all by tomorrow morning, because I've seen it happen before, as you have, but it wouldn't go amiss to soothe her down if you can."

"I'll go up to her at once." Constance put on her expression of gentle tolerance. "A tirade against me had to come sooner or later. Usually it's your father or Sir Daniel or Tom who are her victims. I'll settle her down. As you say, it will all be over by the morning."

Constance chewed the inside of her lip as she hurried to Meg's own drawing room. So that deceitful tosspot had gone behind her back to carry tales to Jeremy. His disregard for what he had heard showed Constance how firmly she had established herself in everybody's eyes as Meg's mentor and friend, and at all costs that image must remain, or everything hoped for could be put in jeopardy. Constance realized she had made a mistake in taking Meg's docility and submittance to her will for granted. She had thought herself to have become such a prop of security to Meg that nothing could assail it, but in Sea Cottage that afternoon Meg had regathered a kind of dignity and forcefulness of spirit about her that Constance had never seen before. Most probably it had been no more than a flash in the pan, culminating in a complaint to Jeremy, but it did decree to Constance that she should return to more subtle tactics in the future to keep the upper hand.

As Constance reached the first floor and turned her steps swiftly in the direction of Meg's own drawing room she decided savagely that Tom was to blame for Meg's rebellion. Admittedly several weeks had passed since he had made some reflection against her that had sent Meg into such a paddy of outrage, but it seemed to Constance now that he had undoubtedly planted a seed of resentment in his mother's mind. In retrospect, Meg's fury with her son could have been sparked off by his making her aware that she was securely under her companion's thumb, no matter that at the time she was reveling in the new social activity it was giving her. Constance wished there were some way to get back at Tom for the harm he had done, but at the present time she could not think of anything, and Richard would not have his youngest son mentioned or discussed.

Richard. Her whole body throbbed in sexual deprivation and she pressed her hands against her breasts until they hurt. Nothing must endanger the plans she had made to link the rest of her life with his, and the grave threat of Meg's rebel behavior must be put down at once.

At Meg's door she composed herself and straightened her shoulders against the difficult task of seeking to make amends with Meg while not losing her own authority at the same time. She found Meg lying in a drunken stupor on the chaise longue, and her anger burst forth again, for she knew it meant that a secret supply had been smuggled in from somewhere.

She soon discovered the emptied brandy bottle, and snatching it up by its neck, she had an almost uncontrollable impulse to smash it down on the disheveled head that lolled on a crumpled cushion. "All right, you stupid cow," she said viciously, knowing that Meg was too far gone to comprehend her words. "This is your very last fling. From now on I'll make sure you never slip back again. At least, not until I'm gone from this house, and then I'll not care a tinker's cuss what you do."

She stalked across the room and rang the bell for the maids to undress Meg and put her to bed. In her present, venomous mood she feared she might strike Meg, and it would never do for questions to be asked about bruises and a black eye. She waited until the servants came, and then she left.

At Easthampton House, Helen and Jeremy were alone in the Green Drawing Room. It was the hour after dinner, and since

Beatrice had not been well enough to come downstairs, Donna and Daniel had gone upstairs to take their coffee with her. Whether Jeremy had had a word with Donna about her withdrawing her father from the drawing room Helen did not know, although she suspected it by the firmness with which he closed the door after them. It had come, the dreaded hour she had hoped to avert by firm talk of a future with Beatrice at Sea Cottage and a show of enthusiasm for the house that she hoped rang true. Apparently it had been to no avail, for she had received proposals before and knew the signs. Doubtless Jeremy was about to do it better than most, which would make a refusal all the more painful and humiliating for him. At all costs she must prevent him saying the words that he would later regret.

"The sale of Sea Cottage is quite settled," she said easily from where she had seated herself in Daniel's wing chair, thinking it best to avoid the sofa, where an amorous embrace was more easily obtained. "I sign the papers tomorrow."

He had come from seeing the others out of the room to stand in front of her in the firelight, which flickered across his handsome face and drew sparks from the diamond studs in his stiff shirtfront. His hands, immaculately manicured, hung by his sides and there came from him a fragrant hint of the French macassar oil that kept his black hair in its deep waves. He was enough to turn the head of any woman, and yet it was inconceivable to her now that once she had contemplated this moment with agreeable anticipation, never dreaming that he would diminish in her eyes to become a mere shadow of the only Warwyck able to ensnare and hold her heart.

"We'll go together and tear those papers up," he said.

She shook her head. For his sake she must accept his statement at its surface level, the way to avert disaster still within her power. "As you know, no other property in the area proved remotely suitable, and it would be foolish to lose Sea Cottage now on the slim chance of finding anything better. The south coast air is renowned for its beneficial effect on invalids, and I'm putting my trust in it and hoping that Beatrice and I will share Sea Cottage as our home for many years to come."

So, he thought, she is set on that house for her sister. All the better. He found any form of illness disgusting and it would suit him to have the invalid in a separate establishment. "I suppose you're right, and I daresay Beatrice will be perfectly happy there." Slowly and leisurely he moved Daniel's footstool a couple of inches with the toe of his polished shoe and sat down on it, bringing himself romantically at her feet. "But you are destined for more in life. You're extremely beautiful, quite the loveliest woman it has ever been my good fortune to meet. I'll never forget the first time I saw you. I had watched you from across the room long before I learned your name." He took her hand and would have turned it to press his lips to the palm if she had not withdrawn it, rising quickly to her feet. Taking a few paces forward, she turned slightly away from him.

"You're wrong in thinking that my destiny lies anywhere but in the total care of my sister and whatever other responsibilities await me at Sea Cottage. Marriage is not for me and never can be."

He rose to his feet and came to stand behind her, taking her by the shoulders and caressing them through their covering of rose velvet, thinking it quite the most sensuous material any woman could wear, and he lowered his head to bring his face close to hers.

"Your self-sacrifice is admirable in principle, but totally unwise. Do you imagine that Beatrice could thrive and get better on the knowledge that you had made a martyr of yourself for her sake? Knowing her, I should say she would be the first to wish you the joy of a husband and children and a home of your own." He tried to draw her backward to lean against him, but she resisted the amorous pressure, her spine rigid.

"Beatrice has always been unselfish," she agreed without hesitation, "and it's only the nature of her illness that has made her afraid and demanding at times. However, in this case neither she nor anybody else I know could persuade me to marry a man with whom I was not in love."

His grip tightened on her shoulders and he twirled her around to face him, nothing in his expression to give away any misgivings he had experienced at her words, his eyes still meticulously adoring, all his power to coax and charm and entice emanating from him like a bouquet. "My dear, sweet Helen—and I've thought of you as my own ever since we met—sometimes one partner in a marriage will love more than the other, and it is enough for both until such time as the stronger passion awakens the other and they meet on a mutual level. You know what I'm saying to you. Come and sit down again. What I want to ask you can't be said standing here in the middle of the drawing-room floor."

His hands had moved to her waist, arching her forward, and she pushed at his arms to break his hold. "You must ask me nothing. Nothing! I've been terribly at fault if I have failed to make it clear to you that anything I might have felt when I first came to Easthampton left me long since. Had you spoken when I first expected you to, things might have turned out differently." Her voice cracked. "I wish to God they had."

He pulled her in to him, his strength overcoming hers. "It's not too late. We can begin all over again. This time you'll be in no doubt of the extent of my love for you, and from the start you and I will know what the outcome must be." He would have kissed her passionately, already blaming himself for holding back in past months, but she twisted in his arms and tore herself from him.

"There can be no new beginnings. Not when I'm going to bear someone else's child."

He had a demonic urge to laugh. Her statement was so utterly unexpected and incomprehensible that the shock of it made it appear like a ghastly joke being played upon him in a nightmare. Then he could have killed her. He could have put his grip about her white throat and throttled her for making all her property and bank notes and shares and investments slip out of his reach when his grasp was almost upon them. The life he had been going to lead melted away before him, taking with it the racetracks, the tables at Monte Carlo, the nightspots of Paris, the money to burn, the women to buy, and all the trappings and social pleasures that would have gone with a country estate and a house in Mayfair.

"Whose child is it?" He barely recognized the rasping voice as his own.

She closed her eyes just once on the directness of the question, almost as if it had had the impact of the violence he would gladly have vented upon her, and although she gripped the back of a chair beside her as if for support, she stood quite straight and still with some inner, unassailed dignity.

"You have no right to ask me that. Nobody has."

The significance of her words sank in. "Do you mean you're not going to marry the man concerned?" he demanded incredulously.

She was very pale. "I told you that marriage was not for me."

He paced across the floor in front of the fire, flapping his hands at his sides. "I don't believe it. I just can't believe it." He came to a halt. "Have you thought of the scandal you'll bring down on your head? You might as well become a hermit at Sea Cottage. No one will receive you. Everyone you've met in this district will cut you dead." A sneer twisted his mouth. "Since you're so concerned for your sister it's a great pity you didn't think of how it would affect her before you—"

Her look, direct and steady, cut him off in mid-sentence. "I knew you never loved me, Jeremy," she said quietly. "Instead, I thought you liked me as I liked you, and I was well aware that my money was my chief asset in your eyes. Naturally you are disappointed. You have my permission to cut me with all the rest when the time comes." She nodded toward the door. "Now I suggest you leave."

He had colored uncomfortably. Gaining control of himself, he decided he should not have given way to derision, and he would make a supreme effort to save what he could from the ashes. It need not be such a great loss after all. "All right, I did want your fortune," he admitted with a frankness designed to disarm. "There's nothing wrong in that. Had your father still been alive you would have had a dowry of comparable proportions, which would have amounted to the same thing. You and I have enjoyed each other's company from the moment we met, and we could have gone on having good times together. I believe we would have made a better match than most." He let his splendid smile show a trifle ruefully. "You see, I wasn't lying when I said I thought you beautiful. I have always thought you a most desirable woman, and I could have made you happier than you think." He saw her pass a hand over her eyes, and was encouraged by her silence to continue. "I could still make you happy. Marry me, and let the rest of the world think I'm the child's father. It will save you from scandal and ostracism, and instead of your baby bearing the stigma of illegitimacy for the rest of its life it will grow up a Warwyck. There's no better name to be proud of."

She thought she would faint. "No," she whispered. Then her voice rose into a crescendo. "No! No! No! For mercy's sake, leave me alone and never come near me again!" She threw her arms over her head and ran from the room, driven to a point beyond endurance. He heard her footsteps rushing away upstairs.

When Tom returned home he found his aunt alone in the drawing room. She was full of the news that Helen had refused Jeremy's proposal of marriage. Tom's feelings were mixed. He thought Helen had probably made the right decision, but he felt sorry for poor old Jeremy. What a blow to suffer.

"Where is she?" he asked.

"In her room."

He decided not to disturb her. He had not had the chance yet to thank her for keeping his secret. He liked her immensely. Had he been older and Nicolette not his life, he might have fancied her himself.

Chapter 18

When morning came Meg opened her eyes blearily to find the curtains closed against the harsh light of day, and Constance standing ready with the draught that would ease the awful pains in her head and banish the worst of the nausea that never failed to afflict her at these times.

"Thank you," she whispered as the rim of the glass was held to her lips, and she sipped gratefully, her mind still blank. When the glass was drained she lay back again with eyes closed, her companion's arm lowering her gently.

"Now you'll soon feel better," Constance said soothingly.

What was in the draught Meg had never asked, thankful only that it did its task well and comparatively quickly. Gratefully she accepted the cloths dampened with eau de cologne that were changed upon her forehead as Constance ministered to her. Gradually her thoughts began to clear. Why was she in this present state? What had precipitated the previous night's indulgence? Then she remembered. Jeremy had let her down in her hour of need. Tears pricked hotly behind her lids and she felt too weak to let them come. Why had he disappointed her? Memory was jogged and back came the image of Constance's look of loathing at Sea Cottage and the insults that were blurted out in an awful moment of truth. Nervously, under fluttering lids, she looked toward her companion.

Fractionally it was almost as if it were the old Constance sitting patiently at her bedside, ready with another refreshing cloth to lay against her temples. Constance, seeing she was observed, leaned forward and smiled.

"How are you feeling, Meg dear?"

Reality returned to Meg. False, false, false! Constance did not care how she felt. Inexplicably, she found herself quite terrified by this complete reversal from the naked enmity of the day before.

"Better," she muttered, all her instincts alive to danger.

"That's good." Constance changed the cloth that cooled a raging head so mercifully. "You mustn't worry about your little lapse. I'm not asking you any questions about it, because as a matter of fact I'm sure that nothing like it will occur again. You were upset over what happened between us at Sea Cottage, and I hold myself entirely at fault."

"You do?" Meg could scarcely believe she had heard aright. She had never heard the woman admit to being in the wrong before.

"I was tired and out of sorts. That's no excuse, I know."

"You called me names," Meg answered accusingly, the fear within her in no way abated.

"I said the cruelest things I could think of in the heat of temper," Constance admitted in contrite tones. "I've been letting worry get me down."

Meg found herself wondering if she was hearing everything that was being said with some part of her ears that had never been active before, because in every word that the woman uttered she heard the ring of falsehood. The spell that Constance had cast over her was gone, all trust irretrievably shattered. "What has been worrying you?" she asked without expression.

"Thoughts of my future and what will happen to me when I leave this house."

Hope, sweet and more intoxicating than anything else in which she had ever indulged, filled Meg's breast. "You are thinking of leaving?" she questioned cautiously.

"It is inevitable. Only consider how far I've brought you along the road to recovery. By working to restore you to your rightful place in this household I've been diminishing my own position." Artfully Constance turned a Judas slant on what lay ahead. "With a little more effort on your part I'll soon be on the outside again as I was before I came to the Grange. It's not easy for a woman to be alone in the world."

"I'm sure my husband will see you right," Meg said, finding it hard not to let her eagerness show through. "You won't go empty-handed from here. He'll make sure you're provided for."

A peculiar glint belied the innocence of Constance's eyes. "Do you really think so?"

"I'm sure of it," Meg insisted. The old courage that she had recovered the previous day had returned to strengthen her.

The odd glint seemed to echo in the lifted corners of Constance's mouth. "You've put my mind at rest. I hadn't looked for any reward. I've simply tried to carry out my duties to the best of my ability."

In her braver mood Meg allowed a long-held resentment to fester forth. "You've never kept your promise to take me to see Lennox's children in London."

Constance's expression did not change. "I've been hoping that the day would come when Mr. Warwyck would take you."

Meg raised herself from the pillows on a rush of angry misery. "He don't want to take me to London. He has his own pleasures there. Ain't there no limit to your taunts, Constance Meredith?"

"I'm not taunting you. I'm giving you the facts. Guard your conduct, continue to strive for sobriety at all times, and eventually your husband will do anything you ask. I would say you're more than halfway to winning him back again." So huge was the lie that Constance half expected it to be thrown back at her, but instead she saw that Meg was looking vulnerably shy on a private longing for such a miracle to come true.

"He's a good man and I've been a disappointment to him many a time." Meg sank back onto her pillows, gazing ceilingward. "But no more. I've turned over new leaves before, and this time I'll keep to it if it kills me stone dead."

Constance refrained from the cynical comment that came to

mind. Meg had said in rough terms exactly what she wanted to hear. She did not believe that Meg would stick to her resolution, but the will to make a fresh effort had been jogged again. Moreover, she could tell Meg wanted her gone, and with that wish combined with a renewed aim to bring Richard back to the marital fold there could not be a more powerful incentive to keep Meg on a sober path. In the meantime she would not let Meg forget that she was still in charge. "In view of what you have said I shall not tell Mr. Warwyck when he returns about last night's debauch."

Meg turned her face sharply and her retort snapped back. "In return I won't say nothing about you calling me a fat bitch!"

The air between them seemed to crackle with the hostility that each felt for the other, and it was with effort that Constance retained a benign expression. "Did you imagine that I wouldn't tell him of my own failings? I have always told him before when I have shown lack of patience or understanding, and the fact that I've never pretended to be a saint, merely a human being trying to do her best in difficult circumstances, has shown him that I'm honest with him at all times and without pretense."

As she closed the door of the bedroom behind her she knew she had cut the ground from under Meg's feet and was still in full control. Meg's challenge had been a pathetic attempt to hold a pistol at her head, the last spark of active mutiny in a minuscule uprising. She doubted that she would have any more trouble there for a while. Once again, truth tainted by falsehood had done the trick. She had always diluted any failures to Richard, having at the back of her mind the need to guard against any tale-telling, thus making sure that he would believe any outburst against her to be grossly exaggerated.

Left on her own, Meg simmered resentfully over being routed, and then turned her mind to whatever practical means were at her disposal for the regaining of liberty. No more drinking, except perhaps for the odd tot or two when she really needed it, and on the strength of this new behavior she would appeal to Richard upon his return to deliver her from the companionship of that villainess. He could not deny her. Always he had done whatever he could for her, and he alone would not fail her as Jeremy had done. Such a pang of anguish racked her on the thought of her favorite son's rejection that she quickly made excuses for him, telling herself that it was not his fault that he had been deceived by Constance's duplicity like everybody else. Only Richard would stand alone from all the rest.

She was certain he would bring her a handsome gift from France. Looking back, she could not remember a time when he had come home empty-handed, for she had always retained a childlike enthusiasm for presents. Yet out of all the things he had given her, nothing could compare with the first gift she had ever received from him at the end of that long-ago summer of tall grass and buttercups when he was fresh out of school and she, although younger than he, had been able to teach him more than he could ever have learned in a classroom. She had kept that souvenir of happier days and had it still.

Pushing back the bedclothes, she lowered her feet to the floor, and had to wait a few minutes for her head to stop reeling before she could move from the bed. Then, staggering a little, she padded across to her dressing table and flopped down on the stool in front of it. She opened her jewel case and lifted out one velvet-lined tray and then another, the contents sparkling in the light softly penetrating the curtains, which were still drawn. At the bottom of the jewel case she found what she was looking for, and unfolded the crumpled tissue paper to reveal the lace-trimmed handkerchief yellowed by storage.

Gently she fingered it, remembering the sun-dappled orchard where they had lain together. On that last day, when the air was full of apple scent from the boughs overhead, he had said he had a gift for her.

"It's a token of my esteem, Meg. It comes with my best wishes and deepest affection."

He had always talked posh like that, born to it and not aware that sometimes she had difficulty in grasping his meaning quite accurately. For a moment of despair she thought he was about to give her money for what had taken place between them during the summer, but instead he had taken a beribboned package from his jacket pocket and inside had been the handkerchief. It was the sort of present that the gentry gave each other, and he was treating her as if she were of his own class. If it had been possible to love him more than she did already, that special courtesy would have brought it about. She thanked him in the manner most natural to her, generously and without restraint.

He had become a partner in his father's business firm by the time their paths crossed again. By then he was in love with Lucy, suffering as decent young men did when courting respectable females, being unable to fulfill his passion until the wedding night, and shamelessly she had taken advantage of that situation to seduce him back into her arms again. Alerted by her own mother to the possibility that Sir Daniel had fathered both Lucy and Richard, she made sure she was close at hand when he learned the truth that had almost destroyed him. Never had he needed her comfort more than at that time, and she had run away with him. He had made her his wife, let her bear him four sons, and drawn more and more away from her over the years.

Meg raised a weary-lidded gaze to her reflection in the looking glass and was sickened by what she saw. Once a young and impish face had looked back at her; eyes now bleary and bloodshot had held a sparkle in their depths. Only her skin retained something of its creamy smoothness that the weathering of sea and salt and rough winds in her fishing days had failed to harm. She trailed a hand from her throat down to the cleavage of her full breasts, thinking how that girl of the past was trapped inside this older, misused body, because inwardly she felt much the same as when she had first won Richard to her. Unquestionably she had been his first love, that tender, inconsequential madness of the heart that leaves its mark when later, more passionate involvements are long forgotten. Suppose, just suppose, that something of the boy she had known remained locked inside him as the youthful Meg still breathed deep within her.

She moaned, clasping her head and rocking on the pounding against her brain. She could not think any more without a drink. Just a little one. Swiveling around on the dressing-table stool, she grabbed at the decanter that held the measure Constance always

put ready after a debauch, the welcome hair of the dog. She drank
a glass empty twice, her teeth clattering against the rim, and restrained herself over what was left, feeling the reviving spirit seep
through her exhausted frame. Once more she reviewed her circumstances. Constance had been wrong in guiding her slowly to a
reconciliation with Richard. No long-standing breach could be
healed by anything but a direct approach with a simple apology
for all that was past, and an appeal for a new beginning.

Hope rekindled strongly. When Richard came home again he
would find her loving and forgiving, expecting to be loved and
forgiven in return. As she had said, he was a good man with a
kind heart, and he would not turn away from her. Nothing could
change the awful pattern of the years behind them, nothing wipe
out the past wretchedness that their marriage had brought upon
them both, or the countless times she had inflicted on him the
most dire distress out of her own misery. But they were old
enough now to make the best of what was left to them, to redis-
cover what still remained of the fisher-girl and the youth who had
loved her. On this tender, nostalgic basis much could be built,
much consolation drawn.

In celebration of all she had settled Meg lifted up the decanter
and tipped it to let the last golden drops fall upon her tongue.

In a solicitor's office earlier that morning, some time before
Meg had stirred from sleep, Helen had signed the documents that
made Sea Cottage hers. That same day a band of cleaning women
scrubbed the property from attic to cellar, and the following
morning horses and removal wagons arrived after two days' travel
with furniture and other items from the family home, which she
had arranged to have taken out of storage. Carpets were laid and
curtains hung. She had already interviewed and engaged the necessary number of servants, and with the two faithful personal
maids who tended Beatrice and herself she moved into Sea Cottage and installed her invalid in quarters that would capture the
most sun and give full view of the sea. It was the first Thursday in
February. In another seven months she would give birth beneath
this roof. Practically she had decided which room should be the
nursery. In it, taking advantage of a breathing space away from

Beatrice and all those busy domestically, she sat on the window seat and contemplated the future without fear and with courage. Whatever happened, and whether girl or boy, one day her child should know the truth of its heritage. On that she was resolved.

That evening at Radcliffe Hall, Nicolette came hurrying down the stairs, ready to leave with Beth, and saw her brother in outdoor clothes waiting in the hall with her chaperone, who alerted her with a warning flicker of a frown. Nicolette slowed her pace, pulling on her gloves. "Where are you going, Hugh?" she asked casually.

"There's a new club opened in Easthampton. I've been invited along by one of the members to see if I should care to join, so I thought I would drive you to the Assembly Rooms and home again when I come away from the club."

"Oh," she said flatly. "Is that sensible? You may want to spend longer there than the lantern lecture lasts."

"No, it will be long enough. I'm hunting tomorrow and I intend to have an early night."

There was nothing she could do. Hugh took the reins and did most of the talking, while Nicolette answered in monosyllables. He glanced at her once or twice, thinking she was singularly uncommunicative, and her face had lost that glow that he had glimpsed when she had come to the head of the stairs. It was as if a candle within her had been snuffed out, leaving a dull void. His memory was jogged. He recalled that she had had the same luminous look over her face on New Year's Eve when Tom Warwyck had pushed himself into that quadrille. At the time his eyes, being young and stronger-sighted than his grandmother's, had spotted what the old lady had not seen from the stairs, for it had registered with him without his being aware of it that his sister's face held a special radiance as she stepped into the dance.

He believed he had guessed the reason. One of the three other young fellows in that quadrille had caught Nicolette's fancy. She had a beau whom their grandmother knew nothing about, and he would wager his last guinea that Nicolette's renewed cultural interests stemmed from the same chap attending the lantern lectures. No doubt they sat together under Beth's watchful gaze and held hands in the darkness as the lantern slides were changed. Now his sister was afraid that her protective older brother was going to discover the truth and put an end to her harmless expectations. Did she imagine he was such a killjoy?

"Don't expect me to join you at the lecture when I leave the club," he said munificently to put her mind at rest. "I finished with history on the day I closed my school books. I'll meet you in the foyer afterward."

At the steps of the Assembly Rooms he saw Nicolette and Beth join the stream of people passing through the columns of the porticoed entrance, buy their tickets, and disappear into one of the halls. He did not adjourn to the club, but entered the foyer and continued to wait until the doors of the lecture hall were closed for the evening entertainment to begin. Crossing over to the oval glass panels in the doors, he looked into the hall. The lecturer had mounted the rostrum and had begun to speak. Hugh scanned the backs of the heads of the audience and spotted Nicolette's cream velvet hat and Beth's brown toque side by side, but no young man occupied the chair next to his sister or any other close to her as far as he could see. Perhaps she chatted with the unknown beau in the interval. He grinned to himself at such innocent pleasures and went off to his club.

Nicolette fidgeted restlessly for a few minutes and then whispered to Beth. "I'm going to see Tom. I'll be back before the lecture ends."

Beth grabbed her arm. "Don't be foolish, lass! What if Mr. Hugh should return early?"

"You heard what he said. I'm sure he won't."

"Sssh!" Someone in the row behind objected to their whispering. Nicolette stood up and tried to cause as little commotion as possible as she left her own row and hurried out of the hall.

She ran all the way to Honeybridge. The pins loosened in her hat, causing it to blow off. She would have left it to its fate if she had not been certain that there would be awkward questions from Hugh if she appeared hatless when they met again. Valuable time was wasted while she gave chase as it bowled merrily back the way she had come. Snatching it up, she held it in her hand as she raced on once again.

Tom, despondent, thinking she was not coming after all, was checking his watch once again with the long-case clock in the hall when he heard her burst open the back porch door. With a whoop of relief he rushed to meet her, and as she stumbled exhausted into the kitchen he swept her up into his arms, making her skirts flutter like flags in the wind.

"What happened? Why are you late?" he demanded, exuberant in having her with him after all, as he carried her through into the hall and across to their own special room, she laughing in her breathlessness, unable yet to answer him. He laid her on the couch, her head on the pillows, and they kissed with a hunger that neither could assuage until she trapped his fingers with her own as he began to unbutton her coat.

"I can only stay a little while," she exclaimed with regret, and gave the reason why.

He sat back and clapped his hands upon his knees in exasperation. "We can't go on much longer with this cat-and-mouse game," he declared hotly. "I've had enough of it. Other people have no right to interfere with our meetings or to set their barriers up between us." He scooped her to him again. "There is a solution if you're willing to take the risk with me."

"Anything!" she cried. "I'll do anything if it means we can be together for always."

"Well, it's only a matter of three or four weeks before *Sea Star* is ready for launching. The big news I was going to tell you this evening is that three important men in the yachting world are coming to see her sea trials. One is a well-known yachtsman, Sir Duncan Watson, whom I met once when racing in a regatta, and the other two seem to have caught wind that I might have something worth seeing, which I believe I owe to Grandfather, although he hasn't admitted to it."

"I'm so glad, Tom." She hugged him proudly.

"After the sea trials, no matter what happens, we'll have a means of getting away together that nobody can stop." So intense was he that the young bones shone in his face. "I'm asking you to run away with me. We'll sail to France and be married there. After we're man and wife in every sense of the word nobody can part us."

She had come to the greatest crossroads in her life. She had to reject all that was Radcliffe, to turn from everything that had gone before in the way of ties and traditions. There was no hesitation in her answer.

"I'll go to France with you. All I want is to belong to you for always."

It seemed harder to part than ever that evening, especially since their time together was so short and such a tremendous decision had been made. He accompanied her as far as the street that opened into the center of the resort where Ring Park lay a-twinkle with gas lamps. He watched her as she took a shortcut through it to cross the road beyond to the steps of the Assembly Rooms. The glass door flashed as she disappeared inside. Then he turned homeward to Easthampton House, whose own lights shone out from the brow of the hill.

Hugh, coming from the club, had driven around a corner in time to see a slim figure enter the building, and had he had less to drink in the time he had been absent he might have focused his gaze a little more accurately. As it was, he was merely left with the impression that it could have been his own sister if he had not known she was securely in that dour Scotswoman's iron charge.

"Did you enjoy your evening?" he asked Nicolette when she threaded her way through the dispersing crowd to reach his side in the foyer, Beth close behind her.

"Yes, thank you," she said demurely. The bleakness had gone from her face and that inner happiness showed through once again.

As Hugh flicked the whip over the horse's head, Nicolette seated beside him once more, he wondered about the identity of the beau concerned. Whoever it was must be harmless enough for the chaperone to allow them to converse, which meant that the fellow was surely well known to the Radcliffe family. He had recognized and been greeted by several possible candidates in this

mystery as everyone had come out of the lecture hall, most of
them dull fellows with more interest in books and music and
other such pastimes in preference to the hunting field and the
cockpit and other sundry sports suited to his more vigorous taste.
He did not blame Nicolette for not letting Olivia know about the
matter, for the old bird was insanely possessive toward his sister,
almost as if she wanted to live her own life again through her
granddaughter, which he found unhealthy and somewhat nauseat-
ing. By chance he had discovered that all Nicolette's correspondence was steamed open by Olivia before the letters were
posted or received, and since nothing untoward appeared ever to
have come to light he could only suppose that the sweethearts
passed love notes to each other during the lectures, provided the
relationship had reached that stage. Nevertheless, he would make
it his business to find out who the fellow was if he could.
Nicolette would be glad to know that he was standing by her if it
came to the suitor wanting to call officially upon her. He almost
shuddered on the thought of how Olivia would react. He would
not mind betting she would show the colors of a true virago.

Chapter 19

Helen had been two weeks at Sea Cottage when a Warwyck carriage stopped at the gate and Meg alighted somewhat unsteadily, clutching at the groom's arm. In dismay Helen put the baby's nightdress that she was embroidering into her needlework table and closed the lid. So far no one suspected her condition. Jeremy had many faults, but it would have been against his code as a gentleman to reveal what she had told him in confidence, and not even Beatrice knew of the morning sickness behind closed doors.

"Show Mrs. Warwyck in," she said to the maid who announced the visitor's arrival. With her fingertips she smoothed her hair unnecessarily. She was stricken that Richard's wife should come to see her in this house, and she was paying in more ways than one for what had happened in a certain upper room. For herself she had no regrets. She would love Richard for the rest of her life, and to know that a child was to come from that one paradisiacal afternoon gave her more joy than she felt she had any right to have.

"Good morning, Miss Edenfield." Meg had entered the room with an air of boldness as if asserting her right to come as a lady into the house where she had once worn fishing rags. "You're nicely settled in, I see."

"Please sit down. May I offer you some refreshment?"

Meg sat down heavily in a silk upholstered chair. "I won't say no. A glass of sherry wine would suit me very well."

Helen had been thinking in terms of coffee, tea, or hot chocolate, but she sent for it, and when it was served merely put her own glass to her lips and no more. She was wondering why Meg had called. Inquiries about each other's health had been exchanged and comments made on the weather. The visitor's glass was already empty.

"Is Mrs. Meredith joining you here presently?" she asked, hoping that was the case. Meg was in no fit state to be out alone.

"I'm on my own." Meg looked conspiratorially satisfied with that state of affairs. "She don't know where I've gone. I wanted to talk to you private. About Jeremy."

Worse and worse. "I can't possibly discuss your son with you, Mrs. Warwyck."

"You must. You've got to. I want you to think again. Since you turned him down he's been in a terrible state." Huge tears sprang to Meg's eyes and she fumbled for a handkerchief in her drawstring purse. "How could you consider remaining a spinster when my dear son wants to make you his wife?"

Helen felt her chest constrict in dismay at the woman's brashness and insensitivity. She forced herself to answer calmly. "Jeremy is a grown man and would resent your interference on his behalf. I implore you to let the subject drop, or else I shall have to ask you to leave."

Meg could have been deaf. "I won't see his life ruined." The tears were running grotesquely, for she had been unable to find a handkerchief. "You played with his affections and led him up the garden path. Why? You should be thankful he wants you. You're nearly thirty and well and truly on the shelf. Believe me, any marriage is better than no marriage at all."

Helen, overcome by the horror of it all, rose to her feet and went to the bellpull. "I'll ask the maid to show you out to your carriage," she said faintly.

"No! Wait!" Meg could not accept that she had failed completely in her mission. She was vaguely aware that somehow she had blundered badly. Her intention had been to be tactful and gently persuasive, but at times her brain did not work as she would wish, and her tongue seemed to run off on its own. It tore her to pieces to see her dear boy thwarted in his aim, for he was in debt again, his inheritance from his great-aunt already dissipated, and although she did not care to recognize the fact, he had become positively vicious toward her in his ill humor when he asked her for money and she did not always have enough to satisfy his needs. It was almost as if he hated and despised her, but she knew that was not true, and if only she could be instrumental in bringing Helen and him together again he would be everlastingly grateful to her and show her the devotion for which she had always longed. "Just think about what I've said, Miss Edenfield. Let me at least tell him that you're willing to see him again. I'm sure when—"

The door had opened. The maid who had been summoned hovered in the background, and it was Constance, her eyes snapping, her smile fixed, who stood in the doorway. "So this is where you are, Meg. I hope you haven't inconvenienced Miss Edenfield by calling a little earlier than the conventional hour."

Helen's immediate reaction of thankfulness that Constance had arrived to remove Meg and take care of her was followed by a feeling of unease that had nothing to do with all that had been said previously. She saw that Meg was afraid. At the unexpected sight of her companion Meg had positively cringed. It had been only momentary, for Meg had cloaked herself almost instantly with a robust air of defiance, but for those few revealing seconds of being caught unaware she had shown a touch of terror in her eyes.

"I've been made most welcome," Meg retorted, tossing her head and making the pink ostrich feathers on her hat sway and dance. She turned to Helen. "Thank you for your hospitality, Miss Edenfield. My husband will be returning home from the Continent any day now. I hope you will call on us at the Grange very soon. Good day to you."

She sailed out unsteadily, and Constance followed. Helen went to the window and watched them depart. As the carriage swung around she caught a glimpse of their faces turned to each other; Meg's was crumpling like a child's in disgrace, and the hard move-

ment of Constance's jaw left Helen in no doubt that the mistress
of the Grange was being severely reprimanded. For the rest of the
day Meg's look of fear returned to Helen. She recalled hearing
from Donna that it was Tom's criticism of Constance that had
boiled up to bring about the rift between him and his parents.
Had he seen it too? Yet overwhelming all else in her mind was
Meg's information that Richard was due home in Easthampton at
any time. He had stayed away long enough to adjust to a life in
which they could never be together. Through her having to stay
in Easthampton against her will it was inevitable that they would
meet sooner or later. She hoped she would be brave when that
day came.

In London, Richard was alighting from the boat train at Victoria, having disembarked from the Channel packet at Dover
earlier that morning. He hailed a hansom cab and went straight
to the Warwyck offices, imposing premises in the City, where
Lennox welcomed him with a hearty handshake, for except on occasional organization and policy matters they got on well, and the
bond between them was strong. There was much awaiting Richard's attention and signature, and he had a great deal to report
himself since he had not been idle during his sojourn on the Continent and had secured some valuable contracts, although he had
failed to secure the German engineer, who had already signed
with an American company. The business talk between the two
Warwycks flowed without pause, and they lunched together at
Roules, where amid crimson damask and gilt ornamentation they
continued their discussions and exchanged facts and figures right
through to the last curl of smoke from their Havana cigars. They
parted in Maiden Lane, Richard seeing by his watch that he
could catch a train to Easthampton within the hour.

Upon his arrival at the coast Richard, as was his custom, went
first to Easthampton House to see his father. It was dark, and the
lights in the windows of the seashell of a mansion glowed on the
brow of the hillock as the cab took him up the winding drive. He
guessed that Daniel would invite him to dine there. He would accept since those at the Grange had no definite date or time at
which to expect him.

Daniel was more than pleased to see his son, for Donna was away for a few days on a visit and the house was exceedingly quiet since the Edenfield girls had removed to Sea Cottage. During dinner he mentioned that Beatrice appeared to be much improved again.

"It is amazing how one so frail can continually take on a new lease of life when it is least expected. Helen told me that this time she thinks it is due to her sister's peace of mind in knowing that roots have been struck and she will remain at Easthampton until the end of her days."

Richard had received this news and details of the move into Sea Cottage from Donna, who was an inveterate letter writer. He made a comment that he hoped the invalid's health would continue to improve, and the conversation turned along other lines. When the cloth was drawn and they sat on with their port he chose the moment to tell his father that he had decided that his plans to take life easier at the Grange had proved ill-suited to his active nature.

"So you are going to throw yourself headlong back into the business," Daniel said.

"That's about it."

"Are you leaving Meg?"

Richard's glance jerked toward him. "No. Things will go on as they are. I'll simply make my London residence a permanent home instead of the Grange."

Daniel sighed deeply. "So that's the way of it. You find you cannot go on living with your wife in one Easthampton house while the woman you love resides in another that is little more than a stone's throw away."

With deliberation Richard tapped off the ash of his cigar before he sat back again in his chair and regarded his father wryly across the polished length of the table. "You never fail to surprise me, Father. Does nothing escape you in this house on the hill?"

"As a matter of fact, I believe a good deal passes me by. Donna's moods of depression seem to be increasing in length and frequency as she broods on some matter known only to herself. Tom comes and goes, living his own young life, and apart from my receiving an enthusiastic daily report on the progress of the building of *Sea Star* he could be spending his hours away from Easthampton House on another planet for all I know of them." He shook his head. "In your case, it happens to be obvious why you have made your decision. Since circumstances compel Helen to remain at Easthampton, then you must be the one to leave it. She is not a woman to live in the shadows of your life. She is too independent and too compassionate. The feelings of other people matter to her, and Meg's would be among them. In many ways she reminds me of Kate."

Richard stared under his lids. He could not remember when his mother's name had last been uttered by Daniel in his hearing. "That is praise indeed," he said slowly.

With a thrusting back of the shoulders that defied any further reference to the comparison made, Daniel rose from his chair and pushed it aside. "Let us go into the library and have the coffee served there." He led the way, Barley getting up from under the table to follow him.

It was after midnight when Richard returned in one of the Easthampton House carriages to the Grange. Tom had come in before he left, and agreeably the boy had been extremely civil to him, easing some of the past tension between them. The controversial subject of *Sea Star* had not been mentioned by either of them, and the evening had ended more convivially in the boy's presence than he could have imagined possible some weeks ago. He supposed it to be due in no small measure to his own desire to mend the rift before leaving Easthampton again. Oddly, he had felt that Helen would have wished him to make the first move, and he had done it.

The Grange was almost completely in darkness, and as he rang to be admitted he realized it was going to be a relief to turn his back on this house at last. It had never given him the contentment he had sought there, for Meg had seen to that, and since Helen had made it possible for him to relegate Lucy to the past it no longer retained any connection with her for him. He would put it up for sale and let Meg choose the kind of house she had always wanted, one that was cozy and comfortable, not grand or too large. With Constance to look after her he could be sure that she would come to no harm.

He was let into the sleeping house by the footman on night duty, and after handing over his hat, coat, gloves, and cane, he made his way along the carpeted corridor to his study. There he found a pile of letters that had not been forwarded to him since he had notified his estate secretary of his almost imminent return, and standing by the fire, he began to open them, throwing those in need of no further attention into the flames. When a floor-board creaked he looked up from what he was reading and saw that Constance had entered and was leaning against the door she had closed after her. He could tell she was naked beneath the frilled silk robe that she wore, and the expression on her face, the avaricious look in her eyes, and the moistness of her half-open mouth blatantly announced her reason for being there. He was struck by a mild surprise that he should not have given her a thought except as Meg's companion all the time he had been away. It was as if those lustful interludes between them had never been.

She let the robe slip open as she came forward, reminding him of a voluptuous Venus he had seen on an Italian canvas quite recently in a gallery in Paris, and he was glad he had not purchased it.

"I thought everyone in the house was asleep," he remarked, not setting aside the correspondence that he still held.

"Oh, Richard darling! How could I miss your first night home when you've been away such a long time?" she exclaimed throatily. "I left instructions that I was to be notified immediately you returned, whatever the hour of the day or night."

"Did you?" He was displeased, seeing it as an intrusion on his own privacy. From the start he had allowed her no special privileges in the household as a result of their intimacy, and although their first coming together had been in this very study, he had afterward made it clear that unless he went to her room she was to make no overtures to him in any other part of the house.

She realized her mistake. She should have waited and not come to him, but she had been too eager, too sexually ravenous to delay another second when she had learned that he was in the house. Quickly she covered her error by pretending to mistake the reason for his cool reply. "The servants have no cause for gossip or speculation. I made it clear that it would be your concern for your wife's well-being in your absence that made it necessary for me to make an immediate report."

He sighed at her connivance, and then decided that perhaps it would be as well to make an end to what had been between them at this very hour instead of waiting until the morning as he had originally intended. "How is Meg?"

"Better. Well on the way to being cured." She seized the chance to establish that point. "But let's not waste time talking about anything except ourselves. We have the rest of the night to spend together." She saw by his manner that she had not yet dispelled the faint air of displeasure that her balking of his instructions had brought about, but there had been other times when she had not quite pleased him, and the tricks and devices that she knew soon made him forget all else. She smiled disarmingly, tilting her head so that her hair rippled on her shoulders, and stretched out her hands to him. "Put away that correspondence for now. Comfort me a little for enduring your absence all this while. I've dreamed of being in your arms again."

Outside the double doors of the study Meg took her ear from the crack, an expression of stunned horror and disbelief upon her face. Richard and that woman. They were renewing an adulterous relationship as if he had never been away. With an awful clarity her first impression of Constance came back to her. A whore's mouth. Wet and red and wanton. Like a warning that she had later forgotten.

Meg moaned under her breath, staggering back toward the staircase, not so much from the effect of her nightcap, which had been reduced recently to hot milk and brandy, as from the shock that was making her walk like an old woman, her peignoir dragging its soft folds behind her. When she put her foot on the bottom tread she stepped on her own nightdress and tumbled against the newel-post, knocking her head. She wept silently, released the hem, and clutching folds of her nightgown, she made her way laboriously back up the flight. She had still been awake when she had heard Richard's return home, and if she had not stopped to comb her hair and find her prettiest peignoir she would have been first to meet him. Never once in all the years at the Grange had she ever gone to meet him at any time when he returned home, and it would have told him clearer than anything that this was no ordinary homecoming for either of them. Instead she had opened her door in time to see Constance flitting toward the head of the stairs, the billowing robe revealing bare legs, and her silhouette against the sconce glow in the hall below had shown she was not wearing a nightgown. There were no servants about except the footman on night duty, who had probably gone back to dozing in his alcoved chair, but Meg, modest herself, knew shame that Constance should be about with so little to cover her, and even then did not believe that the woman could be going to see Richard until, leaning over the gallery rail, she saw her turn in the direction of the study where an arrow of light spread out from the half-open door showed where the master of the house had gone. Heart thumping, suspicion rising like gall, Meg had crept hastily downstairs after her companion and seen her adjust her robe to reveal more of her breasts, flick her hands under her long hair to set it in prettier disarray, and then enter the study, closing the door behind her. Meg had run the rest of the distance and pressed her ear to the door in time to hear them start speaking to each other.

Meg could not bear the ache and fright and desolation within her. On the landing she stood dazed, uncertain which way to turn in a house that had become familiar to her over nineteen years. Her life stretched before her without light or hope, nothing to lift that terrible woman's domination from her. Richard, on whom she had pinned her faith in the certainty of liberation and a new beginning, had gone from her long since beyond any point of reconciliation, and she had failed to see it. With stumbling steps, thumping her shoulder against the wall as she kept close to it for support, she went to seek the only source of solace left to her.

In the study Richard had put aside the correspondence he had been holding, but he made no move to take Constance's hands.

"You had better go back to bed," he said, not unkindly. "I appreciate your staying up to see me, but there is an end to the matter this night."

She was bewildered. "I don't understand. What is wrong? I thought you would be as eager as I for this coming together."

His glance flicked over her splendid curves. All his life he had sought sexual release at times of distress and tension as well as through the needs of passion, the only true lovemaking he had ever known having been with Helen, and this woman could have aroused him as fiercely as ever if he had not come to the end of sullying his own house.

"I would have been," he answered frankly, "if my personal life had not become too complicated. It has to be sorted out and changes made."

"What changes?" she demanded.

"I have come home to collect some things I want before moving back to London and spending most of my time there again."

She came close to panic. "Is there somebody else?"

"No," he answered with perfect truth. The rivals whom she was imagining did not come within a million miles of lovely, loving Helen, who would never be his again.

"Are you sure you did not meet someone abroad?"

"There was nobody. Not even in Paris." Again he spoke with truth. Helen had filled his thoughts and his heart.

Constance could tell he was not lying, as far as any man could be entrusted with straightforwardness, and the only possible explanation came to her. "It's Meg, isn't it?" She did not add the bitter gibe that his conscience had finally caught up with him, but she thought it. She should have known it would happen sooner or later.

"Ah. Meg." He repeated the name on a contemplative note and moved across to stand looking into the white-hot coals of the fire, his hands clasped behind him. "Yes, I suppose it is Meg. As my wife she is at the center of all things in my life and, through no fault of hers, divides me from everything I want most from it."

"What is it you want that you cannot have?" Constance

breathed, trying not to break his new and quiet mood in which he seemed about to reveal some other side of himself that he had always kept from her.

He answered in the same low, ruminative voice. "The freedom to bring love into the open. The chance to build up from passionate beginnings the kind of lasting relationship that few are privileged to know and experience." His strong profile was outlined briefly by the firelight as he glanced toward her before returning his gaze to the burning coals. "When you first came to me you released me from one section of my past, whether you knew it or not, my dear. I wish you had a second key, and then my life could follow a rosier path."

He was not really concerned with how much or how little she understood of what he was saying, for he was setting out his thoughts for himself as much as he was talking to her. If she had had the power to banish Helen from his heart as she had eased him from the bonds of Lucy, he would not be facing whatever years were left to him with a feeling of being utterly alone.

In silent, searing elation his listener had taken his words into herself. Because she saw their beginnings in what he had said, and because he had declared previously that there was no other woman active in his life, she believed he was telling her how things could have been for them if Meg had not blocked the way. Aiming for his protection now paled beside the greater security and attendant advantages that having him in love with her would bring. She moved close to stand half behind him, looping an arm up and around his throat, her forehead resting against his shoulder blade through the thin layers of fine cloth and linen shirt.

"If only it could be," she whispered fervently.

He turned around to her, agreeably surprised that she should desire his happiness so unselfishly, having been more than prepared for an unbridled scene at his drawing their liaison to a close. It caused him to revise his opinion of her attachment for him, thinking that she loved where he had not. He never let his mistresses who had served him well go from him empty-handed, jewels proving as acceptable to the well-bred as to actresses and their ilk, but no settlement of a financial kind could compensate any woman for the rejection of love. In consolation and with some pity he gathered her to him, intending to speak gently to her, but suddenly from somewhere overhead a crash reverberated through the house, making the crystal pendants of the lusters on the mantel jingle together.

"What on earth was that?" He put her from him quickly and went from the study as another heavy thud came upstairs. In the servants' quarters there was a stirring of alarm, and the footman on night duty was already halfway up the staircase.

"Wait!" Richard overtook him as he obeyed, and rushed ahead up the flight. There was no doubt in Richard's mind that the commotion had something to do with Meg, and he would not have her exposed to inquisitive stares if he could get to her first.

On the landing he checked his direction, not going along the gallery toward her bedroom, but turning instead toward his own, where the door stood wide, spilling light, and from which came further sounds. He reached it, took one look at the scene before him, and swung about in time to halt the footman almost at his heels.

"It is all right, Jenkins. Go back to your duties and reassure anyone who has been awakened by the crash we heard that there is nothing amiss." Firmly he closed the door on the man, and then went to the foot of the bed where he had slept alone every night since he had brought his wife and children to the Grange all those years ago. Completely drunk, several bottles clutched to her, Meg was lying untidily across his bed in the room she had made a shambles. One of the doors in the wall-length wardrobe stood open, his clothes and summer hats and tennis racquets tumbled to the floor. Drawers were pulled out with their contents spilled, and he could see through to the dressing room, where similar chaos reigned. The crash appeared to be caused by one emptied bottle being hurled at a cheval glass, which in turn had made some heavy books on a chest tilt and fall in rotation, taking a jade horse with them.

"Meg," he said without anger. "Meg."

She grunted, opened her eyes to look at him muzzily, and then with blatant satisfaction put a bottle to her mouth again, some of the brandy trickling down her chin. He moved around to the side of the bed and tidied her nightgown, bringing it down with the rumpled folds of the peignoir over her sprawled legs. Then he sat down beside her and tried gently but firmly to take the bottle from her clutch, which tightened desperately.

"No!" she screeched.

"Come now. I think you have had enough to enable you to sleep well." He succeeded in getting it away from her, but when he tried to take the rest away she began to fight him, shrieking and screaming, lashing out with fists and nails. Using more force than he would have wished, he managed to pinion her back into the pillows with an elbow and arm while he tossed the captured bottles further down the bed out of her reach. Then he picked her up bodily and carried her through to her own room. No sooner had he placed her on the bed than Constance came in. She had been to her quarters to change into more decorous attire, and her velvet robe was buttoned from throat to ankle. On the way she had looked through the open door of Richard's bedroom and seen the disorder there. She had had the wit to close it shut against the gaze of anybody else going by. Meg, who had gone quiet, was glaring at her from the pillows.

"How dared you do this, Meg!" Constance exclaimed on a crescendo of outrage. It was all she could do to stop from springing forward and beating that swollen, drunken face. In a matter of minutes Meg had destroyed all her chances of getting away from the Grange, perhaps even to London and Richard's own establishment there. Constance thought of all the weeks of effort and strained patience and constant harrying that had drained her energies more than Meg's, and in a single, intoxicated act Meg had wiped out the assurances given to Richard that his wife was almost cured. Cured! Meg lay there for what she was, an incurable alcoholic set on ruining her own life as well as everybody else's. Constance knew what it was to have murder in the heart.

"I does what I likes!" Meg sneered. "From now on I'm goin' t'have all the booze I want, and you'll see that I get it, you strumpet!" Then she began to utter all the foulest obscenities she had ever heard or used in her fishing days until Richard smothered the awful flow by clapping his hand over her mouth, and he bade Constance go from the room.

He tended Meg for the rest of the night, holding her head when she vomited, bathing her face, and before dawn put her in a clean nightgown and smoothed the bedcovers over her, for she slept at last. When he returned to his own room he found that his valet, who could be relied upon to keep his own counsel at all times, had been summoned by Constance to clear away all trace of Meg having been there. Fresh linen was on the bed and the windows stood open to the early-morning sunlight. In the bathroom a bath was being run for him. As he pulled off his jacket wearily and began to unbutton his shirt, he heard Jeremy go lurching past his door, coming home from an all-night party.

Later as he came from the breakfast table Constance had a word with him. "It is only a temporary setback with Meg," she said with assurance. "I'll make sure that nothing like it ever happens again." She had not slept during the night hours, working out what she must do, and there was a below-the-surface meaning to her words known only to herself.

"I wish I could believe that." He passed his fingers in tiredness across his forehead.

"I promise, Richard. You'll see. The day will come when Meg will no longer be a burden to you."

He was touched by what he took to be her loving desire to please him, and with a faint smile he put his hand over hers where it rested on his sleeve. "I leave her in your good care. If anyone can achieve such a miracle, I know it will be you."

She returned a smile that was brave and resolute. But there was no smile on her face when she went upstairs to his wife's bedside. Meg had rolled over and her face was in the pillows.

"I wish you would suffocate," Constance whispered venomously. "It would save me and everybody else a great deal of trouble. You'll get your booze, I swear to that. There's more ways than one of killing a cat, and since you're beyond saving for the Temperance Society I'm going to let you have enough drink to drown yourself in it!"

In the bed Meg bit her knuckles in fear, scarcely daring to

breathe until Constance was gone again. There was no one to help her. No one to turn to. Except Tom! Why hadn't she thought of him before!

Later that day when in stony silence, refusing to speak, she heard Richard talk of plans to sell the Grange, and knew it meant that in all but the unbreakable, legal bond they had come to the parting of their ways. When he said he was returning to London that same afternoon she made no comment or protest. He was condemning her to a life sentence in the charge of Constance, with whom she believed he would continue to associate whenever it suited him.

Jeremy received the news of the Grange being put up for sale with indifference. "Do what you like, sir," he said to his father. "I have no sentimental attachment to the place."

"I cannot imagine that you will want to continue living in a smaller house with your mother, and if you wish you may come to London and stay with me for a while. It is high time you made a new effort to establish yourself with a career, and Lennox has an appointment that he thinks would suit you. It would involve entertaining overseas businessmen and potential customers, but you would have to stay away from any gaming yourself."

Jeremy's lifted eyebrow revealed his interest. "I might consider it."

"Surprisingly, a few businesswomen come into the picture now and again. Next month, for example, an American widow is coming to London to consult Lennox on some matter."

"Hmm. Really? Well, I suppose the best thing to do would be to see Lennox as soon as possible and have a talk with him about this appointment. Would you have any objection to my traveling back to London with you when you leave after luncheon?"

"None at all."

When Richard and Jeremy had departed, Meg took paper and pen and wrote an impassioned plea to her youngest son that he should come and see her. She stated that he had been right about Constance and she had been wrong. She begged him to forgive her, and signed herself as his devoted mother. After sealing it she summoned a manservant and gave instructions for it to be delivered with all speed to Easthampton House.

Unknown to Meg, no servant did anything at her bidding without reporting to Constance. "I'll deliver that letter," Constance said, taking it from the man. "I'm going to Easthampton House for afternoon tea."

She did go. She was calling on Donna, who had returned home from her visit away, but the letter was not left on the salver in the hall there for Tom. Constance had steamed it open, read it, and put it in the fire.

Daily Meg sat at her window waiting and watching anxiously for Tom. When finally she realized that he was not going to come, she blamed herself for having driven her youngest son from her beyond recall, and she gave way to utter desolation. Brandy was always on hand now for her to drink as much as she wanted. All will to resist was gone. She began the last steps to final degradation.

Chapter 20

A six-strong team of cart horses, their brasses shining and jingling, brought *Sea Star* slowly out of the shadows of the barn into the bright March sun, which ran a gleam over the sapphire-blue hull and varnished woodwork. Cheers went up from the men engaged in the operation, Hab snatching off his hat and waving it, while Daniel and Donna, who had come to watch, applauded the fine sight. Tom, directing the moves being made, was too tense to relax until the yacht with her bow pointing seaward was finally trundled into position close to the verge of Hoe Lane, a long wake of crushed and trampled grass stretching far back across the meadow to the distant barn. Only then did a beaming smile take over his face, and he gave a whooping cheer of his own in personal celebration. Work on reeving the halyards followed, and afterward, using tackles, the mast was set up, seeming to pierce the sky from the viewpoint of those gathered about in the grass below.

The final tasks on *Sea Star* had been completed when in the moonlight Nicolette, helped by Tom, climbed the ladder propped against the hull and went aboard. Moth-like, she flitted about, admiring everything, while he explained some of the techniques of yachting to her, and why *Sea Star* should excel above all others in the same class when the great day came for serious competition. They spent the rest of the evening in the little cabin, for the first time not going into Honeybridge. He made a pot of tea in the tiny galley and they drank it out of white enamel mugs, smiling at each other over the rims and holding hands while pretending they were already under sail and on their way to France.

The launching came at dawn a few days later, an ancient slipway off Hoe Lane, which had not been used since smugglers' days, giving *Sea Star* her outlet to the sea. Conditions were ideal, an offshore wind filled her sails, and she took to the water like a swan. Hab had expected that with her new design she would prove capricious, and when they were a mile out where the waves were larger she played a number of tricks on them, making them sweat and shout and swear as time and again they were drenched with spray as she fought their efforts to tune her to their liking. By the time they turned shoreward they were both too tired physically and mentally from the battle for mastery to do any talking. They removed the oilskins and tramped in silence to the Crown, where they downed three rums in quick succession. Then they caught each other's glance, and Hab began a slow, satisfied grin.

"You've laid 'er and she knows it, Mr. Tom. I don't reckon you'll get much more trouble there."

Tom's eyes twinkled, a sense of triumph running through his veins as warm and golden as the rum. "I don't believe I will," he chuckled gleefully. "Drink up, and we'll have another round to get the last chill out of our bones."

Hab's prophecy proved right. The next day Tom had *Sea Star* beating into a stiff westerly, close-hauled on the starboard tack, and the difficulties of handling her proved minor and were soon eradicated. As each day went past she responded more and more sweetly to his control, until eventually he was able to put her deep keel to the test and sailed her closer to the wind than his crew of one man had deemed possible. Hab yelled his exultation, the wind combining with the hiss of the bow wave to carry away his voice, and Tom knew his yacht was ready for her official sea trials.

Nicolette's last meeting with Tom before their elopement coincided with the eve of the sea trials. Little more than thirty-six hours separated them from their departure in *Sea Star* for France, a prospect that filled her with an anticipation that was both delicious and dreadful to her, for try as she would she could not ignore the feeling of premonition that had recently returned to her. Always when Tom's arms were about her and in his strong presence her misgivings were banished, but once on her own again the sense of unease came back. She had found herself going about as though on tiptoe, fearful of upsetting the delicate balance of anything that was linked with her future happiness.

It was with relief that she came out of the evening darkness into his embrace within the welcoming walls of Honeybridge. There she was safe and nothing could part them. Never had she loved him more than this last time together in the haven they had made their own. Never again in all their lives would their privacy be so secret and complete. Never before had she felt quite as she did this night.

Tom was aware of the subtle change in the girl he loved and was awed by it, not quite sure yet whether it was as he believed. He drew her to the glow of the charcoal fire in the dining room, where she did not take the inglenook seat, sitting down instead by the hearth within view of the portrait of Kate, with which she exchanged a long look before turning to him with a little smile. He sat beside her, keeping back all the adoring things he wanted to say to her on this last and special occasion, for he had to go over once again the plans he had made with meticulous care. Nothing must go wrong.

"You will leave Radcliffe Hall at any time in the morning most likely not to cause questions. Beth will drive you to the Pier, leave you there, and then depart on whatever errand that was supposed to bring the two of you into town."

"The library," Nicolette endorsed.

"You will buy a ticket at the turnstile and go along the Pier until you reach the Pavilion. With so few visitors in the resort at this time of year I don't suppose there will be anybody else about except two or three anglers trying their luck."

She nodded. "I wait until I'm quite sure nobody is observing me, and then I let myself into the Pavilion by a side door."

"That's right. You know the one." He took a key from his pocket and handed it to her. She put it away in her drawstring purse. "The Pavilion is the last place where anyone would think of looking for you, and you'll be in the dry whatever the weather until you see me sailing toward the Pier. Then you will come out of the emergency doors and down the iron steps where the paddle-steamer passengers alight. You'll be hidden by the ironwork from anybody's gaze, and I'll have you aboard in no time at all."

She traced two hearts in the powdering of ash on the stone hearth. "I wish we could set out from shore together, Tom."

He leaned forward and drew an arrow through the hearts with his forefinger. "So do I, but *Sea Star* is never without a little gathering of spectators coming to look at her these days, and the local urchins make quite a profit wading and diving after pennies thrown to them as part of the entertainment while everybody is waiting for *Sea Star* to set sail. Someone could so easily recognize you, and the longer your disappearance can be kept from any connection with my first crossing to France, which my family will know about, the better our chances will be of safely tying the knot that no man may split asunder."

She continued gazing at the two hearts. "I wish that knot were tied now, Tom."

"It is for us."

She did not move, and spoke almost in a whisper. "And for Kate. She wants us to know love in this house as once she knew it. When we leave Honeybridge tonight we may never come into it again." Slowly she raised her hands and began to pull the pins from her hair.

He held his breath, not touching her. When the last silken strand tumbled to her shoulders he reached out, burying his hands in her tresses as he held her head and kissed her mouth long and lovingly. Afterward he carried her up the stairs of Honeybridge and into Kate's bedroom.

He had not known he could be capable of such extreme tenderness. He loved her so much that all that happened between them could have been the first time for him as it was for her. She had wanted the brocade curtains closed around the bed, creating a sanctuary within a sanctuary, but a thread of candlelight in the room gradually penetrated the velvet darkness, and he was not denied the sight of her at the exquisite moment of her surrender. Never again would there be anyone but her. Unconsciously he had committed himself to the Warwyck vow of lifelong love to one woman above all others.

When they came downstairs again Nicolette looked about her at the house that had come to mean so much to her, and bade it a silent farewell. At the gate out of the meadow she and Tom took longer than ever before to say good night. She gave no thought to Beth's impatience on this occasion, all else lacking importance beside this parting with Tom, who was as loath to let her go as she was to leave him. When finally she slid her fingers from his she became aware at last of the lateness of the hour, and took to her heels to run the distance along the dark lane out of his sight to the equipage parked in a secluded spot.

She put her foot on the step to climb in, and froze. It was Hugh who sat holding whip and reins as he glared fiercely at her. "Where's Beth?" she gasped in consternation.

He ignored her question. "Get in!" When she still hesitated he jerked the whip forward and shook it within an inch of her nose. "You get in, my dear sister, or I'll flay you here and now."

If she cried out Tom would hear her, but there was still a chance that Hugh did not know where she had been or with whom. Summoning up her courage, she obeyed her brother's command and half fell into the seat beside him, caught off balance as he cracked the whip over the horse's head, making it charge forward. "I want to know what has happened to Beth," she persisted stubbornly, determined not to be browbeaten.

"Very well," he replied with a dangerous silkiness that was more deadly than his previous show of rage. "I took it upon myself to find out why the lantern lectures held such a fascination for you, and do you know what I discovered? You don't attend them at all, and Beth has been leaving in the interval to spend the rest of the time at the Crown while waiting for you to come from your assignations at Honeybridge House. But no more. I put her in the charge of my own coachman with instructions to take her back to the Hall, where I don't doubt she is already packing up her chattels."

So he knew the truth. Her spine seemed to have turned to ice. "You spied on me!" she accused with indignation. As she clutched her purse nervously her grasp met the Pavilion key through the soft leather.

"You probably won't believe me, but I had your best interests at heart. I thought you had a beau I could help you present to Grandmother. How wrong I was." His voice rasped ominously. "You have been carrying on a dirty little hole-in-the-corner affair—"

"No!"

"—with one of those rotten Warwycks!"

"I love Tom Warwyck!"

Hugh gritted his teeth, a nerve throbbing violently in his jaw. "You'll live to regret that statement. My God! You will!"

At Radcliffe Hall he seized her by the arm and hauled her unceremoniously into the house, setting a pace that she had difficulty in keeping up with, being hampered by her bustled skirt and petticoats. As always at this hour, their grandmother had already retired, but Hugh, upon hearing from her personal maid that she was not asleep, insisted that he see her. A few minutes later they were shown into Olivia's bedroom.

Olivia was propped against large, lace-trimmed pillows, her face framed by the frill of her nightcap, a shawl about her shoulders. Her claw-like hands, bare of all except her wedding ring, lay on the embroidered coverlet. "Well?" she demanded uncompromisingly of her grandson. "Why have you disturbed me at this untimely hour?"

Nicolette wrenched herself free of her brother's grip and stood alone. "I will tell you! I'm in love with Tom Warwyck and he's in love with me. We have been meeting for a long time. I have cut myself off from the Radcliffe-Warwyck feud and never want any part of it again."

Shock and rage contorted Olivia's face almost beyond recognition, her eyes seeming to start from their sockets, and her hands began to shake as if she had the palsy. "You wicked creature!" She fumbled with the bedclothes to throw them back and get up, too consumed by temper to lie still. Hugh hurried forward to help her stand, and take her lilac silk peignoir from a chair to assist her into it. "That such a confession of treachery and disloyalty and betrayal should come from my own grandchild," she stormed on. "Hugh! What part have you had in all this? I demand to know everything that has happened."

Nicolette remained motionless with her head high as Hugh recounted his growing suspicions that the lantern lectures were attended for some ulterior purpose; how he had called in on a second occasion and seen Beth sitting beside an empty seat, and how the third time he had followed and compelled the truth out of the woman, who had gaped at him in dismay when he had entered the Crown and caught her sitting there with a glass halfway to her lips. All the time Olivia, who had seated herself by the bedroom fire, drummed her clenched fists on the curved arms of the chair, unable to contain her wrath in stillness. At the end of Hugh's account Olivia turned her blazing gaze upon her granddaughter.

"Come here!" She pointed to a spot in front of her.

Nicolette obeyed, her outward composure revealing nothing of the frightened drumming of her heart. "I'll not allow you to strike me again as you did in the carriage, Grandmother," she said firmly.

Olivia gave a hiss. "I'll not degrade myself with any contact with such wickedness. What has there been between you and this Warwyck lecher at Honeybridge House? How often has he had his way with you? Don't try to pretend innocence with me, because I know that family. Daniel Warwyck seduced my own sister when she was wed to another and he to Kate. Richard and his half sister Lucy almost brought scandal down upon themselves, and the Warwyck fishwife has not taken to the bottle without good reason. As for this present generation, Lennox was wild enough before he settled down, Jeremy is a known rake, and Thomas Warwyck—"

"Don't you dare to say a word against Tom!"

"Hoity-toity," Olivia sneered sarcastically. Then she banged down her fist on the wooden chair arm with a force that made Nicolette jump. "Answer my question, girl! I'll have the whole truth from you if I keep you on your feet before me without food or drink for a month!"

Her terrible, probing voice beat against Nicolette's eardrums. With a dawning horror the girl saw salaciousness blended with the wrath in the old woman's eyes, and was sickened beyond measure by this evil seeking to vilify and contaminate all the joy and love and the perfect happiness that she had known at Honeybridge. She stopped listening to what was being said, shutting herself away by a knack she had developed in childhood to keep a little oasis of quietness in which to read or think in a household of noisy, boisterous brothers; only this time her head started to swim and the room was beginning to sway.

"Steady on, Grandmother," Hugh interrupted, taken aback by the crudeness of the accusations and insinuations being directed at his sister. It was as if some lascivious venom had been unleashed in this little old woman, who had always turned such a prim face to everything. No one was more enraged than he by Nicolette's association with Tom Warwyck, but she was his sister and no common trollop. "I said that was enough! Shut up! I always did think you were off your rocker and now I'm sure of it."

Nicolette had not heard a word. The swaying of the room had got out of control. Her knees folded under her and she collapsed without a sound at her grandmother's feet. Roughly Hugh hauled her up, and with an arm about her waist he dragged her from the room. Incredulously he heard the old woman's voice take on new strength as the tirade was continued as if Nicolette was still there.

In the morning when Olivia came slowly downstairs with one hand on the baluster rail and the other on her stick she appeared to be completely recovered, and Hugh found it hard to associate the dignified image she presented with the old harridan of the night before. Moreover, she seemed to have quite forgotten his insults.

"Where is your sister?" she questioned icily, going past him into the drawing room. It was obvious that her granddaughter's name was never going to pass her lips again. He followed in her wake and answered her.

"She is in her room." He had gone in to see Nicolette and found her fully dressed, sitting calm and quiet by the untouched breakfast tray that had been brought to her. In any other circumstances, and if it had been anyone else but Tom Warwyck with whom she had dallied, he would have felt sorry for her and prevented her banishment. Instead, his resentment was almost unbearably raw, and he wanted her gone from the Hall before his temper got the better of him and he used some violence against her.

"Is she under lock and key?"

"No. I don't think that is necessary. She is completely resigned to being sent away. All she asked was to see Beth Macdonald, and that I refused."

"Where is Beth?"

"Gone. I manhandled her out of the house myself. She had the insolence to demand her wages in lieu of a week's notice."

Olivia tut-tutted at such brazenness. "This morning you will send word to your father by telegraph asking him to come and take his wretched daughter from this house forever. In the meantime I will write a letter to Sir Daniel Warwyck." Normally she never gave her enemy the benefit of his baronetcy when mentioning him, and she used his title now with sarcasm. "He has kept his late wife's home closed up these many years. I am going to let him know that whatever is kept locked up there has been intruded upon by his grandson and Alexander's granddaughter. I hope the shock does not stop his heart." Her lips drew back narrowly and her grandson glimpsed again the evil visage of the night hours. "I want him to suffer long over the violation of Honeybridge House."

At Easthampton House, Donna was trying to cope with one of her depressive headaches and last-minute arrangements for a grand luncheon that was to be served that afternoon when the sea trials were over. She blamed Helen for the oppressiveness of her mood. Helen had set her worrying about Meg when she could least do with any extra anxiety, wanting a truly handsome repast to round off the day for the three important yachting guests of honor who could hold Tom's future with *Sea Star* in the balance. Helen, who was included in the guest list, had donated a recipe for a cream pudding the previous day that Donna had asked for, and it was during the resulting conversation about who else was coming that Meg's name came up.

"Haven't you invited her?" Helen had asked.

"Meg has not relented toward Tom, and in any case Constance advised against it. As I mentioned to you recently, Meg has lapsed back into her old ways and is rarely fit these days to appear in company."

"Perhaps the chance to heal the breach with her son is all Mrs. Warwyck needs to recover again." Helen's gaze was very direct. "Forgive me for speaking frankly, but you are her sister-in-law and it should be for you to judge what is best for her in this case. At least she will attend the sea trials, will she not?"

"Constance says Meg never rises now before noon, and not always then. You don't realize how much she has slipped back recently."

Helen sighed, getting up from her chair to take her leave. "If Mrs. Warwyck were less afraid of Constance I think she might come to assert herself again."

"Afraid? What do you mean?"

"Exactly what I say. I saw her cower that day when Constance came for her at Sea Cottage. I cannot believe that a state of fear is conducive to anybody's recovery."

Helen's words had come back to haunt Donna in the midst of the discovery that the damask cloth that was to have been used that afternoon had an iron mark, adding to the harassment of the day. Her father had already departed, for he was to meet the two businessmen at the railway station. Sir Duncan Watson had arrived the night before and was staying at the Royal Hotel. When a parlormaid interrupted a discussion with the butler about the vintage port, Donna was exasperated to be told there was a visitor.

"I'm not at home."

"It's an urgent matter, ma'am. So I was told."

"Oh, very well."

Donna did not recognize Beth Macdonald and did not know who she was, but her dress and appearance stamped her as respectable working class. "I canna get near young Mr. Warwyck for the crowds on the beach," the woman began, "and I want tae get the money he owes me and be awa' from here."

"Money? What money?" Donna was bewildered.

Beth, who considered that her dismissal had released her from all bonds of secrecy, answered bluntly. "The sum he promised tae pay me as compensation for losing my post as chaperone tae Miss Nicolette Radcliffe when the truth came oot that they have been meeting on the quiet at Honeybridge Hoose for these past months."

Donna sank down in the nearest chair. She knew that her headache would prove to be the worst she had ever had, and at all costs she must keep this woman's shattering revelation from her father. "If Tom has entered into a financial agreement with you—and I have no reason to doubt your word—you will get your due. All I ask is that you wait until tomorrow when today's sea trials are over before taking up the matter with him. I will pay your overnight accommodation, as well as any other expenses incurred, on the condition that you do not breathe a word of this business to anyone else."

Beth considered. She wanted her money, but she was not after a pound of flesh from Tom Warwyck. After all, it would not inconvenience her very much to wait one more day. She gave a nod. "Very well. I accept your offer and will do as you say."

No sooner had Beth been shown out than, unbeknown to Donna, a letter addressed to Sir Daniel Warwyck and bearing the Radcliffe crest on the back of it was handed in to await his return. Lost in her own troubled thoughts, Donna did not as much as glance at it lying on the silver salver in the hall as she went upstairs to change for the splendor of the day's events, now overshadowed for her by what she had learned of Tom's foolhardiness. The reckless boy! Of all the girls in the world he had to go running after a Radcliffe!

Reaching her room, she put a hand to her aching head. This new worry was almost too much to bear, adding to the burden of her conscience toward Meg. That, at least, could be settled. She should have invited Richard's wife in the first place, but it was not too late. At table she would sit Meg under her own observation during the luncheon and see that she was served only watered wine, which should prevent any disasters. As for the sea trials, Meg liked to act the lady in public, and whatever the differences with Tom she would enjoy taking up a place of honor on the Pier. Glancing at her fob watch, Donna decided that if she traveled fast there would be just enough time to collect Meg at the Grange and bring her into town to see most of the excitement.

Such a crush of traffic met her as she drove herself away from Easthampton House in her swift little phaeton that she had difficulty in getting through the stream advancing toward the promenade. Precious minutes began to slip away, and she became more frustrated at every delay.

At the Grange, Constance stuck a pearl-headed pin through her new crimson felt hat with the feathers of an English blue jay sprouting from its ribbon band, and for greater security added a second pin, for the day was blustery with a strong wind blowing, and she wanted to look her best at the sea trials. In addition she wanted to look conspicuous, the striking hat having been purchased with that aim in view, because she wanted as many people as possible to remember that she was present throughout.

She stood back from the looking glass and regarded herself with some curiosity. Who would think she could appear and feel as rigidly calm as she did? The worst time had been steeling herself for what she was to do this day. Many nights she had paced the floor, plagued by an inherent abhorrence at the prospect of taking life, but knowing that unless Meg was done away with there was no chance of the rosy future that would otherwise be hers. She called in a doctor one day, wanting to get a check on Meg's health and see whether the ravages of drink would hasten her demise by natural causes, but the report that Meg's heart was strong and her lungs clear was her death sentence. Constance knew she would have to take matters into her own hands.

The chance had come when Richard had written to Meg that all the indoor and outdoor servants should have a couple of hours off to watch the sea trials. Many of them had seen Tom grow up, and even those who had not were eager to take an unexpected break from routine to see the boat that everyone was talking about. Constance, checking unobtrusively, had discovered the time when hired horse buses would pick them up and bring them home again. The vehicles had just departed. Only two elderly gardeners had declined to go, and the lodge keeper at the gates was remaining on duty. All would be too far away from the house to prevent what she intended to accomplish. She took a deep breath, smoothed the waist of her buttoned basque, and went to carry out her carefully timed and rehearsed tasks. They would take her no longer than three minutes and forty-five seconds.

Meg lay snoring on the pillows. Constance looked down at her with contempt and knew renewed loathing since Meg was the cause of projecting her into the obscene act of murder. When Meg had awakened earlier Constance had been ready with a bottle and glass to reinforce the effect of the previous evening's debauch. Later she had made sure on various pretexts that no less than four of the servants had seen their master's wife in the heavy, sleeping-off condition normal to her at such times, nothing to indicate that there had been a replenishing to induce deeper sleep. Knowing how strong Meg could be if the need arose, something retained from the muscle power used to haul in loaded fishing nets, Constance had decided against any attempt at suffocation with a pillow before putting her plan into action.

As always, Meg's windows were open to the sea air, and the draft was an aid to what she had devised. Taking up a poker, she prodded the coals in the grate to a good blaze, so that smoke from the chimney would be evidence of a vigorous fire with the chance of flying sparks. Going to the chest of drawers and to the large wardrobe, she pulled out a variety of day garments such as a woman in a drunken state might select at random after making a last-minute decision to attend the sea trials. She spread them as if they had been dropped across the floor into a heap at the side of the bed where Meg lay. Carefully she folded back the bedcovers from the sleeping woman and laid more garments over her as if the effort of selecting something to wear had proved too much, and she had fallen back into bed again. Silently Constance took an oil lamp from the bedside and dripped its contents over the clothes lying on and around the bed before laying it on the floor as if it had been accidentlly knocked off its table. She did not risk the noise of deliberately smashing it, knowing that later the heat in the room would do that for her. Although she expected everything in the room to be destroyed by the fire she was shortly to light, she wanted to make sure that in whatever probing inspection afterward, Meg's accidental death would appear to have happened exactly in the circumstances she had contrived.

Lastly, she took the long fuse she had made ready after much experimentation and timing. It would burn slowly enough for her to be away from the Grange and seen on the promenade at the sea trials before the room burst into an inferno. She put one end into the depths of the fire in the grate and saw it take life like a cigarette. Carefully trailing it snake-like across the broad width of the carpet she brought it around the foot of the bed to the pile of oil-sprinkled clothes. All was done. Averting her gaze from her victim, she went from the room and closed the door after her. Downstairs a coachman was waiting with one of the less grand equipages to drive her to the sea. As she settled herself she thought that it would not be long before she was being driven through the streets of London in the best landau or the grand sociable. The thought stopped her mind splitting at what she had done.

She alighted at the Pier. There was a full tide, and the promenade was crowded, some of the spectators having to watch out that they did not get splashed by waves breaking against it. Being connected with the Warwyck family, Constance was able to take up a priority viewing place on the Pier, and she made sure that a number of Sir Daniel's as well as Donna's friends and acquaintances saw her and acknowledged her greeting. Taking up a position by the railings, she looked for Donna, but could not see her in the throng. The hands of the Pier clock moved toward 10:45 A.M. At any moment the smoldering fuse would ignite the room at the Grange. She started violently as a great shout went up. *Sea Star* had been sighted.

At that moment Donna was driving through the lodge gates of the Grange. Due to the trees and the curve of the drive it was not until she came almost to the forecourt that she noticed thick smoke rolling out from Meg's bedroom windows. Alarmed, thinking that coals must have fallen from the fire onto a carpet, she jumped down from the phaeton and rushed into the house. Inside, the hall was filled with dense smoke that plunged into her lungs. She did not call out, for she had remembered that all the servants had been let off duty. Coughing, she soaked a handkerchief in the water of a bowl of flowers, and putting it over her nose and mouth, she ran up the stairs. The smoke was thicker than ever in the upper corridors, and she saw it curling out from under Meg's door like gray ostrich feathers as she drew near. She turned the handle and threw open the door to take in a scene that seemed out of a nightmare. The whole carpet was smoldering away from a charred, black trail winding itself from the fireplace to the side of the bed where clothes lay tumbled. Through the choking smoke she saw that someone lay on the bed, and flew to her.

"Meg! Meg!" She shook her sister-in-law violently, but Meg only rolled away, coughing and mumbling, the covering garments slipping from her. The action probably saved her life. As Donna turned to run around to the far side of the bed to rouse her again her foot caught in one of the garments on the floor, and inadvertently she dragged it across the fuse. Flames burst upward with a roar, and almost instantly fire seemed to be everywhere. Donna, her own clothes alight, heard Meg scream as fire touched her, and saw her reel to her feet from the bed.

"Get out! Come on! The door!" Donna tried to pull her in the right direction, but Meg had become immobilized by panic upon finding herself in an inferno with a fire-raked figure attempting to drag her seemingly toward the worst of the flames.

"Getta way from me! No! No!" Meg hit out wildly in defense, and Donna was knocked to the burning floor.

One clear part in Donna's mind amidst all the searing, physical pain told her she was going to die without ever having made amends for the old crime of leaving Ben Thompson's body on the railway lines without a prayer for his soul. It gave her the strength to stagger to her feet again, and with raw and blistered hands she did the one thing left in her power, and grabbed Meg with all her might to yank her forward and around. Meg received a blow in the back that hurtled her forward. Yelling and screaming, she fell to her knees in the choking smoke by the door, and out of it loomed Richard. He hauled her out of immediate danger into the corridor before dashing back into the room again with arms upraised to protect himself against the scorching heat, certain he had glimpsed someone else there. He found his sister and snatched her from the inferno to smother the flames that engulfed her with his hands and with his coat. She was still alive.

People were starting to enter the house at a run with buckets of water. Villagers had seen the smoke, and the alarm had been raised. He sent someone he recognized for the doctor, and bore Donna to a place of safety. Meg stumbled after him in her scorched and blackened nightgown, holding on to his coattails like a lost child.

None of those crowding the Pier and promenade at the sea trials noticed the sinister plume of dark smoke beginning to make itself visible far away beyond the town. All were caught up in the spectacle before them. Many of the spectators knew little or nothing about boats, but there was not one person present who could not see that this was an exceptional craft. With a flash of blue hull and with white sails curved taut, she sliced through the rough gray sea with a speed that dazzled those accustomed to humbler sailing vessels. Hundreds of telescopes and ancient spyglasses had been unearthed to follow her progress at close quarters, and a street vendor with his wits about him was doing a busy trade selling small brass spy-pieces made in Birmingham. Among the variety of lenses focused on the yacht, only the best were able to give full notion of the split-second timing between the helmsman and his one-man crew in a combination of strength, agility, and sharp intelligence.

Tom and Hab had been able to tell from *Sea Star*'s beginnings that she would always be difficult to handle when strained to her fastest speed, and for some nerve-grinding moments they were hard put to keep her from heeling excessively in the increasingly heavy wind, but the crisis passed and all was well. Cheering went up from the Pier and was echoed by other spectators as *Sea Star* turned shoreward, Tom and Hab exchanging spray-drenched grins and giving each other the jaunty thumbs-up sign. *Sea Star* had excelled herself.

Sir Duncan Watson was waiting in his oilskins, ready and eager to try *Sea Star* for himself, the fiercely strengthening wind an additional challenge. Nobody was standing at the promenade rails any more, not only because the waves were hurling spume and spray across into the road beyond, but because the smoke had been generally spotted at last. Those who lived in that direction were departing hurriedly, their faces anxious for their own property as they whipped up horses and bowled away. Tom, crewing for Sir Duncan, was fully occupied and did not glance shoreward as *Sea Star* cleaved the waves once again.

At Radcliffe Hall the smoke was billowing densely over the treetops, and as the servants ran into the grounds to stare and question where it was coming from, a tradesman brought the news that the Grange was ablaze. In her room Nicolette saw the smoke, but could not tell from which direction it was coming, and supposed it to be a barn or one of the other farm buildings on the estate that was on fire. From her window she saw excited servants hurrying toward the coach house, where the hand-pump fire engine was kept, or gathering to gape and point at the smoke-blackened sky. She peeped out of her room and saw that the maid-servant set to watch over her movements had gone from the chair outside the door, curiosity about the fire having overcome all else.

She did not hesitate. Quickly she threw on her coat and hat, snatched up the small valise she had packed ready, and with her heart thumping against her ribs she hurried to the nearest stair-case. Without seeing anyone she went out through a side door away from the activity of the servants and was off through the trees, making for the spot where Tom had found an easily accessi-ble way in and out of the grounds. By rights she was not expected by Tom to be at the Pier Pavilion until the next day, but she had known from the moment of their secret meetings being discov-ered that it would be up to her to find some new means of getting away from the Hall to keep their special rendezvous. She glanced up at the smoke-filled sky through the wildly waving branches overhead. The smoke *was* dense. She hoped it was not anyone's home, because it would burn like tinder in this high wind.

In the Hall falling away behind her the butler had brought word of the fire to the mistress of the house, the young master having ridden to hounds that morning and being still absent.

"Have I your permission to send the hand pump and all the available male staff to help put out the fire, ma'am?" he inquired in the expectation of an affirmative answer.

Olivia, sitting in her high-backed chair, regarded him coldly. "We send nobody," she rasped. "It is Warwyck property. Let it burn."

Nicolette reached the boundary wall and tossed her valise over it. Hitching up her skirts, she followed it by way of the gnarled branches of an ancient tree. She dropped onto a grassy bank on the other side and fell to her knees unhurt. Springing up at once, she put her clothes in order, rescued her valise from the ditch, and set off across the fields to avoid any kind of pursuit by road, her head down against the rough wind.

By the time she reached Easthampton the tide was going out, the second sea trial was over, and the crowd had dispersed. In the hope of seeing Tom she went along to Hoe Lane where *Sea Star* had been drawn back up the slipway, but he was not there. Two burly fishermen were watching over the yacht and keeping at bay a number of children who wanted to touch and inspect it. She knew that *Sea Star* had not been left unguarded at any time since that damage done to it a while ago. Tom had not said to her that he suspected her brother, but she was very much afraid that Hugh had been responsible.

She wished she could seek Tom out at Easthampton House, but that was out of the question. It would be a double catastrophe if the truth came out there, because then she and Tom would have the combined force of the two rival families set into ruthless action against them. Deciding to reach her hiding place without further delay, she bought some food to sustain her until the morrow, and went to the Pier. Although it had been crowded during the sea trials, it was now deserted, and due to the rough wind the ticket office was closed and the turnstile padlocked. Neither of the souvenir shops on either side of it had been opened yet for the forthcoming season, and after a quick check to make sure that she was unobserved within the archway, Nicolette clambered over the turnstile and drew breath behind one of the shops. All that remained was to get to the head of the Pier.

The wind fought her the whole way, tearing at her as she held on to her hat and beating her clothes against her. With relief she reached the Pavilion and let herself into it. She was just in time. Slashing rain began to beat against the windows.

At Easthampton House later that day Donna's body was brought home. She had lived long enough to whisper a few words to her brother, and then she was gone. The Grange had been reduced to a blackened, still-burning shell, the efforts of fire engines from several areas defeated by the wind that had whipped itself to gale force during the afternoon. Many items of value had been saved, but more had been destroyed. Daniel and Richard and Tom were stunned and grief-stricken at the loss of Donna, whom each had loved and respected in his own way.

When word had spread that the Grange was burning it was Helen who took charge of the three important guests, leaving Sir Daniel free to go to the scene of the fire as well as Tom when he came ashore from the sail with Sir Duncan and had the news broken to him. She gave the guests luncheon at Sea Cottage, and one of her own servants rode back and forth to the fire to bring the latest news. Before leaving for their train the visitors left letters for Tom, the two businessmen inviting him to meet them at the first opportunity when all sad family matters were settled, and the yachtsman offering to sail *Sea Star* in the first important race of the season, which would bring further recognition of her qualities. Helen was left in no doubt that Tom would get the financial backing that he had hoped for.

At Easthampton House she gave the grievous tidings about Donna to the servants, and at her instructions the elaborate celebration table was stripped of its crystal, silver, and damask. She went herself to pull down the blinds at each window in the home already hushed in mourning. Constance had gone with Daniel to the fire, but when she returned on her own with Meg wrapped in blankets she seemed incapaple of looking after her, shivering with shock, and it was Helen who saw Meg into bed and soothed her distress. She was still upstairs with Meg when the coffin was carried through into the music room. Coming down shortly afterward, she found the three Warwyck men coming from there, Richard with bandaged hands. All looked up at her with haggard faces, and in Richard's she saw what the sight of her meant to him at this hour. It seemed the most natural thing in the world that she should go into his arms and put her own around his neck in consolation. Neither saw Tom's look of astonishment or Daniel stir himself in the midst of his grief to give his grandson a tactful tap on the shoulder to indicate that the couple should be left on their own.

"Hush, my darling," she whispered as Richard groaned in the anguish of his bereavement. "You did everything possible to save her."

"If I had caught an earlier train to see the sea trials she would be alive now. I had thought to take Meg with me, and I arrived to find that room aflame."

"Thank God you came when you did, or else poor Meg would have suffered a similar fate."

As Daniel and Tom entered the drawing room Constance looked up from where she was sitting huddled by the fire as if she would never be warm again, and was in time to see Richard and Helen in each other's arms before the door began to close. She went rigid, her cheeks hollowing, and she got up from her chair with the stiffness of an automaton to jerk the door open wide again as Helen put soft lips to Richard's mouth. The shock she had already suffered renewed itself as she watched them kiss in an unmistakably caring way.

He saw Constance before Helen did. His expression changed completely as he faced his sister's murderess.

"Get out of this house and this town," he said dangerously, "and never come back to Easthampton again."

Constance fought for self-control, more frightened than she had ever been in her whole life. "You can't send me away. Not after all we have been to each other and will be again. You mustn't let this woman's sympathy beguile you into thinking that she can take my place. Remember all you said about the kind of future we could look to together."

He stared at her incredulously, completely astounded. "I do not know what you are talking about. I have never for one moment considered any kind of future with you." Such was his tone that even she became instantly aware that she had made a dreadful error of judgment. Later he was to put together remembered snatches of conversation that gave meaning to her extraordinary statement, but at the present time he had no thought but to be rid of the sight of her once and for all. "Donna lived long enough to give me some idea of what she found when she tried to rescue Meg. You were the last one to leave the Grange after all the servants were gone. Be thankful that I have not called in the police."

She was ashen, but her avaricious nature made it impossible for her not to try to grab something for herself out of the chaos she had created. "I have only the clothes I stand up in. A few pounds in my purse. What am I to do? Where am I to go? You can't send me away destitute."

He had never hit a woman before, but he struck her across the face with his fist then, momentarily blinded by the inadvertent reminder that she had been destitute in the past when Donna had lifted her up and brought her to Easthampton, only to be repaid with the most terrible death. He would have dealt Constance a second blow if Helen had not thrown herself forward to restrain him.

Constance had her revenge. At the door she turned with her hand still holding her bruised face and spat the words that he was to remember all his life. "Think what you like about me. There's no proof and never can be. If I should be guilty of anything you have only yourself to blame. Your sister's death lies at your door!"

That night with the incoming tide the gale-force wind became stronger than ever. In the town slates flew from houses, and trees were uprooted. The windows of Easthampton House boomed and rattled under its onslaught as Tom looked out toward the distant promenade where mountainous waves could be seen in the lamplight, breaking over it like individual waterfalls to flood the road. Unless by some miracle the gale had subsided by the morning, Nicolette would know that their elopement that day would be out of the question. The best of yachts would capsize in such waves, or be dashed to pieces against the Pier. At least he knew that his Aunt Donna would have wanted him to go ahead with his elopement as soon as it proved possible, because she had always desired his happiness above all else, and had been more of a parent to him than his own mother had ever been. He had counted on his aunt being on his side when he had made Nicolette his bride, because once she had met the girl of his choice she would have understood why he had not let the name of Radcliffe divide him from his love. He was going to miss Donna more than anybody else could possibly realize. His sadness was heavy upon him.

Morning brought no respite from the gales, which were lashing the entire south coast. Damage to property was considerable, and many windows in hotels and other buildings facing the seafront had been smashed by pebbles hurled by the waves. Sea Cottage had suffered no damage, but Beatrice had been so alarmed the previous evening by the sight of the huge incoming tide that at Daniel's invitation Helen had brought her to Easthampton House for the night. Tom, in mourning black tie and armband, restless as a tiger in a cage, would have gone with his father to the ruins of the Grange, but Richard had many things to see to and had no need of his company. Yet all the animosity between them had vanished. The fact that Richard had come home to Easthampton with the intention of giving support to the sea trials had healed the breach between them without a word being spoken about it on either side. Tom entertained a great deal of curiosity about his father's relationship with Helen, but it was not a matter for discussion, and he drew his own conclusions with a tolerance he would not have expected of himself.

Unable to bear the confines of the crepe-draped house any longer, he went to check that all was well with *Sea Star*, but, as arranged, Hab had had her brought high, out of danger. They spent some time in the cabin talking with great seriousness over the tragic and dramatic events that had taken place the previous day, and before he left again both of them stood to observe the approaching tide with some misgiving. Strands of seaweed on the groins were flapping level in the wind, and the waves were running full and angry under rearing whitecaps.

"It looks as if the full tide at midday will be worse than last night," Tom commented. Then he thrust his hands into his topcoat pockets and strode against the wind's force back to Easthampton House.

Daniel was opening the black-edged letters of condolence that were beginning to arrive in batches. When he picked up an envelope bearing the Radcliffe crest he thought for a few incredulous moments that Olivia was sending him an expression of sympathy. He read it through and was shaken by a wrath so violent that the letter vibrated with a rustling sound as he held it.

"Sir Daniel! What is the matter?" Helen had come from attending Beatrice, and she rushed to drop down on one knee beside his chair. He could not answer her. Alarmed, she dashed for a glass of brandy and he thrust it aside, knocking it from her hand. Tom came into the room.

"What's up?" he inquired innocently.

Daniel gave a mighty roar, getting up from the chair and rising to his full height. "You have dared to invade Honeybridge! You have trespassed and consorted there with a fancy piece whom her own grandmother is casting out for her immoral ways!"

The skin strained taut over Tom's face, making the bones stand out with a burnished look. "Cast out? When is she being cast out?"

"Is that all you can say?" Daniel stormed. "Honeybridge was to stay closed until after my death, and you have violated it and gone against my most sacred wish that none should disturb anything that is stored there!"

Tom had only one thought in his head and shouted his demand. "For God's sake, let me know what is to happen to Nicolette! I love her! I want to marry her! What are they doing with her? When is she to be sent away and where?"

Daniel hurled the letter at him and Tom snatched it up to read it through. Without a word he tossed it from him and went crashing out of the house bareheaded and without a coat. Daniel stumped across to hold aside the mourning blind at the window, Helen following him, and seconds later they saw Tom gallop an unsaddled horse past the house and down the slope to the gates, ignoring the drive and sending clods of plush-like lawn flying in his wake.

He did not ease the pace all the way to the Hall. At the gates he bawled to be admitted, and the startled lodge keeper had one gate barely wide enough before Tom was through it and charging his horse away up the drive. He dismounted and was over the threshold of the house even as the door was opened to him.

"Tell Miss Radcliffe-Stuart that Tom Warwyck has come to fetch her away," he ordered in a tone that brooked no argument.

"The young lady is not here, sir," the footman replied faintly. A Warwyck under the Radcliffe roof! "She has departed."

"Where has she gone?" Tom was almost beside himself at the thought that he had come too late.

"I have not been given that information, sir."

Enraged, Tom seized him by his collar. "Then take me to someone who has!"

Olivia's icy tones spoke from the head of the stairs. "Free yourself, Stephens, and remove that Warwyck person from my house."

Tom thrust the footman from him and made for the stairs, taking them in leaps until he was almost level with the old lady. "Where is Nicolette? I'm not leaving until I know. Neither you nor anyone else is going to keep me from her."

Olivia regarded him with her hooded eyes, giving away nothing of the surprise she had experienced at first hearing him announce he had come to take Nicolette away with him. When the girl's absence was discovered it had been Hugh's immediate conclusion as well as her own that Nicolette had slipped away to her lover. Hugh had been all for going to Easthampton House and reclaiming her as a runaway wherever she happened to be under Warwyck protection, but Olivia had restrained him. She would not risk being humiliated and thwarted by Daniel refusing to surrender the creature out of vengeance. That she could not suffer at any cost. The duty of retrieving the girl must be left to James Stuart, whose parental right to the custody of his daughter could not be refused, and for whose imminent arrival Olivia had been watching when Tom had ridden up the drive. Now it appeared that Nicolette had seen the error of her ways and had accepted that the affair was at an end, simply taking off somewhere in a childish attempt to avoid being sent back to Scotland. She would soon be found. All that mattered was that Tom Warwyck should not find her first.

"All I will say to you," she declared in clipped tones, "is that Nicolette has come to her senses and has gone from your reach by her own free will. You will never set eyes on her again."

"Do you think I believe that lie?" Tom raged. "I know her better than you, or anyone else for that matter. You have lost no time in banishing her under force. She would never have gone willingly. I tell you that I'll find her wherever she is! Nothing exists that can keep me from her!"

He swung about, pushed aside the footman, who had had some idea of pulling him from the mistress's presence, and hurried back down the stairs, jacket tails flying. He had almost reached the entrance doors when they burst open and Hugh faced him, complexion congested, fists cocked and at the ready.

"I saw you from the paddock," he ground out. "Come back to

crow, have you? Damn and blast your eyes! Where is she? I'll have it out of you!"

Olivia screeched out in warning. "Hugh! No more!"

It was too late. Slowly Tom turned his head and looked up under his lids at her, a humorless grin spreading across his mouth. "So you don't know where she is either."

Hugh grasped the situation and articulated cuttingly. "Given you the slip as well, has she, Warwyck? I can deal you a list of places where she is not to be found, just to save you looking there. No hotel or lodging house has seen her. She's not on your boat, because I've had that watched, or in the old barn, or at Honeybridge House."

Tom's eyes blazed. "You've not been there!"

Hugh's gaze was malevolent. "That offends you, does it? Somebody else seeing the little love nest?"

Hugh was prepared for the fist that shot out at him, parried, and dealt out a punch to the throat that sent Tom down on the floor half choked. With his hair over his eyes, Tom, still coughing, scrambled to his feet and came at Hugh with a kill-bull facer that brought the claret spurting from lip and nose. They closed in the fight that had been long overdue, and each exulted bloodthirstily in the chance to smash home at the other. They used the length and breadth of the huge hall like a giant ring, occasionally one hammering the other into a corner, both heedless of vases that toppled from pedestals or statuettes knocked from niches as they swung heavily together, or one sent his opponent reeling back under a blow to the forehead or a punch on the chin. There was gore everywhere, Hugh's nose running like a river, and Tom scarcely able to see out of his left eye from a cut streaming down into it. Their grunts and the thud of blows were magnified by the acoustics of the domed ceiling, porcelain fragments crunching underfoot. The faces of servants peered down the stairwell at them, and others had gathered silently by the baize-lined doors to stare at the scene, but both combatants were totally oblivious to everything except a determination to bring down the other to sprawl senseless before him. Olivia watched, leaning on her stick with one thin-boned hand resting on the newel-post, only her eyes alive in her expressionless face, darting from one to the other of the opponents as the battle went on.

Neither could gain mastery. Retaliation always followed forcefully. When Hugh placed a left-handed hit, Tom let fly with his right, catching him under the ribs, each fighting with skill, and there was no haymakering. Throughout the struggle a conviction had grown in Tom's mind as to where Nicolette was to be found, and his impatience to get to her enabled him to summon up fresh strength when both he and Hugh were tiring. He watched for the opening he needed. His chance came when, after the exchange of more muggers and rib-roasters in full prize-ring tradition on his part, Hugh bore in angrily and Tom met him with a tremendous right-hander on the nose, his whole power behind it. Hugh went flying backward and fell insensible with such impact that his whole frame slithered several yards across the marble floor. Tom waited, swaying on his feet, sweat trickling profusely from every pore, but there was no attempt by Hugh to rise. The fight was won.

He staggered out into the open air and leaned against a stone column, breathing deeply. His clothes were torn, his shirt soaked and in ribbons that flapped in the fierce sea wind. With great effort he got himself on the back of his horse and rode away.

In the house two footmen knelt by Hugh, and he shook his head dazedly as they raised him to a sitting position. He managed to focus on his grandmother at the top of the stairs. "Somethin' wrong," he muttered, pointing to her.

A parlormaid was the first to reach her and gave a frightened cry. The eyes were still brilliant and aware in a face drawn down and contorted beyond the use of speech ever again in a stroke that had paralyzed Olivia's whole body through shock at seeing a Warwyck triumphant at Radcliffe Hall.

Tom's head had cleared and the driving rain had washed most of the blood from his face when he galloped in through the rear entrance to the grounds of Easthampton House. He threw himself down from the horse's back, shouted to the staring stable lads to rub it down and give it warm bran mash, and began himself to put a fresh horse into the shafts of a dogcart. A groom ran to give assistance, noting with a twinkle that the young master had been up to something.

"Did you win the fisticuffs, Mr. Tom?" he questioned with cheeky good humor.

Tom grinned. "I did. Hurry up on your side, will you? I'm fetching a lady."

"Beg pardon, sir, but you're not driving out without sprucing yourself up a bit?"

"There's no time." Tom was leaping up into the driver's seat.

"You'll catch your death of cold. Take this!" The groom had snatched an old hunting jacket of Daniel's from a nail.

"Thanks." Tom shoved impatient arms in it, accepting he would be no husband to Nicolette if he wasted away with the lung fever.

Still the groom delayed him, holding the bridle. "I don't know where you aim to drive, Mr. Tom, but waves is flooding the roads. It's the worst high tide for a hundred years, they say. The Pier is breaking up."

Tom gave him one shattered look, cracked the whip, and the wheels of the dogcart leaped and bounded as he drove around the house, to be hindered again as Helen with a coat thrown over her shoulders ran down the rain-splashed steps, signaling to him to stop.

"Tom! Your grandfather has gone to Honeybridge. You must go after him."

He reached out and caught her by the arm to haul her up into a seat beside him. "I can't. You can go in my place. Nicolette is in the Pier Pavilion and I have to get to her before it is swept away."

She looked at him in horror, holding back strands of hair that the wind had begun to whip loose about her face as he drove for the gates. "Most of the Pier has gone already. Are you certain she's there? Surely she would have left it when she saw the waves."

"Not when she had nowhere else to go and knew I would find her there," he replied grimly. "She would see it as her only chance of eloping with me without her family parting us forever."

He had never seen such a sea. Spring tides were notorious, but these waves were mountainous, smashing against the promenade and cascading over it as if all Niagara had been released. As some of the water dragged back again, shoals of shingle were left in its wake, the broken promenade railings sticking up through the retreating foam like iron fingers, before another gigantic wave repeated the performance. It was impossible to follow the road running parallel to the promenade, and he went by another street to come as close as he could to the Pier. Neither he nor Helen saw Beth Macdonald waving from the pavement to catch his attention. She stamped her foot and fumed. When was she going to trap down the money due to her and leave this town?

Tom stared at the Pier, appalled at the sight that met him. The planking of the long deck had almost completely gone, and even as he watched some more planks rose up as if with a life of their own and were borne away on the huge water. One of the iron arches that ran the length of the Pier had already collapsed, and the remaining framework swayed visibly under each onslaught. The Pavilion itself was lost in spray as yet another rolling wave dashed half over it.

There was an ironmonger's shop close to where he had drawn up in the dogcart. He ran into it, was hastily given all he needed for the task ahead, and came running out again, followed by the concerned shopkeeper and his gaping assistants. Helen's heart sank as she watched him knotting two lengths of rope about his waist and spare lengths across his body, but she did not try to stop him.

"Good luck, Tom," she cried.

He did not hear her. His gaze was set ahead as he went splashing across the flooded road in the direction of the turnstile entrance. A wave descended, drenching him and plastering his hair to his head as it threw him off balance, but he clambered up onto the promenade and had leaped the turnstile before the next wave came. Unknowingly, he took stock of what lay before him on the very spot behind one of the shops where Nicolette had rested the day before. A concrete base extended from the summer buildings for about two yards, all planking gone from it, and stretching ahead was the naked iron base moving on its pillars. In the distance the circular Pavilion looked oddly like a circus tent floating on the churning water.

He edged along to the railings, fastened himself to them with two stout loops at the ends of the double length of the ropes that held him, and began his perilous, crab-like progress along what remained of the Pier. At each paling he had to wait between waves to move one loop of rope to the railings beyond and follow it up with the other, never leaving himself untied for a second. He was buffeted, thrown, doused, and swung, and at times badly scraped and cut by violent contact with the ironwork, but doggedly he continued to move along the railings with an enforced slowness that was agony to him. He was quite unaware that a crowd had gathered to watch him, many of the women crying, and there were shouts and sometimes a scream when a wave washed over him and it seemed that this time he must have gone.

Helen had driven the dogcart on to Honeybridge. Due to the rise of the land Hoe Lane was not flooded, although wide puddles of sea water had drained down from the waves' onslaught at the cliff face. She jumped out at the front gate and found the door on the latch. On the threshold of the dining room she paused. Daniel had opened the shutters, and he sat in a stout mahogany carver pushed back from the head of the long table, an indefinable expression on his face, his eyes fixed on the portrait above the inglenook. She followed his gaze and did not have to be told that the lovely woman in the frame was Kate Warwyck, whose grandson was fighting for his life and that of the girl he loved against the might of a terrible sea. Unable to stop herself, she burst out emotionally in a rush of appeal to Daniel that came straight from her heart.

"Be glad that Tom and Nicolette came here. Be thankful that they knew some happiness at Honeybridge. They are so young and have had such a little time together. God alone knows what lies in store for them this day." Her voice broke and she pressed the back of her hand across her mouth to keep a sob at bay.

He looked around slowly at her, appearing to have difficulty in dragging himself back from the past. For a moment or two she thought he did not recognize her, but it was simply the difficulty of an aged person adjusting to a sudden span of years. "You speak as Kate would have spoken. I told my son that I have been much reminded of her since you came to Easthampton. She never asked anything for herself, you know. It was always for others. I always thought my gift of Honeybridge pleased her more than anything else she had received from me, but when she was dying she told me that she treasured the Championship colors most of all." He returned his gaze to the portrait. "I had never thought to look on her face again this side of the grave, but Tom has brought me to this hour against my will, and miraculously I find that pain is finally at rest." He gave a nod. "Kate always wanted that inglenook opened up and somehow it was never done. I wonder how Tom realized that. Second sight, perhaps, because this house will be his one day. I set that in my will some years ago when I saw that out of all my grandchildren he was the one who cared about the future of Easthampton as I do." His broad hand, scarred from old battles in the prize ring, lifted from the table where it rested, and he pointed to the old salt box set in the wall above the inglenook. "Kate concealed two silver buttons in there once. A blackmailer had tried to use them in evidence against me, not without cause, I grieve to say. But Kate stood by me as she always did and no harm came of it except to the villain, a fellow by the name of Ben Thompson, who ended up in a railway accident. When Kate tried to retrieve the buttons for me we found they had slipped through a crack into the stonework and were out of reach."

Helen could tell that the silence of years had been undammed by the healing return to Honeybridge. For the rest of his days he would talk freely and lovingly of Kate, finding joy in old memories that he had long denied. Out of it he would find the strength and comfort to sustain him in the loss of his daughter, for he would no longer feel alone. Helen prayed that he would have no further heartrending bereavement to suffer. Keeping a brave face, she went across to where he sat and broke it to him what was happening at the Pier.

Nicolette did not see Tom edging his perilous way through the gale-lashed sea. She was huddled in heart-quaking terror on the horsehair sofa in his office, one arm over her head, while the whole Pavilion shuddered and groaned and shifted around her. Now and again there were additional thuds and crashes as more plasterwork cracked away and fell down to the debris lying everywhere. In the skating rink every one of the chandeliers and the gilded cupids from its days as a theater had gone, lying in swirling pools of water that had seeped in.

During the previous night she had not been unduly frightened. Emotionally racked by all she had endured at the Hall before her escape, she had fallen into a deep sleep of complete exhaustion as soon as she had closed her eyes on the sofa, and the worst of the gale had gone unheard. In the morning, full of optimism for the day ahead, she made herself tea in the kitchen that supplied light refreshments to the roller-skaters in the season. Afterward she had explored the whole building out of interest, carrying the lamp from Tom's office to light a path, for the few windows were all stoutly shuttered against the weather. When she opened a door to look out the wind slammed it shut again with such force that she resigned herself with an almost unbearable disappointment to there being no chance of eloping on Sea Star that day. Of one thing she was sure, and that was Tom's realizing she would be in the Pavilion as arranged. He alone would know it was the only place she could hide to avoid discovery, and she guessed that Hugh would be searching ruthlessly for her.

When the incoming tide began to boom around the Pavilion and the shrieking wind tore with renewed fury at the padlocked shutters as if seeking a way in, she experienced extreme nervousness, and only a greater fear of being found by her brother stopped her from leaving her refuge. Eventually, when one wave larger than the rest broke with a noise like thunder to make the whole Pavilion appear to shift on its struts, she knew she must stay no longer. Swiftly she gathered up her valise and ran down the scarlet-walled passage to the foyer, everything vibrating and threatening to collapse about her ears. With frantic hands she wrenched at the bolts of the doors that led out to the deck, and as they burst outward upon release a vast, curving wave of dark green water smashed down before her, hiding the shore and hurling its stinging spray in her face, taking the breath from her. As it drained away she saw with disbelief that the deck was going, and the wave had drained through a gaping hole that stretched the width of it. She was cut off.

Terrified of being swept down into the chasm of churning sea, she fought for possession of the doors against the wind's might, and after a tremendous struggle managed to get them closed. She leaned her forehead against the damp surface of one, gasping to regain her breath, but water gushed in about her feet and she withdrew hastily. Shaking the drops from her hems, she ran back up the sloping passageway to Tom's office, where she flung herself in a corner of the sofa, drawing her feet up instinctively as if to remain out of any further advance by the sea until the last second of life left to her.

Petrified, she remained exactly as she was hour after hour, her eardrums buffeted by the booming of the waves, and with every heave of the slowly disintegrating structure she expected a deluge through bursting walls to plunge her down to swirling depths below. There was such a confusion of noise that when a hammering fist sounded faintly she barely noticed it until, suddenly alert, she became aware that it had a distinct rhythm. With a cry she sprang up and raced back to the foyer, which was ankle-deep in water. As she opened the door Tom half reeled, half fell in and clutched her by the arms. "Quick! We must get back while there's still time!"

But time had run out. "It's too late!" she cried. "Look!"

He swung around in time to see the whole of the Pier that he had traversed with such difficulty buckle and rise up high, before collapsing with its remaining towers slowly down into the mountainous waves. He gave a deep groan.

"That's it then. There's no leaving now." It took all his strength to close the whipping doors, she aiding him until the bolts were secure. Drawing breath, he reached for her and she was in his arms.

In the office he removed what remained of his wet clothes, and she dried his back and helped wrap him in the blanket from the medical supplies cupboard under which she had slept the night before. After first anxious inquiries about the well-being of the other, they became wordless as they kissed and touched each other, their eyes saying all there was to say of this reunion within the clasp of death. She became afraid that his convulsive shivering would stop his heart and part them before their going together when the Pavilion's end came, and after taking off her clothing she slipped under the blanket beside him on the sofa to warm him with her own body. He burrowed his fingers in her tresses, holding her head, and buried her mouth in his. Around them the walls creaked and cracked under the sea's onslaught, and water trickled ominously through the gaudy ceiling that had once been highlighted by gas footlights from a vanished stage. But each no longer looked beyond the other. He was resolved that he would not let the sea drag her from his arms when the last moment came.

Unbeknown to them the Pavilion was awash at a deeper level than before. Only their refuge remained comparatively dry. To those who watched and waited on the land it was an endless vigil. Again and again the Pavilion disappeared from sight in high water and it seemed impossible that it could still be there when the wave had passed on. Daniel stood in the wind and rain, refusing to take shelter. Richard had been sent for, and an emergency message delivered to the Hall brought James Stuart, newly arrived, at top speed to the Pier site, his mother-in-law and battered son left to the care of a doctor and nurses. The two fathers had a long and enlightening talk together.

"If they get out of this alive," James Stuart declared, gray-faced with anxiety, "I'll not oppose a marriage between my daughter and your son. Never, never must they be driven to such lengths again to show the rest of us the extent of their affection for each other."

Helen, who was standing with them, felt Richard rest a hand upon her waist. There would be no such straightening out of life for them. She had Beatrice to care for and he had Meg. In a few months she would have the baby to bring her comfort, but, sadly, there would be none for him. Then it was as if in some way he had read her thoughts, for when she would have moved from his side his grip tightened and would not let her go. Motionless, she stayed with him, his height and bulk protecting her in some measure from the wind that buffeted them constantly while the waves continued to rise and fall, each gigantic heave of water against the Pavilion making her hold her breath in prayer until it had passed on to leave way for the next one.

As she watched she seemed to lose all sense of time. Now and again friends and acquaintances came and spoke to them, but as the Pavilion's end began to appear inevitable people withdrew a distance out of respect for the anguish of the three men whose young kin were most surely doomed. They made lonely figures in their vigil, standing a little distance from each other, only Richard having a companion, his arm still about the woman he loved. None of them took their gaze for a moment from the increasingly fragile structure that swayed visibly under each onslaught. At times it was possible to see pieces break loose and career skyward before being lost from sight as they fell. Always the wind roared and hissed in its constant battle with the raging sea.

It was Daniel who made the first move in the long waiting. He took a few steps forward, heedless of the pebbles cast about his feet by an errant wave. "The tide is on the turn!" he shouted hoarsely. "I tell you that the tide is turning!"

"Are you sure?" Richard demanded. He and Helen had been the first to reach him, James Stuart hurrying up behind them.

"I'm sure," Daniel pronounced sagely. He knew the signs. Those sharper waves, higher and thinner than the rest, were a certain indication. Yet he would have known anyway. Had he not lived and breathed the air and tides and winds of Easthampton since he had first molded the resort with his own strength and power out of a handful of hovels? "The sea is going down."

It took Tom longer to realize that the tide was on the ebb, for the noise of the sea did not abate, but gradually he became aware that there was less force, less vibration, and he knew the danger was past. Nicolette, quiet in his arms, saw the smile dawn in his eyes and on his lips.

"It's over," he whispered jubilantly. "I can tell. We're safe."

Together they began to laugh, softly and wonderingly, and their arms tightened about each other. Bereft of its outer gallery, part of its roof caved in, and with some struts gone, the Pavilion had withstood the full might of one of the worst gales that had ever swept along the south coast.

Knowing it would take a while for the sea to subside enough to allow them to get away, they took their time preparing for their rescue. He made a search of the office and found a waistcoat and a pair of tennis trousers in its cupboard, as well as a spare shirt that he had forgotten he had left there. When she was ready as well, her hair combed and repinned into place, he led her with him to the foyer. Before he shot back the bolts of the door he took her by the shoulders and drew her close, looking down into her face.

"Nothing shall ever part us now," he promised.

A cheer went up from many of those on the land at the sight of the young couple framed hand in hand in the distant doorway. Daniel gave a long, slow sigh of thankfulness. All was well with them. Later today he would take the portrait of Kate home to Easthampton House and set her in her rightful place. She would have liked to know that Honeybridge was to be lived in by their grandson and his bride. Kate would not care that Nicolette had been a Radcliffe. In her heart there had never been anything but love.

95   96   97   99
| | ||| | |